W9-BPJ-226

The Lost Art of
KEEPING SECRETS

The Lost Art of
KEEPING SECRETS

a novel by
EVA RICE

DUTTON

DUTTON
Published by Penguin Group (USA) Inc.
375 Hudson Street, New York, New York 10014, USA
Penguin Group (Canada), 90 Eglinton Avenue East, Suite 700, Toronto, Ontario M4P 2Y3,
Canada (a division of Pearson Penguin Canada Inc.); Penguin Books Ltd., 80 Strand, London
WC2R 0RL, England; Penguin Ireland, 25 St. Stephen's Green, Dublin 2, Ireland (a division of
Penguin Books Ltd.); Penguin Group (Australia), 250 Camberwell Road, Camberwell, Victoria
3124, Australia (a division of Pearson Australia Group Pty. Ltd.); Penguin Books India Pvt. Ltd.,
11 Community Centre, Panchsheel Park, New Delhi - 110 017, India; Penguin Group (NZ), cnr
Airborne and Rosedale Roads, Albany, Auckland 1310, New Zealand (a division of Pearson New
Zealand Ltd.); Penguin Books (South Africa) (Pty.) Ltd., 24 Sturdee Avenue, Rosebank,
Johannesburg 2196, South Africa

Penguin Books Ltd., Registered Offices: 80 Strand, London WC2R 0RL, England

Published by Dutton, a member of Penguin Group (USA) Inc.

First Printing, April 2006
10 9 8 7 6 5 4 3 2 1

REGISTERED TRADEMARK—MARCA REGISTRADA

LIBRARY OF CONGRESS CATALOGING-IN-PUBLICATION DATA
Rice, Eva, 1975–
    The lost art of keeping secrets / Eva Rice.
        p. cm.
    ISBN 0-525-94931-3
    1. London (England)—Fiction. 2. Socialites—Fiction. 3. Friendship—Fiction. I. Title.
    PR6118.I35L68   2006
    823'.92—dc22   2005020738

Printed in the United States of America
Set in Adobe Garamond

PUBLISHER'S NOTE
This book is a work of fiction. Names, characters, places, and incidents either are the product of the author's imagination or are used fictitiously, and any resemblance to actual persons, living or dead, business establishments, events, or locales is entirely coincidental.

For Donald "Capability" Rice,
who helped me invent Milton Magna

Acknowledgments

The Lost Art of Keeping Secrets would have floundered at the starting post if not for the following, so groveling thanks to: Claire Paterson, Eric Simonoff, Molly Beckett, Christelle Chamouton, Rebecca Folland and all at Janklow and Nesbitt, Harriet Evans (editor extraordinaire), Catherine Cobain, Georgina Moore and the brilliant team at Hodder Headline, the amazing Trena Keating, Emily Haynes and all at Dutton. Joanna Weinberg, Edward Sackville, Bee Ker, Paul Gambaccini, Ray Flight (who knows his Teds), Tim Rice, my grandmother Joan Rice, my mother Jane (who is nothing at all like Talitha), and Donald Rice, whose knowledge of great country houses is unrivaled.

Bouquets to Ann Lawlor (who was there at the Palladium when Johnnie Ray played), Sue Paterson, for having the foresight never to throw away her brilliant fifties magazines, Petrus, Martha, and Swift. I would also like to acknowledge Ruby Ferguson as a great inspiration.

She said that we must do something about the rooms. The walls were all damp and fur had settled on some parts of the wallpaper. But we just closed the doors and hurried down to the kitchen where it was warm.

—Edna O'Brien, *The Lonely Girl*

The Lost Art of
KEEPING SECRETS

ONE

The Girl in the Green Coat

I MET CHARLOTTE IN LONDON one afternoon while waiting for a bus. Just look at that sentence! That in itself is the first extraordinary thing, as I took the bus as rarely as once or twice a year, and even then it was only for the novelty value of not traveling in a car or train. It was mid-November 1954, and as cold as I had ever known London. "Too cold to snow," my brother used to say on such days, something that I had never understood. I was wearing my beautiful old fur-lined coat from Whiteleys and a pair of Fair Isle gloves that one of Inigo's friends had left at Magna the weekend before, so was feeling quite well-disposed toward the arctic conditions. There I was, thinking about Johnnie Ray and waiting patiently with two old ladies, one boy of about fourteen, and a young mother and her baby, when my thoughts were interrupted by the arrival of a stick-thin girl wearing a long, sea green coat. She was almost as tall as I, which caught my attention straightaway, as I am just about six foot with my shoes on. She stood in front of all of us, and cleared her throat.

"Anyone want to share a taxi?" she demanded. "I can't sit around here all day waiting." She spoke loudly and quickly and without a hint of self-consciousness, and it was instantly clear to me that although the girl was addressing us all, it was me she wanted to accept her offer. The fourteen-year-old boy opened his mouth and closed it again, then blushed and dug his hands into his pockets. One of the elderly ladies muttered, "No thank you," and the other I think must have been deaf, because her expression remained unaltered by the proposal. The young mother shook her head with a smile of infinite regret that stayed in my mind's eye long after the day had ended. I shrugged.

"Where are you going?" I asked pointlessly.

"Oh, you *darling*! Come on." The girl darted into the middle of the road and stuck out a hand to hail a cab. Within seconds, one had pulled up beside her.

"Come *on*!" she cried.

"Hang on a second! *Where are you going?*" I demanded for the second time, thoroughly flustered and wishing that I had never opened my mouth in the first place.

"Oh, for goodness' sake, just *jump in*!" she ordered, opening the door of the taxi. For a few seconds in time the whole world seemed to hesitate under starter's orders. Somewhere in a parallel universe, I heard myself shout out that I had changed my mind and that she must go on alone. Of course, in reality, I leaped forward and into the cab beside her just as the lights changed, and we were off.

"Yikes!" she exclaimed. "I thought you'd never move!"

She didn't turn to speak to me, but sat straight ahead, staring out in the direction that we were going. I didn't reply at once, but took in the glory of her profile—the smooth, milky pale skin, the long curling eyelashes, and the thick, thick, straight, heavy, dark-blonde hair that fell well below her shoulders. She looked a little older than I, but I sensed from the way that she talked that she was probably about a year younger. She sat very still, her big mouth set in a small smile.

"Where are you going?" I asked again.

"Is that all you can say?"

"I'll stop asking it when you give me an answer."

"I'm going to Kensington. I'm having tea with Aunt Clare and Harry, which is just *too* impossible for words, so I should like you to come with me, we'll have a lovely afternoon. Oh, and my name's Charlotte, by the way."

That was how she said it. Straight Alice in Wonderland. Of course, me being me, I was flattered by her absurd presumption, firstly that I would be happy to accompany her, and secondly that it would be a lovely afternoon if I did.

"I have to read through Act Four of *Antony and Cleopatra* by five o'clock," I said, hoping to appear slightly aloof.

"Oh, it's an absolute cinch," she said briskly. "He dies, she kills herself with an asp. *Bring me my robe and my crown, I have immortal longings in me,*" she quoted softly. "You have to admire a woman who chooses to end her life with a snakebite, don't you? Attention seeking, Aunt Clare would call it. I think it's the most *glamorous* way to go."

"Hard to do in England," I said reasonably. "Not many serpents hanging about in West London."

"There are *plenty* in West London," said Charlotte briskly. "I had dinner with one last night."

I laughed. "Who was that?"

"My mother's latest conquest. He insisted on feeding her forkfuls of shepherd's pie as if she were three years old. She wouldn't stop giggling as though it were quite the most hilarious thing that had ever happened. I *must* remember not to dine with her again this year," she mused, taking out a notebook and pencil. "What's more, her new beau was nothing *at all* like he is in the orchestra pit."

"Orchestra pit?"

"He's a conductor called Michael Hollowman. I suppose you're going to go all sophisticated and tell me you know exactly who he is and wasn't his interpretation of *Rigoletto* remarkable?"

"It was, if a little hurried and lacking in emotion," I said.

Charlotte stared at me and I grinned.

"I'm joking," I admitted.

"Thank goodness for that. I think I would have had to withdraw my invitation right away if you hadn't been," said Charlotte.

It had started to rain and the traffic was worsening.

"Who *are* Aunt Clare and Harry?" I asked, curiosity winning hands down over practicalities like the fact that we were traveling in quite the opposite direction from Paddington. Charlotte sighed.

"Aunt Clare is really my mother. I mean, she's *not* my mother, she's my mother's sister, but my mother has given up on everything in life except for men with batons who she believes will help further her career. She's got it into her head that she's a great, untrained singer," she said grimly.

"And is she?"

"She's certainly got the untrained bit right. She's very neurotic about everything except for what happens to me, which is rather convenient as we have nothing at all in common—except for our delusions of grandeur—so I spend most of my time at Aunt Clare's and as little time as possible at home."

"And where is home?" I asked, sounding just like my grandmother.

"Clapham," said Charlotte.

"Oh."

She may as well have said Venus. I had heard of it, but had no idea where Clapham was.

"Anyway, Aunt Clare is writing her memoirs at the moment," Charlotte went on. "I'm helping her. By that I mean that I'm just listening to her talk and typing what she says. She's paying me a pittance because she thinks I should be honored to have the job. She says plenty of people would give their eyeteeth to hear stories like hers from the horse's mouth, so to speak."

"I don't doubt it," I said. "And Harry?"

Charlotte turned to face me.

"Aunt Clare was married to a very smart man called Samuel Delancey until three years ago. One of those fearfully good-looking but *very* mean types. Anyway, he was killed by a falling bookcase."

"No!"

"Yes, really, it just collapsed on his head as he sat reading *On the Origin of Species*—very ironic, my mother kept saying—and as a result Aunt Clare inherited an awful lot of debt and not much else. He was a pretty scary sort of man, with a clubfoot to boot—ha ha, if you'll pardon the pun. Harry is their only son—he's twenty-five and convinced that the whole world is conspiring against him. It's very dull indeed."

"I'm happy to share the taxi with you, but I don't make a habit of having tea with complete strangers," I said unconvincingly.

"Oh, good gracious, I'm not asking you to make a habit of it. But do come. Please! For me!" Charlotte implored.

Although this was an absurd reason for me to accompany her, as we had only met a few minutes ago, it had the desired effect. There was something in the way that this creature spoke, something in the way that she carried herself, that made me quite certain that no one would ever be able to refuse her anything, regardless of whether they had known her for five minutes or fifty years. In that sense, she reminded me, very strongly, of my brother. I felt I was staring in at the taxi from the street and I saw myself—beguiling, intriguing—because I was in Charlotte's company, and a girl like Charlotte would not have singled me out for tea without thinking that there was something interesting about me, surely? She had quite the reverse effect on me than had the Alicias and Susans and Jennifers of the debutante circuit. With those girls, I felt myself diminish, sensed my shadow growing smaller, my vision narrowing until a great dread came over me that, if I wasn't careful, I would lose sight of every original thought I had ever had. Charlotte, however, was all possibilities. She was the sort of person one reads about in novels yet rarely meets in real life, and if this was the beginning of the novel—well! I was pretty certain I wasn't supposed to get out of the cab until we pulled up outside the mysterious Aunt Clare's house for tea. I had always been a great believer in fate, but it had never believed in *me* until that afternoon. But I didn't want Charlotte to think she had won me over *that* easily. . . .

"You're very persistent. I'm not sure that I should trust you one bit," I said loftily.

"Oh, you don't have to *trust* me. I've always considered trustworthy people to be very boring indeed, and, oh my gosh! I know some boring people. I just want you to *help* me. There is a difference."

"Have you no other friends you could take along with you?" I asked.

"No fun."

"What do you mean?"

She tutted with frustration.

"Look. I can't *make* you come with me. If you can't bear the thought of it, well, that's just fine. Only you'll always wonder about it, won't you? You'll be lying awake tonight thinking, 'Hmmm—I wonder what Aunt Clare was wearing? I wonder if she really *was* a monster? I wonder if Harry was the most handsome boy in London?' But you'll never know, because it will be too late, and I won't come looking for you again."

"Is he?" I asked, full of suspicion.

"What?"

"Is he the most handsome boy in London?"

"Oh, no! Of course not!" At least Charlotte had the grace to laugh at herself, a surprisingly loud, harsh sound like a motorcycle starting. "He's not at all handsome, but he's by far the most *interesting* boy you'll ever meet. You'll love him," she added simply. "Everyone does, after a while. He's irritatingly addictive."

"Don't be silly."

I was cross with myself for asking about him.

"Aunt Clare always has excellent tea," Charlotte went on. "Stacks of butter and raspberry jam and Eccles cakes and all the ginger scones you can eat. My mother has never understood the importance of a good tea."

The cab was rocketing along Bayswater Road now.

"Well, I can't stay for long," I said unconvincingly.

"Of course not."

We sat in silence for a moment, and I thought that she would ask me my name next, but she didn't, and I later realized that it simply wouldn't have occurred to her that she should have. I had experienced, for the first time, Charlotte's great gift for circumnavigating normal behavior.

"I knew you would take the taxi with me," she was saying now. "I saw you waiting for the bus from the other side of the street, and I thought, now *there's* a girl who would be *perfect* for tea with Aunt Clare and Harry."

I wasn't quite sure how to take this, so I frowned.

"Just perfect!" said Charlotte again. "And gosh! I adore your beautiful coat, too." She fingered the fur collar. "What craftsmanship! I make my own clothes. It's become an addiction. My poor mother can't understand me at all—she says it will frighten any sensible men off if they think I spend long hours at the sewing machine like some spinster from D. H. Lawrence. I told her that I don't mind, as I'm not in the least bit interested in sensible men in any case."

"Quite right," I agreed. "So what do you make?"

"Well, I made this coat out of an old traveling rug," Charlotte confessed. "Aunt Clare tells me I'm terrifically enterprising in a voice that means she thinks I'm terrifically vulgar."

"Traveling rug?" I said in amazement. "But it's a wonderful coat!"

I looked at her with new respect. There was obviously a steely work ethic beneath her flighty exterior, and a steely work ethic (being something I am entirely lacking) was something I admired greatly in others.

"It took me forever and the pockets are a bit shabby, but it's not a bad job," said Charlotte. "But when I see a coat like yours! Well! It's in another league entirely."

"You can wear it to tea, if you like," I was astonished to find myself saying. Charlotte hesitated.

"May I really? You don't mind? It would be such a treat." She began unbuttoning her green coat before I could change my mind.

"Here! You try mine," she said, handing it to me.

Charlotte's coat was exquisitely comfortable and warm. It seemed a little slice of her had stayed hidden in its lining, and it felt strange, like putting on a mask. She wriggled into my coat, pulling her mass of hair over the collar. The effect shocked me, not least because she possessed the actress's ability to change the aura around her simply by altering her clothing. It was as if she had been given her costume for the evening and she was instantly immersed in her part.

"Thank you," she said softly. "Do I look a little richer?" She giggled.

"Yes," I answered truthfully.

"Oh! Here we are!" said Charlotte happily. "How extraordinary. No, no, I'm paying. It's the very least I can do. I feel a great generosity of spirit has come upon me."

We had stopped outside one of those large, rather ugly redbrick houses off Kensington High Street. As I stepped out of the cab, the wind whipped through the green coat and seemed to cut right through me. Sure enough,

Charlotte paid, dropping a shoal of coins from her long fingers and into the hand of the driver with the air of a princess bestowing thanks on her footman. I swear I saw the driver bow his head to her before he drove off again. She took my arm and led me up the steps to the house and rang the bell.

"Aunt Clare lives on the top two floors of this monster," explained Charlotte. "After Uncle Samuel died and she'd dealt with all his debts, it was all she could afford. She's quite happy here. Like all intelligent people, she functions very well in extreme disorder."

The door was answered by a plump girl in her late teens, who offered a very dirty look before leading us up two flights of grubby-looking stairs and into Aunt Clare's flat before vanishing, wordless.

"Phoebe," said Charlotte. "Silly girl. She's madly in love with Harry, which is too pointless for words."

"Poor thing," I sympathized.

"Not at all," scorned Charlotte. "Aunt Clare took her on to help her out for a few months after my uncle died, and she's still here now, earning more than she's worth, I can tell you. She never speaks to me, though I gather she quotes long passages from *Paradise Lost* to Harry whenever he sits still." She smiled up at me. "Now, don't run away, for goodness' sake. I'll be back before you know it."

Then she vanished. And that was how I came to spend my first afternoon in Aunt Clare's study.

TWO

Aunt Clare and Harry

NOW, I AM NOT THE SORT OF PERSON who usually jumps into cabs with strangers—that behavior is more my younger brother Inigo's style of operating than mine. I tried to consider what had made me act in such a reckless fashion, and couldn't put my finger on it at all. After all, up until the moment that I first saw Charlotte, my day had progressed in much the same way as every other Monday that year. I had taken the 8:35 train from Westbury to Paddington in the morning, drifted through my Italian and English Literature classes in Knightsbridge until three o'clock, then strolled through Hyde Park dreaming of Johnnie Ray and new clothes. Admittedly, the decision to take the bus from Bayswater to Paddington was uncharacteristic. But I was here now, and for the next half hour, there was very little I could do but follow Charlotte's lead. I was half-nervous, half-curious, and entirely surprised at myself. *Maybe they're kidnapping me?* I thought hopefully. They would soon throw me back onto the streets once they realized that under the expensive coat lurked a girl with no trust fund, no guaranteed income, and no decent jewels. I pulled out the powder compact I had stolen from Mama's dressing table and blinked at myself. My hair needed a comb (I hadn't one) and there was an ink smudge on my chin, but my eyes flashed back at me, defiant. Make the most of this, I thought. I was aware, for the first time in a long while, that I was alive.

*   *   *

I shoved the mirror away and glanced around. The room was small and stiflingly hot. A fire had been lit some hours ago, and with the door closed, I felt suddenly faint. I wanted to take off the green coat, but felt, curiously, that I should not; I sensed it was part of me while I was here. I've always felt my most hungry in the middle of the afternoon and today was no exception; I felt my stomach rumble and hoped that tea would be served soon, though it worried me that there was scarcely room for a saucer. The room was so full of clutter and objects that it almost hurt the eyes. Dominating everything (and how on earth it got into the room in the first place, I couldn't think) stood a beautiful grand piano scattered with papers, pens, ink, and letters. Naturally nosy (a habit passed down through my mother's side of the family), I quickly read the first sentence of a half-finished postcard. The handwriting was clear, turquoise, and joyous. *My Dear Richard—* it began—*You are quite mad and I love you all the more for it. Wootton Bassett was wonderful, wasn't it?* I shifted my eyes to the large table by the window, where a faded top hat plonked on top of a stack of crumpled pound notes gave the illusion of a giant Monopoly board abandoned midgame. I had Aunt Clare down as a bit of a Miss Havisham until I noticed that the large windows were immaculately clean, and clean windows, my mother was fond of saying, are as important as clean teeth. (She rather shot herself in the foot with this expression, as there were more windows at home than one could count and she was never done employing youths from the village to come and clean them. Once an older sort of chap fell from the blue bathroom window and landed in a wheelbarrow of dead roses below. He broke his leg, but adored Mama so much that he came back the next week to finish the job, plaster and all. But back to Aunt Clare's study.)

There were books, books, and more books, stacked in random piles all over the floor and spilling off the shelves, including, I noticed with a shiver of surprise, a beautiful hardback edition of the Darwin book that Aunt Clare's husband was alleged to have been reading at the moment of his untimely death. The room smelled strongly of learning, not in the calm, musty, leafy way that accompanies most rooms containing great literature, but in that more disturbing, sticky-palmed, feverish way that implies cramming knowledge for an exam or feeding an obsession. Whoever Aunt Clare was, she had no time to waste. I sat down on a very low red sofa and stretched my legs out in front of myself. The clock in the hall struck a melancholy five o'clock and I wondered how long I would have to stay here before excusing myself and boarding the train back to Westbury. Already uncharacteristically nervous, I nearly leaped out of my skin when a huge ginger cat emerged from the shadows and jumped onto my lap, purring like a tractor. Now, I don't like cats, but this one really took a liking to me, or perhaps it was drawn to Charlotte's green coat? What I remember thinking, more than anything that afternoon, was that I had never been in such a still house in all my time in London and it made me uneasy; London was not meant for the kind of heavy, low quietness that was pressing down on me now and filling me with the urge to speak out, to declare my presence for all to hear. It felt as if I had been sitting alone in Aunt Clare's study for at least an hour before Phoebe, Aunt Clare, and Charlotte emerged from wherever on earth they had been, but in fact it was less than ten minutes. It seemed that quite suddenly they were there, and the unbearable tension that can only exist when one sits alone in an unfamiliar room in a stranger's house, in a stranger's coat, was broken.

Aunt Clare altered the room in the same way that a vast bouquet of spring flowers would, complementing everything around her with a vibrant, arresting beauty and a strong smell of rose water. She was a large woman, but handsome and excellently proportioned, with huge yellow green eyes, high cheekbones, and, like her niece, thick straight hair, a shade nearer to gray than blonde, all of it piled on top of her head in a beautiful chignon. Fifty-five, I thought, and only just. (I pride myself on being able to guess people's ages, and I'm rather good at it.) I jumped up at once, outraging the sleeping cat, who slunk off under the piano.

"So here she is!" cried Aunt Clare in a singsong voice. "Introduce us at once, Charlotte."

"Oh—this is Penelope," said Charlotte. There was a silence and my eyes opened in astonishment. At no point thus far had I told her my name.

"H-how do you do?" Aunt Clare's tiny hand was as delicate as a budgie's claw in my great paw.

"Wonderful!" said Aunt Clare briskly. "This is my son, Harry," she added, and out of the shadowy corridor emerged a boy. I sighed to myself because Charlotte was right. He certainly was not the most handsome boy in London. He was short, a couple of inches shorter than me, and skinny as a rake in his crumpled white shirt and charcoal gray trousers. His hair was the same dark blond as Charlotte's, only his was not poker straight, but all over the place. He looked as though he had just woken up from an afternoon nap.

"Hello—" I began, and the word choked in my throat. Because when he looked up at me, his eyes threw me completely off balance. I had never seen anything so spooky, so arresting, so brilliantly *original* in all my life. His left eye was a sleepy blue green, while the right was as brown as dark chocolate, and both were framed by thickly black, curling lashes, giving the uneasy impression that he had spent hours in the powder room.

"What ho!" he said sardonically.

"How do you do?" I recovered, stretching out my hand.

He took my hand and held my gaze in a deadpan stare until I blushed scarlet, and noting this, he grinned and actually stifled a snort of laughter. I hated him at that moment.

"I expect you're hungry," said Aunt Clare, eyeing the green coat, now coated in ginger hair.

"Yes," I said, turning to her in relief.

"Phoebe, we'd like toast, and some of Mrs. Finch's raspberry jam, and chocolate cake, and ginger scones, and a big pot of tea, please," instructed Charlotte, beaming at Phoebe. "Ooh, and some of those nice chocolate biscuits, not those ghastly coconut ones, please."

Coconut! I thought.

Phoebe gave her a spectacular glare and vanished again.

"Now, come and sit next to me, Penelope," instructed Aunt Clare, oozing onto the sofa and patting the seat beside her. Charlotte nodded encouragingly. Harry was lighting a cigarette with long fingers.

"Harry has dinner with the Hamiltons at seven," said Aunt Clare. "He's terribly nervous about seeing Marina again."

"Am I?" said Harry in a bored voice. Just then the telephone rang and he shot across the room to pick it up.

"Hullo? . . . She did? The little darling, I knew she could do it. . . . No, thank *you*. . . . Not at all. . . . "

As he spoke, Aunt Clare remained as still as a lioness, barely breathing, her face grim with concentration. (She certainly didn't have my mother's subtlety when it came to eavesdropping.) When Harry had finished his call, he replaced the receiver with a bang, hurried across the room, and picked up a coat from the back of a chair.

"That tip I had for the four fifty came good," he announced. He spoke very fast, scooping up coins, keys, and betting slips from the table beside the door. "And please don't talk about me when I'm gone, Mother, it's bloody boring."

With that he left us, banging the door behind him.

"How rude!" exclaimed Aunt Clare.

"Isn't he?" agreed Charlotte merrily.

"Oh, he's *impossible*!" Aunt Clare went on. "Penelope—Harry has been madly in love with Marina Hamilton for the past year."

"Oh?" I said politely. I knew of Marina, of course, but only from her photographs in the social columns. She and Harry struck me as a most unlikely match.

"They're a most unlikely match," said Aunt Clare. "Marina's parents are that ghastly American couple who bought lovely Dorset House from the FitzWilliamses."

"Ah. Of course."

I knew Dorset House, and the FitzWilliamses were a dull couple, old acquaintances of my mother.

"God only knows what they've done to the place. It's too frightening to think about," said Aunt Clare.

"I've appalling taste in interiors. I expect I should love it," sighed Charlotte.

"Don't talk nonsense, girl," said Aunt Clare sharply. "Anyway, last week Marina became engaged to George Rogerson—who's a large boy, poor thing, but supposed to be terribly nice and very rich—so Harry's having to admit defeat, not one of his strong points at the best of times."

I giggled.

"He's out for dinner with the happy couple tonight, and on December fifth they're throwing an engagement party at Dorset House, which, *naturellement,* I think is too awful for words. Harry's a very deluded sort of boy—he's never been able to take rejection, which is so *tire*some for us all. I only wish his father were here to set him straight."

It was clear to me that Aunt Clare was the influence behind Charlotte's way of talking. They both spoke in a fashion that was at once mannered and completely natural. Charlotte groaned.

"Oh, I wish Phoebe would hurry up with tea. I'm half-starved."

"She thinks of nothing but food," Aunt Clare informed me. "But what of you, child? How exciting to meet one of Charlotte's friends, and such an attractive young girl! Do I know your parents?" She cleared her throat and paused in a fashion that a novelist would describe as dramatic. "You . . . you look terribly like . . . like . . . Archie Wallace," she said.

For the second time I was rendered almost speechless.

"He's—he was my father," I managed to squeak. "He—he was killed. The war—" I trailed off and looked down at my hands, horribly uncomfortable. Aunt Clare paled, and for an awful moment I panicked that she hadn't realized Papa had died.

"Yes," she said eventually. "Yes. I am sorry. I read about Archie. I was so terribly sad." She pressed her hand to her chest. "And you, poor darling. His daughter. Good gracious."

There was something in the way she spoke these words that made me want to comfort her, to tell her that it was all right, that yes, Papa had died, but that, really, I had never even known him. Her eyes clouded over, suddenly dead, and for a few seconds, the room sank back into that weighty silence again. *Oh, help,* I thought. *She's going to cry.*

But she didn't. Instead she said after a small pause, "Of course, he and Talitha were married before they were whelped."

The clouds lifted again.

"Um—I don't think I understand," I said.

"They were babies themselves."

"Oh, I see. Yes, I suppose they were. My mother was seventeen when I was born," I explained to Charlotte.

"Seventeen! How romantic!" she wailed.

"Oh, Talitha Orr was quite the most sensational beauty," said Aunt Clare. "Thoroughly thoroughbred, despite being Irish, poor dear. Glorious hair, and always dressed for men, not women. That was the key to her success, you know."

I laughed. I just couldn't help it. "It's absolutely true. She doesn't really like women at all."

"It's a common trait of beautiful women," said Aunt Clare pertly.

"Is it? I *adore* women. I suppose that means I'm not beautiful," said Charlotte ruefully.

Aunt Clare snorted and rounded on her niece.

"Don't be so damn silly! Your trouble is that you're far too trusting for your own good."

Charlotte raised her eyebrows at me, and Aunt Clare coughed and gave me a slightly salty look.

"You have a brother, don't you?"

"Inigo. He's nearly two years younger than me."

"Does he look like you, dear?"

"I can't see it myself. He takes after my mother."

"Well! Fancy that, Charlotte. Have you met him?"

"No, Aunt."

"How horribly casual you are, Charlotte. It really is unbecoming. You must ask Penelope to introduce you to her brother. He sounds perfectly brilliant."

"Charlotte and I haven't known one another a very long time—" I began.

"Aunt, we met at a party only two weeks ago but we're already the greatest of friends," said Charlotte, shooting me a warning look.

"What party?" demanded Aunt Clare.

"Oh, Harriet Fairclough's wedding reception," said Charlotte, not missing a beat.

"Really? How extraordinarily clever of you, Charlotte, to meet someone as pretty and interesting as Penelope at such a dull affair," said Aunt Clare.

"Wasn't it?" agreed Charlotte.

I gulped. Five seconds later we were interrupted by the entrance of Phoebe and the tea tray.

"Oh, clear the table," instructed Aunt Clare. "Just put everything on the floor."

Being a self-conscious sort of person, I was very impressed by the fact that she felt no need to apologize for the quite spectacular disorder surrounding us. Phoebe poured tea and gave me a plate with my toast and jam as if bestowing a huge favor the likes of which I could never begin to repay. I have to admit that the cake was exceptional, the scones melt-in-the-mouth delicious, and the tea weirdly but deliciously smoky. Charlotte ate as if she hadn't seen food for weeks, stretching over everyone to grab at the scones, shoving cake into her mouth like a child and swigging at her tea as if it were ale, and quite ruining the elegance she had acquired through the use of my coat.

"We never get tea like this at home," she sighed, midmouthful.

"How would you know?" I found myself asking. "You're never *at* home, are you?"

Aunt Clare snorted with laughter.

"How true, Penelope, dear."

"Yet what would you do without me, Aunt?" demanded Charlotte.

"Manage perfectly well, I'm sure."

"No you wouldn't. What would you do without me keeping an eye on your errant son?"

"You know, Harry worries me, girls," murmured Aunt Clare, absentmindedly passing me a pack of playing cards instead of the milk. "I never imagined I would have a son who *gambled*! I mean, it's perfectly acceptable if you can justify it by knowing one end of a horse from the next, but Harry simply hasn't a *clue*. I lie awake at night wondering what can be done about his behavior."

She sniffed again. Unfortunately for Aunt Clare, she possessed the clear eyes, unlined skin, and bright expression of one who drops off for nine hours of uninterrupted sleep as soon as her head has hit the pillow. I fought a desire to giggle.

"He needs help," admitted Charlotte. "No one can deny that."

Aunt Clare helped herself to a slice of cake. "It was all well and good when he was a child," she said regretfully. "We used to laugh about Julian the Loaf back then."

"Julian the Loaf?" I asked, bewildered.

"Oh, he kept a loaf of bread called Julian in a wire cage because I refused to buy him a rabbit. Whether Julian was white, brown, or sliced, I forget. Harry was quite upset when his father insisted that he stop behaving in such a silly way. I must say, we all grew quite fond of that loaf."

"Harry's always been the same," said Charlotte, shoving another scone into her mouth. "Full of ideas. An inventor of sorts."

"Oh! *Always* inventing. But really, I do wish I had put a stop to it when I could have. I should have known from the start, of course. After all, there aren't many children whose first word is 'dumbwaiter.' " Aunt Clare looked pained and I gulped loudly to avoid laughing.

"He's training to be a magician," explained Charlotte. "He's really rather good."

"What sort of a magician?" I asked suspiciously.

"The usual sort. Sleight of hand. Pulling rabbits, or perhaps loaves of bread, out of a hat," said Charlotte with a giggle. "He has a great talent, apparently."

"Oh, it's all very impressive indeed," said Aunt Clare irritatedly. "Very amusing for everyone but his mother. What future is there in fooling people? And how on *earth* he ever hoped to snare a girl like Marina Hamilton with no fixed income I simply do not know. He must be stark, staring mad."

"Oh, Aunt!" said Charlotte airily. "You do exaggerate. Anyway, it's absurd to talk about such matters in front of Penelope, who can be of no help at all." Charlotte smoothed crumbs off the lap of my coat. I felt momentarily piqued by her dismissal, yet recalling this part of the conversation later that night, I recognized a challenging tone to what Charlotte had said.

"How is your mother? Did you see her yesterday?" Aunt Clare asked Charlotte, briskly changing the subject.

"She's unwell at the moment. A dreadful cold that she can't seem to shake."

"Good, good," mused Aunt Clare. "And your sister?"

"Still away."

"Gracious, she's been gone a long time. Still, they say New York is the place to be."

"She's been in Paris for the past two months, Aunt."

"Has she? How futile. It's a Frenchman, I suppose?"

"No. An Englishman living in Paris."

"Worse, and worse," said Aunt Clare cheerfully. "There is no sight so depressing as the English trying to dress French. I should know."

Neither Charlotte nor I ventured to ask her how she should know, but I, for one, didn't doubt her knowledge on the subject. I ate more toast and studied Charlotte. I had never seen a face that altered so much with movement. When she talked, her face took on a slightly lascivious, amused expression, yet when she was listening and still, she looked wide-eyed and innocent, as if an impure thought had never entered her head. She did a great deal of listening (as I imagine was customary for everyone when they took tea with Aunt Clare), but unlike most people, who pretend to listen and then show themselves up for forgetting everything two minutes later, Charlotte really seemed to take everything in, almost as if it were an exam and she was going to be tested on everything later. Aunt Clare was incapable of staying with one topic of conversation for longer than thirty seconds, though the chat repeatedly came back to Harry, as if there were some game going on in which his name had to be mentioned every three minutes. After nearly half an hour of trying to keep up, I decided that enough time had passed for it to be perfectly acceptable for me to go home.

"I really should be going," I said. "I have to catch the train home."

"And where is home?" asked Aunt Clare.

"Wiltshire, near Westbury."

"Milton Magna," said Aunt Clare. "Of course." She spoke the name in what was almost a whisper. Although I was accustomed to people knowing of the house, there was something in Aunt Clare's tone that unsettled me.

"Milton Magna!" said Charlotte. "What a name!"

"It's supposed to be quite the most magnificant building in the west country," said Aunt Clare, recovering her voice.

"It *was,* perhaps," I said. "It's in rather a state at the moment. I mean, it hasn't quite recovered from the war. There was a lot of mess made when it was requisitioned, the soldiers treated it pretty appallingly—" I stopped there, my heart beating furiously. I hadn't talked about the problems Magna faced with anyone, not even my mother. The subject made me more nervous than anything else in the world.

"To watch a great house dying is a terrible tragedy," murmured Aunt Clare. "One of *the* great tragedies known to man. Goodness knows, I've known enough of the ones that have gone. We'll look back on this time in horror, you know, girls. In fifty years, no one will believe that so many beautiful houses were forced to fall."

"We're fighting to keep it alive," I muttered, slurping noisily at my tea to cover up how moved I was by her words.

"Is the house glorious at Christmas?" asked Charlotte, sensing my discomfort.

"It is lovely. Though fearfully cold."

"I love the cold! So inspiring. I'm quite sure we shall all pass out with heat in this room." Aunt Clare stood up, crossed the room, and poked at the fire. "Harry adores a warm house," she said resentfully. "He has no stamina at all."

"He has a warm heart," Charlotte observed. Aunt Clare snorted. *Ah, Harry,* I thought. Always, we returned to the boy.

"So tell me, Penelope. What do you do with yourself? Do you work hard? Do you fixate upon the notion of having a career, like Charlotte?"

"I work one day a week in an antique shop in Bath," I said, seizing the chance to prove my worth. "It's owned by a man called Christopher Jones, who was a great friend of Papa's at school. He knows more about art than anyone else I know. I'm learning all the time about beautiful things," I added lamely.

"With Christoph? I doubt that very much," said Aunt Clare kindly. "He's the most *outrageous* gossip."

"Oh! You know him?"

"Oh, yes." Aunt Clare smiled blandly. "Oh, yes," she said again. Charlotte raised her eyes at me with an expression that said, "Don't ask."

"Penelope, have *you* ever been in love?" Aunt Clare asked congenially, as if wanting to know whether I took sugar in my tea. Swerving off the subject yet again. I blushed furiously. (You may as well know now that I am a terrible blusher; it's a trait I gather I inherited from my father, who had freckles and a pale complexion, like me. I've heard that if one wiggles one's toes at the moment of acute embarrassment or humiliation, it can distract the brain from the task of reddening the face. Well, I spend my whole life wiggling my toes, but I've never noticed any difference to my hot face.)

"Gosh, no!" I said eventually. "I don't really know many boys. Well, my brother has his school friends, I suppose, but they seem awfully young and silly to me."

"How lovely to have a younger brother with pretty friends," sighed Charlotte. *And how lovely they would think* her, I thought.

"Very useful for tennis," remarked Aunt Clare, bafflingly.

Then, on cue, and just as I was preparing to get myself out of the place, the door opened again and Harry was there. Despite Aunt Clare's talk of his insomnia and rage, he looked far from troubled. He looked at us almost pityingly, with a hint of a smirk on his face, his chaotic hair almost hiding his extraordinary eyes. Newfound knowledge of his skills as a magician seemed entirely appropriate; never before had I met someone who looked capable of turning men into frogs and frogs into princes. Charlotte smiled at him.

"Back already?"

"I haven't been out yet. Got trapped with Phoebe in the kitchen," he said in a low voice.

"Oh, poor thing," said Charlotte. "Why don't you have some tea?"

"No, thanks."

"Are you dreading this evening terribly?" Charlotte went on, her voice soft and full of concern.

"Not particularly," said Harry. "I love her, she loves him. It's not exactly the most original story in the world, is it?"

I sipped cold tea to hide my astonishment. Where I came from, nobody spoke like this, least of all in front of their family. Harry lit another cigarette with elegant fingers, and walked over to the fire.

"This house is always so bloody cold," he snapped. "And I wish you would stop talking about me with everyone who walks through the door, Mother."

I presumed he was referring to me, though I wondered who everyone else was. Perhaps Charlotte did this every week? Perhaps I was the last in a long line of mystery guests who were asked to tea with Aunt Clare?

"Penelope's not everyone, she's my friend," corrected Charlotte.

"Then I don't expect her views differ largely from your own."

"I don't know about that," I said, with perfect truth. Charlotte reached over for yet another slice of cake. For a second I caught Harry's eye, but this time, far from making me blush for his own entertainment, he looked straight through me as though I weren't there at all.

"You see what I mean?" demanded Aunt Clare triumphantly after he had left us for a second time. "He has none of his father's ability to sit still and do nothing."

She stood up. "Girls, you must excuse me, I have to see to Phoebe. Delightful, Penelope."

I scrabbled to my feet.

"Oh, thank you so much for tea. I've loved it," I said, suddenly realizing I had. Aunt Clare smiled at me.

"Darling girl," she said. "Do visit again soon." As she left the room, she paused and whispered something in my ear.

"Do remember me to Christopher. Just mention Rome, September 1935, to him, won't you?" She winked, smiled, and was gone.

I left the house soon after. Charlotte saw me to the door.

"You were just wonderful," she said, taking off my coat and handing it to me. "Aunt Clare says I have to give this back to you now. She noticed right away that I'd asked you to swap coats with me. She thinks I'm fiendish."

"Not at all."

"And I *am* sorry to hear about your father. Mine's dead too, you know. Heart attack, which is much less romantic than dying for your country, isn't it?"

"I can't see any romance in death," I said.

Charlotte looked at me incredulously. "Really? You're obviously not even halfway through *Antony and Cleopatra,* then."

There didn't seem to be an answer for this.

"I can't thank you enough for sharing the taxi and sitting through tea," she went on. "It really makes such a *change* to have a guest for tea. Even Harry couldn't resist popping in to have a gawp at you."

"I hardly think he was gawping," I said stiffly. I gave Charlotte her green coat, feeling suddenly foolish and wondering what to say next.

"Well, good-bye then," I said stiffly. "I hope we meet again one day."

Charlotte laughed. "What a thing to say! Of course we shall."

I laughed. "How certain you are! Why on earth *should* we?"

"We all adore you already," Charlotte said, kissing me on both cheeks. "None of us will let you go now. Have a good journey home."

As I walked away, Charlotte called out to me.

"Hey!" she shouted. "Penelope!"

I turned around. "Yes?"

"Do you like music?"

"What?"

"Music. What music do you like?"

I paused. Charlotte looked to me like a jazz fan and I hated jazz. But how could I tell her that I was madly in love with Johnnie Ray? Yet how could I *not* tell her?

"Oh, this and that," I replied uneasily.

"Like what?" she persisted.

"Oh, the usual stuff, a bit of jazz, a bit of—"

"Oh, *jazz!*" cried Charlotte, her voice heavy with disappointment. "How terminally dull. Funny, I didn't have you marked as one of *those.* Harry's addicted to the stuff, can't get enough. Personally, it leaves me utterly cold."

There was a pause.

"I think jazz is rather important," I said pompously, but Charlotte said nothing. *I can tell her,* I thought. *She'll understand.* I took a deep breath.

"But I—I rather prefer, well, actually, I am utterly and completely dedicated to—to—Johnnie Ray," I admitted.

There. I had said it. Charlotte pretended to swoon.

"Thank *goodness*!" she said. "I think he's the dreamiest man alive."

"You do?"

"Of course. How could anybody *not*?"

"Do you think he might come to London and marry us?"

"He'd be mad not to," said Charlotte, without any irony at all.

I hummed "If You Believe" all the way to the station. It was as if I had been watching a play and hadn't realized how good it was until the last scene. On the way down to Magna that night I *missed*, yes, really *missed* Charlotte, Aunt Clare, and Harry. It had taken them just a couple of hours to alter my life, yet I didn't quite know how yet.

It wasn't until I boarded the train that I felt something strange in the pocket of my coat that had not been there when I handed it to Charlotte in the cab. It was a small green velvet box. I opened it up and found a piece of paper inside, folded up. I opened the paper. On it were written two words, in peacock blue ink.

Thank You!

I liked the exclamation mark. Charlotte, I thought, seemed like one herself.

THREE

The Duck Supper

THE TRAIN SPED OUT OF LONDON and I found myself a seat by the window and ordered a milky tea and thought about what Aunt Clare had said about my parents and Magna. She was right—my parents *were* married before they were whelped. Of course, it never dawned on me that my mother was so very young until I got to the age of about eight, and started to pay attention to what other girls' mothers looked like. I remember having lunch at Magna one rainy August afternoon and telling her that it was my best friend Janet's mother's birthday.

"And she's going to be *thirty*!" I squeaked. It seemed terribly old. "How old are you, Mama?" I asked her.

"Twenty-five, darling. Twenty-five and glad to be alive—oh, Penelope, please don't get jam on your dress. No, too late. . . ."

Now I must say something of Magna, or rather of Milton Magna Hall, the house that Aunt Clare so admired. To speak of its beauty would be missing the point of its power. To speak of its power would be missing the point of its chaos. Really, I shouldn't be referring to the house as Magna at all—it's rather like shortening Windsor Castle to "Castle," but when Inigo and I were little, the word "Magna" came easily to us, probably because it sounded so like the word "Mama," and Mama was, after all, the center of our world. When I started working for Christopher, he pointed out our error. I chose to ignore him. My parents met for the first time at Magna, at a cocktail party in June. It goes without saying that my mother's versions of events are always up for debate, but apparently she met my father and knew "within five minutes" that he was the man she was destined to marry. My mother, then sixteen and about to begin three years of studying opera at the Royal College of Music, was not officially invited that night, but found herself accompanying a nervous friend who had asked her along to the party. This nervous friend, the legendary Lady Lucy Sinclair, was supposed to be utterly in love with my father, and was hoping to snare him that night. Of course you can imagine what happened when she turned up with Mama. I have often wondered how Lady Lucy could have been so unbelievably dim as to take Mama with her. Did she honestly believe that anyone would *look* at her when a girl like Talitha Orr was in the room? My mother never tired of telling Inigo and me what she wore to Magna that night—a thin, pale pink satin-and-silk dress from Barkers of Kensington—and years later I would sneak up to the cupboard where she kept it, take it carefully out of its layers of tissue, and try it on myself. Standing in front of my mother's long looking glass in her pink dress sent shivers of excitement and sorrow up my spine. When the soldiers left Magna after the war, the looking glass had been broken, but the dress was still neat in the bottom drawer. Some things are made to survive. I don't think that a thousand wars could destroy that dress.

Mama's father was a doctor, and her mother an Irish beauty, who doted on her two daughters, Talitha and Loretta. I don't suppose that either of my mother's parents imagined in their wildest dreams that one of their daughters would end up living in America, and the other in a house like Magna, but it just goes to show where beauty can land you in life. By any standards, Mama is staggeringly good-looking. When she turned up at the party at Magna, she had barely spent any time outside London. At just eighteen, Archie was not especially tall and not conventionally good-looking, but he had acres of land and, more importantly, acres of *style*. His hair was thick and blond and his snub nose peppered with freckles. He was always laughing. Oh, I know people often say that of people they love, but in his case it was absolutely the truth. Mama once claimed that she had no straight-faced memories of my father. She said it in a voice of despair, which I found confusing at the time, but now I think I understand. When Archie saw her floating across the lawn, he reputedly fainted. When he came to, a minute later, Mama was holding his hand. *Hello,* she said. *How lovely to meet you. I thought* I *was the one supposed to be falling over.*

They were married five months after their first meeting, in the chapel at Magna. Archie's parents tried hard to dissuade him from marrying Mama, whom they considered worryingly pretty and far too young and inexperienced to cope with such a big house, but their protests fell on deaf ears. His bride virtually ran down the aisle and into his arms, a green-eyed, inky-haired fairy in white lace, already three months pregnant with me. It was 1937. Mama gleefully moved her few possessions from London to Wiltshire and awaited the birth of her first child. She had convinced herself that she was expecting a boy, so I came as something of a shock. I looked then, as I have done ever since, very like my father, which in turn seemed to please and irritate my mother, who was happy that I was never going to rival her beauty but a little jealous of the instant connection between infant and father. All this makes her sound self-obsessed, difficult, capricious—and yes, she certainly was—but she was only seventeen. I have to remind myself of this sometimes.

For years after my father left us to fight, my mother would mark the date that they had first met by sitting on the steps leading down to the walled kitchen garden and drinking a glass of elderflower cordial. One year—I must have been about thirteen—I joined her and suggested that we toast their first meeting with champagne. She looked appalled.

"But I was drinking *elderflower* the night that we met!"

"But we could have a proper toast—we could *celebrate* your meeting," I persisted. I don't know why I did; I could see that it was upsetting her to have her ritual shaken like this.

"Penelope, you're so horribly modern sometimes."

"It was only a suggestion, Mama."

"Sit down next to me," she pleaded, and I did, feeling the stone step warm on my thighs in the late-afternoon sun. I rubbed my fingers over a stalk of rosemary and lay back, listening to the hypnotic buzzing of the wasps in their nest in the old pear tree. The garden was the center of the universe, and within its walls lay the whole world, Eden-esque. What else counted outside the dry stone walls of Magna?

I stared at my fellow passengers and wondered if any of them had had as extraordinary an afternoon as I had. I felt so restless, I had to sit on my hands for fear I might burst with wanting to talk about everything. Aunt Clare, more than anyone else I had met, seemed instinctively to understand how living in a house like Magna was a double-edged sword. When you are just eighteen and desperate for something to happen to you (and anything *at all* will do as long as it involves a boy and some nice clothes), a house like Magna tends to give you a reputation before you have even opened your mouth. But it isn't just the age of the place (most of the house was built by a faithful member of the royal household called Sir John Wittersnake in 1462), but its *size* that gets people's eyes lit up. Glimpsed from the road, through a gap in the estate walls or a break in the avenue of whispering limes, Magna sits like a sapphire among the trees—part birthday cake, part ocean liner, part sculpture, part skeleton—a magnificent, ostentatious chunk of history, immediately defining those who have lived within its walls with the same adjectives.

Even at a school like mine, it was hard to make anyone believe that we were not rich. Alas, by the time I was eight, anything of any value had gone the way of all things—to Christie's. People who came to stay could not believe that in the 1950s anyone could live somewhere so giggle-makingly medieval. If you wanted grandeur, there was the Great Hall; if you wanted ruins, there was the East Wing; if you wanted ghosts . . . well, you just needed to live there. The largest room in the entire house was boarded up, destitute, unused, and full of spiders. Before the war, there was a household of forty. Now there were two—a housekeeper and a gardener. Yet nothing could dim the extravagance of the *idea* of Milton Magna Hall. It was most frustrating.

*　　*　　*

At Westbury, I jumped off the train and looked out for Johns, who was usually sent to meet me in the beaten-up Ford, but much to my relief, I found Inigo there instead, lounging against the bonnet of the car, smoking a cigarette and looking fed up. Inigo, being just sixteen, dressed like a Teddy Boy whenever he could, which was not as often as he'd like, as Mama had twenty fits when he combed his hair into the notorious Duck's Arse (D.A., we call it). Having just escaped from school for the weekend, he was still sporting his school uniform, which would have rendered any other boy desperately square. Not Inigo. Several girls on the platform saw him and giggled and nudged each other, which he pretended not to notice, but I know that he had. He shouldn't really have been at the wheel as he hasn't passed his test, but he's actually the best driver I know.

"Hurry up!" he muttered, leaping back into the car. *"Grove Family."*

Inigo is addicted to *The Grove Family*, but we don't have a television, so he has to watch it at Mrs. Daunton's house in the village. She talks through the show and Inigo ignores her. It's an arrangement that seems to suit both parties rather well.

We sped off home, arriving back in the village in no fewer than seven minutes. My mind drifted to Christopher and Aunt Clare's perfectly accurate comment on his ability to gossip. What on earth had happened between him and Aunt Clare in Rome? I would be far too shy to ask him straight out. And wasn't Aunt Clare still *married* until last year? I was so deep in thought that I didn't even notice that Inigo had stopped the car at the bottom of the drive.

"If you whizz out here, I can still make the start of the program," said Inigo. I opened the passenger door.

"How kind. It's such a mild evening," I yelled, as the wind whipped the words out of my mouth.

"Isn't it?"

I glared at my brother, but he just grinned at me, so I walked away before he could see me smiling too. Inigo is impossible to stay angry with for long. In fact, I felt like a walk. The drive is almost my favorite part of the whole estate, though walking up to the house on a stormy night can be a little bit scary. That evening I rounded the corner that gives the first proper view of the house and imagined what Charlotte would think of Magna. It is a house with a dual personality. Once you have taken in the thrill of the medieval building, there's the extra bit that was added to the equation in 1625—a vast wing stuck onto the side of the house where Renaissance paneling replaced bare stone and marble replaced oak. My great-aunt Sarah recorded in her diary that the East Wing looked as though someone's starry-eyed friend had arrived at Magna with a new quill and a fresh sheet of paper and instructions to "lighten the place up a bit." I think she thought she was being funny—after all, she was referring to Inigo Jones, my brother's namesake. It wasn't until I was about fourteen that I realized how famous he had been, how important his work was. Until then, aunts, uncles, historians, servants, tenants, and trippers all had opinions on Magna that ensured we knew the house was more important than its inhabitants.

That's one of the oddest things about living in a house of Magna's size and reputation—*everyone* feels entitled to air their views about the place. Indeed, it inspires the most awkward questions from people who should know better than to ask. I will never forget my first-year art mistress quizzing me over the remarkable Stubbs in the study and did I know precisely which year it had been painted? *Oh, the rearing pony with the funny fetlocks?* I said brightly. *That was sold last year to pay for the roof.* Miss Davidson's thin face paled and I realized that perhaps this was the sort of information I should be keeping to myself.

Eight years later, and there was little of any worth left at Magna. The only way to pay for the damage done by the army, who had requisitioned the house during the war for four long years, was to sell what was left *inside* to pay for the *outside*. When Papa died, it set the clocks ticking throughout the house with an added chill—death duties came even to the families of those who died heroes. I did not understand this at the time, only that it seemed odd to have to give away money just when we had lost Papa. And Mama was hopeless with money—she never stopped finding ways to lose it.

*   *   *

I flung open the hall door and shivered. The Great Hall at Magna is the first thing that anyone sees when they arrive at the house, and it takes some getting used to. I have to remember every time someone new arrives that they are likely to take a few minutes to get accustomed to it. Steadfastly medieval and weighty with dark, paneled wood and low windows, it is dominated by ten life-size wooden figures, arms stretched up to support the ceiling. Apparently they were carved to represent the master masons who built Magna, a motley crew indeed. Inigo always says that the hall is the sort of place that any self-respecting ghost would avoid like the plague. Suits of armor stand at attention in every corner, and where there is no room for another family portrait, a set of antlers hangs proud. A huge bearskin rug covers the floor in front of the fireplace, teeth bared, eyes wide open and staring. The bear was a present from my great-great-grandfather to his future wife ("No wonder she died young," said Mama), and its long claws used to scare me so much that I could never be in the room on my own for fear that it would come back to life, just to get me. As a result of my fear, Mama made sure that when we had a telephone installed in the hall, it was placed right next to the bearskin, so convinced was she that he would encourage me to finish my calls quickly. She wasn't wrong. There were other stuffed animals scattered about the room—a polar bear by the staircase, a zebra skin by the front door—all of which served to make the hall not exactly welcoming, but also not the sort of place that anyone forgets. The whole effect is pulled together by a vast fireplace—five children could stand upright inside it during the summer, yet during the winter, despite being constantly on the burn, it seemed incapable of throwing out much heat.

Well, I stood in the hall and yelled out that I was home, and no one responded with any interest at all, so I poked at the fire for a bit until I realized that if I didn't hurry up, I wouldn't have time to change before supper, something about which Mama was fanatical. I raced up the stairs, two at a time, and careered into the East Wing. "Thank God for Inigo Jones," Mama used to say to us, and I rather agreed with her. In the East Wing, one didn't feel as though there were ghosts listening through keyholes to your every word, or at least that if there *were* ghosts, they were likely to be well dressed and elegant, with an eye for a good bit of plasterwork.

Splashing cold water on my face, I wondered whether to mention my peculiar afternoon to my peculiar family. Best not to, I decided. I didn't want my mother to tell me that Aunt Clare was a "ghastly woman." All women were ghastly in my mother's opinion, and those she had not met (or could not recall meeting) *sounded* ghastly. Men were either "very plain" or "devastating," and there was simply no in-between. I pulled on a clean skirt, squirted on some of the scent Uncle George brought me from Paris, and applied a slash of red lipstick to my mouth and cheeks. My mother liked me made up.

"It's duck," called Inigo from outside my bedroom door, "so expect the worst."

I groaned. There is always a scene when there's duck for supper.

I ran downstairs to the dining room. The dining room feels about as medieval as you can get—rows of gargoyles peering down from the ceiling and that sort of thing—but it's surprisingly light, with tall windows that were forced into the nine-foot-thick walls when seige warfare went out of fashion. The stony silences of Duck Suppers don't fit the room at all; its atmosphere recalls the sound of tankards clanging together, *merrye music* from the lute, and people shouting across the table as they gnaw on the the bones of ye suckling pig. I found Mama already seated at the table. Wearing her least favorite dress—a long, gray wool number that itched and brought her up in a rash—she succeeded in looking both livid and bored. I sank into my chair (fearfully uncomfortable, no wonder no one ever lingered over their port at Magna) and beamed at her.

"Duck tonight," she announced heavily.

"Why, Mama? Is there something wrong?"

"Apart from that appalling, cheap scent you're wearing? I cannot even begin to *think* when my head is swimming in French Ferns."

"You said you liked it last weekend."

"Don't be ridiculous."

Inigo waltzed in, shirt half-unbuttoned and black hair flopping over his eyes. I braced myself.

"Lovely evening," he said, kissing my mother on the cheek. "Don't you just adore this time of year?"

He pulled out his chair and sat down. Inigo is the sort of person who makes a big performance out of the simplest of tasks, exaggerating every move until those in the room with him start to wonder when on earth it will end. That night he chose to elongate the act of stubbing out his cigarette so that by the time the deed was done, I felt quite exhausted just watching him. Once he had finished this, he moved on to the equally dramatic act of placing his napkin on his lap: unfurling it from its neat folds, whipping it into the air, then spreading it carefully over his trousers. We watched all this with irritation (Mama) and surpressed giggles (me). By the time he had finished, our housekeeper, Mary, had served us the wretched duck, tonight combined with boiled potatoes and whole roasted onions. Mary knew Duck Suppers meant trouble and bolted back to the kitchen as fast as her arthritis would allow. I was not hungry, but knew that the sooner this supper was over, the sooner I could get on with the important business of pondering over Charlotte, Aunt Clare, and Harry. I thought I would look them up in *Debrett's* before I went to bed. Where was our copy of *Debrett's* anyway? Duck Suppers were a terrible bore, I thought. But tonight, I was certain that what my mother said was not likely to have much impact over the resounding din of my imagination.

"How was your class today, Penelope?" Mama asked me, her voice soft and steady. I looked her in the eye, which tends to unnerve her in these situations.

"Pretty bearable, thank you, Mama. I think I'm getting to grips with it all."

Mama said nothing, but speared a ring of onion onto her fork.

"What I mean is that I'm starting to understand what he's trying to say," I added.

"And what is he trying to say?" she asked absentmindedly.

"In *Antony and Cleopatra*, I think he's telling us that love conquers all. Fear, death, war, age—everything kneels, humbled in the presence of love."

I felt Charlotte cheering me on.

"What soupy rubbish you talk, Penelope. I don't know where you get it from," said Mama, glaring and shaking the salt liberally over her plate.

"Actually, I quite like that," remarked Inigo.

I chewed on a boiled potato. The draft blew energetically around my feet and I scrunched them up in my shoes. I thought wistfully of Aunt Clare's suffocating study.

Mama took a deep breath.

"I took your dress shoes into town to be mended today, Inigo," she said.

"Thank you."

"And I've ordered you two new pillowcases to match the pair I gave you for your birthday, Penelope. Harrods had them in a green and white check as well as the pink and white. Which would you prefer?"

"I don't mind, Mama."

She stared at her potatoes, offended.

"I think perhaps the green and white," I added hurriedly. "They—they go beautifully with my nightie."

Inigo snorted. Then my mother put down her knife and fork with a clatter and bit her bottom lip. I glanced at Inigo, who nodded his head slightly. It was coming. The reason for tonight's Duck Supper. I held my breath.

"Johns was up on the roof this afternoon assessing the damage above the Long Gallery," said Mama. "It seems the storm did more harm than we thought. He's talking of attempting the repairs himself, but it's imposssible. Everything's imposssible."

Here was the theme of tonight's meal. I suppose I should have expected it, but it alarmed me all the same. Money. Or the lack of it. Of course we had heard her talking about it before, but never as the subject of a Duck Supper. This was something quite different. This required a proper reaction.

"What do you mean?" I asked idiotically.

She looked at me, her face suddenly soft and full of an emotion I dimly recognized as pity.

"Darling, we have no money," she repeated. "Can I make it any easier for you to understand?" Like the curious pause that takes place before blood seeps out from a cut finger, we all sat quite still, listening to the wind bashing the lower branches of the cherry tree against the window, waiting for the inevitable to happen. She sniffed and pulled a hanky from her woollen sleeve.

"Don't cry, don't cry." Inigo could never bear to see her undone. Personally, I found it strangely comforting. She rarely cried, actually. He dragged his chair close to hers and put his arm around her. A great, silent tear dropped from her eye and onto her untouched duck. She twisted her hanky into a ball.

"I miss him," she whispered. I don't think that Inigo heard her, but I did. My stomach seemed to lurch with love for her then—my ridiculous, beautiful, confusing mother. I pushed away my chair and crouched down on her other side, pulling her close.

"It's nearly summer," I said in a shaking voice. "Then we won't mind about the cold and the garden will look wonderful. We could hold another fête here, couldn't we? Or a gymkhana? Didn't everyone say what a success the gymkhana was last year? Magna won't let us starve."

"She's right," said Inigo. "Magna won't let us starve."

My mother kissed my hand. "Darling girl," she said. She kissed Inigo's forehead. "Darling boy," she said.

I held onto that moment for as long as I could. If I close my eyes, I can still see us now, three crouched-up little figures so tiny in the vast dining room, taking up so little space around the long table, dwarfed by the high ceiling and the long, rattling windowpanes of the dining room. I imagined my father walking into the room and seeing us there—his children lost without him and his darling Talitha looking up slowly as if she knew all along that he was going to come back to her. I had gotten into the habit of picturing him as a sort of cross between James Stewart and James Dean, in a beautifully cut dinner jacket, dressed for a wonderful party, shoes polished, a cigarette in one hand, a glass of whiskey in the other. Yet I knew the image was wrong because Papa never smoked. The shrill bell of the telephone caught all of us unawares. Inigo spilled my mother's glass of wine, and she sat bolt upright, green eyes flashing. *She thinks it's him,* I thought, *just like we all do.*

A moment later Mary announced that there was a young lady on the phone calling for Miss Penelope. Inigo raised his eyebrows at me.

"May I take the call, Mama?"

"Who on earth calls at this time?"

But I had already shot out of the dining room.

"Hello?" I was back in the hall again, teeth chattering with cold and curiosity. *The colder the hall, the shorter the call* was one of my mother's favorite mantras.

"Hello? Penelope? Is that you? It's Charlotte here. Charlotte Ferris. We met today at tea, you came with me to—"

"Yes, I know who you are."

"Oh, lovely. I'm sorry to call so late—were you in the middle of something?"

"It doesn't matter at all."

"It does. You were having supper, weren't you?"

"Yes. But really, it's quite all right."

"What were you eating?"

"Duck."

"Oh."

There was a pause, then Charlotte spoke again, her voice as clear and calm as it had been at the bus stop.

"Aunt Clare thought you were quite the best thing that's ever happened to me. I just thought I'd telephone and tell you so. It's always nice to hear that one's made a good impression, isn't it?"

"Gosh, I suppose so." I couldn't think of anything to say to this.

"Well, that's that, then. I just wanted to thank you again. You know—for sharing the taxi and coming to tea and everything. And to say I'm sorry if you found Harry difficult. We caught him at a tricky time this afternoon."

I could hear Mama's heels clicking on the dining room floor and felt suddenly desperate. What if I put down the phone and never spoke to Charlotte ever again? I took a deep breath.

"Why don't you come and stay? Next weekend perhaps. It'll be . . . it'll be . . . fun."

There was a pause.

"At Milton Magna Hall?"

"Of course."

"Heavens, Penelope, we'd love to."

"We?" I asked stupidly.

"Oh, Harry would love it so much. It's just the thing to take his mind off Marina's wedding. It would be *perfect* if we could come together."

"You're both absolutely invited," I said firmly, pushing aside my horror. "The train on Friday night arrives at Westbury at five twenty-nine. I'll send Johns to meet you. Look out for the beaten-up Ford."

"Oh, the thrill of it all!"

"Oh, and Charlotte—"

"Yes?"

"How on earth did you know my name? I forgot to ask you when we said good-bye."

"Name tape, darling. Sewn into the label of your coat. I saw it when we swapped. PENELOPE WALLACE. SECONDS HOUSE."

"Oh." Something in me was disappointed that there was such a logical explanation.

"I wish I'd been to boarding school. You have no idea how dull it was to go to school in London. I always longed to be gossiping in the dorm and organizing midnight feasts around the swimming pool."

"You've read too much Enid Blyton. It was nothing at all like that."

"At least humor me," sighed Charlotte, "and please tell me what I should bring with me to Milton Magna?"

"Twelve pairs of socks—it's colder than the Arctic Circle at the moment," I said, remembering what Aunt Clare had said about Harry's stamina.

"Socks. Twelve pairs. I'm writing it down now. Anything else?"

The bearskin was eyeing me evilly, and Inigo, who was almost as nosy as Mama, was hovering only a few feet away from me.

"No. Just yourselves."

I said good-bye and put down the phone, and grinned lopsidedly at Inigo. Speaking on the telephone at Magna always made me feel slightly off balance. Mama was using the cracked hall mirror to apply a powder puff to her reddened nose. Crying made her whole face swell up, as if she were allergic to her own tears. I felt certain that she would cry more often if it were not so aesthetically unpleasant.

"Who was that?" asked Inigo, instantly.

"A friend. She's called Charlotte Ferris. I've invited her and her cousin to stay next weekend."

"Who is this girl, Penelope? I've never heard her mentioned before."

"She's a new friend. Inigo's always making new friends. I don't see why I shouldn't, for once."

"Well, I couldn't agree more, darling," said Mama, her eyes full of suspicion.

We took our places in the dining room again. Inigo began cutting up a potato into tiny pieces.

"You know, you really should have checked with me before inviting strangers to the house," said Mama with a how-I-am-put-upon sigh.

"I know you'll like them," I said, with more confidence than I felt.

"Where did you meet?"

"Oh, out and about," I said uneasily. Mama would have been horrified if I had told her the truth, not just because she herself would not have been seen *dead* at a bus stop, but also because she disapproved of accepting tea invitations, clinging fast to her own mother's theory that tea should only ever be eaten with one's family, and taken with anyone else, it became common. Exceptions were made in the case of invalids, who merited teatime visits as they were "less likely to be infectious at this peaceful time of day."

"Out and about? How odd!" she remarked.

"I met her with some friends from my literature class," I went on, feeling that dastardly blush creeping in again. Gosh, I was a hopeless liar. Mama poured herself another glass of wine.

"Well! Charlotte Ferris, indeed. Where does she live?"

"I don't know, exactly."

"What on earth *do* you know? Really, I can't think what you find to talk about with anyone, Penelope."

Inigo lit another cigarette.

"She'll be like all of Penelope's friends," he said. "Slightly pretty and very dull."

"Darling, you know that's not fair," protested my mother gleefully, for nothing gave her greater satisfaction than hearing the female species criticized. Unfortunately, what Inigo had said about my friends was perfectly true, but I took comfort from imagining his jaw drop open in amazement as he saw Charlotte for the first time. He would be charmed and disarmed at the same time, a lethal combination.

"She's different," I said carefully. "Rather amusing, in fact."

"Amusing?" asked Mama. *"I'll* be the judge of that. What about the cousin? Is she another great wit?"

"She is a he. He's training to be a magician. Apparently he used to keep a pet loaf of bread in a wire cage."

"How plain," shuddered my mother.

"Plain! That's very good!" shrieked Inigo. "Next you'll be telling me he's 'well bread'!"

I cursed myself for bringing up Julian the Loaf. It was too absurd outside the confines of Aunt Clare's study.

"His name is Harry," I went on. "His mother is called Clare Delancy and she says she knows of you—and Papa," I added, heart thudding away as it always did when I mentioned my father.

"Clare Delancy. Clare, Clare, Clare, *Clare Delancy.* Let me think."

It was my mother's favorite pastime: trying to work out who, what, when, and where were the scores of people who claimed to have met her. It was rare for her to remember anyone. I had been on the receiving end of many a "Who on earth was that *ghastly* woman?"—usually demanded when she had met the person in question at least five times. She dropped her face into her hands to help herself ponder the issue. Inigo drained his wine and seized the chance to feed his duck to Fido.

"What did she look like?" she asked me. Detailed description was all part of the game.

"Well—tall and rather big, and gray rather than blonde, but quite beautiful in a funny way. Much older than you, Mama," I added hastily.

"Big and beautiful? Don't talk nonsense."

"Her husband died last year. Apparently he was killed by a falling bookcase."

Mama snorted. "That's what they all say."

"She lives in a sort of apartment in Kensington and she seems to know all about Magna. I don't think she's the sort of person one could forget."

"Sounds *exactly* the sort of person one could quite easily forget. An overweight widow with too much time on her hands. You're going to tell me that she keeps cats next."

"She does have a cat," I sighed.

My mother looked at Inigo in a what-did-I-tell-you sort of a way.

"Never trust anyone who keeps a cat within twenty miles of London. It signifies very poor housekeeping indeed. Not to mention the smell and the hair—"

"But Fido sleeps on your bed!" Inigo and I protested in unison.

"Fido is a *dog*. The smell and the hair are entirely different."

"Much worse, you mean," said Inigo, stroking Fido with his foot.

"Cat or no cat, I have no recollection of *ever* meeting this woman. What did she say about me?"

"She said you were a sensational beauty."

"Hmmm. Well—"

"She knew that you and Papa were married young, and she said that Magna was wonderful."

"She's welcome to it."

"Oh, don't say that, Mama. You don't mean it."

"I think I can translate this Clare's words as follows," said Mama beadily. "She wants to unleash her—frankly unhinged—son in our direction in the hope that he will marry either you, Penelope, or one of your ripe, rich cousins. Well! There's not much hope of that. No money, house full of dry rot, and absolutely no ripe, rich cousins, more's the pity." Mama gave an unexpected bark of laughter.

"I'd do anything for some ripe, rich cousins," said Inigo, with feeling.

"Frederick and Lavinia?" suggested my mother, referring to her sister's children of about our age.

"Freddie's a dream but Lavinia's awful," said Inigo contemptuously. "I caught her setting a mousetrap in her bedroom last time she came to stay.

She said she couldn't sleep knowing that they were out there. I said I felt the same about saxophone players."

"The mice were terrible last year," agreed Mama.

"Of course, if we had a cat—"

I felt that the conversation was veering off course, as it tended to when my mother and Inigo were involved. I played with my duck and ate my potatoes and onions and drank three glasses of water for Inigo's three of wine. (It was still a couple of weeks before my appreciation of good wine was due to begin.)

Mary brought around spotted dick for pudding, which cheered my mother up, and Inigo smoked while I drank a grainy cup of cocoa. I pushed off my shoes and sat on my feet to warm them up and wondered how poor Harry was going to cope with this kind of cold. After my cocoa I announced that I was going to bed, and stood up to kiss my mother good night. As quick as a jack-in-the-box, she was up too. It was another of her distinguishing characteristics, this necessity to be in bed before anyone else. I think that it stemmed from her days of dramatic exits when she and Papa were first married. She once told me that it was vital to retire to bed early in order to allow those left to talk about one in flattering terms in front of one's beloved.

"Good night, darling," she said with a small yawn. "I *am* sorry about the duck, but really, tonight has been quite bearable after all. Your mysterious Aunt Clare really has been a marvelous distraction."

I smiled and kissed her on the cheek.

My mother liked to be in her bedroom by ten thirty, but I don't think that she ever slept until well after midnight. I watched her and Fido float off upstairs, then wandered to the kitchen to get myself a drink of water. When I returned to the dining room, Inigo was studying the sleeve of a new record.

"Guy Mitchell," he said.

"Let me see."

"You should hear the song. His voice—" Inigo shook his head in wonderment, his black hair falling over his eyes. "I should be in America. Anyone with any sense should be in America."

I giggled. "Not before next weekend."

"No. I suppose not. I shall stay here and ask your new friends awkward questions." He grinned at me.

"What a strange Duck Supper tonight."

"Very odd. We must speak to Johns about organizing another gymkhana. I quite enjoyed watching hordes of ten-year-old girls on ancient Shetlands wrecking the park. Perhaps we should charge more to watch this year?"

I think, even then, that we both knew how futile such events were. In my heart of hearts, I knew that Magna would need to hold a gymkhana every day of the year for the next decade in order to keep going. I pushed such thoughts out of my head, said good night to Inigo, and decided to stick my head around my mother's door and check that she had quite recovered from the Duck Supper. I padded along the first-floor corridor, imagining my mother writing in her diary at her desk, her left hand scribbling fast over the page. As a child, I would tiptoe down the winding back staircase and into her room for words of comfort and a quick peek at the famous black leather-bound journal. When I was small she never much minded me reading it—I don't think that she had any idea quite what an advanced reader I was—but soon after my eleventh birthday she took to hiding it, and secured it with a padlock and key. It went from being a book that I loved and revered to something I rather hated. I would not think about my mother's diary tonight, I decided; it would only depress me. Outside her door, I knocked softly, and getting no response, crept into the room.

"Mama?" I could hear sounds of running water coming from the adjoining bathroom. Open, and resting on her bedside table alongside the laughing photograph of my father that reminded me that he looked nothing like James Stewart and an awful lot like me, was the blessed diary. I hesitated. She had not heard me come in. I don't know what it was that made me step forward and crane my neck over the entry for that day, but I did it, and there's no point in saying that I did not.

November 16th 1954

Penelope has invited a young girl called Charlotte Ferris to stay. She has an aunt called Clare, and although I did not say anything to either child, I think that I know exactly who Clare is. Fancy her reappearing now when—

I fled, and dived into bed, heart thumping, and wondered if my mother's nose had detected the giveaway scent of French Ferns. I couldn't even go and look for *Debrett's*, as I had spotted it heroically holding open her bedroom window, letting in icy blasts of cold November air.

FOUR

Miss Six Foot Nothing

I HALF EXPECTED CHARLOTTE TO TELEPHONE again before the weekend. The ten days that I had to fill before she and Harry arrived yawned in front of me, interminable. I had been looking forward to my time with Christopher in the shop on Tuesday (when I planned on bringing Aunt Clare and Rome jolly subtly into the conversation), but to my disappointment he telephoned me on Monday to say that he was going to be away until after the new year, buying new stock for the shop.

"I shall expect you back in January," he said.

"Are you going to Rome?" I demanded, utterly without thinking.

"Rome? What on *earth* makes you think I might be going to Rome?"

"Oh, nothing, I thought there was a big ceramics conference going on at the moment," I said wildly.

"Ceramics? Heavens, Penelope, don't make me nervous, please!" I heard the sound of shuffling papers. "No one has sent me *anything* about a ceramics conference in Rome," he muttered. "Oh! Unless you mean that poxy affair run by William Knightly? He wouldn't know a decent bit of art if it ran up and bit him on the ankle."

"Ah. That must have been it." I tried not to laugh. "Er—have you *ever* been to Rome, Christopher? Perhaps in your giddy youth?" I blushed at my nerve.

"Of course I've been to Rome, you silly girl. How on earth could I be doing what I'm doing if I hadn't been to Rome?"

"I'll see you in the new year," I said hurriedly. Christopher could be quite intimidating when he wanted to be.

"Don't expect any more money," he warned.

I spent long hours in the library at Magna. I had two exams to take at the end of the summer and scores of essays to complete in the meantime. Three months ago, Mama and I agreed that I should take English Literature and History of Art for a year before spending six months with old friends of Papa's in Italy, where presumably I would learn to speak the language while floating around Rome and Florence (Mama was unaccountably suspicious of Venice and Milan). There were plenty of girls my age with the same kind of plans, which made me feel comforted and bored in equal measures, but since meeting Charlotte, the comfort factor had been entirely swamped by frustration. I could not imagine a girl like her following the herd for one moment. She would think me jolly dull for doing so. I wouldn't be able to pretend to her that I was enjoying my studies. I had been looking forward to the English course, but soon found the endless dissection and analysis of the books utterly destructive. I wanted to read, but not to write about what I had read. Shakespeare was the greatest trial. I had adored watching *The Merchant of Venice* and *The Winter's Tale,* but had no interest at all in talking about the minutiae of the text. My History of Art classes were almost as tricky. Staring at photographs of the *Duomo* in Florence or the interior of Salisbury Cathedral struck me as quite pointless. I needed to smell the buildings, to hear the sharp clip of my heels on their floor. My appreciation of great art was too literal for study. I would even go so far as to say that I could not understand any art unless I was up close to it, until it filled all of my senses with its presence. I said this to Christoph once. He called me naïve beyond my years, which I said didn't make sense. He said that proved his point entirely.

The days before Charlotte and Harry arrived at Magna for the first time made working even harder than usual. I couldn't shake the feeling that something important, something vital, was hovering just out of my reach,

something that would change everything forever. Accepting tea with Charlotte had set my life off course, had swung me off the familiar tracks that I
had traveled on all my life so far. I tried to work, but most of the time ended
up drinking cocoa while listening very quietly to Johnnie Ray, old blankets
wrapped around my knees to keep out the cold. By Wednesday, I quite understood Cleopatra's demands for mandragora. Time and again I considered
sneaking back into my mother's room for another look at the mysterious
diary entry, but I stopped myself just short of doing so. I was afraid of being
caught, but more than that, I was afraid of what it might say. She had not
mentioned our visitors since the Duck Supper, but I sensed they were on
her mind. Oddly, I did notice that *Debrett's* had been taken away from her
bedroom window and replaced by a vast dictionary. Whether or not there
was any significance in this, I could not tell, and dared not ask.

Relief came one morning when Mama suggested that we travel to London to take a look at the new season's dresses.

"You must have at *least* two new frocks for Christmas parties," she said,
spreading a thin layer of marmalade over her toast. "You are my daughter
and you *will* look beautiful."

She put down her knife and stretched her hand out to me, her face full
of sympathy. She often looked at me like that, and I never held it against
her because her pity was so genuine. With the party season fast approach-
ing, it distressed her that I was not a fraction as spectacular as she. I don't
think that it occurred to her that it was possible to be even passably pretty
if one was tall with freckles and a friendly smile. For my mother, female
beauty was all about wide eyes and gypsy-dark hair and making grown men
faint.

"I don't know that I need any new clothes—" I began.

She tutted with frustration.

"Oh, Penelope, don't be ridiculous. You must have at least one new
dress, and that is my final word on the matter."

"But they're so . . . so expensive," I stammered. "You said yourself that
we have no money to spare. I'm sure we should be mending the piano or
fixing the fireplace in the study—"

"Johns will run us to the station. Would you change into a skirt, darling? Hurry up!"

I scuttled out of the room and bounded upstairs.

I have always found shopping with anyone a trial, but shopping with my mother was a hazardous experience that I tried and failed to avoid as much as possible. It was not just that our tastes differed—like any girl close to six foot, I liked simple designs and modest shoes, while she favored the flounce of Parisian couture and five-inch heels—but more than that, her size and beauty meant that shop assistants gravitated toward her, leaving me kicking my (flat) heels in the background. I don't want to sound too sorry for myself, but there can be very little more disheartening for an eighteen-year-old girl than being outshined by her thirty-five-year-old mother. As I pulled on a pair of stockings and a black skirt, it struck me that that the thrill of meeting Aunt Clare, Charlotte, and Harry was probably intensified by the fact that my mother had played no part in it.

Oh, how I wanted to be too intellectual for new clothes! Stacked up on the chimneypiece in my bedroom were five fashionably lettered invitations on thick white cards from girls called things like Katherine Leigh-Jones and Alicia Davidson-Fornby. I had never met either of those two, but my mother insisted on my accepting both invitations, swearing that the Leigh-Joneses kept llamas in Devon and the Davidson-Fornbys had the best cook in Hampshire. I resisted the temptation to say, *Well, so what?*—but then, I resisted the temptation to say most things to Mama. I was, in spite of the fact that she was almost a foot shorter than I, quite afraid of her—far more so than Inigo, who was younger than I but fiercely opinionated. As a result I was caught between the need to do exactly as my mother wished and the desperate urge to break away from her. More than ever, both sides of thirty-five were acutely aware of the widening gap that the war had placed between the generations, and Mama was more difficult than most. The fact that we seemed to have so little in common frightened me, and my years at boarding school had only intensified the sneaking suspicion that she was quite unlike everyone else's mothers. I vividly recall the gasps of admiration when

I arranged my mother's photograph on my chest of drawers on my first night away.

"What a pretty lady," said the girl called Victoria in the next bed to mine.

"Is she your mother?" demanded Ruth, a moon-faced child with a loud voice.

"Yes."

"She looks like a film star. When was that taken?"

"Just a few weeks ago," I said, startled by all the interest.

By this time all eleven girls were crowding around my bed.

"She doesn't look like you," observed Ruth tactfully.

"I think she does," said Victoria.

"No, she doesn't. *She's* got black hair." Ruth pointed a pudgy finger at the glass of the photograph frame.

"They have the same eyes."

We didn't, of course, but Victoria could sense my discomfort. I smiled gratefully at her and asked if she wanted to share some Nestle's condensed milk from my tuck box (after rationing ended, I craved the stuff). We were best friends from that night onward.

"Penelope! We don't want to miss the train!" shouted Mama. I slipped my Johnnie Ray fan club magazine inside an old issue of *Tatler* and bolted downstairs.

On the way to London, I thought about Harry and his great love for the mysterious Marina Hamilton and why my mother had not yet told me how she knew Aunt Clare. Sometimes I save all my thinking for the train—I find the hypnotic rhythm of the carriages rattling over the tracks makes it an excellent location for reflection. Mama read the *Times* and said things like "I don't know *why* we bother" every time she turned a page.

At Reading, a group of Teddy Boys made a terrific racket as they boarded the train. There was something about Teds that rather thrilled me, although I knew they were always getting into scrapes with the police. None of this lot was very handsome—thin, angry mouths and none of them a day over seventeen—but I couldn't tear my eyes away from the loudest of the group. He took his comb out of his pocket no fewer than fifteen—*fifteen!*—times on that journey, and there was beautiful red velvet on the lapels of his drape jacket. Mama kicked me under the table when she saw me staring—she lived in abject fear of me running off with a Ted, though the chance alone would have been a fine thing. Her main reason for not liking them was that they all had spots, for my mother strongly believed that clear skin was second only to good hands in her list of the important physical features for potential husbands. Poor Mama, her beauty was such that the boys on the train could not resist staring at her and nudging each other when she stood up at the end of our journey. She wore a gray-and-white-checked skirt and a slim wool coat and a slash of red lipstick, her tiny ankles and shapely calves encased in her best silk stockings. When she dressed up for a trip to London, she was as glorious as any Hollywood star.

"Silly, silly silly," she huffed irritatedly as they wolf whistled at her on the platform. "For goodness' sake, stop smiling, Penelope—you're encouraging them."

"They're not looking at me," I said, with perfect truth.

"Selfridges first, I think," said Mama as the cab rattled off.

"We could have taken the bus," I pointed out.

"In these shoes? Come on, darling."

"You gave the porter an enormous tip, Mama."

She ignored me, and I really didn't blame her. The trees in Hyde Park sparkled silver in the vague November sunlight and I hated myself for reminding her of our Duck Supper dilemma. I huddled into my coat and wished I had remembered the Fair Isle gloves. My mother opened her purse and extracted her lipstick and powder.

"I think Inigo was right about the gymkhana," she said, raising her eyebrows at her reflection (she had exquisite eyebrows). "It was *such* a boost for Magna last summer."

Irrationally, I felt a surge of annoyance. It had been I, not Inigo, who had mentioned holding another gymkhana at Magna. There was never any trace of spite in my mother's words, but her intrinsic assumption that any sensible suggestions had to come from Inigo, and not me, drove me to distraction.

"People are so very grateful," she went on. "It gives them something to talk about, doesn't it? Mrs. Daunton at the shop hasn't drawn breath about the number of cakes she sold. 'All but three fairy cakes gone, Mrs. Wallace,' she kept saying, 'and only one flapperjack left.' "

I snorted with laughter, in spite of myself. My mother was a superb mimic. She laughed too. I noticed the cabbie glancing in his mirror to grin at us, and the next moment he rocketed over a bump in the road, unseating Mama and sending my hat flying off my head. Well, that finished us off completely. When my mother got the giggles, there was no hope for anyone; she was as infectious as measles.

"One flapperjack," she repeated, taking out her handkerchief and wiping her eyes. "Oh, help, we're nearly there. Pull yourself together, Penelope!"

She overtipped the driver too.

There was something gorgeously theatrical about Selfridges, with its intoxicating smells of powder and perfume and the rows of salesgirls with shapely fingernails and Thursday-afternoon smiles. It was impossible to imagine anything bad happening to anyone in such a place, and as always, I felt my intellectual resolve weaken. I wanted everything, everything, *everything*—in fact, I felt myself positively winded by my need to consume.

"Second floor," said Mama briskly. "Up we go."

She attracted the attention of a dopey-looking blonde creature in evening wear and put her to work straight away.

"What's your name, darling?" my mother asked.

"Vivienne," announced the creature firmly.

"Really?" asked my mother doubtfully.

Vivienne widened her eyes.

"Well, Vivienne, we're going to need your help. My daughter here needs new dresses for the party season—nothing black, you understand. She has wonderful legs and good cheekbones, you see? We must make the most of them."

"Good cheekbones," intoned Vivienne. "She's very tall," she added accusingly.

"Six foot," agreed Mama.

"She looks even taller," said Vivienne.

"Well, I'm not. I'm six foot nothing," I snapped.

Vivienne looked like she didn't believe me, but showed me to the fitting room and took my measurements, while my mother stalked around the floor, her exquisite, spidery fingers reaching out to feel every dress she passed. I could hear her murmuring away to herself as I stripped down to my underwear. *Beautiful, ghastly, too old.* I thought of Charlotte in my coat and how much better she had looked than I had.

Vivienne handed me a red and black satin dress with lace edging.

"These colors are all the rage in America right now," she said. "Truly. You'll look like a film star."

I had my suspicions about that one. The dress felt tiny in my hands, like a doll's clothing.

"I think the size may be a bit small," I called, treading my foot down heavily on the hem.

"For goodness' sake, just try it and see," barked my mother impatiently.

Of course, I couldn't do it up, nor could the wretched Vivienne.

"The dress is too short and too narrow for me. I'm too big for it, Mama," I mumbled, hot with annoyance.

"You're what they call big boned," diagnosed Vivienne with all the sympathy of the terminally petite.

"Nonsense," snapped my mother. "Get her the dress in a larger size."

Vivienne scuttled off.

"Vivienne, my foot," snorted my mother. "I heard that woman over there calling her Dora. I don't know what's wrong with young girls of today."

This sounded comic coming from one who looked no older than Vivienne herself. Occasionally, I think my mother's youth frightened her; it reminded her of how much more living she had to do without my father.

"I'll tell you what," said Mama. "Why don't I try the dress on too? That way you can see how it looks on someone else. It's the only way to view a dress, really." She shot into the fitting room before I could change my mind and emerged a minute later in the same red dress that I had discarded. Vivienne, arriving back with the larger size, stood transfixed.

"You look absolutely beautiful," she announced. "Nobody would think you had a daughter as old as she is," she added with a nod in my direction. "You look more like sisters."

"Give me strength," I muttered under my breath.

"It is a wonderful color," agreed my mother, turning around in front of the long mirror to view herself from all angles, an immodest smile on her face.

"You don't think I look too old for this fashion?" she asked. I did not bother to answer her, knowing perfectly well that Vivienne's sighs of envy were enough to quash that particular fear.

"Maybe I should try it in green," mused Mama.

"Or we have it in a lovely pink," encouraged Vivienne.

"Good God, no. Not pink. *Never* pink."

"I'd like to look around the shop for a while," I interrupted. "I promised Inigo that I would try to find that new record he wants."

"Don't be long, darling. Oh, and please don't encourage him by buying him anything silly."

I think I knew that I was going to bump into Aunt Clare. Of course, it's easy to say that now, but when I saw her, writing a check in the menswear department, it did not surprise me in the least. She looked big, as she had looked in her study, yet eye-poppingly elegant in a beautifully cut bottle green skirt and blouse. For the first time I noticed how surprisingly tiny her feet and ankles were and I wondered how on earth she didn't topple over the whole time. I pretended to be terribly interested in mannequins of a suave-looking cricketer and a laughing golfer and waited for her to look around and notice me. She certainly took her time. To give myself some excuse for being there, I reached up and removed the cap from the cricketer's head and examined the label. I caught the end of her conversation with the salesman.

"My son will be thrilled," she was saying. "He does *need* a new tie. And cerise is such a *different* color, isn't it?"

"You've made an excellent choice. It's one of our most popular designs this season."

"Oh, is it? How disappointing."

"I wish your son the very best of luck with his interview. I would *love* to work in the airplane business."

"It *is* a thrill."

If I am giving the impression that I regularly eavesdropped on people's private chatter, then I am very sorry; it was not something I was used to doing and what happened next was punishment enough for my behavior. It pains me to recall that I lost my balance while standing on tiptoes and wobbled forward at the wrong moment, sending the unfortunate cricketer crashing to the ground. Aunt Clare's assistant sprang into action.

"Excuse me, Madam, but someone seems to have upset our 'Man for All Seasons' display," he cried, leaping over to the scene of the crime, where I was trying to heave the cricketer back into place.

"I'm so sorry," I gasped. "I lost my balance."

"These displays are very fragile. Our customers are not advised to handle the goods worn by our models." He pointed to a sign with precisely this message.

"I know," I said sulkily.

"Are you interested in anything you've knocked over?"

"Well, I—"

"Of course she is. We'll take the cap." It was Aunt Clare, hot on the scene. She winked at me.

"Oh! I really don't need it. I was just looking—"

"The cap *has* been slightly squashed," lied the assistant.

"Put it on my bill," said Aunt Clare airily.

He nodded and oozed off and Aunt Clare and I were left alone. I was struck by how different she looked outside the confines of her drawing room, though it was hard to say exactly why.

"You really don't have to buy the cap. I was just looking. It's expensive. I don't need it."

"Ah! You shouldn't have said that. No sooner has one announced that one does *not* need something, than the occasion arises when one does. If I don't buy this for you now, you are almost certain to find yourself at silly mid on without adequate coverage."

I laughed. "But I don't play cricket."

"Your brother does, I suppose?"

"Yes, but—"

"Well, that settles it."

"You could give it to Harry?"

"Harry? Playing cricket? Pigs might fly," said Aunt Clare bitterly.

So may he, by all accounts, I thought.

"What a treat to see you again so soon," she went on kindly, squeezing my arm. "We so enjoyed having you over for tea. I must apologize for Harry's behavior. He can be so difficult. Still, I have an interview with a family friend who works in the aviation trade. Building planes, that sort of thing. I think it would suit him rather well."

From my brief encounter with Harry, I could not imagine anything suiting him less.

"He and Charlotte are coming to stay next weekend," I said brightly.

"Of course!" said Aunt Clare. I could not tell whether she already knew about their visit, and I suddenly regretted telling her in case it was something that Harry did not want her to know.

"I was on my way to the record department," I went on. "I'm looking for something for Inigo. He likes the new pop sounds, you know, Bill Haley and all the American singers—"

Aunt Clare looked horrified. "How shattering. Are you here alone?"

"I've left my mother trying on half of Christian Dior's collection."

"She's here?"

"On the second floor, yes."

For a split second, Aunt Clare looked momentarily taken aback.

"You must send her my very best regards. Darling child, I must be going. I only came here to collect a vase, I seem to have left with half the shop."

She kissed me on both cheeks.

"Do look after Harry," she added.

"Oh, of course we will."

I watched her stride out of the shop, parting crowds of shoppers as she went.

I knew that I would not mention her to my mother.

*   *   *

We left in high spirits. My mother, fat with Vivienne's adulation and only too willing to put our financial crisis on hold, had bought herself three new frocks. Vivienne, to her eternal credit, had found me a sparkly mint green dress that suited my "difficult" coloring. It sat next to me on the train, wrapped in white tissue and enshrined in a huge black Selfridges bag. That dress seemed half-alive to me.

When we arrived back at Magna, we found Inigo in a state of great excitement as the second post had delivered a package from Uncle Luke in Louisiana, USA. Just the sight of the American stamps was enough to send Inigo (and me) into a bit of a frenzy. Everything good, everything exciting, and everything worth talking about came from across the Atlantic, and we had the good fortune of having bagged an American uncle.

My mother's older sister, Loretta, had married an American soldier called Luke Hanson and had moved to the United States after the war. Now, four years on, Loretta was nearly as much of a Yankee as her husband. My mother liked to give the impression of being appalled by her sister's willingness to embrace a country she considered deeply vulgar, but secretly she was as envious as hell, and who could blame her? She and I were fascinated by stories of refrigerators in every kitchen, proper washing machines and spin dryers, drive-in movies and Coca-Cola. Inigo, obsessed by the new wave of American music, found having a contact in the promised land itself a considerable bonus, and Luke greatly enjoyed irritating my mother by feeding Inigo's desire for all things new and shiny from America. We had barely walked through the door and put down our bags before he started.

"Uncle Luke's sent me the new Guy Mitchell record!" he announced.

"He's not your uncle," sighed my mother.

"He's married to my aunt. That makes him my uncle. And he sends me records. That makes him the closest thing to God around here."

"Inigo!"

"Let me see," I demanded, dropping my bags on the floor.

"Oh, no you don't. I don't want your grubby little fingers on my records. You can look, but you can't touch."

"Oh, don't be unfair!"

"Let her see it, Inigo."

He shot me a warning look and handed over the sacred item.

"What a funny size for a record," I said, examining its unfamiliar shape.

"It's a forty-five," he explained. "Soon the old seventy-eights will be done for."

"I don't believe you."

"It's true."

"Who on earth does Luke think he is?" snapped Mama, who feared change.

"You wait till I show this to Alexander," said Inigo. (I had been more than slightly in love with Inigo's best friend until last summer, when he drank too much at my birthday party and threw up in the asparagus beds. You can imagine what my mother had to say about *that*.)

"How can you play it? Surely it won't work on our old gramophone?" I asked quickly.

" 'Course it will. It just plays at a different speed, that's all. Forty-five rotations per minute instead of seventy-eight. It couldn't be easier. I've already listened to it about twenty times waiting for you two to get back."

Mama looked at me and raised her eyes to heaven.

"Oh, come on, Mama, we *must* hear the record. Just think, we're probably the first people in England to play it!"

"Oh, all right," sighed Mama. She hesitated for a moment, then said, "That reminds me, darling. I won't be here next weekend."

"You won't?"

"I'm going to Salisbury to stay with your godmother. Three nights I'll be gone."

"Aunt Belinda? But we haven't seen her for years!"

"Exactly. Too, too long. You're quite capable of looking after your guests yourself. You must have a word with Mary about food."

At that moment, Inigo's new record blasted out from the drawing room.

"Tell him to turn it down, Penelope," groaned Mama. "My poor head!"

*   *   *

Inigo and I sat up for two hours that night listening to the new record after
Mama had gone to bed. We kept the volume so low that it was hard to hear
at all. Inigo was in raptures, studying the sleeve, trying to make out every
word Guy Mitchell was singing, occasionally even imitating his voice. He
was remarkably good at it.

FIVE

Snowfall and Forty-fives

MY MOTHER KEPT TO HER WORD and set off for my godmother's house in Salisbury on Friday morning. She seemed anxious to get away, hardly bothering with the usual lectures about not using the telephone for too long and remembering to walk Fido and hose him down if he rolled in anything that had conked (dead sheep were his favorites, or the occasional late badger).

"Mary will be keeping an eye on you" was her parting threat. I noticed her diary stuffed into the outside compartment of her traveling case. She, like Gwendoline, obviously liked something sensational to read on the train.

"When will you be back, Mama?" I asked her, wrestling with the conflicting emotions of panic and excitement that swamped me when we had Magna to ourselves.

"Oh, Sunday night, Monday morning. I'll telephone and let you know. Good-bye, darlings."

We watched her climb into the car next to Johns. He would be off to the station again in a matter of hours to collect Charlotte and Harry. Inigo pranced around the hall.

"I think I might go to the pictures later," he said, skidding to a halt beside me. "I can take the bus into town this afternoon and be back before supper."

"Oh no, please. I need you here to help when they arrive," I bleated.

"I'll be back by the time they arrive."

"But what if you're not? I need you, Inigo."

He snorted with laughter.

"What *is* it about these people? I've never known you get yourself so worked up."

I scowled at him. "I'm *not* worked up. I just want everything to be right, that's all. Oh, and please don't play your new records the second they walk through the door. I thought we could play some jazz after supper for Harry."

"Oh, stop, the excitement's killing me."

Inigo hated jazz, as did anyone who had embraced American popular music. I used to feel myself torn between the two; jazz seemed so much easier to deal with, being much more academic, much less confrontational. Then I went with a school friend to see *There's No Business Like Show Business* at the pictures, and Johnnie Ray seeped into my consciousness for the first time. It is true to say that those two hours in the velvet seats of the Odeon Leicester Square changed everything, and I didn't care who knew it. I don't think that it was just because Johnnie made me want to faint and fall over (for that was just symptomatic of the power of the man); it was more to do with the spark of his performance, the *newness* of his movements. He looked to me like the man I wanted to marry, and when he opened his mouth and sang, the whole world could have stopped and I would not have noticed. I left the cinema in a daze, stirred with yearning and desire for the first time, jittery and disoriented by the sudden, stomach-flipping onset of adoration for a real *man*, and not one of Inigo's friends could compete with Johnnie, this vision of loveliness, this American dreamboat. It took me time to admit it to Inigo, but nothing in my halfhearted collection of jazz records matched up to one night of watching Johnnie Ray on celluloid. When it came down to it, his emotion, his heartache was something that I understood, where jazz was something that I just *pretended* to understand. Knowing that Charlotte felt the same way about him was like discovering that we both spoke the same secret language, but I had enough sense to realize that boys like Harry would have no time for him at all. I dusted down my Humphrey Lyttelton records and propped them up beside the gramophone.

It was nearly lunchtime. Mary, who last week reached her seventy-fourth birthday, was sitting in the kitchen, flipping through my mother's copy of *The Lady.* On the back of an unpaid bill from the grocers in town were Mama's instructions written in her splashy peacock blue handwriting: *Friday night—Boiled ham and potatoes roasted in their jackets. See Penelope for vegetables. Saturday morning—Toast and marmalade (new jar in dresser), boiled eggs. Saturday lunch—Leftover ham and bread with pickled onions and tomatoes. Saturday night—Chicken pie with mashed potatoes, fruit salad. Sunday morning—Boiled eggs. Let them have a pot of Mrs. Daunton's gooseberry jam for toast. Sunday lunch—Chicken soup, boiled ham and bread, fruit salad.*

I gulped, thinking of Charlotte's vast appetite. Despite her ability to cook at astonishing speed, Mary failed time and time again to produce food that tasted of anything. Once, my mother hinted at the need to flavor one's ingredients when cooking. Mary had oversalted her next fish pie to such an extent that even Fido spat it out in disgust.

"She did it on purpose," I said. "She couldn't take you interfering."

"Yet she's such a dear," my mother would say. "Your father was so fond of her." (Women over sixty-five made it to "dear" status, no longer seen as a threat.)

"She's useless," Inigo would retort. "And she smells of mince."

But it was no good. For as long as Mary could brandish a rolling pin, she was in. My mother nearly had a blue fit when the prettiest girl at the bakery in town asked if there was any cooking she could do up at the big house. I don't think that the greatest chef on earth could have shifted Mary from her throne.

"Mrs. Wallace has left her instructions," she said, picking up the list.

"Yes. Has rationing actually ended?" I asked cheekily.

"Get away with you! Most folk'd never set eyes on a chicken pie during the war. And get your hands off those apples. I need those for the fruit salad."

"Mary, can we do a cake today? And perhaps some biscuits or scones?" I pleaded.

"I'd do a trifle," she sniffed. "Only there's no jelly." She closed the magazine. "Terrible pains, I've had these past few days. Oh, it's the cold, you know. Never known wind like it, not since before the war."

"It *is* chilly."

"Snow's due," she said gloomily. "Johns says so."

"I'll cycle to the shop and get you some jelly," I said impatiently. "Anything else you need? Couldn't we do something a bit different today? I don't know—a coconut cake or something?"

Mary snorted. "Where do you think you'll find a coconut around here, dearie? They don't grow on trees, you know."

I glanced out of the kitchen window at the pregnant gray sky. Two magpies were fighting over the last of the nuts on the bird table under the stark skeleton of the cherry tree.

"Two for joy," cackled Mary. "I'll do you a nice magpie flan if you want."

By the time Inigo and I had finished our cheese sandwiches at lunchtime, I was starting to panic about keeping the house warm and giving our guests such terminally dull food. We would be considered one of those ghastly families that invited people to stay, then watched them slowly freeze to death over the fruit salad—and who wanted fruit salad in this weather? We needed hot food—apple crumble and cocoa, I thought. I was about to bolt upstairs and put extra rugs in the guest rooms when the snow started to fall: Great powdery flakes covered the windowsill in the drawing room within minutes.

"It's going to settle!" cried Inigo, opening the drawing room window and jumping onto the lawn. Fido leaped out next, barking with joy and going ridiculous, as dogs do when humans behave like dogs. Inigo scraped the first flakes of snow off the top of the gardening fork that Johns (no doubt warming himself up with a double brandy in the Fox and Pheasant) had not bothered to put away. I couldn't resist clambering outside too. I stared upward at the falling snow until I was dizzy, laughing as I caught the biggest flakes on the end of my tongue. Within minutes, the garden and fields beyond had their winter drear hidden, and became enchanted. Of *course* it was going to snow for Charlotte and Harry, I thought, then started to fret in case their train was delayed. I needn't have worried.

They were two hours early, something that my mother would never have forgiven them for were she ever to find out. I opened the front door, the empty log basket under my arm, and they were standing there, poised to ring the bell.

"We were about to knock," grinned Charlotte. "You must be psychic."

Incongruously carrying a tennis racket and a bottle of champagne, she was wearing her green coat again; but this time her thick, mousy hair was tied back in a long plait. Without the swinging curtains of heavy hair, her face was considerably altered: She seemed less Alice in Wonderland, more heroine of the upper sixth.

"You're early!" I cried accusingly. "Gosh! And I was about to send Johns off to meet you!"

"I know. I expect you think we're the depths. We heard that the snow had started out here, so we took the earlier train, then caught a bus from the station. It dropped us just at the top of your drive. We only just made it—we were sliding all over the road. Hello, Penelope," she added, kissing me on the cheek. Their footprints up the drive were already nearly covered.

"Isn't it just dreamy? Everything's pure Narnia," she sighed.

"Come in, then," I said awkwardly. "The logs can wait while I show you to your rooms."

Harry, his nose fire engine red with cold, was not wearing enough clothes. He still had that I've-seen-it-all-before amused look on his face (a pretty hard expression to carry off in the Great Hall at Magna, I might add), and his hair had been flattened by the dirty-looking tweed cap he clutched in his left hand. Were it not for his shoes (stylish-looking brown leather brogues, the sort that all jazz fans like to wear), he could quite easily have been mistaken for an eccentric traveler, the sort who had miles to go before he slept and all that. I half expected to see his horse snorting in the shadows behind him.

"How are you?" I asked him idiotically. "Shall I take your coat?"

"No, thanks," he said, walking into the hall. He nodded at Inigo.

"Like the rug. Did you shoot it?"

"Oh, strangled it with my bare hands," he drawled.

Charlotte giggled. "Bear hands," she said. "Very funny."

She was staring at the bookcase.

"The Great Gatsby!" she breathed, taking it from the shelf. "Oh, help, it's a first edition! Oh, double help! It's signed by the author! Harry, it's actually *signed*!"

"My great-aunt knew the Fitzgeralds," I said. Oh dear, I hope I wasn't boasting.

Charlotte shook her head in wonder.

"That's just blissful. Isn't it just your favorite book of all time?"

"I . . . it's . . . I haven't read it for a while," I admitted.

"She's never read it!" revealed Inigo. "Penelope loves books, as long as she doesn't have to open them. Hurry up with the log basket—my toes are about to drop off."

I could have cheerfully murdered him.

"Charlotte and Harry, this is my brother, Inigo," I said, through gritted teeth.

Harry stuck out his hand.

"Hullo," he said.

I crossed my fingers behind my back. *Please let Inigo like him,* I prayed. (Inigo tended to make split decisions about people that were quite irreversible. He loathed my school friend Hannah after ten minutes of conversation, despite or perhaps because of her unrequited crush on him. Conversely, he admired our local vicar, even after he was caught gulping from a bottle of brandy in the vestry. "The Lord works in mysterious ways," Inigo kept saying, which baffled Mama and me.)

"How was your journey?" he asked Harry conversationally.

"It was packed," interrupted Charlotte, "and *so* slow. I was like a wound-up spring all journey, waiting to get here. I've heard from everyone that Milton Magna is one of the most amazing houses ever built, and now I can see that it is. I don't think I've ever looked forward to a visit so much."

None of our friends tended to wax lyrical about Magna—they were too

stuck-up perhaps, or too accustomed to being in beautiful houses. Charlotte faced neither of these issues. Inigo's face softened when she had finished her little speech.

"You must be Charlotte," he said, shaking her hand. "Penelope was
right, for once."

"What does that mean?" Charlotte asked him.

"Oh, nothing, nothing. Come on then, Penelope will show you upstairs
and I'll try to keep the drawing room fractionally above freezing. No mean
feat, I can tell you."

By the time he finished this sentence, he had spoken more to Charlotte
than he had ever spoken to anyone else I had ever invited home. He shot
me a defiant look, as if to say, *You see! I can be nice to people when they merit
it!*

"You're in the Blue Room, Charlotte," I said. "Shut up, Inigo, and show
Harry where he's sleeping."

The Blue Room was part of the East Wing, at the far end of the corridor,
with a view of the chapel from one window and Mama's ducks from the
other. It was one of the few rooms in the house that still looked reasonably
presentable after the war—that is to say that the ceiling wasn't about to collapse, and the carpet hadn't worn through yet. Being a room stuck out on
its own, it had been unused by the army, which had saved it from the
tramping of boots and the heavy presence of lingering soldiers. It was
haunted, of course, but that had never bothered me. I opened my mouth to
tell Charlotte about the way the windows rattled on the stillest of summer
afternoons, and shut it again. There was never any telling how people were
going to react to ghosts.

"Christmas!" said Charlotte, looking around. "Why is this the Blue Room?"

It was a fair question. The Blue Room was in fact wallpapered in faded
pink and white flowers that Mama had chosen shortly after she moved into
Magna with Papa, before talk of war had even begun. It had been the first
room in the house that she had chosen to redecorate, and as it turned out,
it was the *only* room that she was to redecorate before Papa left to fight and
we moved to the Dower House.

"It was blue in my grandparents' day," I explained. "Mama tried to get us calling it the Pink Room, but of course, that never stuck."

Charlotte hurried over to the window.

"The snow," she breathed. "It's not ever going to stop."

Indeed the snow did seem to be falling faster and faster: great silent flakes careering down from a pale gray sky that pressed down on the house like a vast pillow.

"Isn't it lucky we got the early train? There's no way we would have made it, had we waited," she said, turning back to me, her green eyes shining.

It was amazing how easy I felt with her, despite all my worrying. She was so utterly familiar to me, like a character from a favorite book come to life. I joined her by the window. The kitchen garden lay still under its white blanket, which gave me an odd sense of freedom. Silently, I thanked God for giving me temporary respite from the location I associated so strongly with the night my parents met. Turning back to the room to check that Mary had dusted the chest of drawers, I noticed with horror one of Lavinia's mousetraps under the dressing table. Mercifully minus *le pauvre papa souris*, it was all set to go with a piece of molding cheddar sitting as bait. Charlotte looked at me, then followed my eyes down to the floor.

"Oh, mice are snidge!" she said. "There's no need for that in here."

"Snidge?"

Charlotte grinned. "Sweet, of course. I never mind mice."

"It's my cousin. She thinks that they follow her wherever she goes."

"Nice to think I'm not the only one with an odd relation," said Charlotte, sitting down on the bed. "Don't mind Harry though, will you? He was so pleased to be asked here."

I nearly pointed out that it was she who had asked him, but instead I just smiled.

"Where's your lovely mother?" Charlotte asked, looking around as if she expected her to leap out of the wardrobe.

"Away this weekend."

"Oh, how disappointing. I was *so* looking forward to meeting her."

"She's gone to visit my godmother," I said.

"How strange, in this weather. Gosh, I feel exactly like Anna Karenina, don't you?"

I laughed and thought, *Please don't make me admit that I haven't read that, either.*

"This is the most romantic house I've ever seen," she went on. "Oh! Do look, is that a dovecote?" (She pronounced it "doo-cut," which Mama always used to insist was the correct way to say it.)

"Yes. Actually, we call it the pigeon house. Mama adores anything with wings and feathers. It was a twenty-first-birthday present. Papa gave it to her."

"How romantic!" exclaimed Charlotte. She turned back into the room and scanned the objects beside her bed. I had picked some winter roses for her. A scattering of white petals had already fallen onto the table. She didn't comment on the flowers, reaching instead for *Good Housekeeping.*

"Ooh. 'How to Be the Perfect Hostess,' " she read. "I trust you've been studying this, Penelope?"

I blushed. I had. I changed the subject.

"I bumped into your aunt the other day."

"She said. In Selfridges, wasn't it? Apparently you sent something flying and she came to your rescue."

"It was quite funny, actually."

I told her all about Aunt Clare buying the cricket cap for Inigo.

"How typical," said Charlotte with a grin when I had finished the tale. "Never was there anyone so unsuited to being poor as Aunt Clare. The sooner she remarries, the better."

I couldn't tell if she was joking. "Do you think she might?"

"Possibly. She has no shortage of admirers."

Christopher, for one, I thought.

"I find her impossible to fathom," Charlotte went on. "She's so frightening sometimes, she *thinks* like a man, you know. That's perhaps what they like about her, I suppose. Gosh, I hadn't thought of that before." Charlotte frowned.

"Mama doesn't understand money, either," I confessed. "She gets terribly worked up about preserving energy and not using too much electricity, then she'll whizz up to London and spend a fortune in Dior."

"My mother only spends other people's money," said Charlotte. "She was out with the conductor again last night. She's got into the most hideous habit of telephoning me every time she's seen him to report on how they spent their evening."

"And how did they spend last night?" I asked.

"He took her to Sheekeys, lucky thing."

"Oh." What and where was Sheekeys?

"I asked her what Mr. Hollowman was conducting at the moment, and she said, 'Electricity, darling,' which made me feel ill."

I laughed.

"At least she's enjoying herself. I worry for my mother. She seems so *lost* sometimes."

"At least if she's lost, you know where she is," said Charlotte grimly. "My mother never stays in one place for longer than three days at a time. Gosh, Penelope, I must have a pee."

The Blue Room had a pokey little bathroom with a small window, but the bath was ocean deep and long, so that you could stretch your legs right out and still not touch the end of it, and that, in my view, made up for the tiny basin and yet more peeling, pink flowery wallpaper. Charlotte peered into the cracked looking glass.

"I look like the captain of the lacrosse team," she said ruefully.

"I used to *be* captain of the lacrosse team," I said. "It's a lethal game." I pulled my cardigan off my right shoulder. "See?"

"Oh, Penelope, that's horrible," cried Charlotte.

I grinned. I liked showing people my scar. It wasn't very big, but it was there all right, and it had hurt like hell when Nora Henderson—an amazon among sixteen-year-old girls—had crashed the chipped wooden edge of her lacrosse stick down on my shoulder.

"I didn't have you down as the sporty type," said Charlotte. "Like I said, it's greatly to my disadvantage that I didn't go to boarding school. I think it would have done me the world of good. Knocked off all my edges and all that. I'm just the type who would have benefited from a bit of discipline on the playing fields."

I blinked. Charlotte said the oddest things. It was hard to know whether to laugh or not.

"I play a bit of tennis now, but not much else. Inigo and I used to ride all the time," I said.

"Ride?" Charlotte looked as though she had never heard of the concept.

"Horses. Well, ponies really. Look, there's Banjo." I pointed out of the window.

Johns, buoyed up with brandy, was leading my reluctant pony through the orchard toward the stables. With the snow swirling around them, and Johns in his thick overcoat and hat, they looked like something out of Thomas Hardy.

"Isn't he sweet?" cried Charlotte. "Can we go and give him an apple later? The horse, I mean—not your man."

Not likely, I thought, remembering Mary's fruit salad.

"Banjo's a bit snappy with people he doesn't know," I said. "He took a chunk out of my great-aunt's twinset last spring."

Charlotte looked alarmed.

"I must change," I said, aware of my scruffiness.

"Oh, don't worry about me," said Charlotte. "I'm always fine."

I absolutely believed her.

On the way back to my bedroom I passed the Wellington Room, where Harry was staying. I hesitated outside the door, then panicked, thinking that he would have heard my footsteps stopping, so decided to knock and check that he was settling in. He opened the door, still wearing his coat.

"Oh, you poor thing, I know how cold it can get up here," I said. "I've got hot-water bottles for us all, so you should survive the night." Why did he make me feel so stupid? I only had to look at him and I felt about eleven years old.

"Please don't worry, I don't really feel the cold at all. I just like to *pretend* I do to annoy my mother. It's become something of a habit."

I must have looked confused.

"Do you *like* annoying her?" I asked him.

Harry laughed. "I read somewhere that only very ordinary men adore their mothers."

"That's ridiculous."

"But funnily enough, it's true."

"I thought your mother was wonderful."

"Of course she is. But wonderful people nearly always combine their wonderfulness with other characteristics that drive one utterly crazy."

I liked the way he said "crazy." He couldn't completely pronounce his *R*s and the echo of a *W* sound hung there instead. Any more than the echo, and it would have sounded absurd, but as it happens, it gave him a vulnerability, a humanness under the magician's cloak. He looked at me thoughtfully.

"Can I ask you something?" he went on.

"Of course."

"Won't you come in?" he asked, suddenly serious. I suppressed the urge to laugh out loud.

"Yes, thank you," I said instead.

The Wellington Room suited a magician, being dark and spooky and filled with grisly portraits of the most alarming of ancestors. In the corner of the room stood a suit of armor that I was convinced I had seen perambulating around the knot garden at midnight a few years ago. Normally, I would have housed a guest in *any* room but this, yet in Harry's case it seemed the perfect fit. He certainly *looked* at home; his suitcase spilled heavy books, jazz records, and ink-stained pieces of writing paper onto the faded ocher and russet rug on the wooden floor.

"I hope you like it in here," I said. "It's kind of different."

Harry looked around in surprise.

"*Like* it? It's like something out of a horror film, only slightly more scary." He stretched a hand out to touch the bat's-head carvings around the fireplace. "I love it," he added simply. "What self-respecting magician wouldn't?"

"I've always felt that any ghosts at Magna are pretty friendly, by and large," I said awkwardly. Harry pulled a packet of cigarettes apparently out of thin air and sighed. There was something distinctly feminine about him, I decided, though I was certain he'd be horrified if anyone ever told him so.

"Do you miss her terribly?" I was amazed to hear myself asking. *Oh, help,* I thought two seconds later, *I shouldn't have asked that.* Harry glared at me for a moment.

"I don't like being without her," he said at last.

"I'm sorry. I shouldn't have asked you. It's none of my business."

"None of mine, anymore," said Harry lightly. His glare had been replaced by that steadfastly amused look once again, so I plowed on.

"Do you think her the most beautiful girl in the world?"

Harry laughed this time.

"Have you ever met her?"

"No," I confessed, "but I've seen her in the magazines."

"She's not a very nice person," said Harry. "She's like a fox—she kills for the hell of it. It's like being in a terrible motor accident—one never imagines that it's something that might actually happen to you."

"Where did you meet her?"

"The Jazz Café." Harry picked up a silver cigarette box from the bedside table. "Oh, it's engraved, how touching. TO MY DEAREST LINDSAY, WITH ALL MY LOVE, SARAH. Who are they, please?"

"Oh, Great-Aunt Sarah," I muttered impatiently. "I never knew her." Now was not the time to get into *that* story.

"So you met at the Jazz Café?" I prompted him. *Marijuana, espressos, and jazz, oh my!* I thought.

"She was talking to a friend of mine," Harry went on. "This guy from school I'd never liked, but I went up and said hello anyway. He introduced me to Marina, and that was it. The spell was cast. For a whole month we met every night—but I never once saw her during the day. Well, it never seemed strange to me at the time, but it *was,* of course. You have to see your lover during the day at some point, don't you? Otherwise the whole thing remains a dream. Perhaps that's what she wanted." He stared at me, as if he had only just considered this. "She was absolutely hooked on magic," he went on, "and she never wanted me to explain how I had done anything. She said that nothing in her life ever surprised her anymore except for watching me. And I'm a sucker for that sort of flattery—everyone is, aren't they?—so I carried on trying to surprise her. I got addicted to the way her

eyes lit up at the end of a trick. She knew people—so many people—
Americans, Italian counts, Indian princesses, and they would crowd around
the table to watch me. I suppose I got addicted to that, too, idiot that I am.
At the end of every night I drove her back to her parents' place. She never
invited me in."

"Why not?" I asked stupidly.

"I wasn't exactly what they had in mind for Marina. She never said, but
she didn't need to. But she liked me, I know that much. I was uncharted
territory for her."

"Why? Because you were a magician?"

"Oh, no!" Harry grinned at me. "Because I was poor, of course. Rich girls
always go through a phase of lusting after men with no money. Haven't you?"

I flushed. His directness unnerved me.

"I'm not rich," I said pertly.

Harry looked at me as though I were mad.

"Anyway, all this was six months ago now," he said. "Just when I realized
that I was in it up to my neck, she told me she couldn't see me anymore."

"In what up to your neck?"

"Love, sweetheart. Love."

"Oh, *that*. I see what you mean," I said, sounding absurd. "How did she
tell you?"

"Oh, the usual. She cried a lot, like girls do, and told me that I would
be better off without her—which is true—then a couple of months later, I
pick up the paper and read that she's engaged to George Rogerson. The least
magical man on the planet."

"Why is she marrying him, then?"

"He's loaded and has lots of important friends. I hear he's a wonder on
the golf course. Irresistible, don't you think?"

"So why did you go to dinner with them the other day? Wouldn't it be
easier not to see her, to try to forget her?"

Harry sat down on the bed and offered me a cigarette from Aunt Sarah's silver box. I had filled the box earlier that day, so at least I knew they were fresh.
It wouldn't do to refuse one; I could see that Harry wanted me to join him.

"Thank you," I said, taking one.

"I *had* to see her with him," he explained, flicking open his lighter for me, "even if it was only to make sure it was really happening. She sat at the other end of the table giving me these odd looks. I couldn't make out what she was trying to say."

"Couldn't you—I don't know—turn George Rogerson into a toad, or something?" I asked.

"I thought of that. But then, of course, someone else got there before me."

I giggled.

"I'm going to get her back," he said calmly.

"How?"

Harry stood up and wandered over to the window. From the back, I could see that the ends of his trousers had been trodden down by the heels of his shoes. He looked as though he could have done with a Selfridges session with Mama. Yet for all his disheveled appearance, he remained peculiarly stylish. He was, like Charlotte, the sort of person who could wear a cardboard box and make it look right.

"Well, it's like this," he said. "There's one characteristic Marina has—something that she could never hide whenever we were together—her Achilles' heel, if you like. I want to play on it until she breaks. Use it until she comes back to me."

"What is it?" I asked, imagining Marina with a fearful stutter or an inability to read.

"Jealousy," said Harry. "The green-eyed monster. She could never relax when other women were around. She used to say that if she ever saw me with another girl, she'd curl up and die."

"And you *want* her to do that? She wouldn't be much use to you dead."

He looked surprised by my insolence and frowned.

"What she meant is that she'd find it very hard to take," he said, as though speaking to a small child. "Do you understand? She needs to think that I've moved on, that I've found someone even more fascinating and thrilling than her." He inhaled on his cigarette very deeply.

"Good God, it's an English smoke, of course. How stupid of me. Wills, is it?" he said lightly, opening the window and crushing it to a pulp in the virginal snow on the windowsill.

"I'm sorry," I said.

"It's all right. I would never have noticed that sort of thing before I met Marina. She taught me the most infuriating habits that I just can't shake. I can't smoke anything but Lucky Strike, I can't sleep without a dose of Southern Comfort, I call men 'guys,' and I have this awful suspicion that without the Americans we might not have won the war. It's hell, I tell you."

I laughed, though I wasn't sure whether I was supposed to. Harry grinned and carried on talking. "But what does that matter? The point is that when Charlotte turned up at tea with you in tow, I just knew you were the one. Everything about you—it's perfect. Your height, your hair, your house. All three fit together to make the perfect nightmare."

"Hang on a minute! I don't think I know what you mean," I spluttered.

"You can help me, Penelope."

"What on earth are you talking about?" I asked suspiciously, picturing myself sideways in a wooden box, about to be sawed in two.

Harry stretched out his arm and pulled something out of his suitcase. It was a large cream envelope with Harry's name on the front.

"Open it," he said, handing it to me.

I pulled out a thick piece of card. It was an invitation.

" 'Mr. and Mrs. Hamilton request the pleasure of your company at a party to celebrate George and Marina's engagement,' " I read. " '7pm, Dorset House, W1. Carriages, 1am. Cocktails and dancing. December 3rd.' Gosh! That's in two weeks' time!" I handed it back to him. "Well, I hope you have a good time."

Harry shoved the envelope back into his bag.

"You'll do it, won't you?" he asked softly. He didn't look at me this time; he kept his eyes to the floor and his hair fell forward as he waited for my re-action. I took my time before speaking again because I still wasn't quite sure what to say.

"So you want me to go with you, to get her to realize how much she really loves you?" I asked slowly.

"Something like that. You know, you're just the sort of girl she would *really* hate," said Harry with feeling.

"Charmed," I said icily. I wasn't at all sure about this boy. Firstly, what he was suggesting seemed ridiculous. And rude. And thrilling. Secondly, he had found one of his own wretched American cigarettes in his coat pocket and was using the silver cup I had won for Best Cleaned Tack, aged nine, as an ashtray.

"She can't *stand* tall, blonde girls like you—and you're younger than her, too. If anyone's going to get her back up, you're the one to do it. That's what I thought when I first saw you. You were just too perfect for the job."

I opened my mouth to say that it was an extraordinary idea and really, who on earth did he think he was, rolling up to my house and asking me to go around pretending to be madly in love with him, but I was interrupted by Inigo yelling up the stairs that there was a bat in the library and could I come and deal with it. Off I went, leaving Harry hanging.

Although I am adept at getting bats out of a house, it took quite some time to rid the library of this one. Rushing upstairs and changing for dinner at breakneck speed to avoid freezing to death, I felt strange knowing that Charlotte and Harry were in the house too. I had imagined the moment of their arrival ever since I had replaced the phone to Charlotte ten days ago, and had pictured myself chic in my mother's scent, drifting downstairs carrying a vase of flowers or a small pile of relevant books, while Mary opened the door to them both and took their coats. As it happened, Mary had seemed to have vanished off the face of the earth, Inigo had made a fool of me, and I had been caught out in a knitted cardigan with a huge hole under the arm.

I sat down on my bed and stared out of the window, thinking of Harry and Marina Hamilton in the Jazz Café (which required quite a lot of imagination as I had never been to the place myself, nor had I ever even drunk an espresso) and wondering if this was one of those Key Moments in life where you are offered a chance to do something out of the ordinary that will mean Nothing Is Ever the Same Again. I wondered if he had said anything to Charlotte about his idea—perhaps it was her suggestion? If I had been entirely honest with myself, there was a greater proportion of me that was flattered and excited to be asked to help Harry than there was irritated by the idea. Yet extending that honesty further, this excitement came much more from the possibility of seeing Dorset House again and attending a truly marvelous American-style party than it did from spending time with Harry. *Perhaps Johnnie would be there,* I thought, then scolded myself for being so silly. It was starting to get dark now; the branches of the lime trees at the top of the drive glowed ghostly pale. The snowfall had altered the scenery for our weekend, had opened up more possibilities, made memories of it before the first nightfall. I would take Charlotte to meet Banjo tomorrow. I smudged on the tiniest bit of lipstick and slid into my new Selfridges shoes. They were already bitterly uncomfortable. My mother was always talking about "wearing shoes in," but what she really meant was to break through the pain barrier so that you no longer noticed how much they were pinching. I wondered how she was, and whether she was regretting her hasty exit from Magna.

"Snow on snow," I muttered to myself.

"Are you ever coming down?" yelled Inigo.

I wobbled dangerously in my heels and thought how lost the effect would be now that my guests had seen me at my scruffiest. I paused for a moment, then kicked them off and pulled on my usual scuffed red flats. Racing down the stairs, three at a time, I forgot about carrying flowers and looking intellectual and smelling grown-up. There would never be any point in pretending in front of Charlotte. What's more, I thought wryly, Harry was a magician, so he was always going to be able to see through me.

Charlotte was sitting by the gramophone in the drawing room, changed into black trousers and a thick white jersey. She had pulled the sleeves down over her hands.

"You got my requests, then," she said with a grin.

"What?"

"Snowfall and forty-fives."

I could put up with Harry, I thought, as long as it meant I could spend more time with Charlotte.

SIX

How to Live at Home and Like It

ALTHOUGH INIGO AND I ALWAYS HAD WINE with Mama at supper (she refused to drink on her own), neither of us had ever consumed the amount of alcohol that we did that first weekend with Charlotte and Harry. Inigo raided the cellar and stripped it of the last few bottles of Moët (Mama only ever pretended to like champagne) and Charlotte produced a large bottle of brandy that she had stolen from her mother's drinks cabinet. Both she and Harry drank like adults, without much fuss and without seeming to be terribly affected by the amount that they were putting away. I tried my best to keep up. The dining room, with its dark wood and even darker carvings, made one feel twenty times more fizzy than one actually was.

"Fancy eating in here every night!" exclaimed Charlotte, eyes widening at the portrait of a set-faced Isabelle Wallace over the fireplace. "Gosh, who's *she*? I wouldn't like to get on the wrong side of *her*."

"That was my grandmother," I said. "I don't remember her. Mama says she was very fierce."

"Looks it. Good nose, though."

"She used to call our mother The Moaner."

"What does she moan about?" demanded Charlotte, champagne spilling over her fingers as she refilled her glass.

"Oh, everything," I said. "It's easier to list what she doesn't moan about. Mostly it's to do with the house, the garden—not having enough help, no heating, no electricity in the East Wing."

"Couldn't you two do something about all these things?" said Charlotte. "Put together some kind of fail-safe moneymaking scheme?"

"Funny, we hadn't thought of that," said Inigo coldly.

"Hadn't you?" said Charlotte in surprise, not registering the sarcasm. "The second I finish working for Aunt Clare, I'm *off.* I've got it all worked out."

"What?" asked Inigo.

"I'm going to make and sell clothes. Rent a shop somewhere and make a fortune."

"What makes you so sure people will want what you sell?" asked Inigo. (Why was it that Inigo never seemed to worry about that sort of thing, just said what he was thinking at all times?)

"Oh, they'll want my clothes, all right," said Charlotte. "Only I have to act quickly. There are a stack of other girls out there wanting to do the same thing."

"Are there?" I asked doubtfully.

Charlotte nodded.

"This girl I knew from school, she's getting together her own clothing business," she said, biting into a piece of bread. "I couldn't *bear* it if she sold her first pair of shoes before I did."

"Will you be part of this empire, too?" I asked Harry.

"Not likely." He looked at me speculatively. "What are you going to do with your life, then? Marry Johnnie Ray, I suppose."

"Ideally," I said, taking on board the snub, "but just in case he doesn't fall for me, I'm going to Italy next summer."

"Fascinating," said Harry. "Speaking of art, who painted the little watercolor in the corridor outside my bedroom, the snow scene?"

I nearly gasped. He was challenging me, without a doubt, and I didn't like it *one bit*—mainly because (inevitably and infuriatingly), I didn't have a *clue* who painted the wretched picture.

"It's a little van Ruisdael," said Inigo, eager to show off rather than rescue me, "one of Mama's favorites. She says she'd rather sell her soul than that painting. I think it was a present from Papa."

"God, I love the Dutch. Such emotional use of color," proclaimed Harry irritatingly.

"Why can't I meet some amazing man who'll buy me paintings?" said Charlotte dreamily. (I might mention at this point that she had slurped through her tomato soup and was now dipping her bread into what remained in my bowl. She did all this so coolly that no one batted an eyelash. That was the thing about Charlotte. She managed to turn her unconventional behavior into a bit of an art form.)

"Not much good if you end up having to sell every painting you're given," I commented.

"But just to know that there was a man who was prepared to buy them for you. That would be enough for me, I think," said Charlotte.

"Have you had lots of boyfriends?" Inigo asked her.

"Inigo!" I said furiously. "For goodness' sake!"

"Oh, it's quite all right," said Charlotte grinning. "That's what little brothers are for, isn't it? Asking questions like that?"

"Not so little," growled Inigo. "I was sixteen last month."

There was a pause. I noticed Harry shoot me an edgy look that I was at a loss to decipher. *Well, answer the question, Charlotte!* I thought. For all that Inigo shouldn't have asked it, I was as keen as he was to know the answer.

"I'm mad about a boy called Andrew," she said calmly. "A the T, Harry calls him. Andrew the Ted. According to my mother and Aunt Clare, he's very unsuitable. I think it's about the only thing they've agreed on in years." She laughed loudly.

"Why don't they like him?" persisted Inigo, and this time I said nothing.

Charlotte took a big gulp of champagne.

"Oh, he's a Teddy Boy, nothing more than that," said Charlotte. "Drape jacket, skinny trousers, perfect duck's-arse hair, radiates discontent. Aunt Clare thought it was all fine at first—she kept on saying how good it was to meet boys who were a bit different. Then, when I showed no signs at all of getting bored with him, she got a bit worried. 'I was out with a different boy every week when I was your age!' she kept saying. As if that made any difference to me." Charlotte stared at Inigo as she talked. "Everyone became nervous because A the T had no money and no real prospects. Standard stuff, really. In the end it got to me. I needed Aunt Clare more than I needed him, I suppose, and I've never been much good at deceiving people.

I told Andrew it was no good, that we had to stop seeing each other, that it wouldn't ever work out." Her long hair fell forward and brushed the side of her empty soup bowl. "Romeo and Juliet, eat your heart out," she added ironically.

I felt a wave of pity for Andrew, who I imagined would never be entirely free from the spell that Charlotte cast. I also felt envy—to have a boy fall in love with me was a great ambition of mine. Harry caught my eye and gave a brief shake of the head. I cleared my throat.

"What have you seen at the pictures lately?" I asked no one in particular.

"Rear Window," said Inigo loudly.

That first weekend with Charlotte and Harry at Magna came as something of a revelation. Without the overwhelming weight of Mama's presence, it felt as if the house was shaking itself out of a long sleep. For the first time in my whole life, the weekend actually meant freedom. We had just two nights with Charlotte and Harry, but it may as well have been thirty. I can see Charlotte and me now, drunk on champagne, dancing powdered snowy footprints over the dining room floor and shouting to make ourselves heard above the intoxicating sounds of Johnnie Ray and America. Always America. I had worried that Charlotte and Harry would be bored at Magna, would need entertaining as many of my friends from school had. In my mind I had a long list of distractions for them—backgammon, the wireless, the television set. I needn't have bothered. Not one jazz record got past Charlotte's insatiable desire for Inigo's rock 'n' roll collection, and backgammon? Who needed backgammon when we had a magician and a pack of perfectly good playing cards?

After dinner, we lit the fire in the ballroom and turned up the volume on the gramophone. Charlotte told me about her father, Aunt Clare's only brother, Willie, who had fought in the Great War and had died of a heart attack at the very start of the last one, and more about her mother, Sophia, and her string of unsuitable suitors.

"The conductor is allergic to everything," she said. "Even wine, which strikes me as just plain selfish."

Harry told me to pick a card from the pack I had unearthed from the kitchen drawer. I hugged it to my chest.

"Now what?" I asked him. "Do I have to tell you my favorite color or what day of the week I was born so you can work it out?"

"Four of clubs," yawned Harry. "Saves time."

I tossed the card out onto the table with a cry of amazement.

"Do it on me," demanded Inigo, inspecting the card.

Harry, deadpan as ever, performed the same trick seven times on both of us. Next he made a huge red silk handkerchief vanish before our eyes, re-producing it two minutes later from Inigo's jacket pocket on the other side of the room. He was wonderful as a magician, and the more he practiced his act on us, the more the tension seemed to drain out of his body, replaced by an air of engaging insolence that seemed to say, *I'm going to fool you again, but only because I like you.* He seemed much older than the rest of us—which he was—but it wasn't just his age that gave me this impression; his whole persona had an old-fashioned drama about it. Another thing that set him apart from the rest of us was his ability to drink and *not* get drunk. After only half a glass of champagne, my head started to fizz and spin. Everything became hysterically funny; nothing seemed impossible.

"How is it that you're still standing?" I asked Harry as he drained his fifth glass.

"Practice," he replied.

At five in the morning, Inigo said he had a terrible craving for eggs with sol-diers, but we left them in the water too long while Harry showed us a trick involving a vanishing soup spoon and they ended up hard-boiled. We peeled off the shells (difficult when we had all drunk more than we ever had before) and dipped the eggs in the salt jar, and I cut us uneven doorsteps of white bread and buttered them in the sort of way that Mary would have de-scribed as liberal. Charlotte made us all scalding mugs of strong, sweet cof-fee and Harry impressed me by tipping the remains of his whiskey into his with a sigh of despair. Then we pulled on our boots and crunched over the snow toward the bench that overlooks the duck pond, armed with traveling rugs and scarves.

"What a place to live!" Charlotte kept saying. "Who skulks about in the house at the bottom of the drive? We passed it on the way here."

"The Dower House? That was where we lived during the war. When we moved back to Magna, we used to get lost the whole time," said Inigo. "The Dower House isn't small, but you can hear someone shout to you wherever you are in the place. At Magna, you're practically in another time zone in the East Wing."

Charlotte giggled. "We spent most of the war in Essex at my great-aunt's place. All we wanted to do was get back to London. Everything sounded so bloody exciting up there and we were stuck out in the middle of nowhere."

I murmured in agreement.

"I felt cheated by the end of it all. Aunt Clare stayed up in town and, as far as I can tell, had a ball. She was forever lunching at Fortnums with falling rubble in her hair. She said the war was drunk-making stuff."

The garden sat so still in front of us, listening carefully to every word, I thought. As the gray dawn began to break, I ran up to the house and put Johnnie Ray on again, throwing open the ballroom windows so that the cold air was suddenly full of that voice and of America, and we all sat perfectly still, not speaking, barely daring to breathe, or so it felt to me. I trembled on the bench and clamped my teeth together to stop them from chattering. It felt as if there were sparks coming out of my fingertips—everything was most reverently alive. My head buzzed with caffeine; I felt dizzy from lack of sleep and the coldness of the sharp, frosty morning in my smoky lungs. When the song finished, two and a half minutes later, something was different. I think we all felt it separately, each of us alone with our own little reasons for why the balance of the earth had shifted.

"It's good, isn't it?" said Charlotte eventually.

"Better than good," I said.

As day broke, the sunlight broke through the clouds, and diamonds danced on the snow. Magna, and everything that surrounded it, glittered.

After one weekend with Charlotte, I could not imagine that there had ever been a time when I had not known her. I became aware of the aura of chaos that surrounded her (she only had to sit down to upset something—a cup of tea, the marmalade jar, the sugar bowl—and she never put anything away after she'd looked at it), yet these aspects of her character, which would in any normal person be considered flaws, only added to her charm. The reason that she spilled things was because she gestured wildly whenever she told a story. The reason she never put anything away was because she was so easily distracted—the sunset over the fairy wood or a book she had just noticed in the library would absorb her completely so that whatever she had been doing was forgotten. She never stopped talking, and though she didn't eat much at mealtimes, her sweet tooth continued to be as fervent as it had been that afternoon at Aunt Clare's. While we chatted after lunch and dinner, I was always aware of her monitoring Mary's loud footsteps around the kitchen and pantry, so that a sort of game between the two started to emerge.

"Penelope, I think Mary's popped out—do you think we could sneak into the kitchen for something to fill the gap?" she would hiss at top speed in the middle of a conversation. She possessed the pastry chef's flair for detail, making everything that she was going to eat look mouthwatering to the onlooker. Mary's fruit salad, after Charlotte had soused it in brown sugar, squeezed the juice of a lemon over it, and dipped her spoon in honey, seemed positively ambrosial. Open and shut went the door of the pantry at all hours of the day and night. There was a nasty moment on Sunday evening.

"Someone's been at my pineapple tart," Mary said ominously. "There was half of it left when I put out the lights last night. Not enough for one helping this morning."

"Bats," Charlotte said solemnly. "They'll eat anything."

Mary didn't quite know what to make of Charlotte.

On Monday morning, just before we set off for the station, I took Charlotte to see Banjo. I found a couple of squares of cooking chocolate for us to suck, and we leaned over his stall in a satisfyingly horsey way. Charlotte told me that she was not much of a rider, but she certainly charmed my pony, who was usually very sniffy with strangers, by filling him up with carrots stolen from Mary's supplies in the larder.

"Don't you just *adore* the way he crunches them?" she said, offering him the carrot like an ice cream cone. "I spent all of my formative years begging my parents for a pony of my own. I never much liked the idea of actually riding, but what *heaven* to groom them and decorate them. I had to make do with a rather plain-looking rocking horse. Not the same thing at all."

"I used to make my own rosettes, out of ribbons and cardboard from the back of cereal boxes," I admitted. "I never won anything myself. Banjo was too strong and too naughty. At the county show one year he carted me out of the ring when I was supposed to be performing my individual display."

"Couldn't you have argued that that *was* your individual display?"

I laughed. "Can't say I got the chance to. I was disqualified."

"How shaming," said Charlotte. "The *torture* of childhood. Aren't you glad to be out of that hell?"

"I don't really feel like I *am* out of it. That day that I saw Aunt Clare in Selfridges, and I knocked over their display, I felt about twelve."

"That's the beauty of being eighteen. You can blame everything on not knowing what on earth you're doing. I do, the *whole* time."

This struck me as odd as Charlotte seemed to me to be someone who knew exactly what she was doing at all times. She bit the top off the one remaining carrot.

"My mother thinks I should find a rich man to marry. She's always talking about how I'll 'come good' once I've found a husband. She hates having me at home—plowing through the books in her library and kicking my heels up at night. She thinks I'm lazy."

"Are you?"

"Of course. Any sensible person is. Aren't you?"

"I don't know," I said, thinking of my studies. "I never did very well at school. I like writing, though, making up stories," I went on lamely. "We weren't encouraged to make up anything at school."

"School has nothing to do with anything," said Charlotte scornfully. She blew air into her gloved hands. "Shall we have a walk around the garden now?"

The glare of the sun on the snow bruised our eyes.

*   *   *

We walked back across the field, climbed over the fence, crossed the drive, and entered the walled garden through what is known as Johns's Gate—because at eleven o'clock every morning he's always to be found standing there, smoking his pipe, Fido at his feet waiting for the crusts from his cheese sandwich. He doffed his cap at Charlotte and me.

"Lovely day!" said Charlotte, bending down to pat Fido.

"Beautiful," agreed Johns, nodding at Charlotte—Gabriel Oak to Bathsheba—as he opened the gate for us.

The walled garden is not perhaps what you would expect from a house of Magna's austerity. It is all curves and romance, and in the snow, especially so.

We threaded our way around the outermost path, crunching our boots in the snow.

"How odd," said Charlotte, "to find such a picturesque garden here. Is it William Kent? It is, isn't it?"

"Um, yes," I said brightly. The name rang a bell at least. "Gosh, Charlotte, how do you know all of this stuff? You're shaming me by knowing more about Magna's history than me."

"People who live in great houses either know everything or nothing about them. I can see arguments for both, actually. There's something very grand about living in a place this size and not having a clue what year the first brick was laid."

We stopped by the little marble Apollo, peering out over the knot garden. Charlotte put her gloved hands on his feet.

"The more you know, the more intimidating it becomes, I suppose," she said.

"When we were little, all Inigo and I did in the garden was stuff ourselves with fruit," I said. "And yews and the box hedges—they were perfect for games and hideouts. There wasn't anywhere in the garden that we didn't make our own." I pulled at the branch of an apple tree and an inch of snow slithered onto the ground with a soft plop. "The ladies from the W.I. were up here all the time during the war, picking fruit. Mama stood about issuing orders, but she was never much good at getting her hands dirty. She kept on saying that no war was going to turn her into a dowdy old woman with rough hands."

I felt disloyal saying this, but at the same time, talking like this came as a relief.

Charlotte exclaimed at everything—at the snaky boughs of the apple and cherry trees still laden with snow, at Mark Antony, our cockerel, crowing fit to burst from the roof of the henhouse—yet all the while succeeded in creating a strange impression of having planned everything herself. Her face suited the cold weather; when her nose shone red and her cheeks glowed pink, she looked like a model from the front of the knitting patterns that Mary was always sending off for.

I led us into the fairy wood.

"Gosh!" said Charlotte, picking up a handful of snow and molding it into a ball. We ducked under the first cluster of branches, then followed the path that weaved through the wood and would eventually lead us out at the top of the drive. The world was cast in white and silver, with the occasional burst of color from the scarlet berries of the holly trees. I couldn't have planned a more spectacular morning if I had tried.

"I suppose Harry's shown you the invitation," said Charlotte at at last. "I tried to persuade him that you would have far better things to do than hang around with him at some dumb party of Marina's—but he just said that anything was worth a try and you looked like the sort of girl who would get under Marina's skin. I think that's a compliment, by the way."

I laughed, embarrassed.

"I must admit that I'd love to see what they've done to Dorset House."

"Harry's pretty good company at parties," said Charlotte, throwing her snowball into the air and catching it again. "He's one of those rare characters who improves with drink."

"Do you think he's wasting his time trying to get her back?"

"Who knows? Being as dedicated to oneself as Marina is leaves so little time to focus on anyone else. I think she *did* love him, though," she added unexpectedly. "I only saw them together a couple of times. He claims he made her laugh. Girls love that, don't they?" There was that regretful tone to her voice that she had had last night when she talked about the mysterious Andrew. She cleared her throat and threw her snowball away. "You wait till you meet her! Harry was never good-looking enough for a girl like Marina," she said. "Too short, and way too different. I can't imagine the Hamilton family settling for someone as asymmetrical as Harry."

"What—what happened to his eyes? Was he born like that?"

Charlotte groaned. "Oh, don't! I was dreading you asking me that question." She bit her lip and took a deep breath. "His eyes are odd because I stabbed him in the eye with a pencil when I was only two years old. He used to have two blue eyes. After my attack, one of them turned brown. Aunt Clare was horrified and convinced that he was going blind, which he wasn't—though his vision in his brown eye isn't entirely twenty-twenty."

I squirmed. "Poor Harry!"

"But isn't it appropriate, for a magician?"

"He's certainly got the right look for the job," I admitted.

"I'm always telling Aunt Clare that he couldn't possibly be anything else because his eyes are too fairground for anything sensible. Would you honestly put your faith in a banker with one blue eye and one brown? It looks so indecisive, doesn't it?"

"It's sort of like Johnnie Ray's story," I said eagerly. "Dropped on the ground and losing his hearing as a little boy, yet remaining even more determined to succeed—"

"Like Johnnie Ray, only not quite as successful," said Charlotte drily. "Aunt Clare despairs of him, as you know. She wanted him to be the sort of son who would make a fortune in the city and buy her a wonderful house in Mayfair. She considers herself extremely unfortunate that Harry's ended up like he has."

"My mother's terrified that Inigo will bomb off to America and try his luck at a career in music," I said. "She's more frightened of that than of him having to do National Service."

"All mothers are terrified of their sons, I think," said Charlotte. "I hope I have nothing but daughters myself."

"My mother doesn't think much of me, most of the time. She can't understand why I'm not already married. My father fainted when he first saw her."

"No! Really?"

"Oh, yes. It's one of Mama's Great Truths. You should only ever stick with a man who's prepared to pass out when he claps eyes on you."

"Jolly sensible if you ask me. Andrew never fainted," said Charlotte. "He wouldn't have dreamed of it. Still, he liked me enough to ask me to marry him."

"He *what?*"

"Oh, yes. He wanted to marry me." She kicked at the snow. "It ruined everything."

"What did you say?" I demanded.

"No, of course."

The stillness of the morning gave her words resonance; her voice hung thickly in the frozen air.

"Aunt Clare would have gone crackers," she said, "and I wouldn't have blamed her. He's utterly and totally wrong in every way except for one."

"What was that?" I asked her, knowing the answer.

"I was mad for him," she said simply. "Still am. Mad for A the T."

Then she changed the subject so fast that it could not have been more clear to me that I shouldn't ask anymore.

"Where did your parents meet?" she asked me.

"Here, at Magna. It was mid-June."

"June! It sounds like another country!" said Charlotte.

Yet even in the grip of winter, I could sense the heady fertility of that minty summer night in 1937. Under the diamond-hard November earth, another soft summer lurked, with its time-old promises, and heavy bees and love at first sight.

"What's your favorite one of Johnnie's songs, anyway?" asked Charlotte, swerving onto a different subject yet again.

"Oh, you can't possibly ask me that!" I wailed. "I'd feel awful picking a favorite."

Charlotte laughed. "Don't be so jolly wet, Penelope."

*   *   *

On Monday, just after Charlotte and I returned from the fairy wood, I found Harry in the library absorbed in Keats.

"The train leaves in an hour," I announced. "Would you like something to eat before you go?"

"No, thank you."

I turned to leave him, sensing he wanted some time on his own.

"The Long Gallery," he said suddenly. "Could you show it to me, before we go?"

"Oh," I said, surprised and not at all pleased. "It's all boarded up, I'm afraid."

"So?"

"We can't get in."

"But you live here!"

"I know."

Harry shrugged and went back to his book. I hovered, livid.

"Oh, all right then," I said ungraciously. "Just five minutes. And don't come running to me if you crash through the floorboards and never walk again."

"How could I come running to you if I—"

"I know, I know," I interrupted him crossly.

The Long Gallery is one of the oldest rooms in the house. Originally, it was used as a sort of exercise pen for the ladies who wanted to stretch their legs in an afternoon, but didn't want to venture outside in the cold or rain (or snow, as the case may have been). Inigo and I used to spend hour upon hour up there, because it is the perfect room for children—ideal for any number of games and far away enough to make as much noise as we liked. We loved the Long Gallery then. The black oak floor shone from centuries of footsteps swaying on the uneven boards. The barrel-vaulted ceiling gave us the exact sensation of being on a ship, and when the wind blew, one could almost feel it creaking and careering over the waves.

But I myself didn't like to spend time in the Long Gallery anymore. You see, we were up there, Inigo and I, playing a variation on marbles (the variation being that we didn't know the rules but simply whizzed the glass balls along the floor and challenged each other to get them to the end of the room without zooming off course) when Mary came upstairs to tell us that Papa had been killed. The Long Gallery died after that, became haunted. Its door remained locked; Mama admitted defeat and said that it was the one room she simply couldn't cope with any longer. Inigo and I were glad; though at eighteen, I felt a kick of shame whenever I thought of it languishing away on the top floor—a room for centuries so full of life, so spectacular—left to the mice and spiders and woodworms. I felt too old to be afraid of it now.

"Follow me," I instructed Harry, and he did—all the way up the stairs, four flights of them getting thinner and thinner with each ascending floor—until we were outside the Long Gallery. I turned the rusting key in the door and creaked it open as though Hitchcock were directing me; I half expected the world to turn black-and-white in that moment. I stood impatiently in the doorway while Harry stepped carefully inside the room. Today wasn't the day for me to overcome my Long Gallery demons. I felt angry out of all proportion to this situation. In that moment, I thoroughly disliked Harry for making me open the door.

And off he went with his first question.

"What year does this room date from?" he asked, running his hands along the wall.

"It's medieval, much like the rest," I said breezily. He shook his head.

"The medieval period was pretty long," he said. "Any idea which decade within which century?"

"Thirteen twenty-eight," I said wildly.

"I'd like to stay here all night."

"Not a good idea when you've a train to catch."

He lay down on the floor and closed his eyes, which I found intensely irritating. He was doing it to annoy me, I thought.

"Have you ever slept a night up here?" he demanded horizontally. *Always* he was demanding, and every question he asked me sounded like an accusation, heavy with the assumption that my answer would always be wrong.

"No," I said. "Too cold and scary."

He closed his eyes again, with the annoying smirk back on his face. *He thinks I'm pathetic,* I thought.

"Actually, I don't like to come up here anymore," I said defiantly. "I was up here when I heard that my father had been killed. It's not a room that makes me feel very happy anymore."

"How strange," Harry said simply. I hated him for it, and I hated myself for telling him the story, because it weakened me, and more importantly, I realized that I had only told him to make him feel bad.

"You shouldn't waste a room like this," he said. He stood up and blinked and crossed the room to one of the windows and stared out at the snow-covered lawn.

"What a place to look at the planets!"

The first dim sparks of what would soon become brilliant white stars were appearing over the dark blue velvet horizon; the night was closing in on us, oceanic. All I wanted was to get out of the room as soon as possible. I felt myself heavy with melancholy and the soft romance of ages past—I could even hear the church bells tolling "Evensong" into the sharp air, reminding me of Papa's memorial service and Mama's tears.

"We had better go," I said, not liking the sound of my own voice. "You don't want to miss your train."

Harry turned to me with a burst of laughter.

"You can't wait to get rid of me, can you?"

"No, not at all."

"You know what you should do?"

"What?"

He pushed back his hair.

"Come up to London. I got myself into this whole silly mess with Marina, but at the very least it got me out of my mother's clutches and into the dark corners of the Jazz Café. I think you need to do the same."

For a moment I glared at him. At least I *think* I glared. My glares are pretty ineffectual as a general rule. Inigo says they make me look as though I'm sitting on a thistle.

"You're eighteen, for God's sake," Harry went on. "If you don't get out now, you never will."

"Get out?"

"Yes, get out. I can only imagine the kind of pull that a house like this has on one, but you'll never find Johnnie Ray out in the sticks."

"I'll certainly come with you to the party, if that's what you're worried about," I said pertly.

Harry laughed. "That's a start. Oh, and don't worry, if you get bored, Dorset House is stuffed full of the most amazing new paintings. Perfect for someone as interested in art as you," he added. He just couldn't help himself, I thought sourly. I chose to keep a dignified silence as we made our way back downstairs.

If we had been outside, I would have stuffed a snowball down his neck.

SEVEN

Me and the In-Crowd

IF MAMA SENSED THE CHANGE that had taken place at Magna after the snowy weekend, she didn't show it. She arrived back from her three-day sojourn with Belinda weighed down with her usual selection of baffling presents—a fir cone dressed as a hedgehog dressed as a nurse for me, a pair of hideous lime green slippers for Inigo, a woolen toothbrush holder for Mary—and announced that she had never had such a jolly time with *anyone* as she had had with my godmother.

"She's such a darling, but she really has become the most plain woman," she announced gleefully. "Such a shame. Goodness, when I think of her when we first met! She was such a beautiful girl, the longest eyelashes you had ever seen." This was another one of my mother's classic devices: Give praise to good looks that are long gone. I felt rather sorry for poor Belinda.

"She surrounds herself with extraordinary men, of course," she said. "All of them closer to seventy than forty, but quite fascinating. The food was inedible, but then when is it ever *not*? All the men were too busy gassing away to care much. Oh! I must talk to Johns about the dining room table."

I don't think this was true. I don't believe that she needed to talk to Johns in the slightest, but she obviously had no plans to ask us about our weekend. I was both relieved and highly irritated. Inigo did not seem to notice. I brought the subject up with him later that night after Mama had gone to bed.

"Odd, that Mama didn't mention Charlotte and Harry," I said, poking at the fire. "You'd have thought she'd be dying to know how it went."

"Of course she is," said Inigo in surprise. "You are *slow* sometimes, Penelope. She wants to appear nonchalant, but inside she's boiling over with curiosity and general *what happened*–ness. I wouldn't bother telling her a thing. She'll crack sooner or later, mark my words."

"Why does everything have to be so complicated?" I asked crossly. "You know, sometimes I get the distinct impression Mama's keeping something to herself."

"Concerning what?"

"Concerning Clare Delancy."

"Where did you get that idea?"

"Oh, I don't know," I said. "I just feel it, like a Thing from Space." Naturally, I didn't want to admit that I'd been snooping around in Mama's diary.

"Why can't she just be normal?" I said.

"Don't wish that on anyone," said Inigo with a shudder. "And don't be silly, Mama's incapable of keeping anything to herself."

I went to bed after that. There seemed to be no point in arguing. Mama didn't crack the next day, or the next. Nor did she crack when Harry telephoned me to make arrangements for the party. So in the end, of course, it was I who buckled under the pressure.

"It's Marina Hamilton's party tomorrow, Mama," I said. "Everyone's talking about it."

"Are they?"

"Well—yes. I think so."

"If you only *think* so, there can't be too much to talk about."

"I've heard they've flown a chef over from Paris who's going to cook omelettes at dawn," I said determinedly.

"How revolting."

"Apparently Marina designed her dress herself."

"If she looks anything like her mother, it would be more accurate to tell me that she has designed her own teepee. Tania Hamilton has a frame like the figurehead of a pirate ship."

I played my trump card. "Well anyway, I shan't be home tonight. I'm going to stay with Clare Delancy after the party."

"Who?" asked Mama, looking genuinely baffled.

"Oh, Mama, I asked you about her at our last Duck Supper. She said that she knew you and—and Papa. She's my friend Charlotte's aunt—"

"Ah, yes. Charlotte's aunt. The cat lover."

"Amongst other things. She likes cakes, too, and writing, she's—"

But Mama had moved on.

"Yes, yes," she said irritatedly. "Do remember to tell Johns what time you want collecting from the station tomorrow. Oh, and, Penelope, for goodness' sake, put your hair up. You can't have it hanging around your face tonight like a spaniel's ears. And tell Mary to give your shoes a quick rub before you go."

"Yes, Mama."

There was no doubt in my mind that she knew exactly who Aunt Clare was.

That afternoon I climbed onto the train to London and fretted for most of the journey (Was my hair *really* better up? What if I could find nothing to talk to anyone about?), so that by the time the train pulled up to the platform in London, I quite felt like running for the hills. At Paddington I was met by Charlotte in her green coat, carrying, of all things, a wire birdcage.

"Parakeets," she said, rolling her eyes. "Harry's giving them to Marina as a wedding present. I imagine he sees some dark irony in it. I think he's just plain cruel. I was thinking of setting them free in Hyde Park. What do you think?"

I giggled. "Harry would never forgive you."

"I wonder to myself—do I actually care? Come on, we'll get a cab back to Kensington Court."

Phoebe, marginally more unfriendly than the last time we had met, showed Charlotte and me into Aunt Clare's study, where Harry was reading the paper. He jumped up when we walked in.

"Your birds have arrived," said Charlotte sardonically, balancing the cage precariously on top of a book called *Wild Animals I Have Known* on Aunt Clare's desk. One of them squawked incredibly loudly and I jumped.

"Penelope. You look princess-ish," said Harry, yawning.

"I haven't dressed yet."

"Didn't say you had. Would you like a drink? I've asked Phoebe to open some champagne for us before we leave."

"Where's Aunt Clare?"

"Upstairs on the telephone," said Harry. "She's delighted with herself for refusing to come tonight. I think it's the first invitation she hasn't accepted all year."

"I'm surprised she's not coming, if only for the free drink," said Charlotte. "Apparently they're making real American cocktails. There have been so many rumors circulating about this party, it can't fail to be anything other than the most enormous disappointment."

"Nothing Marina does is ever a disappointment, unfortunately." Harry peered at the birds. "They need a drink."

"So do we," said Charlotte. "Phoebe gets more and more hopeless."

On cue, Phoebe clattered into the room with a bottle and some dusty-looking glasses. She was the most joyless girl I had ever seen, even succeeding in making the pop of the champagne cork sound melancholy. I took an enormous gulp, and my eyes watered.

"It's warm," shuddered Charlotte in disgust. "Nothing worse. I think I shall save myself for the daiquiris tonight."

"The Daiquiris? Aren't they that terribly nice couple who breed Norwich terriers?" came a voice from the doorway. Aunt Clare bustled into the room.

"Penelope dear, how delightful." She kissed me on both cheeks. "How are your cricketing skills?"

"Oh—the cap. Gosh, I still feel bad about that."

She gave me a wink. "Don't, darling. Don't ever feel guilty about anything—such a waste of time. Now I'll have some champagne please, Phoebe. Mercy! What on earth are those poor birds doing on my desk?" She clasped a hand to her chest.

"They're off to the party with us, Aunt. They're part of the 'Marina, Don't Do It' campaign."

"No wonder they're green."

"Sick as parakeets," Charlotte giggled.

Phoebe took me to my room to change. It was a nice room—clean and plain with a fire dancing in the grate—and someone had arranged some flowers on the dresser. I washed my face and changed quickly into my green velvet Selfridges number. Up and down, up and down, went my spaniel's ears, as I struggled to make sense of my hair. Why, oh why, couldn't I be one of those naturally stylish women, like Charlotte or Mama? After twenty minutes, I knocked on Charlotte's door to ask her what to do.

"Mama says I should put it up."

"Which, of course, you should. Here." Charlotte grabbed my hairbrush and some pins. She looked beautiful in the most understated way possible. All she had done was brush her hair and change into a blue silk dress, but her natural style meant that she could have worn anything and looked right. Her height was a great relief to me too, for I had spent most of my school days slouching next to girls of five foot, embarrassed of my conspicuousness. Charlotte stood just an inch smaller than I, making her carry herself utterly without self-consciousness.

"I like your dress," she said.

"It's a bit tight," I admitted. "Mama refused to buy me the bigger size. I feel a bit nervous, Charlotte."

"Are you?" she asked in surprise. "Lucky you. Nervous is exactly the right approach to any party."

"I don't know how I'm supposed to act," I admitted humbly.

"Don't do anything except smile and look as though you're having a good time," she instructed.

"I hardly know Harry. The whole thing feels jolly awkward."

"You know his name and he knows there's a Watteau hanging outside your bedroom at Magna. I should think that fact alone would be enough to send Marina into orbit."

"The Watteau or the fact that Harry knows it's there?"

"Both."

Charlotte grimaced as she concentrated on my hair.

"To be quite frank, I'm bored witless by the whole Marina Hamilton saga," she said through a mouthful of hairpins. "Still, events that take months to develop in the cold light of day can be whizzed through in just a few hours at the right party. I'm hoping that Harry will go through the lot: anger, despair, humiliation—followed by revelation, hope, and finally, triumph. It's the mix of drink and cigarette smoke that does it. There you go, just as your mother requested." She swung me around to look in the mirror.

"Oooh, gosh, it's lovely!" For it *really* was. Charlotte dabbed a powder puff over my nose, swished a soft brush of rouge over my cheeks, and stood back to admire her handiwork.

"Pretty good, if I may say so. Not that you needed much. I'd do anything for your freckles." She frowned into the mirror at her creamy pale face. "When I was little, I used to paint them onto my nose with brown ink swiped from Mummy's best pen."

"Oh, shut up."

"She thought I was quite mad, *comme d'habitude*, poor old Mummy. Aunt Clare thought it was funny, which annoyed her even more."

But I had something now, something that Charlotte had given me when she had put up my hair and made me look just how I always imagined I could look. For the first time in my life, I was going out with a quality that had hitherto dodged me. I had caught a large dose of confidence.

"Idiots!" said Charlotte under her breath, as a bank of camera lenses opened fire on us. "Do you think any of them realize that the building behind them is far more fascinating than any of the fools inside it?"

Despite the rain, the crowds had gathered behind the railings of Dorset House to watch the guests arriving for the party, hoping for a glimpse of Princess Margaret, I supposed. As we stepped out of our taxi, one or two of the photographers had shouted out Charlotte's name and asked her what she was carrying.

"Parakeets," she said solemnly. A moment later, an efficient-looking man had swept up and taken the cage from Charlotte.

"Oh! They're a present!" she cried.

"For Miss Marina? Will she know who they're from?"

"I doubt it."

The man took out a pen and card and handed them to Charlotte, who handed them to Harry.

"From me," he wrote, and the rain smudged the ink.

"How on earth will she know who 'me' is?" I asked him, slightly irritated.

"Because no one else will give her anything that can't be worn, sprayed, eaten, drunk, or sat on."

It was entrancing to view Dorset House again with adult eyes. I noticed with a surge of surprise that it looked Italian to me now, like a Roman villa, with its three stories of long arched windows, pale stone, and long, level low-pitched roof. The portico was ablaze with torchlight, and a string quartet played bravely under its shelter.

"Doesn't it look romantic in the rain?" I sighed.

"Everything looks romantic in the rain," observed Charlotte.

"Except cricket pitches and occupied taxis," said Harry.

When I was little, Mama used to take me to Dorset House for tea with Theodore FitzWilliam, who was two years my junior and a very wet blanket. Tonight there was nothing of the chilly atmosphere of those miserable childhood visits. The first thing I noticed was the warmth in the place— every room had been properly *heated* (something that would surely have killed old Lord FitzWilliam stone dead had he walked in)—and the faded, pinched nobility of the war years had vanished, replaced by an all-consuming, glittery American glamour.

"Get me a drink," demanded Charlotte.

Like everyone else, we had arrived fashionably late. All around us people surged forward into the glorious hall, shaking off their coats and hats and filling the house with a deafening roar of chatter, while in front of us, a gay throng crowded the grand staircase in all its newly restored, white-marbled glory. As a child, I recalled the vast columns that stretched up to the first-floor gallery looking frightening and ghostly, as though they might collapse at any moment. Now they gave the impression of having been dipped in Californian sunlight. My ears were full of fascinating conversation.

Well, how are you? You look soaked to the skin, poor thing. Of course, this weather's been a terrible shock for Vernon—he's grown so used to the temperatures in L.A. . . . I don't believe I've seen you since the Governors Ball! . . . Borrowed the earrings, but not the necklace. Asprey's, such kind people. . . . Oh, I received flowers from Marilyn last week with a note that simply read, "Joy." . . . I found her such a sweet thing, such a talented actress, my dear, and so very vulnerable.

Charlotte and I giggled, and I worried for half a minute that I should have worn better shoes, then realized that everyone else was far too concerned with his or her own appearance to bother about mine. We followed the crowd up the staircase and into the saloon, and I thought how odd it was that usually when one returns to a place one had known as a child, it seems to have shrunk, yet Dorset House felt ten times larger than it ever had before. Automatically, Harry gravitated toward the long line of windows.

"Typical," said Charlotte. "Here we are, in one of the most spectacular rooms in the whole country, and all he wants to do is stare outside. Oh, yes, I'll have one of those, thank you!" she added, stealing a cocktail sausage from a passing waiter.

"You're welcome, Miss," he said, bowing his head, his face as serious as a surgeon.

The saloon had *not* been ruined by the Hamiltons, I realized; rather, it had been revived with extreme consideration. They had drawn attention to things that I had never noticed before—the nymphs and unicorns that frolicked along the curve of the ceiling and the five candelabras that lit the room with the sort of soft glow that makes everyone look twenty times more seductive than he really is. Charlotte read my mind.

"Beware of good lighting," she warned, as full of wise advice as I expected her to be. "It's almost as dangerous as alcohol."

Harry returned from the window and stuck close by to give the impression of being with us, but he seemed to know an awful lot of people, and they all seemed very pleased to see him. Occasionally, in the middle of a conversation, he would look my way and grin, though I supposed this was all part of the act—for the benefit of Marina, were she ever to appear. Charlotte knew plenty of people too, including the infamous Wentworth twins, Kate and Helena, who struck me as too beautiful and scary by half. They smoked thin cigars and were never out of the gossip pages. Kate was the cover girl of this month's *Tatler.*

"How *are* you, Charlotte?" demanded Helena.

"More to the point, how's your darling aunt?" asked Kate.

At that moment, Hope Allen, the least fashionable girl from my Italian class, with the skin of a rhinoceros, spotted me and hurried across the room to say hello. Dressed in an unflattering off-white crinoline, a heat rash creeping over her plump shoulders, she would have made me feel sorry for her, were it not for two things that made her unbearable to me. Firstly, she had borrowed my best Italian dictionary last year, dropped it in the bath, and returned it to me with crinkled pages and minus the whole of the letter Z. Secondly, she had an awful habit of sniffing during lectures. She never carried a handkerchief.

"Penelope! What are *you* doing here?" she yelled, speaking aloud what I had been wondering about her. "You look different. It's your hair, isn't it?"

I nodded, my heart sinking with shame. Why should the only person I knew at this gathering be Hope Allen? She glanced around and her eyes lit upon Charlotte, deep in chatter with the Wentworth twins.

"Heavens! Don't look now, but that's Charlotte Ferris and the Wentworth girls over there," she hissed, swinging her back to them. "I read something about Charlotte in the *Standard* last month. They said she was the only girl in London who can wear Dior, identify a great claret, *and* talk to the Teds," she added in one of those whispers that comes out louder than a normal voice. I wanted the polished floors of the saloon to swallow me whole. And I had my doubts about the *Standard.* The only thing I had ever heard Charlotte say when consuming wine was "yum."

"She's a friend of mine," I said with as much dignity as I could muster.

"No! How long have you known each other?" gasped Hope, virtually winding me with the insult of her astonishment.

"A couple of weeks. We came to the party together."

"Ahhhh!" said Hope slowly. "Now the hair makes sense—" she stopped and clutched my arm. "Oh, how *divine*, Harry Delancy's here too. I've always thought him frightfully attractive in that smoldering sort of way that short men can be."

"Smoldering?" I repeated blankly, trying to edge away from Hope.

"Yes. They have to try that much harder, you know, short men. They make terrific husbands as a result. It's worth remembering, you know."

"Right."

By a stroke of good luck, this painful exchange was terminated by the frantic signaling from a huge hairdo on the other side of the room.

"Oh, I'll have to whizz off," sighed Hope. "That's my mother over there, you see? Talking to the woman in gold?"

"I see."

"Oh, you *must* introduce me to Charlotte later," went on Hope. "I've met her before, with my cousin George. She won't remember me, of course. That type never does."

Cousin George. Hope was George Rogerson's cousin. No wonder she was even more pleased with herself than usual tonight.

"Who on earth was that unfortunate creature?" demanded Charlotte as Hope waddled off.

"Hope Allen. She says she's met you before."

"Can't have. I'd remember a pig scarer like her."

I giggled.

But I thought about what Hope had said about Charlotte and the *Standard*. As far as I was concerned, the description was as accurate as the press had ever been. And was she *really* that type, that rare type who had the luxury of picking and choosing exactly who she remembered and forgot? I vowed that I would be one myself by the end of the evening.

Harry slid up to us with an empty glass.

"You should try one of these," he said. "Once you've had three, stand over there in the corner of the room and look out at Hyde Park. It's the closest I've ever got to the sensation of flying—" His face stiffened and Charlotte and I followed his gaze.

"There she blows!" whispered Charlotte, "Harry's dream mother-in-law."

Resplendent in a pearl-festooned silver gown with a matching tiara, Tania Hamilton was greeting new guests with a presidential air. She was a pocket battleship of a woman, even wider and shorter than Mama had suggested, but she had the unapologetic air of a woman enjoying life to the full. She steamed up to us, holding her cocktail glass in front of herself like a torch.

"Well! Mr. Delancy, how *delightful!*" she exclaimed, and instantly my ears tuned in to the seductive American accent. "How *brave* of you to come—George will be *so* thrilled. And who are your friends? What a pity your mother couldn't be here this evening." She beamed, her relief at Aunt Clare's absence palpable. Harry was saved having to respond to this by Kate Wentworth, who slunk up beside him and put her hands over his eyes.

"Guess who?" she growled.

"Crown Princess Giselle of Spain?" suggested Harry. Kate exploded into giggles.

"What a wonderful party, Lady Hamilton," said Charlotte, ignoring Harry. "I'm Charlotte Ferris, Mr. Delancy's cousin. This is my—*Harry's* friend—Penelope Wallace."

Lady Hamilton clasped Charlotte's hand.

"Of course! Charlotte! What a treat. I've heard so much about you!"

"Oh, dearie!" said Charlotte with an immodest smirk. I tried not to giggle.

"I love your house," I said brightly. "My mother says I used to come here when I was little, when the FitzWilliamses lived here."

Curses! I thought the moment the words had left my mouth. *She won't like that information one bit.*

"I expect you think we've stripped the place of its old charm and made it all so *grotesquely* American," laughed Lady Hamilton, not in the least bit worried. "My husband tells me they were going to pull the place down if we hadn't bought it. So really, it's a case of the Yanks stepping in and saving the place once again, ha ha ha! Have you three tried all the cocktails tonight? I have a passion for brandy Alexander, so intoxicating. Oh, would you excuse me, girls? I believe the princess is arriving."

She surfed off into the crowd.

"I thought she was rather a poppet," said Charlotte. "I liked her sense of humor."

"She has no sense of humor," snapped Harry, who had disentangled himself from Kate Wentworth. "Here," he added, swiping two cream-colored concoctions from another phantom-faced waiter, "and don't ask me what's in it."

All I could tell was that it was delicious, and sipped through a straw, it tasted of coconut and sugar and countries with names I couldn't spell. We drank one each, and then Charlotte suggested we try a different drink, and just as we were setting forth on our third, Harry's face hardened, for standing talking on the opposite side of the room, exactly as he had described her to me, was Marina Hamilton. She was much shorter than I had expected (as the very glamorous always are) *and* thinner, and ten times more alluring. Dressed in a hot pink dress with a dazzling string of diamonds around her right wrist and a knockout cluster of rubies on the ring finger of her left hand, she looked a million and one dollars. How on earth Harry expected her to feel concerned at *my* presence, I could not think. Laughing, drinking, smoking, and sparkling, she moved as though she were *someone*. Even from as far away as we were, her famous cackle rang out above the music and the chatter. It was ten minutes before she spotted Harry, and even then she merely flicked her eyes in our direction and raised a glass. *That's that, then,* I thought.

"She's coming over!" hissed Charlotte.

And she was. Disentangling herself from a gaggle of girls, Marina was heading in our direction. I watched her, transfixed. Her pink dress was pure Cinderella and clashed gloriously with her piled-up red hair, yet the way she walked was pure Marilyn.

"I *thought* it was you," she said to Harry, leaning forward and kissing him slowly on both cheeks. "Daddy insisted on this crazy lighting tonight, which tends to make everyone look like they're staring at everyone else, when actually all they want to know is who the cocktail waiters are. Hello, Charlotte. *So* pleased you could come. Oh, and you must be Penelope. How smart of you to find such a simple dress."

"Selfridges," I blurted.

"It matches your Mai Tai. Have another."

For a moment I was baffled, then realized that Marina was talking about my drink. Quite apart from the obvious appeal of her accent, her voice was like her laugh—rich with smoke and jazz.

"Trader Vic's cocktail recipes are the best," she went on, running shiny red nails over her diamond-studded wrist. "My God, what an amazing man he is! Did you know that when he introduced the Mai Tai to Hawaii a couple of years back, it was so successful that he ran the world's supply of rum dry within a year? I think that's kinda fabulous. You should see his restaurant in Los Angeles, Charlotte. We go there on Sunday evenings in the summer and drink Screwdrivers. It's the best fun you can have with your clothes on," she added, her eyes glinting wickedly. "I recommend getting as drunk as you can, honey. The drink is so darn good tonight that you'll wake up tomorrow still high. And if you stick to the rum drinks, you won't even feel it. Trust me."

There was a brief pause.

"I love your dress," I blurted.

"Oh, George bought it for me," said Marina, lighting another Lucky Strike. "I saw it in Harrods yesterday afternoon and he got it for me on the sly. He's kinda like that."

"Sly?" I asked brightly. Charlotte giggled and Harry smirked. Marina roared.

"Oh no! He's as far from sly as sly could be! I meant he's the kinda guy who can't resist treating me to things, y'know? And boy, is he *funny*! You know, back in August we were at this swell party in the Sporting Club in Monte Carlo, and Ari—you *do* know Ari Onassis? No? Well, Ari just could *not* stop laughing at George. He found him *so* hilarious. You know, I could not *be* with a man who didn't make me wanna shoot myself laughing."

She coughed suddenly, a hacking, unladylike noise, and her eyes watered a little. "Nothing like a funny guy," she gasped eventually. "It *matters*, doesn't it, girls?"

She went on and on, and we listened, through a haze of Mai Tais and jazz. She name-dropped incessantly, asked no questions about us at all, and was blush-makingly rude to several of her waiters, yet she was impossible to dislike. I could have listened to her stories for hours—if only for the fact that she was the first person of my generation I had met whose life had not been limited to England. And did she *really* know these people? Was I standing next to someone who had actually had a proper conversation with Marlon Brando? As she carried on talking—her life in America, her life in London, which was better, oh, she couldn't say, they were so different but the weather in Los Angeles was sublime—I had a good chance to study her face. None of her features was individually remarkable—her eyes too close together, her nose too upturned, and her mouth too wide—yet together they formed a perfect, coherent, fox-like beauty. To this day I cannot say exactly how this was achieved except to suggest that it was something to do with her coloring—her enviable hair and her skin, milky clear except for a fetching dusting of palest indigo under each eye, confirming her lust for life postmidnight. I could quite easily see how Harry had fallen under her spell. He stood beside me, watching her talking but not, as far as I could tell, listening to a word.

"You must stay for breakfast," Marina concluded, flickering her eyes to Harry for a split second. "Omelettes and champagne."

"How delectable. Your parents certainly know how to throw you a party," said Charlotte.

At this point a gawky-looking man in braces launched himself at Harry with a cry of delight and bore him off in the direction of the band.

"Who was that?" demanded Marina. (Knowing who was attending one's own party was obviously not *de rigueur*.)

"Horace Wells—he was at school with Harry," muttered Charlotte. "Terrible stutter."

"Oh, *Horrie!*" cried Marina. "My God! He must've married Lavinia Somerset, after all. Good for him!"

"I have no idea," said Charlotte.

Marina barked her wicked, smoky laugh.

"Aren't we ridiculous? Listen to us! We sound just like our mothers, yakking on about who and where and when!"

I felt a momentary frisson of flattery that Marina was referring to the three of us together, which was swiftly replaced by horror at what she was saying. The burst of self-awareness on her part was admirable, but surely she could see that Charlotte and I were as different from her as were English and American cigarettes? She drained her glass.

"You know what, girls," she said conspiratorially, leaning in toward Charlotte and me, "I said to George that I didn't want a big wedding, no more than five hundred people. We tried to cut back the numbers even more, but it was *impossible*."

I hardly dared to look sideways for fear of the giggles.

"You are the most marvelously well-suited pair," said Charlotte. Marina sighed and looked, I thought, not entirely pleased with this.

"Well, George is such a traditional kinda guy. He wants everything done just right. You know he proposed on my birthday?"

"How darling of him!" I managed.

"A toast, I think," said Charlotte with a wicked smile. "To unimaginable happiness."

"To unimaginable happiness," we all repeated, but I saw Marina edging herself around so that she could keep tabs on where Harry had gone.

"Listen," she ordered, beckoning us in to hear her whisper and swamping us in Chanel No. 5 and hairspray. "I hate the idea that Harry's taken it badly," she murmured. "You know me, fickle as anything," she went on, forgetting that we didn't know her at all. "Harry *thinks* too much. He certainly thinks too much of *me*," she added, her face completely straight. Then she said, "Look after him, will you?" leaving me dumbstruck.

But Charlotte laughed. "Does he, indeed? Gosh, but that's an interesting theory. Penelope's not one of our family anyway, are you?"

There was a short silence while Marina absorbed this news. I could almost hear the whirring of her mind as she tried to figure out exactly what this made me.

"I thought—I thought she was your sister," she said finally.

"Penelope? If *only*," said Charlotte. "No, she's my friend. She's Harry's— er—friend too." She let the word "friend" hang ambiguously in the space between us. I blushed.

"Friend?" demanded Marina. "*Friend?* I thought you were all related."

"Oh, we only met recently," I said hurriedly. "Very recently indeed."

Marina opened her mouth to say something, but was interrupted by her mother gliding toward us, towing a horse-faced girl in green sequins.

"Marina! The Garrison-Denbighs are here! Look at Sophia's rubies, aren't they superb?"

Marina tutted with irritation.

"I'm talking, Mother," she hissed, shooting poor Sophia Garrison-Denbigh a look that stopped only just short of loathing.

"It's quite all right, Marina. We've monopolized you for long enough," said Charlotte smoothly. I smiled at Sophia.

"Your necklace is beautiful," Charlotte said to her, truthfully.

I pulled Charlotte away and announced that we should go and see what the Hamiltons had done to the gallery.

The Picture Gallery ran off the saloon and had been altogether abandoned in the FitzWilliamses' day. I remember Mama telling me about the tired red-fabric walls that were covered in darker red rectangular patches where every single painting had been taken down and sold. I laughed out loud when I saw how the Hamiltons had covered up every one of these unfortunate areas with new paintings, paintings in bright colors with bold lines the likes of which I had never seen before. In the center of the room stood a perplexing piece of sculpture in the shape of what looked like a man with a square head shielding his eyes from the sun. Several people clustered around, talking about it and using words like "intelligent" and "priceless" and "daring," while in the corner of the room, the jazz band played.

"*New York Movie,* 1939. She looks a bit like you, Penelope," said Charlotte, squinting at the painting in front of her of a blonde woman standing on her own in the cinema.

"Who dunnit?" I asked.

"Man called Edward Hopper, apparently." The Hamiltons had taken the liberty of labeling their art as though we were in a museum. I daren't even imagine what Aunt Clare or Mama would have had to say about this.

Charlotte's eyes lit on the next canvas. "Now *this* is remarkable. Mark Rothko."

It consisted of an orange square with a darker orange bit at the top and bottom. Something about it unnerved me. I wasn't sure that I understood it, but I found it hard to drag my eyes away.

"It's amazing what some people pass off as art nowadays," observed the good-looking man next to us.

"I think it's brilliant," said Charlotte quickly.

"My nine-year-old son could have painted it."

"Ah, but he *didn't*, did he? That's the point, isn't it?"

The man laughed and raised his glass to Charlotte.

"You're right, you know. You're *absolutely* right."

"Do you really like it?" I asked her when he was out of earshot.

"The only thing I know for certain is that I want to think the opposite of what *he* thinks," said Charlotte with feeling.

"You know him?"

"Oh, yes. Patrick Reece, former lover of Aunt Clare's, circa forty-seven. He took me and Harry to the theater a couple of times. I remember in the interval of *Blithe Spirit* he asked us if we'd like to try a little pot," Charlotte shook her head. "Can you *believe* that? Of all the nerve! Harry had the presence of mind to steal his entire supply of the stuff in the second half of the play and sold it to another one of Aunt Clare's devotees the next afternoon." She frowned at the memory. "Thank goodness he didn't recognize me out of my school uniform."

"Do you make this stuff up?"

Charlotte looked at me in surprise.

"No, worst luck. Oh, *do* look over there!"

It was Harry. He was sitting on a hard-backed chair just behind the band, his eyes half-closed, his whole being absorbed by the music. Girls with red lips, perfect hair, and swoonsome perfume laughed around him; boys drank around him; one man in a beautiful pinstriped suit actually flicked the ash from his cigarette onto the top of Harry's head without either party noticing. Charlotte grabbed two more drinks from the nearest waiter.

"These are Sidecars, apparently," she said. "And if anyone tries to tell me where they originated, I may well murder someone."

"With a Screwdriver?" I suggested, taking a huge gulp.

"Isn't she unbelievable? What on earth do you think she and Harry ever talked about?"

"Maybe she was tickled by stories of Julian the Loaf?"

"Highly unlikely. Oh, do look, the princess is wearing even more rubies than that unfortunate Sophia girl."

"Should we go and talk to Harry?"

Charlotte giggled wildly. High on rum, I made my way through the crowds and across the room to Harry's chair. He didn't see me at first, so I stretched out a hand and touched him lightly on the shoulder.

"Hullo," I said brightly. "Want to get another drink?"

He looked up at me, a cigarette dangling from his mouth. Candlelight and jazz suited Harry. His strange eyes with their heavy lashes set him apart; his skinny frame lengthened by his disheveled black suit.

"Huh?" he said. "Oh, it's you, Penelope. Here." He removed the cigarette from his lips and passed it to me. I took a puff. It had a strange flavor and smell and made me feel even more dizzy than I already was.

"Are you all right?" I asked him, feeling foolish. What was it about Harry that *always* made me feel foolish?

"Shall we play Dead Ringers?" he asked me, pulling up a chair next to himself. "Sit down, I'll tell you how."

I flopped down on the chair next to him.

"Finish this off," he said, handing me his cigarette again, and I took another three puffs and chucked the stub into his empty cocktail glass.

"Right," I said dreamily. "How do you play?"

"The idea is to point people out who look like famous people and for the other person to guess who you're thinking of. You'll soon pick it up."

He leaned in toward me. "I'll start." His eyes scanned the room.

"How about her—that woman, the one to the left of Charlotte, in the green and white dress—"

I thought for a moment. "Fanny Craddock?" I giggled.

Harry laughed. "Absolutely and utterly right. Your go."

"All right, all right." My eyes swam around the room. It really was the most gorgeous party. Sitting there with Harry, watching everything and everyone gave me the sensation of being in the cinema.

"How about the man there, playing the trumpet, in the band?" I hissed. "Louis Armstrong?"

"Yes!" I squealed. "And isn't it funny that he's playing the trumpet too!"

"Penelope," said Harry heavily, "that *is* Louis Armstrong."

"Oh, my word!" I exclaimed and collapsed giggling. Really, I couldn't help it.

"You're one of those girls who gets silly after one puff of marijuana, aren't you?" sighed Harry.

"One puff of *what?*"

A stout man with a schoolboy's smile and immaculately combed blond hair was bearing down on us. Harry struggled to his feet.

"George!" he said, offering him his hand. "Great party!"

So *this* was George, I thought hazily. He was fatter and shorter and uglier than I expected, but like Marina, he exuded enough wealth and self-confidence to make him curiously attractive. I sat tight and clapped hard as the band finished their latest number.

"How are you, Delancy? And who's this?" George smiled at me and I swayed a bit.

"How do you do? I'm Harry's—er—I'm a friend of—I'm his—his—friend." I beamed at George, wondering why I could see three of him. His faces broke into a series of wide smiles.

"Ahh!" he said slowly. "I see! *Well!*"

He roared with laughter and looked at Harry with new respect.

"You know, Marina's been worried about you, Delancy," he said in a low voice. (I expect he thought that I wouldn't be able to hear him, but growing up with Mama trains one rather well in the eavesdropping department.) " . . . kept insisting that you'd taken the news of our engagement very hard. Advised me not to invite you tonight, would you believe! Now I see she had nothing to worry about." He shot me an amused look. "Pretty little thing, isn't she?" he added in an undertone.

"Penelope's six foot," said Harry lightly. "That makes her three inches taller than you, doesn't it, Rogerson?"

George looked livid for a second, then laughed.

"Damn right, old man," he said, grinning. "Damn right. Well, enjoy the rest of the party. Have you heard? Omelettes at dawn."

He did a rather good mime of someone flipping a pancake, slapped Harry on the back again, and waltzed off.

"Omelettes at dawn," repeated Harry in brilliant imitation.

I fought off another attack of the giggles and raised my glass to Hope Allen, who was being spun around the dance floor by Patrick Reece. When the band took a break, she cantered toward me.

"*So* good-looking, don't you think?" she demanded breathlessly, grabbing my cocktail from my hand. "Paddy Reece. Brilliant mind. Known him since I was twelve." She leaned in toward me with another one of her deafening whispers. "Used to take me to the theater and offer me cocaine in the interval."

"Really?" I giggled.

She drained the rest of my Sidecar.

"Thanks," she said, handing me back the empty glass and shooting a meaningful look in Harry's direction. "I'm off. Apparently there's someone playing the bagpipes on the stairs."

She staggered off in utterly the wrong direction.

"Bastard!" muttered Harry. "We were only ever offered lousy old weed. And *never* more than once. I could have made a fortune from a bit of coke."

Despite being high on cocktails, I was genuinely shocked. Drugs were unthinkable to me, something I had never talked about, and certainly never tried.

"Gosh, Harry. Have you no shame?" I asked primly.

"Absolutely not."

Just then, the band struck up the first chords of "Shake, Rattle, and Roll," and the whole room lurched and exploded around me. Charlotte was grabbed by a good-looking boy with red hair (some cousin of Marina's, perhaps?) and Harry turned to me challengingly.

"Want to dance?" I think he expected me to refuse.

"Of course!"

"Come on, then. And for goodness' sake, kick off your shoes."

I did, and we swayed around the dance floor, Harry holding me very tight, which was just as well because if he had let go, I might very well have fallen over. Harry, for all that he was short and skinny and odd looking, was the best dance I had ever had. All right, he was practically the *only* dance I had ever had, but what did that matter? Dorset House, newly rich and seething with youth, seemed to be laughing with us all. Models, actors, royalty, beauty—and Harry and I—collided for three minutes of blissful havoc on the Picture Gallery floor. Mark Rothko's orange squares swam in front of my eyes. It felt half-holy to me.

I closed my eyes and imagined that Harry was Johnnie Ray.

EIGHT

All the Honey

AFTER MIDNIGHT MORE FOOD EMERGED, and ravenous as wolves, Charlotte, Harry, and I sat down to a Parisian breakfast. As the night became the morning, Harry became more agitated about Marina and George. He stubbed the end of his cigarette out on Charlotte's plate.

"She could at least have spared me the indignity of watching her marrying someone so fat!" he groaned. "Look at him! That's his tenth vol-au-vent!"

"And you're *counting*?" said Charlotte, looking disgusted.

I thought of my Uncle Luke, whose trousers always looked too tight and who could never resist a Mars bar.

"What does it matter that he's fat?" I demanded. "You shouldn't judge people like that, Harry. He can't help his weight."

(I regretted these words as soon as they were out of my mouth, but something had to make room for the two omelettes.)

"Don't be such an idiot," snapped Harry. "He's fat because he never stops eating. If he were as in love with Marina as he should be, he wouldn't be able to eat a thing in her presence."

"And you're speaking from experience?" I asked.

"Unfortunately, I am."

"Did she eat in front of you?" Charlotte asked curiously. Harry glared at her.

"All the bloody time," he snapped. "She's American. They're like that."

"Marina's been shooting me sinister looks for the last half an hour," I said hopefully. "Do you think she's feeling the first stirrings of loathing and jealousy?"

"Probably not. I imagine she's thinking how unfortunate the back of your dress looks since you sat down on that ashtray."

"You shouldn't have left it on the chair!"

"You should have *looked* before you sat down, like any normal person!"

"Normal person! Aren't you the boy who kept a loaf of bread in a cage?"

"Don't bring Julian into this!"

"Why should you care if my dress is ruined anyway?"

"It isn't ruined—any good dry cleaner will get ash out of satin," said Charlotte soothingly.

What she had said earlier about a good party playing host to every conceivable emotion was true. I had gone from wishing that my dance with Harry could go on forever, to wanting to walk out of the room and leave him to go to hell.

"She mustn't see you rowing," Charlotte went on warningly.

"Why not? I thought that all lovers ever did was row," said Harry. His fists were tightly clenched, and he must have nearly bitten through his bottom lip with the tension of being in the same room as Marina and George.

"Do you want to leave?" I asked suddenly.

Charlotte raised her eyes questioningly at Harry.

"Nothing left to stay for now the omelettes have happened," he said. He looked shattered all of a sudden and my heart went out to him. We left the Picture Gallery and made our way out of the house, back through the saloon, and down the stairs. I glanced back over my shoulder before we left the building. It was how Dorset House should be, I thought, and how silly anyone was to think otherwise. It was a house *made* for parties. What was the point in living somewhere with a staircase that beautiful, that romantic, if one didn't fill it with princesses and politicians and butterflies? An older sort of woman with a handsome face and a gawp-worthy string of pearls around her neck was standing at the bottom of the stairs waiting for her coat. She smiled when she saw me.

"Did you enjoy the party?" she asked me, shrugging her fur over her shoulders.

"It was the best party ever," I said truthfully.

"They're terribly generous, the Americans," she said.

"Aren't they?" I agreed. And more generous than even they knew, I thought, waving her good-bye with a giggle. Charlotte and I had pinched a cocktail glass each as a souvenir.

I don't recall our taxi ride home with any clarity at all. I know that Harry ranted on about Patrick Reece and said very little about Marina, but also that he paid the driver at the other end. I remember falling into my bed and being aware of the fact that the room was spinning, and waking up the next morning at eight o'clock with a pounding sensation throughout my body, cursing Marina for her lies about good-quality alcohol reducing the chances of an agonizing headache. I had heard about these headaches before, but had never had one myself. A hangover seemed to me to be thoroughly exotic and grown-up. What would Mama say? I washed and dressed and drank three glasses of water from the basin next to my bed and felt a little better. I could hear Aunt Clare's voice issuing orders in the kitchen. I peered at myself in the mirror. Pale as a ghost and puffy eyed.

Charlotte was eating breakfast and reading the paper in the dining room, showing no signs at all of the suffering that I was experiencing.

"Get yourself a bowl of porridge," she ordered as I entered the room. She had pulled her hair off her face into a low ponytail and was wearing the thick white jersey she had favored when she had come to stay at Magna. Despite so little sleep, her bright-eyed spark was indestructible, her back straight, her long fingers steady.

"Oh, I'm not sure I could manage it," I said, sitting down and pouring myself a cup of tea.

"Don't be silly. I always have porridge after parties. It's the only sensible thing to eat, isn't it, Aunt?"

Aunt Clare swept into the room carrying a pile of papers.

"What's that?" she said vaguely. "Charlotte, we've a huge amount of work to do today. I expect you ready at the typewriter in twenty minutes. Oh, hello, Penelope dear, I trust you slept well?"

"Very, thank you."

Charlotte spooned porridge into a bowl for me and oozed a spoonful of golden syrup on top.

"There's more if you want it," she said, and went back to reading the paper.

It *was* good porridge, thick and made with real cream and not all lumpy and watery like Mary's. Aunt Clare asked only one question about the party, but Charlotte told me later that this was because she agreed with Oscar Wilde that only dull people are brilliant at breakfast.

"Was Tania Hamilton wearing peach? She always wears peach!" was all she managed, and when we replied simultaneously in the negative, she merely rolled her eyes and went back to eating toast. I found myself consuming two bowls of porridge and then felt so stuffed and hot that I decided I must leave Kensington Court at once, if only to get some fresh air into my lungs.

Charlotte stood on the doorstep and said good-bye to me.

"Harry's still asleep?" I asked her for the sake of something to say.

"Oh, gracious, no. I don't think he's back yet."

"Back?"

"He disappeared off to some jazz bar in Notting Hill after you went to bed," said Charlotte. "Just grabbed his box of tricks and off he went. He makes most of his money doing late-night shows. Or early-morning shows, as the case may be."

"Goodness," I said. "What stamina."

As I turned to go, Charlotte pressed a magazine with Johnnie Ray on the front into my hands.

"Something to read on the train," she said. "I expect you've already seen it, but it talks all about London and how much he loves performing here."

I stared down at Johnnie's perfect face on the cover of *Melody Maker*.

"We have to see him when he comes to London," said Charlotte. "I don't care who we have to mug to get tickets."

With Charlotte, one never knew whether she was joking or not.

Back at Magna, I found Mama flicking through *Tatler* and sipping weak tea. Like Aunt Clare, she asked few questions about the party, but in Mama's case I felt that it was less to do with protocol and more to do with resentment that it had been I, not she, who had seen Dorset House again. Deep down, Mama would have done anything to see inside the place under its new American ownership, even if only to despair over the new paintings. I longed to throw remarks around about the generosity of the Americans, and Marina's hot pink dress, and Louis Armstrong and omelettes and cocktails and Patrick Reece and Mark Rothko, but I knew better than to try to push things onto Mama that she, essentially, *feared.* Instead, I tried to plow through an essay on the difference between Egypt and Rome in Act One of *Antony and Cleopatra,* and in the afternoon helped Mary with the dusting, which is an awesome task in a house like Magna. At supper, I could bear it no longer, and decided that at the very least, I would bring up the subject of Charlotte and Harry and see what that provoked from Mama. What was the point, I thought in despair as I powdered blusher over my death-pale cheekbones, in having a mother at all if I couldn't talk to her about anything that interested me? It felt dead, like living with a shadow sometimes. Living with another ghost.

Yet Mama, unpredictable as ever, was one step ahead of me. We sat down together for supper (just the two of us as Inigo was back at school) and she waited until Mary had served us our vegetable-and-barley soup until she came out with it.

"Darling, I think you should invite your new friends here for New Year's Eve," she said calmly.

I gulped. "Charlotte and Harry?"

"Yes. The girl and her cousin—the one who keeps the stack of pancakes in the rabbit hutch or whatever it is he does. I'd like to meet them."

"It was a loaf of bread," I said, "and I didn't think that you liked having guests for New Year's?"

"I don't—ordinarily," said Mama lightly, dipping her bread into her broth. "I feel that these two merit a change of attitude. I thought they would get on rather well with Uncle Luke and Aunt Loretta. Perhaps you would like to telephone them after dinner and see if they'd like to come and stay?"

"Oh, Mama, I don't want you to feel—to feel put out," I said. "There's no need to—"

"Penelope, I've made up my mind. I'd *like* them to come and stay. Now let's not talk about it any further, or you'll start making me nervous."

She took a gulp of wine to emphasize the point.

"Thank you, Mama," I said quietly.

What she was up to, I had no idea. I finished eating and raced to the hall to telephone Charlotte, sliding over on the zebra skin and nearly falling over.

"Steady, darling!" cried Mama irritatingly.

Aunt Clare picked up the telephone.

"Oh, hello, Aunt Clare, I mean, Mrs. Delancy," I said breathlessly. "It's Penelope Wallace speaking."

"Good evening, Penelope Wallace Speaking. How are you tonight?" came Aunt Clare's amused voice.

"Oh, very well. Thank you again for your wonderful hospitality," I said quickly. "I loved breakfast this morning, and I slept so well last night. We had the most marvelously fun time at Dorset House."

Away from the breakfast table, Aunt Clare clearly felt she could probe a little more.

"And Harry?" she asked in a low voice. "How was he? I hope he didn't make a fool of himself."

"Oh, not at all," I said. "There was just about the best jazz band I've ever heard to distract him. Louis Armstrong was playing with them."

"I am pleased that he asked you to the party," Aunt Clare went on, who obviously had no interest in jazz. It was also clear to me that she had not been let in on the part of Harry's "Winning Back Marina" plan that involved me as bait.

"You're so much prettier than Marina. So much better for Harry," she went on.

"Oh, I don't know," I said uncomfortably. Heavens, the last thing I needed was Aunt Clare thinking that Harry really *had* taken a shine to me!

"I knew the moment you walked into my study that you would be the one to sort him out," she went on.

"Not at all. Mrs. Delancy, I was wondering if I could talk to Charlotte," I said, desperately steering her off the subject of Harry and me.

"Oh, darling, she's not here. She's out at the pictures with a friend from school."

Who? I wondered irritatedly.

"Would my son do instead?" Aunt Clare added coquettishly. "I must catch Phoebe before she goes. Here he is, dear."

Horrors! I thought. Had Harry heard everything she had been saying?

"Oh, um—"

It was too late.

"How are you, sweetheart?" Harry sounded amused and not remotely embarrassed.

"Does your mother think you're falling in love with me?" I hissed.

"Probably. It takes the heat off the truth somewhat."

"So you can concentrate on winning Marina back without worrying that she thinks you've lost your mind?"

"Exactly. She thinks you're wonderful, which makes my life so much easier. Guess what she said to me this afternoon? 'So pleased you've come to your senses and realized that Penelope's so much better for you than the American.' " Harry laughed. He sounded as though he were still drunk.

"So how will you explain the fact that we're not engaged in a year's time?" I said. "And what will she think if the plan works and you go running back to Marina after all?"

"Oh, don't worry about that," said Harry breezily. "She has very little faith in me—she's already convinced I'm going to mess things up. When I do, it will come as no surprise at all."

"Wonderful," I said sardonically.

"I made forty pounds last night."

"Forty pounds!" I gasped, momentarily full of admiration.

"Indeed. It was this great little trick with a piece of string and a passport that did it. Incredibly simple, but people can be *so* stupid and *so* drunk. I must take you out to dinner to thank you for your sterling work so far."

"So far!" I cried, forgetting to keep my voice down. "I'm not sure that this is going to be going any further."

"Why were you calling, anyway?" asked Harry idly. "Want to invite us to stay for the New Year?"

"Well—yes, actually. How did you know?"

"Wild guess. And we'd love to come. And don't worry about my mother. She travels to Paris every New Year to stay with my uncle Cedric. At least, that's *her* story."

I heard the sound of Aunt Clare reentering the room.

"I must go, sweetheart. I'll pass on your invitation to Charlotte."

"I'm not sure you should be calling me that—" I began, but he had already hung up. When I replaced the receiver, Mama was straightening the zebra rug and trying not to look as though she'd been listening.

"All organized, darling? Are they coming to stay?"

"Yes," I said heavily. "They're coming to stay."

"I must telephone Fortnums tomorrow. We'll need all kinds of everything if we're having guests." (You may think that this kind of chat suggests that we were never out of the place, but in fact I don't think that Mama had ordered food from Fortnums since before the war. I wanted to say that we couldn't possibly afford it, and what on earth was wrong with the village shop and Mrs. Daunton's mince pies, but I just couldn't bring myself to. Anything that distracted Mama from our dire financial crisis was a good thing, even if it meant spending yet more money we didn't have.)

My mother, when she put her mind to it, had a flair for decorating and an eye for detail. Since Papa left us, her efforts to create a festive atmosphere at Magna had been halfhearted—and phrases like "I'm at a low ebb, darlings" and "I simply don't have the energy" echoed around the house even more during December than at any other time of the year. We all slumped, and the house felt silent and sad and weary. But the end of 1954 was a different story altogether. The morning after Charlotte's phone call, Mama ordered Johns to cut down huge armfuls of holly from the fairy wood, and the next day she specified the tree that she wanted for the hall. A week later, Inigo returned from school, bursting with energy and getting under everyone's feet.

"Do put something cheerful on the gramophone while we dress the tree, Inigo," ordered Mama, and some kind of spirit of goodwill must have descended upon Inigo, for he chose a scratchy recording of *HMS Pinafore* instead of his new Bill Haley disc.

"*This* is music," sighed Mama, and the wind snaked under the front door and the dark night spat hailstones against the windows, and Buttercup lamented and the sailors roared, and Magna felt far out at sea. I pricked my fingers on pine needles and thought of all the other men like Papa who would never see their family decorating the tree, and arguing over records. Papa would never hear Johnnie Ray, I thought, and this fact, for reasons that were not quite clear to me, shocked me very much. Mama dusted down the ancient nativity scene for the hall table.

"I remember the second year we were married, your grandmother nearly losing her mind with worry when the archangel Gabriel was dropped and his halo broke," said Mama in that high voice she reserved for telling stories about things that still bothered her.

"She made me feel so small, like a blasphemous child. I heard her saying to Archie, 'Well, of course, you've married a child, this sort of thing is bound to happen.' She never got over it."

"Silly woman," I said automatically.

"The thing that she never knew was that it was *Penelope* that broke it," Mama went on, taking my hand. "I could never have told her that. I couldn't bear the thought of that awful, condescending voice ticking off *my* daughter."

"No, Mama, *you* were the only one allowed to do that," said Inigo.

There was a silence. I don't know where these words came from, for normally, the blame-me-for-breaking-the-halo story filled Inigo's heart with adoration for Mama, the beautiful young misfit condemned for my babyish carelessness, but this year he had thrown down the script. Mama looked puzzled, more than anything, by his unexpected response.

"Darling, I hope you're not going to go through one of those awkward phases I've been reading about in this month's *Vanity Fair*."

"If it's in *Vanity Fair*, then I'm very much hoping to go through it."

"You need an early night, darling, you're obviously overtired."

"I'm not tired."

"Oh, Inigo, please don't exhaust me with answering back."

"I'm not answering back."

There was a pause, and then Mama said something that raised a lump in my throat.

"Funny," she laughed softly. "I rather miss the old boot now."

Mary, entering into the spirit of things with uncharacteristic good cheer, hung a wreath on the front door. She even fashioned a pained-looking fairy for the top of the tree using pipe cleaners and some silver foil. On Christmas Eve I spotted her gray-stockinged legs carefully ascending the stepladder in the Morning Room doorway.

"What on *earth* are you doing, Mary?" I demanded, curiosity forcing me to abandon my copy of *Housewife* in the middle of an article called "Is Mother Ever Wrong?" (Yes, frequently, in my view.)

"Yer mother wants this up here," Mary announced, brandishing an armful of mistletoe at me. "Johns bought a whole load back with 'im from Hereford last week, the socking great Romeo. 'Old the ladder for me, won't ye?" she huffed.

"Who would you like to kiss you under the mistletoe, Mary?" I teased.

"Marlon Brando," she answered promptly, her face reddening as she struggled with the branches.

"Mary!" I was genuinely astonished.

"Good arms," she said. "Nice to see a man with good arms."

There was a pause as she concentrated on knotting the mistletoe to the moth-eaten antlers of the stag above the door.

"Well hung," I added, and I think I saw a twitch of a smile on Mary's thin lips.

On Christmas Day, Inigo and I linked arms with Mama and walked through the garden to church. It was one of those rare December mornings of cloudless blue sky and bright white sunlight, when the grass scrunched frostily underfoot and the church bells really did seem to peal with tidings of great joy for all the world, but especially for us, in our corner of the world, our piece of little England. Being of a romantic disposition, I had always liked attending church, but since the war, the family pew (as uncomfortable now as it must have been when it was first carved in 1654) had felt too big for just the three of us. I had a sudden wave of longing for Papa, for the presence of a man to protect us.

"A very happy Christmas to you," came a low voice from the pew behind, and I turned around to see Mrs. Daunton, rosy with the cold morning, smiling at Inigo and me. Next to her sat the vicar's beautiful daughter, who seemed to me to be wearing an awful lot of pancake and pink lipstick for a Christmas service. She gave me a small smile that seemed to unite us in something I couldn't quite explain, but probably had something to do with being younger than everyone else. Her father spoke about John the Baptist and how he prepared the people for the coming of Christ, and I tried hard not to think about clothes and music, and all the other things that just seemed to pop into my head at the wrong time. We sang "O Come All Ye Faithful" and Inigo and I nudged each other during the *now in flesh appearing* line because the way it was phrased made it sound like Jesus was starring in a film. Mama looked down at her hands during the service, and I thought about her thinking about Papa and wondered if Aunt Clare was thinking of him too. When we filed out into the churchyard an hour later, Mama stood and talked to people about the village, and the gymkhana, and the proposed expansion of the village stores. There was no denying it— Mama's star quality was her great gift. She had fame in the village, and there was great public sympathy for her in the big house, "rattling around like a pin in a trunk," as I once heard her situation described.

"Penelope thinks another gymkhana is a wonderful idea, don't you?" said Mama, cueing me up for a long conversation with Mary's sister, Lucy, who was fifteen years younger than Mary and lacked her sister's woeful outlook on the world.

"Weren't we lucky with the weather last year?" she began. "I can't think what we would have done, had it rained. . . ."

I nodded and smiled and tried not to tune in to Inigo's conversation with Helen Williams, which included words like "cinema" and "Marlon Brando" and finally, "Palladium" and "Johnnie Ray." By the time we waved good-bye and set off for Magna half an hour later, I was fairly bursting at the seams with wanting to know what Helen Williams knew and I didn't.

"She says Johnnie's coming to London again next year," said Inigo casually.

"I don't think you should have been discussing John Ray in church," reproved Mama.

"Johnnie, Mama, *Johnnie!*" I snapped in exasperation.

"And we weren't in church, we were standing outside," said Inigo, maddening as ever.

Throughout all of that Christmas, the Duck Supper of the previous month hung over the three of us and with it, the incomprehensible, unthinkable notion that we couldn't afford to be where we were any longer. That we had nothing left to offer Magna except for ourselves—and what use were we? In the back of my mind I felt we were being cruel to the house—it was suffering because of our lack of money and romantic convictions that something would come right in the end. One evening, I caught Mama rummaging through a crate of old junk from the cupboard in the Blue Room. For a wild moment I wondered if she was looking for something of Charlotte's, for she was the last person to have slept there.

"What are you doing, Mama?" I asked her.

"Searching for hidden treasure," she said, without the slightest trace of irony.

I wanted to tell her not to be so stupid, and what on earth was she expecting to find, but I hadn't the heart. And of course, there was always the hope inside me that perhaps the answer to our prayers *would* reveal itself among a box of moth-eaten blankets, crumpled newspapers, and broken toys. Could it also contain a teddy bear worth thousands of pounds? Or the discarded necklace of a long-forgotten ancestor? We dreamed on, but I was horribly aware that dreaming was getting us nowhere.

A week later, after lunch, Luke and Loretta arrived. They had set sail from America on Boxing Day and, after five days at sea, stood in the hall and marveled at us. Inigo and I couldn't have been more excited had they sailed in from Mars.

"My word!" exclaimed Luke in his delicious Southern drawl. "Who on earth are these two, Lolly?" (Mama despised Luke calling her sister "Lolly"; nicknames were to be avoided at all costs, which makes one wonder why she named me Penelope.) "You two are grown so tall!"

Inigo and I both adored Uncle Luke, who was six foot five with a wide, smiling face and huge yellow green eyes, the sort of man who looked as though he were perpetually making hay while the sun shone. It would be disloyal to my mother and my aunt to say that Loretta was a much easier, sweeter, less beautiful version of Mama, but I thought it just the same.

"The *image* of Archie, isn't she, Luke?" she whispered, shaking her head in wonder.

"The very image!" agreed Luke, enveloping me in a bear hug.

"Your daddy was the very best man I ever met," he went on. "An' I only met him the three times, didn't I, Lolly? Funniest man I ever did meet. Biggest feet an' all."

Papa was never more real than he was through Luke's memories of him.

"An' you, young man," he went on, addressing Inigo and his duck's-arse hair this time. "Well, bless my soul. You look like a young Elvis Presley to me."

"Who?" I giggled.

Charlotte and Harry arrived two hours later. Mama received them in the Morning Room and Charlotte plied her with presents—a huge ham, a box of violet creams from Harrods, a bottle of lavender bath oil from Swan & Edgar that I intended to swipe as soon as possible, and a fruitcake that weighed almost as much as Mary.

"How wonderful!" Mama cried. "You are clever. Oh, Penelope! Do save the ribbon on that ham—it's too wonderful to throw away."

Dear Mama. She was wearing a new pair of cream trousers with a high-necked black sweater. With her black hair swept into a perfect chignon, she looked the epitome of style, yet the room she sat in shamed us all. The curtains hung sorry as teardrops, ripped and faded beyond any kind of chic; the mauve wallpaper—unchanged since my great-grandmother's era—peeled miserably around the once-beautiful Inigo Jones cornices. The ceiling was stained yellow with age and dry rot, and Mary had not removed a bucket that had caught water from a serious leak on the floor above a week ago. Sensitive as a heat rash to my friends' reactions to my mother, I noted Charlotte's jaw dropping and Harry's face becoming strangely watchful. I knew precisely what they were thinking: We knew she was young but we didn't expect her to be *this* staggering. Why on earth doesn't she do something about the house?

"Penelope, show Charlotte and Harry to their rooms," said Mama with a soft smile. "How *delightful* to have the house full of beautiful youth. It's how it should be, you know."

I wanted to gnash my teeth, but I wasn't sure how, so I let her go on.

"Dinner will be at eight o'clock," she said. She looked suddenly tired. "I'm not sure I have the energy to stay awake until midnight, but you young ones can celebrate. My sister, Loretta, and her husband, Luke, are here from *America*." She paused to allow the force of her disdain to sink in. "They're recovering before dinner." Her eyes shifted to Mary's bucket on the floor.

"Oh, Lord," she said quietly. "I meant to get rid of that."

I stepped forward and picked it up.

"Charlotte and I will be down at the stables this afternoon," I said. Mama took a cigarette from the silver case that Papa had given her for her eighteenth birthday.

"And what about you, Harry?" she asked. "Do you ride?" She asked the question perfectly innocently, but it hung in the air so evocatively that he actually blushed.

"I don't," he admitted finally.

"Ah, well. I hear you're a magician?"

"I hope to be one day."

There was a short silence, and then a strange and spooky thing happened. Harry glanced up at the ceiling and the lights in the drawing room flickered and went out, and we would have been plunged into blackness, were it not for the amber glow from the dying embers in the fireplace. Mama gasped and pressed her hand to her chest, and Charlotte and I cried out at the same time and grabbed each other in that instinctive yet altogether undignified way that girls do when this sort of thing happens. Power cuts were par for the course in a house like Magna, but the timing of this one seemed a little too appropriate to be true.

"Harry! Stop it!" hissed Charlotte, her face livid with dancing shadows, and miraculously, the lights came back on again, and the pirates groaned back into life, and the fire looked cold and small once more.

"It wasn't me, for goodness' sake," said Harry innocently, "though I'm very happy for you to believe that I can pull off stunts like that—it can only be a good thing for my reputation."

"Well!" said Mama slowly. "That was *quite* something. Whatever can we expect next? Books flying off the shelves? Wardrobes spontaneously combusting?"

"Oh, please no," I whimpered in alarm.

"I don't go in for anything like that," said Harry. "I'm rather a traditional sort of magician, in fact."

"Sounds like a contradiction in terms," said Mama. She didn't look tired any longer. She liked this sort of thing.

"Would you like me to take a look at your fuse box, Lady Wallace?" asked Harry.

"Oh, would you? And please, you must call me Talitha."

The next minute Inigo exploded into the room brandishing the dustpan and brush. "The lights went out and I knocked this off the hall table and the frame's smashed." In his hand was the photograph of Papa in his uniform. I braced myself for tears from Mama, who usually considered this sort of thing a Bad Omen. Instead, she smiled at Inigo.

"Well, it can't be helped. Leave the photograph for Johns—he can take it into town and have it reframed."

"That's it?" asked Inigo suspiciously.

"Whatever do you mean, darling? Accidents happen."

Not around here, they don't, I thought.

My mother was dynamite by candlelight—she used it like an actress to enhance her mystique, her gypsy-green eyes and her film-star vulnerability; against the backdrop of the dining room in all its medieval glory, she looked even more bewitching. She placed herself between Harry and Uncle Luke. Mary, set-faced with the effort of catering for more than the usual total of three, whisked us through our prawn cocktails, and I fancied I could read Harry thinking, *Well, why on earth not serve something comforting like soup on such a cold night?*

"So you're a magician?" Loretta asked Harry. *Here we go again*, I thought.

"I'm training," explained Harry. "It's a long process. It's not the sort of thing that there's any point in being just halfway good at."

"I can imagine," said Mama. "No good making someone disappear, then not knowing how to get them back again!"

"I don't know," I muttered to myself.

"And how about you, Charlotte? And you, darling Penelope? What do girls like you do with yourselves nowadays?" asked Loretta, turning her kind eyes toward me.

"Now *that's* a question," I sighed.

Charlotte paused and glanced around the table to assess whose attention she had. This sort of behavior from her made me slightly nervous; Charlotte was still an unknown quantity to me, someone capable of saying almost anything. I chewed hard on a rubbery prawn and hoped that she wouldn't be too outrageous.

"Girls like me," she contemplated slowly, "well, most of us spend a few months in Europe learning to speak beautiful French or Italian. Then when we arrive back in England, we go to plenty of smart parties where we hope and pray that some nice, rich young man will see us standing on the edge of the dance floor. Then I suppose we marry him and have children." She gave me a glittery little grin. "Well, that's what I've heard, anyway. It's all the rage among the girls I went to school with. Personally, it leaves me a little bit cold. I want to earn my own money. I intend on making a great deal of it. Then perhaps marrying Johnnie Ray, if Penelope hasn't got there first."

Uncle Luke gave a shout of laughter.

"Penelope's off to Rome in September," said Mama quickly. I think she felt slightly surprised that someone other than herself was capable of being the center of attention. "She's been desperate to see the Sistine Chapel in the flesh for as long as I can remember."

"Yes," I said automatically, but found myself thinking, *Have I?* It was hard to cast my mind back to a time when I felt desperate over anything but Johnnie and music and waltzing off to parties and eating chips. Yet Mama was right; a few years ago and after reading a dire romantic novel set in seventeenth-century Rome, I had longed to go to Italy.

"I adore the thought of Italy," said Charlotte dreamily. "My aunt refuses to let me go. She thinks I'll fall in love with a foreigner and never return."

"She's absolutely right," said Harry.

"And what, may I ask, is wrong with falling in love with a foreigner?" asked Loretta, pretending to be shocked. "Good gracious, I married one!"

"Uncle Luke's not foreign, he's American!" said Inigo indignantly. Luke threw back his head and roared at this—a great rumble of rich noise with the odd high squawk thrown in for good measure, and it set us all off, though I couldn't really see what was so amusing.

"I can't see Penelope marrying an Italian. She's far too in love with England," said Harry idly.

"More's the pity," said Mama.

"What do you mean by that?" I asked Harry, but my heart was beating faster because it wasn't often that people said things about me that I had not even realized myself until that moment.

"I've never known anyone so English as you," agreed Charlotte. "The way you look, for a start, like something out of an Enid Blyton story. Gosh, your freckles are so perfectly placed that after our first tea, I had a bet with Harry that you drew them on with a pencil."

"So that's why you asked me—"

"Exactly."

"I still don't see why that makes me terribly English. Just having freckles—"

"Oh, but it's not just that, is it?" said Charlotte. "It's the way you talk, the things you say, the sort of stuff that shocks you, like some of the things Marina was saying the other day, the stuff that *doesn't* shock you, like getting into a cab and having tea with me at Aunt Clare's when you'd never met me before—"

"Ahem!" I coughed loudly. Mama was still unaware of how I had met Charlotte.

"Don't sound ashamed of it," said Harry. "I think it's a very, very good thing. I wish I was like you."

"You're the *worst*," said Charlotte. "You're an English eccentric. Nothing could be more tiresome."

"December thirty-first, 1954," announced Inigo, who was hot on proclaiming times and dates. "Just two minutes of 1954 left. Farewell, sweet rationing," he added with glee.

"Can you believe it?" said Harry.

"It's odd," said Mama, "but when I heard that meat was coming off rationing, I felt sort of empty. Frightened that we might start to forget, I suppose. Oh, I'm being silly, I'm sorry." She picked up her glass and her hand was shaking and I knew that she hadn't really meant to say what she had just said. Papa was the one being whom she never used for effect. Luke reached out and touched her arm.

"Nothin' silly 'bout that," he said softly. "Ah know just how you feel." He smiled at Charlotte and me. "You young ones have honey days ahead. And thank the Lord for that."

"Amen!" I cried.

"May the new year bring us all the honey we can eat!" added Charlotte.

"All the honey!" we repeated, and raised our glasses, and Inigo ran to the gramophone and put Frankie Laine on. When the grandfather clock in the hall struck bleakly at midnight, I sensed its surprise and resentment at being drowned out by the American pop music that blasted from the hall. Inigo grabbed me and Charlotte by the hand and we danced out of the dining room, kicking off our shoes and spilling champagne down our fingers.

NINE

Modern Boys and Guinea Pigs

JANUARY 1ST, 1955, was the first time that I can remember feeling hot in the hall. Hot from dancing and laughing, hot from the quivery, odd anticipation for the new year. Inigo ran upstairs and came down with his guitar and played along with every single record that we put on—Frankie Laine, Guy Mitchell, Johnnie, of course—he knew all of them, and though Charlotte and I sang along with everything (like the fans we were), it was Inigo who had every groove of the vinyl ingrained in his being. He approached pop music like a scholar, cursing himself on the rare occasions that Luke asked him a question he could not answer. The mathematics of the records enthralled him as much as the music—what color was the label? How many minutes and seconds, precisely, did each song last? Then, at half past one in the morning, Luke slipped upstairs and came down carrying two records on a label that none of us had ever seen before.

"Think you might like these," he said. "This boy's gettin' kinda big where we come from. Mah friend Sam's got him on his record label. We saw him jus' a couple of months ago at the Louisiana Hayride—crowd went mad for him, y'know. Sam thinks he's the greatest thing he's ever seen. Ah think you kids'll love this record." (I loved the way Uncle Luke said record, "rec-ud.")

"Who is he?" asked Charlotte, flopping onto the chair next to me.

"He's a white boy, though you'd never believe it, hearing this. He's this funny hillbilly cat—sorta your school weirdo type—but *man,* he's good too.

Loretta says he's a good-lookin' kid. I wouldn't know, but I guess she's right," laughed Luke.

He put the record on. When I heard Uncle Luke's hillbilly cat singing "Blue Moon of Kentucky" for the first time, the only thing I remember thinking was that I didn't believe for one moment that the singer was a white boy. Certainly, the voice was something else, and hearing new records from America was always exciting, but I doubt I would have given any of this much more thought that night were it not for Inigo.

"Play it again! Flip it over—what's the other side?" he demanded. "Can I keep it?" His face was white as a sheet, as if he had been given a terrible shock.

"Y'know, I should've played ya the other side *first*," said Luke, grinning. "This is the *real* eye-opener."

When I tell people about the first time I heard Elvis singing "Mystery Train," they don't believe me. For the rest of the country—unless, I suppose, Sam Phillips had other friends from Memphis who had traveled to England at the end of December, armed with records from his tiny label, which I sincerely doubt—Elvis did not break through until the start of 1956. Yet there we were in the hall at Magna, in the primitive hours of 1955, listening to the man who would become known as The King. I wish I could say that I knew, from that moment, that Elvis was going to change everything. I wish I could say that I had some extraordinary sense of something new and important happening, but I just *can't*. I liked the songs, and I was intrigued by the sound of the white-boy singer, but that night my judgment was blurry with champagne, and I felt sick with violet creams and dancing. It wasn't until after Luke and Loretta had left two days later, after Inigo had drummed the songs into my brain with his constant playing and replaying of the records, that it dawned on me that he was something a bit different—yet for Charlotte and me, Johnnie was still the brightest star in the firmament, irreplaceable, untouchable. Inigo was quicker than us like that. For him, the Messiah had arrived. It was almost as if he did not know what to do with himself. The revelation of Elvis and the New Sound was so great to him; he would have happily swum across the Atlantic just to meet him. From that night on, he became possessed.

*   *   *

Only half an hour after Elvis made his debut in Wiltshire, England, Mama demanded that we take him off the gramophone and play some jazz.

"You can't dance to this white guy of yours," agreed Harry. "We want a bit of something we can really move to." He clicked his fingers rapidly, a gesture that would have made anyone else seem absurd.

"If you can't move to the hillbilly cat, you can't move to nuthin'," observed Luke, and I thought how nice it would be to have him around all the time, just to be on hand to make remarks like that in his addictive Southern drawl.

"What do you think of our boy Elvis, girls?" asked Loretta. "He's pretty sweet in the flesh, I might tell you."

"He certainly *sounds* good," I said politely.

"Don't ask them, they're Johnnie Ray–obsessed," said Inigo dismissively.

"You are?" asked Luke. "You girls'd rather hear Mr. Emotion than my man Elvis Presley?"

Charlotte looked thoughtful. "Johnnie moves us," she said simply. "That's why we like him so much."

"Love him," I corrected her automatically.

Luke roared with laughter. "The Million Dollar Teardrop?" he cried, wiping his eyes with the mirth of it all. "Y'know, girls, ah'm not altogether sure that he's the kinda guy who'd love you two back, if y'know what I mean. Hee hee haa haah hee!"

I didn't know what he meant, *really* I didn't, but I smiled and looked as though I did.

"Hats off to y'all," said Luke. "But I think you'd be on to a surer thing with young Presley here. He's got somethin' the like of which ah've never seen before."

"It's the way he *moves*," said Loretta.

"You wouldn't expect it from a young guy like him. But when he sings, he moves like he's lost control of his whole self. Tell them, Loll."

Loretta gave us a wicked look. "We watched the girls watching him when he played the Hayride. It was like nothing I've ever seen before, really something extraordinary. He just ripped the place up."

Inigo hung on to every word.

"He sings so raw," said Luke. "Up-tempo songs, not all slush like your man Johnnie. For what it's worth, I'd keep watching."

I had my doubts. Can you believe that? I had my doubts.

While this conversation had been going on, Harry had taken it upon himself to change the record, and suddenly the hall was full of Humphrey Lyttelton and jazz.

"Feel this!" said Harry. He stood in the middle of the hall, arms lanky and loose by his sides, cigarette hanging delicately between his fingers, smoke swirling up around him like a genie. Spotlit by the remaining candles on the chandelier, easy in his suit and correspondent shoes, he looked very grown-up all of a sudden. I felt a million miles from him.

"Won't you dance with me, Penelope?" he asked. My eyes flickered toward Mama.

"Go on, then," she said rather roughly. "Surely those dance classes you took last year taught you something, Penelope."

"Oh, Harry, I'm sorry," I said, flushing scarlet. "I can't dance to jazz," I added lamely.

"How can you not dance to jazz?" he asked me, half laughing. "You're ridiculous. *All* girls under twenty are ridiculous."

"Because Johnnie hates jazz," interrupted Inigo. "She has no interest in anything that Mr. Ray hasn't deemed noteworthy."

"Come here." Harry pulled me toward himself and spun me around.

"No!" I pulled away, horrified in front of Mama.

Harry laughed. "Don't be so silly."

"And a happy new year to you too," I muttered, hating him again.

"I think she looks beautiful," said Mama tersely. I shot her a grateful smile. (Sometimes, and always at the times I least expected it, Mama really came out on my side. I think it was because she took criticism of me as a personal insult to her.)

Harry just laughed.

Charlotte was talking to Loretta at great speed about American fiction.

"I'm crazy for Salinger," I heard her say.

I shook my head, suddenly hot. "I think I might take a breath of air."

"Have you read *The Catcher in the Rye?*" demanded Charlotte. "I thought it was blissful."

I slipped out of the hall, through the dining room, into the kitchen, and out of the back door. It was a chaotic night. Gray, shadowy clouds skidded over the cold, pale moon, and although I could make out the stubborn form of the Plough, there seemed no order to the rest of the firmament; the stars looked wild and unscrewed to me, as if there were nothing there to stop them shooting toward the earth at any moment. Instinct and champagne drew me and my beautiful frock out onto the black velvet lawn and through the door in the wall that led to the kitchen garden. I might add at this point that I had consumed more champagne than I ever had before, which had the useful consequence of washing away fear in a sort of blissful wave of carelessness. *I'm not afraid of the dark!* I thought, and shouted it out loud, just in case there were any badgers or barn owls that may have been interested.

"Nineteen fifty-five!" I said. Then louder, "NINETEEN FIFTY-FIVE!" I laughed. The year ahead was a blank page, and surely all anyone could ever want was blank pages? I turned around, feeling tiny, swaying and sinking into the mud in my heels, to face Magna, imagining the centuries slip back and back until the day the first stone was laid in its creation. Nothing, not the dedication of Inigo Jones, nor the years of hard work from those austere, painted faces that lined the walls in the drawing room and the hall, made me anything other than the most important person to have lived at Magna, the one who understood and loved the house the most. I could almost see the place breathing from where I stood, and I closed my eyes and felt myself terribly, terribly modern. Like I say, I was also terribly, terribly drunk. I struck up a conversation with Johnnie.

"Oh, Johnnie," I sighed. "Will I ever see you sing again?" I closed my eyes for an answer. I imagined him standing next to me, talking into a microphone, a band lined up behind him ready to strike up at any moment.

Come to the Palladium! I heard him say. *I'll sing for you, I'll cry for you, Penelope. Can I call you Penny?*

"Oh, I'd rather you didn't, Johnnie. Nobody does."

I felt cross with myself for making him ask a silly question like that. I reached out my hand; I wanted to touch him, to know that he knew me, that he understood me like I thought he would—

"Penelope! Where on earth are you?"

It was Mama. Johnnie and his orchestra vanished with a regretful smile and a wave, and I watched Mama wrapping her coat around herself and taking little steps in her Christian Dior shoes down toward the kitchen garden. Fido followed her, plunging ahead, his nose to the ground.

"Where are you, Penelope? For goodness' sake, you'll catch your death of cold."

"I'm here, Mama."

"Oh! Gracious, you frightened me! Who in heaven's name were you talking to?" she demanded, eyes flashing torch-bright into the box hedge.

"I was talking to Johnnie."

She looked irritable, as well she might. Her sacred space for private contemplation about Papa was not the spot for chatting away to pop stars.

"Do come inside. People will think you're quite mad."

We walked up to the back door, and I found myself holding her hand.

"Did you like dancing with Harry?" she asked me.

"Not really. He's so rude to me, Mama. I'm sure he would much rather have danced with *you*."

Mama answered me briskly. "You've had too much to drink, darling. It's not attractive. You'll end up like your grandmother if you're not careful."

Oddly enough, this remark was enough to sober me up completely.

Everyone collapsed into bed soon after this. Inigo wanted to carry on listening to Elvis, but Mama told him that she would have to remove the gramophone from the house if he did not give it a rest.

"Well—good night, y'all," said Luke, his arm around Loretta. For some reason, the sight of them both, making their way upstairs together, tired but happy, and ready to make their return journey the next day, choked me unbearably. Magna needed the rock-sure stability of people like Luke and Loretta. Without people like them, the house swayed, unhinged.

*   *   *

Charlotte led me into the library and shut the door quietly behind her-self. Kicking off her red shoes, she flopped into the reading chair and started pulling grips out of her hair at terrific speed. Rooms came alive when Charlotte was inside them; the library was no exception. Her vitality gave a curious glamor to the rows of dust-covered first editions, and her literacy and unquenchable thirst for reading somehow justified the unashed cigarette swaying dangerously close to the hopeless oil painting of *The Lake, Milton Magna on Mid-Summer's Eve, 1890,* by good old Great-Aunt Sarah.

"Harry seems happy tonight," she said, placing heavy emphasis on the word "happy." "He seems to have forgotten all about the American girl."

"Marina?"

"Yes, of course Marina—who do you think I was talking about, Ava Gardner?"

I giggled.

"It won't last," sighed Charlotte. "He can only ever forget about her for short bursts of time. Then it comes back again, worse than ever."

"How tiresome it must be," I said, "being in love. I was always led to believe it would be the most wonderful thing ever."

"Who on earth told you that?" said Charlotte in amazement. "I've never known it to be anything other than torture."

"Andrew?" I asked softly.

She twisted a finger around her hair, something that I noticed she tended to do when she felt uncomfortable. Andrew and Charlotte remained something of a mystery to me. I had tried to talk about him more—to find out when Charlotte had last seen him, how often she thought about him—but it was tricky. She kept him to herself most of the time; he was a piece of her that I sensed I would never be able to touch. She guarded her time with Andrew, and what she said about him seemed attentively planned, selected with care so that I knew enough, but not enough at all. That night, it seemed that she couldn't quite resist talking about him.

"He's just so *nice,*" she admitted.

I laughed. I just couldn't help it.

"Of all the things you could have said about him!" I said. "I never would have expected you to say he was *nice*."

"It's hard to find nice boys," said Charlotte sadly. "I miss him so much sometimes, it hits me completely out of the blue. Pathetic, really. I feel myself desperate for a dose of him." She frowned. "Now, where did I put my glass of wine?" she added quickly. And that was it. And as it happened, she kicked her wine over onto the rug at her feet, but as it was impossible to tell what color the rug was supposed to be in the first place, I didn't suppose it mattered much. We lounged around talking until five in the morning. I had never spent so long in that room in the entire eighteen years that I had lived at Magna. By the time we crawled up the stairs to bed, I felt quite different about the library. Charlotte pulled books off the shelves and read me chunks from her favorite authors. Not only was it the first night I heard Elvis, but the first night I heard Coleridge. In turn, Charlotte asked me to tell her the stories behind the watchful faces of my ancestors. When all the faces seemed to jumble into one and I could not remember who they were or what had made them great or terrible, I made it up. I had the feeling that Charlotte didn't really care what was true and what wasn't. What mattered to her was a good story.

The next morning, an hour before Charlotte and Harry were due to take the train back to London, I knocked on the door of the Wellington Room and creaked open the door, and found Harry muttering to himself with an outsized, upturned top hat in his hands. He looked up when he saw me.

"Quick!" he whispered. "Stick your hand in!"

"I'm sorry?"

"Into the hat!" he hissed impatiently. "Close your eyes!"

Obediently, I closed my eyes, stuck my hand quickly into the hat, and felt something soft. I gave a bit of a scream, which I think Harry must have expected, because when I opened my eyes, he was grinning and looking smug.

"Take a look," he said. I peered cautiously into the hat and gasped when I saw the tiniest of rodents, no longer than my hand. It was entirely white, except for a dusting of charcoal over the nose.

"Oh, Harry!" I gasped. "It's *precious*! It's a hamster!"

"It's a guinea pig," he corrected me.

"But how did you get—?"

"Don't ask silly questions that you know I will never answer," he said quickly. "I thought I'd give her to you." He blew a lock of hair out of his brown eye. "To say thank you for having me," he added a little heavily.

"But—"

"Rabbits are somewhat passé," said Harry quickly, "but guinea pigs strike me as rather amiable creatures. You can keep this one inside if you want—it seems a bit cruel to shove it into a cage outdoors when it's used to the interior of a luxurious hat like this."

"But, Harry, this is a living animal, not a loaf of bread," I said, casting my mind back to the legend of Julian. "What shall I do with her?"

"You're not supposed to *do* anything with her," said Harry. "Just make sure she has water and carrots and a bit of attention." He lifted the creature out of the hat. "She has a look of Marina about her. In fact, I think she should be called Marina, don't you?"

I laughed. "Well, I suppose I should thank you," I said. "No one's ever given me a guinea pig before."

"I should hope not," said Harry.

Luke and Loretta left half an hour after Charlotte and Harry. As usual, saying good-bye to guests at Magna always made me feel more sad than saying good-bye to people anywhere else in the world. It was a gray, wet afternoon with the sort of efficient, blustery wind that encouraged the jackdaws to clack and shriek around the chapel like fighter pilots—even Banjo had stirred himself for a determined, hightailed gallop around the field. I hovered in the shelter of the front door with no shoes on, watching Luke load suitcases into the car. Mama fussed behind him, not really helping but wanting to leave him with the best impression she could. In the back of my mind, I knew that it had always irked her that Luke had only ever had eyes for her older sister, though it would have horrified her if it had ever been any other way.

"Look after your mother," whispered Loretta, scrunching over the gravel and kissing me on the cheek. "Don't fall in love and leave this place without making sure she's a little happier."

"I have no intention of doing either of those two things," I said indignantly. Loretta laughed.

"Harry was right," she said, "you are so utterly English sometimes. Don't change, will you?"

The car rounded out of the drive, and we waved until they were out of sight, laughing when Luke honked the horn and scattered the rabbits into the hedge. The sight of them reminded me of Marina the guinea pig, and I shot upstairs to my room, where Harry had installed her in a cardboard box lined with last week's *Telegraph*. (Ironically, the gossip pages featured a big piece about the Hamilton party, and I had to lift Marina the rodent *off* a photograph of Marina the human being to read it. There was a good deal of guff about the daughter an M.P. I'd never heard of vanishing with the piano player in the jazz band, which perplexed me, as I remember the aforesaid musician being about ninety and toothless, but what do I know?) When I finally finished reading, I had a stiff neck and Marina the rodent had scuttled under my dressing table. It took me twenty minutes to get her out again. Perhaps when the weather improved I could set her free in the garden, I thought hopefully. Where on earth had she come from? Surely she hadn't just appeared out of Harry's hat? After he and Charlotte left, the house seemed deathly quiet. Even the hiss and crackle of Radio Luxembourg fading in and out on Inigo's wireless could not dent the void left by their departure. That night, I shoved a carrot into Marina's box, pulled on a pair of thick socks, and climbed into bed. Through the gray and pink curtains in my bedroom (I don't think they had been washed since before the war and they would probably disintegrate on contact with soapy water anyway), I sensed a bright moon. I thought about Harry and Johnnie, about the flickering lights and the guinea pig, and about Luke and Loretta and Magna. I thought about 1955 and how I would be feeling at the end of the year. I thought about Mama and tried to imagine how it would have been had Papa not been killed.

TEN

Five O'Clock and Later

A WEEK LATER, Charlotte and I were sitting on a bench in Hyde Park finishing cheese rolls. My lectures had finished early, and the afternoon stretched out before us, cold and blue in the winter sunlight. I had all but abandoned the friends I had made on my course, and I was starting to realize why Charlotte prefered loafing around with me to the girls that she had grown up with. We bumped into them very regularly—beautiful, perfumed girls with white smiles flashing—and afterward Charlotte would always say how depressed they made her, how their engagement rings had made them shadows of what they were in the sixth-form common room. Only last week she had pointed out the girl who had been head of the school in the year above her.

"There goes Delilah Goring," she said sadly, as a girl in a fox-fur stole and a cream hat crossed the road on the arm of a tall, redheaded man. "Or rather, what *was* Delilah Goring."

That afternoon in the park, Charlotte was quieter than usual, and I knew her well enough by now to understand the difference between Charlotte Dreaming and Charlotte Speculative.

"Anything wrong?" I asked. Charlotte threw her crust to a passing pigeon.

"Why should there be?" she demanded.

I said no more. I knew that the best way to get Charlotte to talk was to feign lack of interest. Sure enough, she pulled something out of her pocket and handed it to me.

"Read it," she instructed. "It arrived this morning."

The handwriting was terrible, the spelling atrocious, but the turn of phrase Byronic.

I have to see you, it ended (and *have* was underlined). *If we met one more time, then I think I could get over you and lern to forget you and whot hapened betwene us. I will wait for you outside the caff on T.Court Road on Friday at 5pm. Yours for allways faithfuly, Andy.*

"Funny thing is," said Charlotte, "I don't want him to learn to forget me."

"Gosh, he'll be there in an hour," I said, checking my watch.

"I know."

Charlotte bit her lip. "I'll go," she said. "Will you come too?"

"Oh, Charlotte, I don't think I'm invited."

"I'm inviting you. You can make sure that I leave after half an hour. If I go alone—" she trailed off.

"Of course I'll come," I said. "I'm *longing* to meet A the T."

So we tripped along Tottenham Court Road until we got to the caff. Mama would have *died.* I was nervous, because it was getting dark, we were somewhere way off my usual track, and Charlotte's demeanor had changed completely.

"We'll just wait here," she said. "He's always a few minutes late. It preserves his dignity." It wasn't especially cold, but her teeth were chattering.

"Here he is," she muttered. "Oh, help . . ."

Andrew appeared very suddenly, a cigarette between his teeth, his hands in the pockets of his jacket. He had beautiful hair—black, thick, and shiny, and coiffed in a perfect D.A.—its glossy perfection emphasizing the chiseled frailty of his face. He wasn't especially good-looking, but was fearfully attractive and, much to my satisfaction, he disproved Mama's theories about all Teds having bad skin; his face was as white as porcelain and utterly blemish free. He flicked wary, gray green eyes at Charlotte. She was taller than he, but so intense were her nerves that she looked small and unchar-acteristically shy.

"You all right?" he said.

"Fine. This is my friend Penelope."

Andrew nodded at me.

"Hullo," I said.

"Tea?" said Andrew lightly.

Charlotte shook her head briefly. "I'd like a cigarette and something stronger than tea," she said. Andrew grinned.

"I hear Babysham's all the rage with the ladies these days."

He pushed open the door of the caff.

A number of Teds were sitting inside, smoking and laughing. One of them nodded at Andrew when we walked in, and a couple of them stared at Charlotte and me.

"Ignore 'em," advised Andrew.

The air was heavy with smoke, the tables greasy. Someone put a record on—it was a dance-hall song that I hadn't heard before.

"H-how have you been, Andrew?" asked Charlotte, her legs jittering under the table. "Everything all right at home?"

Andrew lit a cigarette and passed it to her. "What do you think?"

"Your father?"

"Still drinking. Still shouting. He stamped on two of my new records last week for no reason at all. Broke my arm last month when I tried to stop him hitting Sam."

I gasped in horror. Andrew gave me a mocking smile.

"Bastard. It was the new Bill Haley and His Comets disc, just got hold of it, too," he added resentfully. His eyes lit up for a moment. "You should hear it, Charlie."

Charlotte kicked me under the table, which I presume meant I was to ignore the nickname. She started to shred her napkin.

"And work?" she asked him. "Still working hard?"

"Sacked last week. Got into a fight."

"Oh, Andrew," wailed Charlotte.

"Wasn't my fault," he said moodily. "Bloody nothin's ever my fault. I'm just good at takin' the blame."

"Yes," agreed Charlotte. "You're right there."

Andrew leaned forward and took her hand in his. At first Charlotte looked as though she might pull away, but she couldn't.

"You look more beautiful than words can say," he said. It was as though I weren't there at all. Charlotte's eyes welled up.

"Don't," she said weakly.

Help, I thought, and busied myself studying the menu.

"Ah, but it's the truth, girl. The truth, for once." He pulled his hand away again and got his comb out from his pocket.

"So how's that auntie of yours?" he asked her. "Still grooming you for Prince bloody Charles, is she?" But there was no bitterness in his voice now. Charlotte grinned, at once more like her usual self.

"Oh, my good gosh, no," she said. "He's not *nearly* rich and sophisticated enough."

We sat with Andrew for well over an hour. He was funny and charming, considerate and sweet, and if he minded that Charlotte had bought me along too, he never once showed it. The place filled up around us, all these velvet-collared boys, deep in their own world, talking records and clothes and riots in the streets. What struck me most of all was how *young* they all were. I mean, where were their mothers? People walked past the caff and peered in at us, which made me feel dangerous and safe at the same time. It was a nice feeling, an exciting feeling, a sensation that I had never got with any of the dull boys I was used to. I wanted everyone to see me—I wanted Hope Allen to think that *I too* could talk to the Teds. *This is living!* I thought proudly. Soon after our arrival, three of Andrew's friends came and squashed up on our table.

"We heard he was meetin' you, Charlie," said the first, a good-looking boy with bloodshot eyes.

"Had to come and say hullo," said the other.

"Digby, Ian—how are you both?" asked Charlotte delightedly. "This is my friend Penelope."

They gave me a thorough looking-over. The one called Ian spotted my lecture notes bulging out of my bag.

"I prefer the flicks to reading books," he said sagely.

"Have—have you seen anything good lately?" I stammered.

"This an' that," he shrugged. "Brando. I like Brando."

Perhaps he admired Brando's "nice arms" like Mary, I thought.

"I like your jacket," I said admiringly.

"I only wear the best."

"My brother would love it."

He looked thoughtful for a moment.

"Your brother could prob'ly afford it. Hang on." He rummaged in his front pockets, and pooled the contents in front of himself on the table; a rusty razor blade, a bag of tobacco, two combs and a tub of grease, a bicycle chain, and three chocolate wrappers appeared before the stub of a pencil.

"Got anything to write on?"

I pulled the Italian dictionary that Hope Allen had wrecked out of my bag.

"Use the back page of this."

"Italian?" asked Ian incredulously. "Now you're jus' showing off, girl."

I laughed, light-headed with the attention he was paying me.

"Here," he said, scribbling fast. "This is the address of the bird who knocks up zoot suits for all us lot. Genius, she is. Used to work on Savile Row. Charges us a quarter of what she used to charge the toffs. Tell your brother to tell Cathy that Ian Sommersby sent 'im. Cathy'll give 'im the best deal in London. All right? Ian *Sommersby*. Don't forget the name." He ran his fingers through his D.A. and looked so serious, I nearly giggled.

"Thank you," I said, pocketing the address.

"What's he called, your brother?" asked Digby.

"Um—Inigo."

"*Indigo?*" Digby cracked up, his whole face creased with the amusement of it all.

"Bloody queer name, that," observed Ian.

"I suppose so."

Andrew nodded at me. "Charlie knows how to dress," he said. "For a toff, she knows her threads."

"And for someone with no class, no job, and no money, you brush up very well indeed," said Charlotte dryly.

Andrew laughed loudly. "Sod off," he said good-naturedly.

I blanched a little. I had never been told to *sod off* by anyone, least of all a boy in jest. Charlotte just smiled.

Half an hour later, she reluctantly decided that we should leave. Andrew grabbed her and pulled her into a kiss, and a few boys wolf whistled.

"You want one?" Ian grinned.

"Oh, I'm fine, thanks," I muttered.

"Not posh enough for you, is he?" laughed Digby.

"No, I mean, yes, I mean—" I felt hot and silly.

"Aw, leave her alone," ordered Andrew idly.

It was dark by the time we left the place. Andrew vanished with Ian and Digby, and Charlotte and I decided to walk home. Charlotte didn't talk and I didn't think to make her. I was quite happy. I wanted time to think myself. Then, just as we got to Marble Arch, a face appeared out of the window of a Jaguar, waving at us and ordering the driver to pull over—which he did, to the consternation of the bus driver behind him. It was Kate and Helena Wentworth. Charlotte was forced out of her silence as they spilled onto the pavement.

"We thought it was you! We could tell. No one else in London has legs that long and hair that thick!" exclaimed Helena. "We've just got into the car after lunch, would you believe it? We've been at Claridge's since midday. Sophia G-D's birthday 'do. Possibly the most mind-numbingly dull experience of my life thus far."

"Sophia with the rubies," I remembered. "We saw her at the Hamiltons' party, Charlotte. Marina was terribly rude to her." *And hark at me!* I thought, giggling inside.

"Oh, we've only met her a couple of times ourselves," said Kate quickly. "She seems a sweet thing, such an unfortunate face, poor lamb. She was embarrassingly pleased we had turned up at all, actually. Marina was there, under sufferance and drinking like a fish, and George too, looking larger than life. But it was your cousin Harry who made the whole ordeal bearable," she went on, blushing slightly.

"Really?" asked Charlotte grimly.

"He was our after-dinner entertainment. *Such* tricks! Gosh, he's improved since I first saw him at Clara Sanderson's coming-out ball last year. I was longing to find out how he does that marvelous one with the cigarette and the ten-shilling note, but as soon as lunch was over, he vamoosed. Said something about getting back to some cove called Julian Mac Something."

Charlotte snorted.

"He is just *so* talented!" Kate went on gushingly. "I could watch him performing for hours on end. He did the sweetest thing with his napkin, folded it into a mouse shape and made it run up everyone's arms—it was *killing!*"

Methinks Kate has a thing for Harry, I thought in astonishment. What on earth was it about him?

"So what have you two been doing this afternoon?" asked Helena, smiling at me in a very friendly way. (Being seen with Charlotte not just once, but twice, clearly merited acceptance.)

"Are you out to dinner? We were thinking of heading straight to Sheekeys for an early dinner," said Kate.

Sheekeys! Charlotte was in love with the place, I knew, because she talked about it whenever she was hungry. I could sense her considering the downside of Kate's suggestion—spending another couple of hours with the Wentworth girls—against the upside—a plate of Dover sole that she probably wouldn't have to pay for. She didn't take long to make her decision.

"Yum," she said decisively. "We'd love to join you."

"Wonderful!" said Helena delightedly. "Do jump in!"

"To Sheekeys, Bernard!" ordered Kate.

So off we went to St. Martin's Lane, Kate and Helena talking nineteen to the dozen, Charlotte moving smoothly into the gossipy, flighty mode that I had seen her in during the Hamilton party. She didn't mention that half an hour earlier we had been sitting in the caff on Tottenham Court Road with A the T and company; in fact, I began to wonder whether it had happened at all. Sitting in Sheekeys, gulping down Pol Roger, and listening wide-eyed to the twins' chatter made me feel quite dizzy. Was this the same city, I wondered? Was I the same person with these girls? Was Charlotte? People looked over at our table and nudged each other; they recognized Kate and Helena, and fell quiet from time to time to try to hear what they were saying, which wasn't difficult, as neither girl thought to keep the volume of her voice within the confines of our table. Charlotte asked a lot of questions, many of which she already knew the answers to, so she didn't have to talk much and could focus her attention on what she was ordering and eating. She was clever, though, throwing in the odd scandalous snippet of gossip just to keep our end up and make the twins feel they were getting their money's worth out of their evening; then it was back to the fish and the sautéed potatoes. We left just before midnight. The girls were very friendly with me, especially after Betty Harwood, who wrote "Jennifer's Diary" for *Tatler*, came up to say hello and asked to be remembered to Mama. I could have hugged her.

Back at Kensington Court, Charlotte peeled off her coat and her shoes and flopped onto the sofa. Aunt Clare had gone to bed and Harry was nowhere to be found.

"Probably still bringing people back from the dead at Sophia Garrison-Denbigh's," said Charlotte. "Gosh, Sheekeys is good. I could have eaten those pancakes three times over."

"Was it strange?" I blurted. "Seeing Andrew again."

I thought she wouldn't answer, but eventually she did.

"It's silly, isn't it? Andrew's no good for me because he's too common and too poor. Marina's no good for Harry because she's too rich and too vulgar. Was there *ever* a condition so idiotically pathetic as that of the penniless toff?"

"Worst of all worlds," I said dully. "Losers, all of us."

"At least you have Magna to give you some semblance of wealth."

"Not much good when there's a high possibility of the ceiling collapsing on all potential suitors."

Charlotte gave me the ghost of a smile.

"What are we going to do?" She buried her face in her hands.

I was partly horrified, having never seen Charlotte with her guard down like this before.

"A the T—he *was* nice, you were quite right to say that about him," I said quickly. "And *so* pretty. I can't think why Aunt Clare objects so much. Surely—"

"Did you hear what he said about his parents?" she asked heavily.

"Yes, but—"

"It's not fair on Aunt Clare," said Charlotte. "She's waited all her life for me to marry the right man. And she's right about one thing. It would never last. A the T—he's the boy you fall for before your *real* hero comes along. He's too young for me, too. I realized that today. I need someone older, someone to keep me in line."

"Is that what you think, or Aunt Clare?"

"What does it matter? He'll do his National Service next year. That sort of thing changes a boy like Andrew. I'm not sure I'd want him after that."

I didn't say anything, but I wasn't convinced and neither was she.

We sat in silence for a while, listening to the tick-ticking of the clock. Charlotte stared straight ahead, frowning, knotting her fingers together. It was the first time I had felt cold in Aunt Clare's study. Eventually, I spoke up.

"Mary thinks Marlon Brando has nice arms."

Charlotte stared at me as though I were mad. Then she started to laugh and suddenly we were all right again.

Harry arrived back soon afterward. He jumped with surprise to see Charlotte and me still up.

"What on earth are you two doing?" he demanded. "Waiting for Godot?"

"No, just you," said Charlotte. "We've heard from reliable sources that you've been whooping it up *chez* the nouveau riche."

"I nouveau *wishe,*" snapped Harry. "It's been a painful day. I got stuck with the Wentworth twins for longer than is healthy for any man."

Charlotte looked at me and grinned.

"We just had dinner with them."

"You did? Well, you're gluttons for punishment, then."

"Gluttons, certainly," said Charlotte. "We went to Sheekeys."

"They paid?"

"Naturellement."

"Well, I suppose that's something. I don't know what it is about those two, but every party I've been to in the past year has involved sitting next to one of them. People obviously think we're kindred spirits."

"Kate seems rather keen on you," I said slyly.

"Don't," said Harry coldly.

"She's jolly beautiful," I pointed out.

"Until she opens that mailbox of a mouth."

"Did you make enough money to justify the whole grisly experience?" asked Charlotte.

"Just about. I was booked for another two lunch parties this week, so it's not all bad." He looked tired suddenly.

"So you're in it for something other than the thrill?" I asked, rather surprised. "I always imagined that magic was far too sacred to make money from."

"Nothing is too sacred to make money from, Penelope," said Harry irritatedly. "Do you really think I'd hang around girls like Sophia and Kate for my own amusement? They're enough to send anyone running for the hills."

"Why do you do it, then?" I said.

"Because I love magic, I'm good at it, and I can put up with all of it when I'm paid as much as I was paid tonight." He pulled out a stack of crumpled pound notes from the inside pocket of his jacket and tossed them onto the table. Charlotte gave a low whistle.

"Nice work," she said. "I expect it'll all be gone by tomorrow evening."

"It won't," said Harry sharply. I had never seen him so agitated. He looked at me and sighed. "How's the founder of the Johnnie Ray fan club tonight?" he asked.

"Very well, thank you," I said firmly. "And if only I *were* the founder! We've missed out on tickets to his Palladium shows. Mama threw my fan-club letter away before I read it," I went on, aware of the sourness in my voice. "We could have had discount tickets. As it happens, we're left with none at all."

"Shame," yawned Harry, picking up last week's *Country Life*. I wanted to scream at him.

"I don't suppose we can expect you to understand a tragedy of this pro-portion," said Charlotte irritatedly.

"You're right, I don't. If you'd missed out on tickets to see George Melly or Humphrey Lyttelton, yes, I could muster up something that resembled sympathy. But not getting to see Johnnie Ray? I should consider it a narrow escape."

Charlotte threw a cushion at him, which missed and knocked a little or-nament of a rather ugly milkmaid off Aunt Clare's table and onto the floor, where it broke. For some reason, this seemed to annoy Harry very much.

"For God's sake!" he snapped, picking up the pieces. "You're not thirteen anymore, Charlotte." He stared at the bits, trying to work out how it had smashed. "I suppose I could try and fix this—"

"Oh, just wave your wand over it," suggested Charlotte airily.

Harry glared at her. "When are you going to stop being so bloody thoughtless? It's so typical of you not to give a damn about anyone else's things."

Even I was amazed at the vehemence of his tone. Charlotte recovered fast.

"Well! Since when have you cared about Aunt Clare's china collection? I've heard you say yourself that that dog was a hideous piece of tat she should never have bought. And as for thoughtless! Talk about the pot call-ing the kettle—"

"Oh, shut up. Just *shut up!*"

Harry put the broken milkmaid into his top hat, and for a moment I thought he really *was* going to magic it back together. Instead, he looked straight at me with those ever-changing magic eyes.

"You look good in black," he said softly.

"Goes with the mood," I said, rattled.

He sauntered off to bed, taking his top hat and wand with him. The next morning the milkmaid was back on the table, smiling blithely, as good as new. Charlotte and I examined her under the light and couldn't see a single crack. You had to hand it to Harry. He had style.

ELEVEN

My Beautiful Youth

WHEN I WAS EIGHTEEN, I spent a great deal of time absorbed in magazines. My favorites were *Vanity Fair,* which Mama ordered and I read feverishly as soon as she put it down, and *Woman and Beauty,* which was aimed exclusively at young housewives. Even though housewives represented a section of society as alien to me as the creatures in the outer-space comics that Inigo devoured, I was quite addicted to reading about them. I kept a stack of magazines in my bedroom, and another downstairs in the Morning Room for flicking through while waiting for Mama or Inigo to appear, and their pages worked their magic on me more effectively than even I was aware. By the time I had whizzed through "The ABC of Unusual Holidays," I felt desperate for a hill-climbing trip to Austria. "Tartan, Tartan, Everywhere!" found me rummaging through the mothy depths of my great-grandmother's old trunk in search of a kilt I could fashion into "this season's look." I was quite overcome (and more than a little bit ashamed) of my need to spend money. When, oh when, would I be "Free as Air in My Loveliest Clothes"?

In between the boredom of my studies, I did everything I could to make money, and tried to keep a strict policy of giving fifty percent of all that I earned to Mama, and therefore, to Magna. Once the excitement of Christmas and New Year's was over, I went back to working for Christopher once a week in his shop in Bath. The shop was placed between New Sounds, the best record shop in Bath, and Coffee on the Hill, the best café, which meant that I frequently ended up out of pocket before I had even left the town center, and very little found its way back to Magna. Inigo, who was away at school much of the time, was even worse than I. He sold comics, chocolates, and even cigarettes to his fellow pupils on the black market. I confronted him about it one weekend.

"Don't you think you should stop spending so much money on yourself and give something to Mama?" I asked, drowning in guilt myself as I had just spent five shillings on a slap-up tea with a school friend in the café after my Tuesday shift.

"I don't want to give Mama my dirty cash," said Inigo gravely. "It's black money, Penelope—everything I do at school is illegal. It wouldn't be right to pour it into Magna. It would be like cursing the place."

"Whereas spending it on yourself is quite acceptable."

"I've already sold my soul to the devil for the sake of rock 'n' roll."

"Oh, you've got an answer for everything," I said crossly.

One thing that I did start to do at this time was writing stories and sending them off to the magazines I so adored. This was the one thing in my life that I did without considering payment; all I wanted was the thrill of seeing my name in print. I ransacked my imagination for romantic tales of good-looking heroes and beautiful women and frequently stayed up writing late into the night, eating Cadbury's chocolate sandwich biscuits (which, like all biscuits, tasted especially good after midnight) with Marina the guinea pig snuggled into the crook of my arm. I had some letters back from friendly enough editors, all saying that they liked my style, but that I was not quite right for their magazine, and perhaps I could send them something when my writing had matured? At the time, I felt rather stung by this, but a few months later, when I wrote a story that came right from my heart and onto the page, I realized how right they had been. But I am going too far ahead.

I told myself that I was making a difference to Magna—perhaps the money I earned would go toward Mary's salary, or a new spade for Johns, new candles for the dining room? It was a gesture that made me feel better, but it scarcely touched the surface of the problems we faced. I was horribly aware of the yawning chasm of debt that we were sinking into, and I felt helpless. Since the night of our Duck Supper before Christmas, Mama had not mentioned money. The odd thing about Mama was that she liked to think of herself as a doomy sort of person, but there was a natural optimism in her that refused to be defeated, however hard she squashed it down, and I know that she never lost faith completely. She scoured the cellars for buried treasure and had the few remaining paintings in the library valued by a dealer in London; perhaps Aunt Sarah's pesky oil of the lake was worth millions after all? No, said the dealer, no more than a couple hundred pounds, and he winced when he heard that Mama had let a Stubbs go for a fifth of its value three years after the end of the war. In the back of her mind, Mama clung fast to the hope that Inigo would find a rich girl to marry. She had more or less given up on me. The fate of other big houses did not augur well. My childhood rang out with the names of great, lost houses. Broxmore, Draycott, Erlestoke, and Roundway—Wiltshire houses all—each reduced to rubble through tax or fire or death. Houses like ours were a rare breed, but not quite rare enough. Each loss struck Magna like a blow upon a bruise.

When I thought of it, I felt dizzy with worry, and the fastest way to forget was to go shopping. I craved new shampoos and lipstick (Gala of London did the most delicious makeup), cigarettes (I didn't really like smoking, but as *things* in their bright, squashy packets, cigarettes were the last word in essential style), coffee, and the cinema. After rationing, this new life was intoxicating, and there to be reveled in before it was taken away again.

Of course, all this time I was thinking about Johnnie and the fact that he was coming to England in April, and how on earth Charlotte and I were going to get tickets to his sold-out shows. Every time I thought about the mere fact of him being in England, my knees felt weak; once, when I imagined being in the same *room* as him, I actually had to sit down and have a glass of water. I played his records as often as I dared at home—it was not Mama who objected as much as Inigo, who had moved on to Elvis Presley and saw little point in listening to Johnnie Ray anymore. Despite the fact that I was still living at home (and, of course, we had no money to make living at home any easier than it had been in the previous years), there was a sense of something uprising, a feeling of gathering momentum that had started in America and was making its way to our shores. I was a teenager, and even if this was nothing more than a label for a section of the population that had always been there, it somehow felt as if it meant more now than it had the year before.

Before I met Charlotte, I had done nothing but stare out of windows. She was unafraid of most things and most people; she thought nothing of bunking a train fare, but she would make sure that she did so with a ham sandwich and chocolate eclair from Fortnums about her person. If ever she was caught, she would turn out her pockets to reveal the most extravagant packed lunch imaginable in the smartest of bags and the ticket collector always let her off. I recognized pieces of myself in her and she encouraged the rebel in me to emerge. Certainly, I would be happy to sneak into the cinema after the film had started. But in those shoes? Never!

London intoxicated us both, and in the first weeks of 1955, whenever we could, Charlotte and I would take a trip into the West End, where we would stare at beautiful hats in Swan & Edgar and talk about what we would sell if we had our own shop. Charlotte was drawn to bright colors and sparkly window displays like a magpie, and her eye was second to none.

"I wouldn't have dressed that mannequin in that drear trench coat."

"Oh, I rather like it."

"Typical you. Penelope, you must try and develop better taste."

"My taste is impeccable, thank you very much!"

"You're too trad, by far."

"Just because I like to look vaguely respectable—"

"Don't use that word in my presence."

I put on my worshipping voice. "Oh, Charlotte, you're so *weird*, you're so *different*. . . . I wish I was like you!"

In response to this, she pulled the ribbon out of my hair and ran off down Oxford Street. She was good at being teased, and the better we knew each other, the more we played up to our differences. My conscientious following of all the latest trends complemented her refusal to conform, and we battered the seriousness out of each other. She also had a habit of nudging me violently when nice-looking boys walked past us. They were confused by Charlotte, with her eccentric clothes and her height and her confidence. She did not radiate the faint-worthy, womanly atmosphere of Mama; rather, she threw something completely different at them—sex, I suppose— and they weren't used to getting that from someone with such class.

I don't mean to create the impression that Charlotte and I spent all of our time swanning around London and buying clothes; for quite apart from my lectures and endless rounds of essays, I had begun working for Christopher again. Charlotte liked visiting me in the shop, and Christopher became defensive and offhand in her presence which was, I felt, a surefire sign of his fascination with her. As an old Etonian, he was of very little interest to Charlotte. She said that men who had been to boarding school never understood women, but she admired the way he ran his shop and she liked to watch him talking to customers. She constantly fired questions at him (Why did he put that particular bowl in the window? What was the difference between running the business in the winter and the summer? Why didn't he play music in the shop?) until he was groaning with irritation. I wondered what Christopher would say if he knew that Charlotte was Clare Delancy's niece—I still hadn't summoned the courage to mention her to him.

For most of the week, Charlotte was entirely at the mercy of Aunt Clare and her memoirs. During January, Aunt Clare got into the amiable habit of inviting me over to Kensington once a week, for tea. These teas usually took place at three thirty on a Friday, when she and Charlotte had finished working, and never went on beyond five o'clock. They were an hour and a half of pure fascination. Her study itself remained a valuable insight into the life of a woman who never ceased to surprise me. One of the most curious aspects of the room was how the level of chaos—the number of books, the state of perpetual disarray—never altered. No one ever seemed to tidy up or put anything away, yet there was never a visible increase in dust or clutter, which gave one the odd sensation of walking onto the same film set every week. *On the Origin of Species* never moved from the place I had noted it on my first visit, and every Friday I ran my eye over the same postcard to Richard about Wootton Bassett. As a result, the room seemed preserved in amber, which would have been quite disconcerting were it not for the variety in atmosphere each week, which ranged from high elation at the completion of an exciting chapter (*and so began a lifelong friendship with the art of keeping secrets* was a favorite of mine) to bitter irritation when Aunt Clare was "lost for adjectives."

"One can only use so many words to describe the heat of the Far East," she complained one afternoon, "and I believe I have ransacked the English language for every one of them."

"Dry, oppressive, stifling, overwhelming?" I suggested with all the flourish of one who had never been east of Paris.

"Already used all of those," dismissed Aunt Clare. "Except for 'overwhelming.' I was *never* overwhelmed. Perhaps we should make that point, Charlotte? *Despite the intensity of the heat, I was never overwhelmed.*"

Tap, tap, tap went Charlotte's long fingers at the typewriter. She typed enviably quickly, much faster, I am sure, than any of the girls in the popular secretarial courses, and she rarely messed up the manuscript with any mistakes. *Never overwhelmed,* indeed. I could believe that, for the harder Aunt Clare worked, the younger and brighter she looked. (Charlotte said it was all to do with the therapeutic nature of writing one's autobiography and that we should try it too. I said I was quite keen on this idea, but if anyone ever read it, I should age seventy years overnight out of sheer nerves.) "That will do for today, Charlotte," Aunt Clare would say when Charlotte started to sag. "Cover that machine up at once—I can't bear to look at it any longer—and send Phoebe in with tea."

Ah, tea. I became as greedy as Charlotte when it came to tea in that house. There was something about the taste of hot buttered toast with gooseberry jam in Aunt Clare's study that could never be replicated anywhere else. On a couple of occasions, Harry joined us just as I was stuffing a second piece of chocolate cake into my mouth, or reaching for a third ginger scone. He never seemed to notice, and he never ate much himself, but boys, I have noticed, don't get as fanatical about sweet things as girls. The more time that I spent with Harry, the younger he seemed to become, and I revised my view of him as having always seemed a man. Twenty-five did not seem so jolly old after all, and although he still refused to accept my fixation with Johnnie Ray and pop music, I realized that, like Charlotte and me, he was just beginning to live. The war had scuppered most of his teenage years, and for that I felt desperately sorry. Then, one afternoon, Aunt Clare and Charlotte had not yet arrived back from a trip to Barkers to buy more ribbon for the typewriter, and Harry and I found ourselves alone for the first half an hour of tea. He stood by the fireplace, smoking a cigarette, murky eyes as amused as ever. Sometimes I felt quite easy with Harry; other times, I felt crippled with shyness.

"How do you find your new job?" I asked awkwardly.

"Quite easily. Apparently one takes the bus to Oxford Street and walks the rest."

"I meant—"

"I know. I'm sorry."

"Is your boss a nice man?"

"Probably."

"What do you mean?"

Harry gave me a look. "Can you keep a secret?"

"Yes." (*Who, on hearing these words, ever says no? I wondered.*)

"I haven't been into the office once. I called up on the first day and said that I had accepted an offer from another firm."

"Harry!" I exclaimed, thoroughly shocked. "How on earth are you going to hide *this* one from your mother?"

"Oh, she's lost interest in me now that she thinks I'm employed. Right now she's so gripped by getting the rip-roaring fable that is her life story into print, I don't think she'd notice if I grew another head. No doubt she won't bump into Sir Richard until Christmas, which gives me eight months to get my career in magic off the ground. And I should warn you that I won't listen to anything you say, unless you wish to praise me for my enterprising cunning."

"Nothing cunning about not having any money," I said pertly.

"I'm playing the circuit on weekends. That keeps me in smokes. Anyway," he went on, "I've always been hopeless at math. If I hadn't dropped out, they would have sacked me within a week."

"It sounds like you've got it all worked out."

"I'm a magician, it's in our nature to have everything worked out. How are you, anyway? Weeping for Johnnie as usual?"

"Oh, shut up. I don't tease you about your obsession with the American."

Harry grinned. "Touché. *Au contraire,* you were rather helpful to me over the American. Which brings me onto something else—" He paused and I felt a flutter of dread mixed with a flicker of excitement.

"What do you mean by that?"

"I need you to help me again."

"Oh, no. No way." I shook my head vigourously.

"At least let me explain." He threw the last of his cigarette into the fire. "Then you can make your own mind up."

"I'm not listening!"

Harry grinned. "George is organizing a soirée for Marina's birthday. Nothing fancy, just fifty close friends for dinner at the Ritz."

"How terribly low-key of him."

"Isn't it? It's taking place next month, so you've a couple of weeks to fret about it."

"Why should it be of any concern to me?"

"Because Charlotte's been invited. And you and I have been invited. And we've both accepted."

"I don't understand," I said grimly, understanding perfectly.

Harry gave me a pleading grin. "Think about it, sweetheart."

"Marina won't want *me* there—"

"Well, that's exactly the point, isn't it? George was only too keen to make sure you would be accompanying me so that Marina gets the message, once and for all, that I've lost all interest in *her.* As far as he's concerned, once I'm well and truly spoken for, he has nothing else to fear. You should have read the letter he enclosed with the invitation. *I do hope your sweet friend Penelope can come. Marina thought her a perfect delight.*"

"It didn't say that!"

"Yes, it did!"

I digested this for a moment.

"No. I won't do it again. I just won't." Something in me felt furious with him for even asking me. Harry said nothing, so I plowed on.

"I still can't quite make out where all this is heading. All I know is that I'm the one who's going to get hurt."

"You've been reading too many magazines. You won't get hurt."

Harry crossed the room to where I was standing and stood right up close to me, and irrationally, all I could think about was how long his hair was getting. I tried to make myself a little shorter by slouching slightly on one leg like a horse at rest. Harry, observant as ever, laughed.

"If only you weren't so bloody tall," he groaned. "It's the only thing that makes us implausible."

"I don't see why," I said defensively. "Plenty of men like tall women."

"Oh, I don't doubt that for a second," said Harry, confirming that he was not one of them, "but there's something very suspicious about a tall girl falling for a shorter man."

"I don't think so," I said. "Height should never be an issue in the face of true love."

Harry grinned. "You're getting the hang of this," he said approvingly. Then he put his hands on my shoulders and bowed his head in shame.

"Call me what you like, but I've got one last chance to get her," he said, returning to the topic at hand. "She was shaken by you after the engagement party. This could push her over the edge."

"Charming. I thought you were madly in love with the girl."

"I am, I am!" he said, crossing back over to the fireplace and reaching for another cigarette. "And if she marries Rogerson, I'll never forgive myself, and neither will she."

"And you honestly believe this plan will work?"

"I know the way her mind works. One more night of you and I together, and she'll snap."

"Then what? When she's finished snapping?"

"She'll come back to me, of course."

"And what about me?"

"Well, sweetheart, I can't imagine that you'll be too heartbroken to let me go. Of course, you could pretend to be, that would be rather nice—"

"But I'll forever be seen as the poor girl dumped for the rich American."

"I imagine it will make you a source of great fascination to the rest of the male species. Men love girls they can protect from the evil of a former lover."

"Girls of six foot don't tend to radiate the need for protection," I snapped.

"Don't be so silly. You'll seem like a beautiful baby giraffe with a broken leg. They'll want to nurse you back to health."

I gave him my best what-are-you-talking-about look, which never normally comes off. I think I did quite well this time, probably because I genuinely meant it for once.

"As far as I can see, there's nothing in this for me at all. The first time it was all a bit of fun, but this is taking things a step too far, Harry," I said firmly.

"I've thought of that too."

"What do you mean?"

He lowered his voice a little.

"You need payment this time. Something to make the whole, horrific ordeal worthwhile."

I was about to open my mouth and say that nothing on earth would persuade me to think that this was anything other than a terrible idea, but something in me paused to listen to what he had to say next. Harry pulled something out of his pocket.

"Here."

"What—what are they?" I muttered, but I knew even before I had finished asking the question.

"Two tickets to Johnnie Ray at the Palladium in April. Rare as guinea pigs, I can tell you."

"How did you—" I whispered, heart hammering, trying hard not to whoop.

"Let's just say the roulette wheel, several dry martinis, a collection of rich gamblers, and a sprinkle of magic were involved. From what I've heard about him, Johnnie Ray himself would be proud of me." He grinned. "I'll leave it up to you to tell Charlotte."

The next thing that happened was that we heard the front door opening and both of us nearly jumped out of our skins. Harry shoved the tickets back into his pocket, pressed his finger to his lips, and stalked off, leaving me struck dumb in the middle of the room. Five seconds later, Charlotte burst through the door.

"Oh, Penelope, you're here! Goodness, you must be starving."

I nodded, but for once, tea was the last thing on my mind.

"This whole city has gone quite mad," said Aunt Clare, sweeping into the room and kissing me hello. "I've never seen so many people shopping in all of my life, and I've never felt so violated by the power of advertisements! All I wanted was a simple ribbon for the typewriter, but I've come home with two new skirts, a bottle of perfume, and a book that I am quite sure I will never get around to reading."

"Why did you buy it then, Aunt?"

"I liked the title. We must think of a good title for my book, Charlotte. Something rare and controversial."

"How about *My Autobiography*?" suggested Charlotte, who was looking fed up.

Aunt Clare gave her a withering look and flopped onto her chair.

"This need to buy everything one reads about it is quite frightening," she said. "Still, Harry has his job now. We should be grateful for small mercies. Goodness, Sir Richard is *such* a friend."

I hardly knew where to look.

"I wouldn't get *too* complacent, Aunt," warned Charlotte. "You never know with Harry."

"Oh, he'll be quite at home in accountancy. He's always loved figures," said Aunt Clare vaguely. Charlotte raised her eyebrows at me and I stifled a giggle.

Unfortunately, I didn't get a chance that afternoon to talk to Charlotte about Harry and his outrageous suggestion. Tea finished at five as usual, but Charlotte had to leave ten minutes early for her mother's birthday drinks.

"The conductor's throwing her a party," she said gloomily. "I'm quite sure he'd be out of the door faster than you can say *Nabucco* if he knew that she's *fifty*-three, not forty-three, today."

I rather hoped that Charlotte would invite me to accompany her. She didn't, of course.

Because she left earlier, I took the earlier train home. This was going to prove to be one of those momentous decisions made without the slightest realization of its momentousness. It had been tipping down with rain for most of the afternoon, and the carriage smelled sweetly of damp clothes and wet newspapers, of tobacco and British Railways tea. I listened to the comforting rattle of the carriage on the tracks, and watched through the window as we slipped out of London and toward the soft, friendly stations that marked the journey back to Magna. The rain stopped after a while and the evening looked beautiful in a nearly spring sort of a way. For the first time, I felt aware of lengthening light, the elbowing out of the winter.

As we pulled out of Reading, the man opposite me looked up from the *Financial Times* for the first time since leaving London, and smiled at me. I caught my breath, because he had the most amazing face I had ever seen. It wasn't just his beauty, which was obvious in an older-movie-star way (I put him at about forty-five), but his eyes—huge, soft, brown, and full of kindness—that took me by surprise. I had never thought that glamour and kindness could be happy bedfellows, yet this man's features were doing their best to prove me wrong. He didn't even have to shift in his seat for me to notice that he oozed self-confidence in a distinctly un-English way.

"Strange weather," he said, and—joy of joys!—there was the unmistakable American accent.

"Isn't it?" I agreed.

He grinned again and went back to his paper, and I noticed how beautiful his hands looked. *Manicured!* I thought in amazement. I wanted to hear him talk again.

"But then, we're used to that in this country."

He laughed. "Sure we are," he said, and smiling, turned back to his paper.

"Do you—do you live in England?" I asked falteringly.

"Some of the time," he said. "Most of the time, in fact."

"Gosh," I said, "you're American, aren't you?"

"Damn, I thought I'd shaken the accent off at London airport," he said mockingly, but there was amusement in his eyes. Not that haughty, *Isn't this all a bit of a jolly jape?* look of amusement that Harry wore. This felt *real* to me. He was back at his business again, so I wrenched my questions back and stared out of the window and thought about Harry's request. Johnnie and a night out at the Ritz seemed too good a chance to pass up. And yet . . .

"You look like there's something on your mind," said the stranger. I gave him a quizzical look.

"What would you do," I asked him quickly, "if somebody wanted you to do something for them that you weren't sure you really wanted to do?"

"What is this very terrible thing?"

"A smart dinner party," I mumbled.

"*All* good dinner parties should make you feel odd and out of place to start with," said the stranger briskly. "The combination of good wine and good-looking people throws most folk completely. The question is, can you rise to the occasion? Can you turn it around and make the night work for you?"

I stared at him, openmouthed.

"I don't know," I answered truthfully. I thought of our triumph at Dorset House, and Marina's irritation at my presence. "I suppose I could have a go," I said.

He laughed out loud at me.

"What would you rather be doing," he asked, "if there was some place else you could be rather than at this dinner party? Dancing to poor old Johnnie Ray, I suppose?"

My eyes widened, and as usual, my heartbeat skipped at the mere sound of Johnnie's name. Spoken by an American, it sounded even more delicious.

"How on earth did you know about Johnnie?" I cried. "That's psychic!"

"Not really," said the stranger, pointing at the magazine Charlotte had given me—I always carried it with me for the train. "There's no hope, I'm afraid. I've heard he hypnotizes young girls like you. God knows, one can hardly blame the man."

I felt myself flushing scarlet.

"I do like the new sounds," I admitted. "My brother's addicted to them."

"There's big money to be made in it all," said the stranger. "Big money indeed."

Then the ticket collector came through, and an awful thing happened— I couldn't for the life of me find my ticket.

"I know it's here somewhere!" I fretted, turning my coat pockets inside out to reveal a half-eaten ginger scone that I had wrapped in a bit of paper to eat on the journey home. Why couldn't I be like Charlotte, who always kept her cool in situations like this? The ticket collector, who was a sour-faced man with a hacking cough, looked ready for the kill.

"I don't have enough money for another ticket," I muttered.

"You'll have to alight at the next station," he said smugly.

"Oh, but I'll come back with the money tomorrow!" I begged. We were still a good half an hour from Westbury and the rain had started again. My American hero reached into the breast pocket of his coat and pulled out a leather wallet.

"Now look here, my man," he said, like they do in the films, "I'll pay her fare."

"You traveling with this young lady?"

"I am now. How much does she owe?"

"Two shillings and eightpence," said the ticket collector sulkily.

"Here you go. If my companion finds her ticket before she reaches her destination, we shall expect our money back."

"Certainly, sir," said the ticket man, shuffling off with a spluttering cough.

"Thanks most awfully," I gasped. "I must take your address so I can send you the money as soon as I get home. I *did* buy a ticket, you know. I'm generally an honest sort of person who doesn't normally get into these sorts of scrapes."

"How disappointing," said my new friend with a wicked smile. "And of course you must *not* send me the money. I would take that as a terrific insult."

"Oh, please, I'll feel sick if you don't let me pay you back. At least let me have your address, just to write and thank you."

He relented at this, and a shiny, black ink pen appeared from nowhere and he scribbled something on the back of a ticket stub. I wanted to see where he lived, but thought it was rude to look with him watching, so I shoved the ticket straight into my pocket with the unfortunate ginger scone.

"My mother would be horrified if she knew I had accepted a ticket from a stranger," I said.

"She need never know," he said with a wink.

I thought he had probably had enough of me causing trouble, so I thanked him again and buried my head in my book, while he studied a number of typewritten pages, tutting and swiping his pen through bits he probably didn't agree with. At the next stop, which was Didcot, he packed his papers away and stood up. He was taller than I had imagined he would be, which only enhanced his fearful glamour.

"Well, I'm off here," he announced. "Nice to meet you, mysterious lady with no ticket. I hope Mr. Ray appreciates you. I have a funny feeling you may be wasted on him."

I thanked him yet again, and said good evening and watched him leave the train. He was met by a man in gloves and uniform, who relieved him of his suitcase. A minute later I thought I was seeing things as I watched him climb into the passenger seat of the most beautiful black car with cream piping down the sides.

"Blow me! It's a blinking Chevrolet!" exclaimed a boy of about thirteen, a couple of seats behind me, his glasses falling off his nose in excitement, and at once, all faces that could pressed to the window to have a look.

"I knew 'e was American," said the boy smugly. "Could tell from the way 'e was talkin'."

"Rich American," said the man next to him.

The car was quite the most exotic thing I'd ever seen, especially in a place like Didcot. Several little boys gathered around it, flummoxed with admiration, waiting for it to start off, which it did with a great roar and a cheer from the crowd. My friend even stuck his hand out and waved at them. They loved it.

Mama met me at Westbury, which was unusual.

"Johns wanted the afternoon off," she said, cranking the car into gear (Mama was a good driver, which always struck me as being somewhat out of character). "If only you could find a rich man to marry you, Penelope! All our troubles would be over," she sighed.

"Don't be silly, Mama," I said automatically. But I reached into my pocket and felt my stranger's address, and as soon as we arrived home I rushed upstairs to my room and pulled it out of my pocket to study. It was a ticket from last week's performance of *La Traviata* at Covent Garden. Royal Box, I noted in awe, and nearly fainted when I read the price in the corner. I turned it over to find out where he lived. This is what he had written:

I must not lose my head over pop singers.
I must be myself at smart dinners, love Rocky

I gave a half cry and clutched the ticket to my chest. "I must not lose my head over strangers on the 5:35 from Paddington," I whispered. I went to bed that night with my fingers still covered in black ink.

TWELVE

Inigo Versus the World

I WANTED DESPERATELY TO TELL CHARLOTTE all about my encounter with Rocky (was that *really* his name?), but I did not dare to make a phone call to her until six o'clock the following evening, when at last Mama vanished for a bath and I could be sure she was not in earshot. Mama had ears like a bat, and the matters up for discussion that night were especially delicate. Were Mama to hear me telling Charlotte that a strange man (oh, and an American too) had paid my fare home, and that I was planning on going to see Johnnie at the Palladium in exchange for pretending to be Harry's lover, I don't think she would have been too delighted.

"Charlotte!" I hissed.

"Oh, hullo. You're late calling today."

"We need to meet tomorrow. Urgent matters to discuss."

"I can come to Magna. Aunt Clare's given me the day off." Charlotte was hard pushed to keep the glee from her voice.

"I'm working in the shop until lunchtime. Shall we meet for lunch in Bath? Twelve thirty at Coffee on the Hill? You can get the early train, can't you?"

"Yet more expense," said Charlotte cheerfully. "Of course I can."

"Oh, and I've two essays to complete by tomorrow night," I said quickly. "You'll have to help me."

"What are we talking about here?"

"Tennyson."

"*The curse is come upon me,*" quoted Charlotte.

"What?"

"'*The Lady of Shalott.*' Really, Penelope, you are hopeless."

"You'll help me, then?"

"I can certainly do your handwriting. I'm getting rather good at it. What are the urgent matters we need to discuss, anyway?"

"I can't possibly tell you now," I said, but I was bursting inside with the need to talk about Johnnie Ray and Rocky and what Harry had proposed.

"Harry's been horribly smug all day," said Charlotte, reading my mind. "It's nothing to do with him, is it?"

"It might be. I'll tell you tomorrow."

"*Penelope!*" came Mama's voice from behind me.

"There's my cue," I muttered. "See you tomorrow."

"You're far too mysterious. It doesn't suit you, Penelope," complained Charlotte.

Inigo was home from school that night, and Mary had made an insipid stew for our dinner.

"So warming on a cold night," she said stoutly, ladling it onto her plate. Earlier on I had noticed the first daffodils of the year outside the kitchen door and I had cried out loud with delight. Daffodils packed a glorious punch at Magna, such bright, assured successors to the exquisitely shy snowdrops that crept up the verges of the drive with heads bowed at the end of January. I loved them for the confidence they instilled; their merry, sunshiny heads bobbing in the wind seemed to make a mockery of the idea that Magna could not survive. Winter was being edged out of the picture by spring—lovely, lovely spring—and that evening, I felt it all around us, crouching in the wings, waiting to burst out and trample the dark evenings to the ground.

"Good week at school?" I asked Inigo automatically.

"Pretty horrific. I got lines."

Mama dropped her fork with a clatter onto her plate. She always overreacted to Inigo's misadventures, and he got a strange thrill from relating them to her.

"What on earth for?"

"Listening to the radio after lights out."

"You're a silly boy," said Mama angrily. "Why on earth did you get caught?"

"It was that dronesome prefect, Williams-May. I got off lightly, actually. Thorpe was caught doing the same thing last night and got caned before breakfast."

"What's wrong with you two?" demanded Mama. "You're always so damn *care*less. Your father would be horrified!"

"You're always telling us how radical Papa was at school!" complained Inigo, edging a watery onion to the side of his plate.

"But he was never *caught*! And he was captain of every team!" Mama's voice got higher and higher with excitement.

"Except for hockey," chorused Inigo and I together.

"Except for hockey. And who on earth wants to play hockey?"

"I can't think, Mama. All I want to play is the guitar."

Inigo stood up and pushed away his chair and crossed the room to the window. Mama looked at me with a see-how-I-suffer expression on her face.

"Do sit down," she sighed, changing tack.

Inigo paced a bit and eventually sat down on the windowseat and stared out into the night.

"Pass me my lighter, will you, Penelope?" He fished in his pockets and pulled out a squashed packet containing only one miserable-looking cigarette.

"Won't you sit down with us and finish your stew, darling?" asked Mama reproachfully. She didn't really like getting cross with Inigo, but I could sense her discomfort. She was unequipped to cope with any scenes not instigated by herself.

"No, thank you," said Inigo. "I find Mary's stew unutterably depressing."

There was a silence and I felt like screaming with laughter and sobbing at the same time.

"You used to love stew," said Mama in a wobbly voice. "It used to be a treat, something we all looked forward to—"

"During the war, when we looked forward to Papa coming home, too," I said.

"But he never did come home, did he?" finished Inigo, rubbing his hand up and down the back of his head as he did when he was talking about Papa.

That's done it, I thought, waiting for tears, but for once, Mama did not cry. She looked weary, older suddenly, crushed. Then her face hardened and she rounded on Inigo.

"And I suppose you think playing the guitar will make you rich? Will save Magna from the tax collectors? Will pay to reopen the Long Gallery? You think singing will keep the place standing? You think—"

"Yes, I do!" Inigo shouted. He stood up and shook his hands out at us in frustration, and the ash from the end of his cigarette floated gently to the floor.

"I *do*!" he repeated. Mama gave me a despairing look, yet I looked back at her full of triumph, for I believed everything that Inigo said.

"You see, Mama!" I cried. "He's thinking of Magna! He'll sing and play for Magna! I *know* he will!"

Inigo ran forward to Mama and actually fell at her feet.

"*Please*, Mama," he said. "You have to believe me."

"How many people do you know who've made a record? How on earth would you do it?" asked Mama, but I could tell she was softening a little. Inigo stood up again.

"I could go out to Memphis, to Uncle Luke's friend Sam Phillips's place. He could get me into his studio for a day or two, I could start off there, just like Elvis Presley—"

"How on earth would you get to Memphis in the first place?" demanded Mama.

"Aeroplane."

Mama laughed, without mirth.

"And I suppose you've made enough money selling booze and cigarette cards to do just that? Afford yourself a trip to America and back on an aeroplane?"

"I don't have to come back."

Mama burst into noisy sobs. The house felt so quiet around her; I almost hated the place for not providing more noise, more distraction from this most awful sound. I felt rooted to the spot, a spectator watching my own drama. I wanted so badly to help Mama, but there was a part of me that hated her for crying, that hated her for wanting to keep Inigo and me here with her, trapped as she was.

"How did this happen? It must be my fault! It must be me!" she wailed. Everything, even Inigo's obsession with music, had to come back to her.

"It must be me!" she repeated. "I'm an awful mother! I'm a terrible person!" She reached out for something to clean herself up, but distressingly for everyone, she chose the napkin that Inigo had spat his onion into. With eyes blinded by tears, she drew it to her face and blew heavily, thereby squashing the onion onto her delicate nose. For the next few seconds, she teetered on the brink of further tears but, being Mama, soon found it impossible to do anything but throw back her head and laugh and laugh. I think she despaired of her sense of humor sometimes, for it was something uncontrollable that was inclined to interrupt perfectly good misery. She had no idea of the power her laughter had over Inigo and me. When Mama laughed, really laughed, nothing else in the entire world mattered.

Later that night, after Mama had gone to bed, Inigo and I played a hand of rummy in the library.

"Were you serious?" I asked him. "About going to America?"

"To Memphis?" said Inigo. "To make a record? Of course I was serious."

"But *you*? Little old sixteen-year-old *you*? Making a *record*? In *America*? No one we know makes records. It isn't possible, is it?"

"Elvis Presley makes records."

"But we don't *know* him—he's just some singer Uncle Luke's met!"

"Good enough for me."

"What's so great about him, anyway?"

"Everything. You're just frightened because he's even better than Johnnie and you know it."

"Of *course* he's not!"

"I'm sorry, Penelope, but there it is."

"Why don't we hear him on the radio, then? How come he's not playing the Palladium next month?" I heard my voice growing hysterical, but Inigo just grinned at me infuriatingly and rearranged his cards.

"When Elvis Presley makes it, he's going to kick everyone else out of the picture," he said, not even bothering to raise his voice. "It really is that simple."

"Show me a photograph, and I'll be the judge of that," I snapped. "It's not like he could possibly *look* more dreamy than Johnnie."

"He doesn't need to wear a hearing aid, if that's what you mean. Uncle Luke's sending me pictures of him."

"Uncle Luke says he looks weird."

"Weird is only ever a good thing," yawned Inigo.

"Oh, you're *impossible!*"

"Not at all. I can just see that there's life after Johnnie Ray."

"But who's going to remember Elvis Presley in twenty years' time?" I cried. "No one! But *everyone* will remember Johnnie! You've only heard him singing four songs!"

"You can believe what you want," said Inigo, "but I know that there's something different about Elvis Presley. I just know it. Can't say why or how. I just *do*."

We played the next round of cards without talking.

"I'm not saying I don't like him," I admitted grudgingly as we stomped up the stairs to bed. "It's just that he's not like Johnnie."

"He's certainly not like Johnnie," agreed Inigo. "He's not like anyone. He's just Elvis Presley. That's enough."

The next day I left for work before Mama had even surfaced for breakfast. She claimed to dislike the fact that I had a job in town, saying that she hated the thought of anyone she knew entering the shop and seeing me behind the counter, yet privately I felt that she was glad to get me out of the house for a few hours. She was so lost in her own self sometimes, so completely immersed in memories of Papa and her youth, that on occasion I perceived that my presence felt clangingly out of sync with her; I seemed to belong to a time that she did not want to be a part of at all. I was too modern for her, perhaps, and if there was one thing that Mama did not want to understand, it was modernity.

It was one of those abnormally warm February mornings that shocks the system into thinking that winter has fled overnight. I cycled to the station on the Golden Arrow, my ancient but reliable bicycle, and jumped on the train to Bath. Fifteen minutes later, I arrived at the shop and removed my coat and sweater and sat on the stool behind the counter, dangling my legs and thinking about Rocky while waiting for Christopher to arrive. I liked the hours that he and I spent in his shop. We talked about very little of any importance—we just sat drinking Robinson's lemon-barley water, which he said was good for the soul. I liked him because he was a piece of Papa that I could reach out and touch, and he liked me for the same reason. That morning as we wrote splodgy price tags for four new tea sets that had arrived the day before, I knew it would only be a matter of time before Charlotte came into the conversation. I had also vowed that today would be the day that I would ask him about Aunt Clare and Rome.

"Price them all as high as you dare," Christopher advised me. "People are drinking tea like it's going out of fashion at the moment." He pretended to be concentrating very hard on refilling his ink pen. "Does Charlotte drink tea?"

"She does."

"She does?" repeated Christopher. "Well, there we have it. Perhaps you could offer her first refusal on the green and white set in the window? Wouldn't she like that? She could have it half-price. I always felt green was her color—don't ask me why—perhaps it's to do with that ghastly coat she always wears."

"I like her coat."

"Oh, it must be me, then. I'm too old."

"Never. Oh, help, I've forgotten how many I've done now."

Christopher looked at me curiously.

"You're terribly distracted this morning. Is something wrong?"

"Not really," I said. "Just thinking."

"Well, don't think, dearest. We've too much to get through."

We were interrupted by the tinkling of the bell as the front door opened and our first customer, an elderly lady carrying a basket of needlework, entered the shop.

"I'd like to look at the green and white tea set in the window, please," she said, removing her hat.

"Oh, good heavens, I'm frightfully sorry, but it's already reserved," said Christopher pleasantly. "Remove it from the display, please, Penelope."

The woman turned to leave, but Christopher was one step ahead.

"Now. A lady like you," he said, guiding her back into the shop, "should *really* be serving tea from a mauve set."

"Mauve?"

"Or china blue," considered Christopher, "to match those marvelous twinkling eyes."

"Oh!" she squeaked.

I giggled to myself. Christopher was successful because he believed every word he said. I wrapped the green and white tea set in newspaper and vowed to offer it to Aunt Clare, not Charlotte.

"Of course, Victorian tea cozies are so attractive," Christopher was saying with the air of one discussing Chanel's latest collection. "I simply can't get enough of them."

I watched him cross the shop to what I called the trinket drawer. For a man who had spent so much time in the air force, Christopher was still fabulously pretty—his face was unlined and his hands so soft that it was impossible to imagine him doing anything out-of-doorsy at all. He dressed in a manner that verged on dandyish (stopping just short of pink neckties) and was nothing short of obsessed with his shoes, yet he was equally interested in beautiful women, never failing to comment on the appearance of every female who entered the shop. He had been very brave during the war, Mama had admitted to me one evening last summer, braver than any of us would ever know, but she didn't like to see him too much now, claiming that he reminded her of Papa. As absolutely everything in life reminded her of Papa, I felt it was rather silly of her to block out Christopher, whose *joie de vivre* and ability to find silver linings in both clouds and smoking jackets never failed to make me feel better about just about everything. As soon as we were alone again, I took a deep breath.

"So, you have been to Rome? Once upon a time?"

He gave me a knowing sort of a look.

"Yes, as well you know, I have been to Rome. And before you carry on with this unsubtle probing, I might as well tell you that yes, I adored Clare Delancy for the ten days that I knew her, and yes, I know she's Charlotte's aunt."

I was stunned. "How did you know?"

Christopher took off his glasses.

"The moment Charlotte first walked into the shop, she reminded me of someone, and I spent the next few days trying to work out who that someone was. Then it came to me. Lovely Clare Delancy. Rome, 1935." His eyes misted over. "I always thought Clare had the most glorious hair I had ever seen. And that *perfect* nose! Charlotte is the only other woman I've ever known with that perfect Roman profile. I guessed right away that they must be related. When I heard her talking about Aunt Clare last week, I put two and two together." He looked quite smug. "Good bit of detective work there, for you." He bent his knees up and down. "Just call me Dixon of Dock Green."

I laughed. "Well, Charlotte's aunt asked me to remember her to you," I said.

"She did?" He was so stunned—he actually stopped moving for a second, which was so unlike him that I felt slightly alarmed.

"I'm amazed she has any recollection of my existence," said Christopher, trying hard not to sound too pleased. "The day after I left for England, she took up with some Austrian count. The following month, I heard she was dining out every night with an eye doctor from Bristol. And all the time she was married to some good-looking bore with a clubfoot. Yet she was so entertaining, so rare, and so damned good-looking—she was quite beyond blame."

"Do you think she ever had her heart broken? You know, really smashed into pieces?"

"Goodness knows. Heavens, your generation talk a lot of rubbish, Penelope. Hearts smashing into pieces, indeed."

"Well, answer the question," I said impatiently.

Christopher blew his nose on a huge square of blue and pink silk. (He always had the most extravagant handkerchiefs.)

"I doubt anyone broke her," he said. "Women like that are far too interested in who and what's around the corner to become too attached. That's where I imagine the similarity between her and her dear niece extends beyond mere outward show."

But he was wrong there, of course. I remembered the way Charlotte had been off her food around A the T and it made me worry that she would never love again.

"Do get on, Penelope," said Christopher irritably. "That's quite enough thinking for one day."

I rather agreed with him.

Half an hour later, Charlotte burst through the door. She beamed at Christopher.

"Lovely day, isn't it, Mr. Jones? I've come to collect your assistant for a vital lunch engagement."

"I thought we were meeting at Coffee on the Hill?"

I still hadn't got used to Charlotte's maddening habit of arriving early for absolutely everything.

"We can walk there now. I'm bursting to hear your news—" she stopped in her tracks, her eyes fixing on the window display. "Oh, what a beautiful scarf!" she cried, pulling a rust-colored Sevillian shawl from off the top of a hideous old sideboard that Christopher had never been able to shift. "How much?"

"For you, one pound," said Christopher, not batting an eyelid.

"Oh, come on! You can do better than that!" cried Charlotte, wrapping the shawl around her shoulders and flouncing in front of the big mirror behind the counter. It looked wonderful on her, I thought enviously—was there anything that Charlotte could not conceive of wearing? I fervently wished that I had had the presence of mind to realize two weeks ago, when Christopher first brought the scarf into the shop, that it was more than just the "bit of old tat from Spain" he had described to me, for clearly it was a work of art, a beautiful piece of seduction that Charlotte could easily choose to wear to see Johnnie in the Palladium, and then he would fall in love with her and her exoticness, and not even so much as glance my way—

"One pound," repeated Christopher.

Charlotte sighed and replaced the shawl. "Too much," she said, shaking her head.

"Ten shillings," ventured Christopher, no doubt hating himself. Charlotte fixed him with a stare. "Nine," she said.

"Nine and eightpence."

"Done."

Charlotte whipped out her purse and handed over the money before he could change his mind.

"You're a hard woman, Charlotte Ferris."

"Hard, my foot," I scoffed. Charlotte folded the scarf into her bag. Her eyes took on a thoughtful look.

"You know, Christopher, you and I should think about going into business together."

Christopher kept his cool.

"I'd never survive with you at the helm," he said. "I couldn't trust you as far as I could throw you."

"Ooh! You're unkind!" squeaked Charlotte.

"Did you pay your train fare here?" demanded Christopher coolly. He was *so* attractive when he was like this, sort of like a good-looking head-master who made one feel guilty for thinking naughty things about what he did when he wasn't working.

"No, I did not pay my fare," said Charlotte defensively, "and what's that got to do with anything?"

"It simply proves my point."

"Well, I could have lied to you and pretended that I *did* pay it," pointed out Charlotte. "Instead, I chose to tell the truth."

"Big mistake," said Christopher airily. "I'd have taken you more seriously if you'd stuck to the lies. And, Charlotte," he added briskly, "say hello to your aunt from me, will you?"

Charlotte didn't miss a beat.

"Of course I will. She talks of Paris with such fondness."

"It was Rome."

"Ah, you were Rome? I'm sorry, I get so muddled."

"You're very like her, you know," said Christopher.

"People say I look more like Aunt Clare than like my mother," said Charlotte boastfully.

"No, it's not that," said Christopher thoughtfully. "It's your attitude. Too clever by half."

Charlotte kicked up her heels and blew him a kiss and we burst out onto the street into the bright February sunshine. I thought how lovely it would be to have the nerve that Charlotte had. It felt to me like all one would ever need in life.

I suppose Coffee on the Hill was the first place in town to catch on to the fact that now the war was well and truly over and that money could be made from catering directly to the new youth, so the new youth gravitated toward it, magnetically drawn to the pastel colors of the ice cream sundaes and the smell of heat and youth. They sold ham sandwiches and cheese on toast, and bucket loads of Heinz tomato soup with white bread, and cigarettes and glasses of warm red wine that seemed to us like the last word in sophistication. All the while, the records kept playing and playing, and if you got to the place and there wasn't too much of a crowd, you could ask the waitress for Johnnie Ray, and two minutes later, you could listen to him singing while you ate. Charlotte and I liked the corner table by the far window so that we could glance down the hill toward the market square as we talked, ate, and smoked. It was the best table to be looked in on and also the best table from which to stare out at the Teds who congregated on one of the benches in the square. Charlotte's face was grim with concentration where Teds were concerned, all the time looking for A the T, though what he would be doing in Bath I don't know. There was no doubt that these groups of velvet-collared boys had a hold on Charlotte; she flicked her hair more than usual when we saw them, and she spoke in a hushed voice as though they could hear through glass.

I ordered a plate of chips and a glass of orange juice, and Charlotte a bowl of chocolate ice cream and a glass of lemonade. I waited until Charlotte had consumed most of hers before starting to talk, as she was never really able to concentrate until her stomach was full. All around us the tables were filling up—mostly with clusters of giggling girls—but occasionally a couple entered the room, a girl and a boy who sat close together but said very little—struck dumb by their own brilliance, I thought. Struck dumb by the wonderfulness of being together and away from home. People watching in Coffee on the Hill was heady stuff.

"Why do you think Christopher's not married?" asked Charlotte idly.

"Why, do you want to marry him?" I giggled.

"Shut up. I was only asking." She actually went a bit pink.

"He was married once," I said. "His wife died a year after they were married."

"Gracious. How inconsiderate. How?"

"She fell off a horse, I think."

Charlotte looked thoughtful for a moment, then changed the subject as swiftly as if she were changing a record.

"So," she said, licking her spoon. "What did you want to talk to me about, then?"

I didn't really know where to start, but I supposed that Harry's offer was as good a place as any.

"It's Harry," I said.

"Don't tell me. You've fallen in love with him."

I shrieked. "Don't be ridiculous!"

"Thank God. I've been fearing it for the past few weeks, you know."

"Why?" I asked her, temporarily thrown.

"I don't know. Just something about the way you look at him sometimes. It makes me nervous, you know. Like you're seeing things in him that no one else sees. Oh, do signal to the waitress—shall we get a pot of coffee?"

"You're utterly wrong," I said. "I couldn't be less enamored of him. Especially at the moment. He's put me in a very difficult position."

Charlotte raised her eyebrows.

"Oh, help. I hope he's not falling in love with you. I hadn't even *considered* that." She looked horrified for a moment. "Sorry, that wasn't meant to be rude, it's just that he's been so obsessed by bloody Marina I never imagined he could—"

"Charlotte, will you be quiet and let me talk!"

"Go on, then." She sucked the remains of her lemonade loudly through a straw.

I took a deep breath. "Harry wants me to pose as his—his—friend again," I said primly. "At the dinner that George is giving for Marina. He says you've been invited too.

"Hmm. I have, worst luck."

"Well, in exchange, he's got us both tickets to see Johnnie. He thinks that my presence will rile Marina to such an extent that he'll win her back, once and for all. He says that this will be the last of it, one way or another. I don't know what to think. I can't think of anything worse, but then I keep on thinking about Johnnie and all my fears vanish."

Charlotte called over the waitress. "One pot of coffee, please," she ordered. "And make it strong."

"Not too strong," I added, and the waitress raised her eyes to heaven.

"Now," said Charlotte briskly, "I think he's jolly silly to think that this plan of his will work. He's not competing with George—he's competing with his money and his connections, neither of which Harry could ever hope to obtain in a million years. So I suggest that you humor him and turn up at the party, act like his lover, then take the tickets and run for the Palladium as fast as your legs will carry you."

"But I'm living a lie! I'm *not* Harry's lover! I wouldn't know how to be anyone's lover, worst luck."

"It's not something that anyone learns—one makes it up as one goes along," said Charlotte airily.

"Quite literally, in my case."

"Nobody's expecting you to do anything ghastly like spend the night with him." Charlotte liked saying this sort of thing to me because it always made me blush.

"It's not that," I said, frantically wiggling my toes. "It's just the false pretenses of the thing. Then if Marina does leave George, I'm the one who's left on the sidelines, heartbroken."

"But you won't *really* be heartbroken."

"I know I won't—not really—but everyone else will *think* I am. I'll be seen as Harry's castoff."

"Could be worse," mused Charlotte. "Men adore a castoff."

"Funny, that's what Harry said too."

We paused while the waitress poured our coffee.

"You must know, already, what it is you're going to do," said Charlotte. "You must have known from the moment Harry talked to you about it all. What's the decision? Yes or no?"

I took a scalding gulp of coffee. It was sweet and strong and filled me with courage.

"Well, yes, of course."

"I knew it," said Charlotte. "You won't regret it. Anyway, I'll be there to make sure that nothing gets out of hand. I think it'll be rather fun. And we get to see Johnnie," she breathed, "in the flesh! I must make certain that Harry hands over the tickets before the party," said Charlotte. "No tickets, no lover."

"Good idea." Buoyed up by Charlotte's encouragement and dizzy with the kick of caffeine, I felt my heart crashing against my ribs. "Oh, and another thing—"

"Yes? Gosh, *another* thing?"

I had planned to tell Charlotte about Rocky, planned to ask her opinion, share my story of how we met on the train and how he had written his name down on the back of the opera ticket, but all of a sudden, the words caught in my throat and I realized, to my astonishment, that Rocky was something I wanted to keep to myself for the moment. He wasn't absurd like Inigo's friends, or too young and dangerous like the Teds from the caff, nor was he out of reach like Johnnie Ray—he was a real live man, someone who had listened to me, and made me think.

"I haven't anything to wear to the party," I said.

When I got home that evening, I pulled on my Wellingtons and walked out to Banjo's field with an apple. Banjo crunched it up into little pieces and spat much of it out again—his teeth were pretty ineffectual in his old age—

and I put my arm around him and smelled that lovely pony smell and stared back at Magna, which from a distance looked not at all weary, but tall and strong, like a phantom ship on the horizon. A great lump came to my throat at the idea of Inigo leaving us and going to America, and Mama disintegrating even further without him, and Papa never coming back, and I realized how horribly fragile everything was, and I closed my eyes tight and prayed for something to save us all. When I opened my eyes again, Banjo had dribbled the remains of the apple over my blouse, and I thought how unlike books life is, and how absurd Charlotte had been to imagine that I could be in love with Harry. The only reason that he had got right under my skin was because he had dangled tickets to see Johnnie under my nose. I wandered back home, hitting down nettles with a stick and singing Johnnie Ray and wondering if I would ever see Rocky again. Men, I thought, were more trouble than they were worth. Really, one should stick to books where one sees the hero coming a mile off.

THIRTEEN

The Long Gallery

CHARLOTTE TELEPHONED ME to say that Harry had shown her the tickets to Johnnie's concert, but that he was not prepared to give them to us until the dinner was over.

"Did you really see them?" I asked her in a loud whisper, for Mama was lurking.

"Of course," said Charlotte. "They're genuine, all right. He must have pulled a fair few strings to get hold of them."

I remembered what Harry had said about the roulette wheel and rich gamblers.

"You're absolutely sure they're real?"

"As sure as I've ever been. April twenty-fifth, 1955, Johnnie Ray at the Palladium. Doors open at seven thirty."

I shivered uncontrollably with the excitement of it all.

"George's party takes place on Friday night at eight o'clock," went on Charlotte. "Oh, and your date wants you to dress demure."

"Oh, he does, does he?" I said grimly.

"I said to him that you've only ever dressed demure, and who on earth do you think she is? If I were you, I'd head straight for the nearest corset and suspenders. Oh! Hang on, darling, he's grabbing the—"

"Hullo? Hullo?" Harry sounded amused and very slightly drunk.

"Yes?" I said, as icily as I could manage.

"I'm so pleased you're coming with me, sweetheart. We're going to have a terrific night. Just relax and I'll take care of you."

"Somehow those words don't fill me with confidence."

"Listen, would you mind awfully if we turned up separately? I feel like we could manufacture much more of a scene if you arrived after me, you know, just as everyone's sitting down to dinner? *My face softens with delight at the sight of my lady love.*"

I could hear Charlotte protesting in the background.

"Anything else?" I asked sarcastically. "A kiss at the end of every course?"

"Perfect."

I stifled a giggle. He was preposterous.

"Oh, and Penelope?"

"Yes?"

"Sweetheart, you're far too tall to wear heels. I meant to say that to you last time, only I was too distracted by the American to talk. Now I'll see you at the Ritz. I'll be there by eight, and I'll expect you there at twenty past. Remember, demure but delightful. I'll do the rest."

"Who else will be there?" I bleated, suddenly panicked.

"Oh, everybody you will have read about this year in all the gossip columns but nobody that you actually know."

I fell silent, imagining the horror of it all.

"Penelope?" I heard Harry's voice soften. I couldn't help liking the way he said my name—he hung longer than most on the "el" bit in the middle, and even longer when he was a little bit over the top with wine.

"What?"

"If it's too awful, I can turn the whole lot of them into rats."

I allowed myself to laugh.

"Pity you can't send me a fairy godmother too."

"Can't I? We'll see about that. Listen, I'm going to stay with an old school friend the night after next. He lives about three miles away from you."

"Name?"

"Loopy Turner. Well, Lorne Turner's his real name. Deafeningly loud, has a fearfully pretty sister called Isobel?"

"I know who you mean. They live in Ashton Saint Giles. He's very short, isn't he?"

I gulped as soon as I had said this, realizing that he was probably a little taller than Harry.

"To you, every man is short. What do you say to my plan?"

"Oh, all right," I consented. "Shall I see you on Thursday afternoon?"

"I'll get to you at about three," he said.

"Very well. Oh, and, Harry, just so you know, Isobel Turner's the most awful girl. She came to Sherborne for a couple of terms. She used to eat chalk."

"Just the way I like them," sighed Harry.

I replaced the telephone and ran straight into Mama, who was conveniently arranging some daffodils in the hall.

"What was all that about, darling?"

"Oh, nothing much. I'm going to a party with Harry on Friday. He's coming here on Wednesday afternoon to go through plans."

"Plans?" demanded Mama, and I cursed myself for saying too much.

"Oh, just talking me through the evening. It's a smart affair," I said hurriedly.

"What on earth are you going to wear?"

"I don't know. I'll find something. Maybe the dress I wore to the party at the Hamiltons'?" But I knew that I couldn't possibly face Marina in the same outfit.

"You should have something new," said Mama. "Something new and sensational. How on earth do you expect anyone to notice you if you're always wearing the same thing at every occasion? There's nothing for it. Aunt Sarah's watercolor must go."

"Oh, Mama! It's not worth it!" I wailed.

"It will be if you get yourself a suitable husband," said Mama grimly.

"Oh, for goodness' sake!" I said, starting to lose my temper.

"I don't know why I bother," said Mama. "If you want to look like a bag lady, that's quite all right with me. I shan't be there to pick up the pieces when you're unmarried at *thirty*!"

"Just because you were married before you were whelped!"

"I beg your pardon?"

I would have cried if it hadn't been wildly funny at the same time. I saw Mama's mouth twitching, but I didn't want to give her the satisfaction of seeing me giggling.

"Inigo's package from Uncle Luke has arrived," Mama announced. "Photographs of this Ellis Presley. I don't think it's right that he should be sending him such things. It encourages this teenage wildness I keep reading about in the papers."

"Elvis Presley," I corrected her. "And don't you think Inigo deserves a bit of wildness, Mama? Gosh, I think we all do."

I shook my head and left her standing there in the hall holding a daffodil to her chest. Poor Mama, I thought. Like so many women of her generation, she was ill prepared for teenagers. She was still four years off forty, and looking back, she was more beautiful at that time in her life than she was even on her wedding day, yet she had lost so much, suffered so much, that it had aged her very soul.

Inigo came home from school the next day and ripped open the brown parcel that contained his yearned-for photographs. There were five pictures in all, and in four of them Elvis was smiling—standing next to Uncle Luke and his friend Sam Phillips, even holding up a bottle of beer with Loretta. He had the most amazing hair, pale brown and shiny like a shampoo advertisement, and the most beautiful eyes that seemed to laugh into the camera, full of light and life. But the fifth image was different. He was onstage, and he had a guitar around his neck, and his legs stuck out at odd angles, and a sneer was on his lips, and just looking at that picture made me uncomfortable. There was something unsettling but thrilling about the fire in his eyes that made me feel as if he were staring right at me and might at any moment climb right out of the photograph and into the room to kiss me. Inigo put on the new record that Uncle Luke had sent him, and we plowed our way through a bag of apples and studied Elvis as he sang.

"I want to look like him," announced Inigo as the record came to an end. "I could look like him if I tried."

"Your hair's wrong," I said.

Inigo stood up and combed his hair forward, Ted-style, and slung his guitar around himself and stood like Elvis stood, his right leg cocked out in front of him. I giggled.

"You look like you're in pain," I added.

Inigo ignored me and struck a few chords of the song that Uncle Luke had first played us, "Blue Moon of Kentucky," and I was forced to stop laughing, for he had the art of imitation perfected. At the end of the first verse, he swung around the room, jiving away as if possessed by the spirit of Sam Phillips's recording studio, and I beat my hands on the surface of the dining room table in time to his playing, and stamped my feet, and the sharp heels of my shoes made a terrific sound on the wooden floor. It took me all my life up to that moment to realize that without noise, Magna may as well have crumbled and fallen to dust. Without youth, the house was just a shell, a shadow. We may not have had the money to keep the house how it deserved to be kept, but we had the energy to fight its demise for all we were worth. Funnily enough, when Inigo stopped playing, there was a five-second silence followed by a deafening crash as an ugly purple vase and a vast stack of sheet music that had been balancing in an unhappy alliance atop the piano cascaded to the ground, hitting several untuned keys on the long journey floorward. Giggling madly, Inigo and I scuttled around picking up pieces of broken glass and pages of Cole Porter and Beethoven.

"I hope it wasn't worth anything," I said, placing a shard of the vase inside last week's Sunday *Times*.

"Probably was," said Inigo. "But it was hideous, so who cares?"

Mama appeared five minutes later, her hands over her ears.

"What was all that appalling racket?" she cried. "My nerves are in shreds, children. And, Penelope, Mary has just announced that you've been housing a rodent in your bedroom? Really, it's no wonder this place is falling apart."

"She's a guinea pig, Mama," said Inigo, in dignified tones.

"And I won't hear a word said against her," I added cheerfully.

Marina the rodent certainly continued to thrive in the confines of my bedroom. She really was the most amiable creature, who had grown accustomed to the sound of my voice. She made odd, purring sounds when she was hungry, and loud squeaking noises when she was afraid. Mary, though disapproving, had to confess that Marina was at least a clean pet, and I think she was secretly glad that she lived upstairs, and not anywhere near the kitchen. Mama was harder to convince.

"She's doing no one any harm, Mama," I said. "When the weather improves, she can move outside—I'll get her a friend!"

"I don't want them breeding all over the estate, Penelope."

"They won't breed! I'll be sure to get another female!"

"Don't be silly. No two guinea pigs are ever the same gender. Even *I* remember that much from my school days."

This was to be one of the few issues on which Mama was proved to be entirely correct.

On the afternoon of Harry's visit, Mama decided to spend the afternoon in Bath.

"Do make sure you offer him a proper drink when he arrives, darling," she said. I was surprised that she was leaving me alone with him. It wasn't like her to be so cavalier, but I supposed she felt that there was no danger of Harry falling for me, and even if he did, he was out of the question because he had no money. It was a thunderous afternoon and the house was hemmed in by heavy black clouds. Mama pulled on her head scarf and tightened it around her chin.

"I'll be back in time for supper," she said. "Do remember to feed Fido, and if the weather worsens, make sure he's not left on his own. You know how thunder scares him."

And me, I thought.

I was glad when Harry arrived, because the sky had grown so dark and fierce that I felt nervous alone. Magna did that to one, sometimes. It wasn't so much the idea of ghosts that set one on edge; more the feeling of being trapped indoors forever by the gathering storm outside—and fancy having a dog who couldn't protect you from devilish weather, I thought crossly. As soon as the storm really began, Fido ran under the table in the dining room and wouldn't come out again. I didn't hear the doorbell at first, as the rain had just started hammering against the windows in the hall, and I was singing at top volume to keep me dauntless. When at last it rang out in the hall, it frightened me half to death. I imagined myself opening the door to a ghoul or gorgon or some other fantastic creature, but to my relief, when I peered outside, just Harry was there. A little damp, and very magician-like in a long black overcoat, but just Harry all the same. His wicked eyes flashed bright against the blackness of the afternoon.

"Perfect weather for a round of golf," he said, handing me a bunch of freesias.

"Do come in," I said with a curtsy.

The front door slammed behind us like something out of a horror film.

"Cripes!" said Harry. "This is really the way to see this place, isn't it?"

"I hate this weather." I shivered. "Shall we have a cup of tea?"

"How about a brandy and then up to the Long Gallery?" said Harry at once.

"Why do we have to go up there?" I wailed.

"Because you need to get over your silliness about it. And I'd like to stare out at the garden and the storm. I've got a couple of new tricks to try out."

"Do you always get your own way?"

"Not at all. Look at me and Marina."

I hesitated. "I don't mind going up there if we take the gramophone."

"And that means listening to Johnnie Ray all afternoon?"

In the end, we concocted a funny sort of midafternoon snack to take up to the Long Gallery. I found a half-finished ham in the larder that we hacked into strips to eat with a loaf of bread and some of Mary's homemade pickle. I put this lot on a tray along with the remains of a plum pudding and a couple of chocolate sandwich biscuits each. I boiled up some water for tea, and Harry produced a bottle of brandy from the back of his car. Mama would be horrified, I thought.

When we got upstairs, the sky had turned from dark gray to a threatening, angry violet. The rain bashed violently against the windows and the wind tore at the walls. We stood at the top of the winding staircase that led up to the Long Gallery. This time Harry turned the key.

"All aboard," he said, stepping inside.

He was quite right. The yellow and indigo light of the storm clouds bouncing off the uneven wooden floor gave the room the luster of a ghost ship far out at sea. Cautiously, I stepped inside and shivered. Harry plonked down the gramophone and I busied myself choosing a record to play, and a few moments later, Johnnie's voice filled the room. . . . This year, 1955, was doing its very best to chase away the fourteenth century.

"Want to see something?" asked Harry. He strode off down the middle of the room and came to a halt in front of the longest window.

"A trick?" I asked hopefully.

Harry pulled out a black cloak and appeared to be concentrating very hard.

"What are you doing?" I whispered, but the sound of the wind whistling over the walls stopped Harry from hearing me.

"Come over here," he instructed. I slid over toward him. He was so good now that when he was performing, he seemed to tower over me, Gandalf-like, despite his diminutive frame.

"I've only tried this a couple of times," he admitted under his breath, "but I needed a room like this to pull it off properly."

"Pull what off?" I whispered, scared of breaking the spell.

Harry closed his eyes, and all of a sudden, whipped the cloak away.

"Fly!" cried Harry suddenly. "Fly!"

Three white doves, feathers ruffled and thoroughly confused, flapped wildly into the air. One of them flew up to the top of the room and perched on top of a portrait of Capability Brown. Harry opened his eyes.

"Not bad," he said. "Needs work."

"You're telling me," I cried. "Get them out of here, for goodness' sake! Where did they come from? Oh no, they're not from the pigeon house, are they? Mama will go stark, staring mad if anything happens to any of her birds!" I was genuinely irritated at the same time as being unwillingly knocked out by the beauty of the trick. Harry moved with such fluidity, such style when he was performing that it was impossible not to watch in excitement.

"They're not your mother's birds," said Harry, gathering up his cloak and folding it neatly. "But I thought I could leave them here for now. She won't mind, will she? Tell her they're a present from me, to thank her for her—her hospitality."

"*Hospital* will be the word if we don't get them out of here fast. Mama will kill me for this. We shouldn't even be up here in the first place—"

"They add to the atmosphere, don't you think?" interjected Harry, removing a white feather from my hair.

"Oh, it's very Noah's ark. Perhaps we should invite a couple of the sheep up here too?" I snapped.

Harry said nothing, but gave a low whistle, and all three of the doves flew toward him.

"You'll be calming the storm next," I said pertly.

Harry grinned.

"I've been rehearsing with these three for quite some time," he said.

"How did you get them here?" I asked curiously.

"Magic," said Harry automatically.

I chose not to ask any more.

"Well, you can keep them up here until we've finished our picnic," I consented, "as you seem to have such astonishing control over them."

"Picnic!" said Harry. "We need a rug for that."

He pulled off his overcoat and spread it out for us to sit on, and we tucked into the ham and pickle.

"Do you think we're the latest in a long line of people who've sat up here during a storm and felt as though the house was going to fall down?" asked Harry.

"Probably. I know my father used to—to sit up here," I said without thinking. Blast, I didn't think that I had wanted to talk about Papa.

"He did?" asked Harry, taking a slug of brandy from the bottle.

"He—he was afraid of his father, so he used the Long Gallery as a sort of refuge. It was always his dream to captain a ship and he used to pretend he was in charge of the *Cutty Sark*."

"Isn't it odd?" said Harry. "You get a house as staggering as this at your disposal, but you still dream of getting out of the place. It just goes to show, doesn't it? You can't always get what you want. Shall we have a cigarette?"

"I'd rather have your chocolate biscuit," I confessed.

Harry lay flat on the floor and smoked.

"Lie down," he instructed me. "You can feel the storm shaking the ship."

I hesitated.

"Don't worry, I'm not going to jump on you," said Harry archly.

I blushed.

The elements raged around us, and when we closed our eyes, we really weren't at Magna at all, but somewhere way out in the Atlantic.

"Tell me a story," Harry demanded.

"A story?"

"Yes. Go on. You want to be a writer, don't you?"

It was another challenge. With our heads resting on Harry's coat, our feet were almost touching. Something hung in the air between us, something so delicate that anything other than lying as still as statues and whispering felt like a threat to it. What *was* it? I didn't know. I breathed in the now-familiar scent of Harry's cologne mixed with the sweetness of the brandy from his breath.

"You smell nice," I admitted.

"It's Dior pour Homme," he whispered in a mock-romantic French accent. "Isn't it just the thing *pour snaring les femmes?*"

I didn't reply.

"Tell me about your great-aunt Sarah," said Harry, and he was whispering so softly now that I could hardly hear him. "The one who painted the watercolor you all detest so much."

"All right," I replied, and at that moment, Johnnie started to sing "Walkin' My Baby Back Home" and I sighed with the loveliness of his voice.

"She was quite barking," I began, "and apparently a great wit. She rather frightened people because she had a loud voice and a limp from falling off her pony, aged seven. She wanted so badly to be a great painter. Apparently she fell madly in love with her art teacher, a redhead called Lindsay Saunders, and decided that the only way to win her heart was to—"

"What?" interrupted Harry. "*Her* heart?"

"Oh, yes," I said. "Aunt Sarah was one of—you know, one of those women who—who prefer the company of women."

"How thrilling," said Harry. "I think I'm going to enjoy this story."

"It hasn't a very happy ending," I said. "Her art mistress went off to India to study out there and married some important ambassador or other. Poor Aunt Sarah never quite recovered from the shock of her departure. She married a man called Sir John Holland, who knew all about her past and refused to let her paint. She was broken after this, having lost her only joy in life. In the end, her bad leg grew worse and worse. She had terrible arthritis and died rather young."

"Tragic," said Harry with feeling. "You must hang on to her painting and never mock her interpretation of the lake again."

"I always thought she sounded rather nice," I said, "although I never knew her. She was too tall, like me, and freckled and blonde."

"And not very good at painting," said Harry lightly, "and funny? And oddly beautiful?"

I said nothing but listened to us both breathing. Outside the hail rained against the window and the clouds had turned black again and I shivered— half with cold, half with something else. Then that precious, unnamed thing that had grown heavier and heavier around us was broken when one of the birds landed on my chest and I shrieked with shock. Harry sat up and laughed.

"I think she wants the last of the bread," he said.

The mood changed after that and, oddly enough, so did the weather. The storm passed, and the rain stopped and a blast of late-afternoon sunlight caught us by surprise. Johnnie sang on, and Harry drank a brandy and imitated Johnnie singing, which was really very funny, and we argued a bit about jazz. Then he showed me three or four new tricks and tried to teach me a simple sleight-of-hand thingy with the ace of hearts that I couldn't quite pull off. We didn't venture back downstairs until it was nearly dark and the doves were starting to look as though a night up in the eaves of the Long Gallery would be rather nice. Fido started to pace a bit and I realized he should have been fed an hour ago.

"I should really be going," said Harry.

"Of course," I said. "Are you sure you won't stay for supper?"

"Oh, no, I told Loopy I'd be with him by seven."

"It won't take you long to get to Ashton Saint Giles," I said, "as long as there aren't too many branches across the roads."

"Should I mention you to Isobel?" asked Harry. I had to drag my mind into gear to think of whom he was talking about.

"Oh, no," I said in horror. "She didn't like me one bit. We had to be partners in dance class, and I was always the man and used to stand on her pretty little toes."

"I wish I'd gone to Sherborne Girls," said Harry wistfully.

"Come on, let's get the birds settled before you go," I said.

Half an hour and several white feathers later, we said good-bye and Harry climbed into his car. He wound down the window.

"I loved this afternoon," he said suddenly, "and are you in any way over your hatred of the Long Gallery?"

I grinned. "Oh, I think so." I paused. "Thanks to you and your ridiculous magic."

"See you at the Ritz, then."

"Oh, help, yes. At the Ritz."

It wasn't until after Mama had returned from Bath, soaked through but delighted because she had found a beautiful set of (overpriced) candlesticks for the dining room table, that I realized Harry and I had not discussed Marina once.

FOURTEEN

Somebody Stole His Gal

THE FIRST WEEK IN MARCH began with a fit of squally showers and sudden bursts of blinding sunshine, as the last dregs of the cold winter drifted away for another year. I left the window in my bedroom open during the day, and found the first disoriented honeybee of 1955 lurching around my bedside table like a drunk. I lay around the house in my denims, pretending to write essays while flicking through the new magazines and longing for money to spend on clothes. I listened to Johnnie and thought about Harry more than I ever imagined I would—and it disturbed me. Sometimes he was impossible to picture in my mind; other times his face would come to me clearly and I would think, with great relief, *Oh, it's all right! I don't find him attractive after all!* He wasn't good-looking like Rocky, yet I couldn't push aside our night on deck in the Long Gallery. I found myself wondering whether he had thought about it since, or whether Marina had occupied his every waking consideration. I spent hours in front of the mirror trying on outfits for the dinner at the Ritz with disastrous results. I had neither Charlotte's creative flair nor Mama's penchant for immaculate tailoring, and whatever I wore looked dull rather than demure. For all that I didn't want to attend the dinner, there was no way that I wanted to look half-baked, though I wasn't sure exactly who I was trying to impress. I telephoned Charlotte several times, but always seemed to catch her when she had just finished a particularly grueling session with Aunt Clare, and as a member of that elite proportion of the population who never needed to question whether they looked right as long as they looked arresting, Charlotte had little time for my dilemmas.

"Just go with what you feel comfortable in, darling," she kept saying.

"That's just the problem. I don't feel comfortable in anything."

"Don't wear anything, then. Must dash, ginger scones."

Still, there was no place more enchanting than Magna in the spring, and Mama and I were the best of friends on the mornings that we awoke early, linked arms, and walked from the kitchen garden to the pond and back, our lungs full of the whispered sweetness of viburnum flowers, hearts brightened by the huge swaths of crocuses bobbing regally beside the overgrown paths that threaded around the outskirts of the back lawn. We felt the delicate warmth of the sun on our faces and realized how much we had missed it, and I breathed in the scent of the box hedge that marked our route around the fruit cages during the war and reminded me of our days in the Dower House when, in the height of summer, we helped the ladies of the W.I. pick raspberries and black currants. I thought about New Year's Eve and it seemed an age ago to me already.

"The garden looks wonderful, Mama," I would always say when we arrived back at the house.

"It's chaos, darling."

"I like chaos."

On the night before the Ritz dinner, one more remarkable thing happened to me. In fact, it was something so remarkable, it was all I could do to contain my astonishment and delight, and not go shouting with glee all over the house. I plodded upstairs to my bedroom a little after eleven, closed my curtains, and flopped down on my bed, worrying as ever about what to wear the next day. Now that the hour was drawing near, I was considering pulling out of the whole thing, even if it meant sacrificing Johnnie. And anyway, I thought, surely Harry would be kind enough to give me the tickets even if I ducked out of my role? No, I dismissed this thought almost as soon as it entered my head. Harry was not the sort of man who would take kindly to being messed about. There was time for one last, sorrowful glance at my drear clothes before the dawn broke. I stood up, then stopped dead as something caught my eye through a crack in the wardrobe door. I don't want to sound too C.S. Lewis about what happened next, but suffice it to say that I padded across the room and pulled open the wardrobe door and stuck my hand in. What I encountered was not Narnia, but something even more enchanted. It was a pink box, ribboned in black and labeled PENE-LOPE, which eliminated my two seconds of concern that this was simply Mama racked with guilt and stuffing the packaging from her latest purchases out of her own line of vision. I dragged it out with a small cry of delight, my heart thumping in my chest, and pulled off the ribbon and lifted the lid. Inside was a lot of expensive-smelling pink and white tissue, and wrapped up within the tissue was something with a label that sent my heart racing. Selfridges. Like a child taking a much-longed-for turn at the lucky dip, I stuck my hand in and pulled out a handful of soft, black material with the most glorious sheen of glitter. It was a dress, a perfect, adorable, dream dress, the like of which I could never have imagined, yet now that I was holding it, I could not imagine living without it. I scrambled to my feet again and flung off my nightie.

"Oh!" I whimpered, for I couldn't help it, and if anything like this has ever happened to you, then you will know exactly how I felt. It was as if the dress had been made to measure. It was demure, all right, but it was the first time that I had ever worn anything that made me feel so much like a woman. The first thing I thought when I looked at myself in the mirror was that I looked capable of extremely sophisticated conversation, and it shocked me, but above all else, it excited me. I found another box, smaller this time but equally delicious, containing a glorious pair of Dior heels, the sort that Mama would die for and I would surely never be able to walk in. In with the heels was a packet of super-elegant stockings, and almost hidden away under the last bit of tissue paper was a Yardley lipstick in an elegant red color called Rosebud. Who had done this? Mama? It simply wasn't her style, and she would never have encouraged a dress like this anyway. Harry? It had to be, yet how had he got into my room? How had *anyone* got into my room? I remembered with a shiver that I had kept my door locked all day for fear that Mama would send Fido up to root out Marina the rodent. I had kept the key in the pocket of my trousers.

I rummaged frantically for some sign, some indication of how he had performed this most sensational of tricks. Of course, what I found told me nothing, except that as a magician, Harry was getting better and better. A card was attached to the underside of the box, and inside the card was a simple note written in turquoise ink.

FROM YOUR FAIRY GODMOTHER.

Whoever on earth she was, I thought, she had terrific taste. I packed the clothes, shoes, stockings, and lipstick carefully into my wardrobe again, and shoved the boxes under my bed, vowing to dispose of them before Mama, Mary, or anyone else found them. The next morning, after a surprisingly sound night's sleep, I peered under the bed, wondering if it had all been a dream. Instead, I found Marina the rodent asleep in the shoe box, like an ornament among the pink tissue paper. Like her namesake, she knew what side her bread was buttered on, I thought.

If Harry didn't win his great love back, at least the guinea pig appreciated the way he did things.

I awoke praying for good weather because although my fairy godmother had been considerate enough to provide me with a dress to die for and sensational heels, she had not considered what I should cover myself with, should the conditions from cab to Ritz prove inclement. Mama was fond of telling me that it was unladylike to arrive anywhere without a coat, whatever the time of year, but nothing I owned looked right over my new outfit. In the end, I settled for a thick coat in Black Watch tartan that Mama had borrowed off Loretta one Christmas and never returned. It looked terrifyingly wintery and austere, but at least it had a Harrods label and a bit of oomph. I left Magna with a do-or-die feeling in the pit of my stomach and spent the train journey nearly jumping out of my skin in case Rocky happened to be on board again, which, of course, he wasn't. Once in London, I jumped into a taxi and fairly flew along Bayswater Road and down

Kensington Church Street and found myself outside Aunt Clare's front door well before six o'clock. Charlotte answered the door. Her hair was still in rollers, but she could have turned up at the Ritz without taking them out and still looked like the most stylish girl in the room. She wore a red dress with silver shoes that made her even taller than I. Charlotte had no problem with heels and towering over boys. In fact, I think she rather enjoyed it.

"Thank heavens you're here. Harry's been going spare all afternoon, convinced you were going to get cold feet," she said, bundling me into the house.

"I have got cold feet," I said. "The train was freezing."

She grinned and pushed an errant roller back on top of her head.

"Aunt Clare's dying to see you. She's becoming more and more impossible as we near the end of this blasted book. Oh, and she's convinced that Harry's madly in love with you, which is why you're always taking off to parties with him, so humor her, will you? Pity you missed tea today, it was lemon shortbread. I would have saved you a piece but I thought, well, you need to look as skinny as possible for tonight. People stop eating when they fall in love. Think of me and A the T in the caff and how I couldn't even manage a plate of toast." Charlotte shook her head in confusion at the memory.

Aunt Clare was sipping champagne in her study.

"Ah! How are you, dear girl? Charlotte, *do* shout to Harry that she's here."

"Hullo, Aunt Clare," I said, kissing her and breathing in the familiar rose water scent.

"He's been in such a state, you know, skipping about like a grasshopper all afternoon, worried that you were going to let him down. Goodness, I can't think *what* you've done to him, Penelope."

"Oh, nothing at all, I should think," I said hastily.

"I haven't seen him this animated since the old king died," went on Aunt Clare. "He even asked Phoebe to polish his shoes this afternoon. You can imagine how well *that* went down."

The door opened, and Harry entered the room, fingers wrapped around something that I, in my state of anxiety and confusion, took to be a magic wand. *Phew,* I thought, *I don't want him at all, not one bit.* He looked scruffier than ever, his hair stood on end, and his clothes were crumpled.

"You're wearing odd socks," said Aunt Clare reprovingly.

"They match my eyes," said Harry, grinning at me. He held out what I had thought was the magic wand.

"Cheese straw?"

"Oh, no, thanks."

Then, quite without warning, Harry crossed the room, held me close, and kissed me slowly and carefully on the mouth. Cheeks burning, I pulled away, too shocked to respond with anything other than the briefest of squeaks. Aunt Clare's face softened, and I think her eyes must have welled up, for she pulled out her handkerchief and dabbed her eyes.

"Have a wonderful night, darlings," she said thickly. "You know, during the war, whenever we heard the wailing of sirens, we would head instinctively Ritz-ward. I remember Chips Chanon telling me how like a pantomime the war felt once one was safely inside the Ritz for oysters at luncheon. Dear Chips, I must write to him this evening. Make a note of that, Charlotte."

Dear Aunt Clare. If ever there was a tangent, she was off on it.

Charlotte rescued me and dragged me upstairs to get ready.

"Did you see what he did?" I asked her.

"What?" she demanded, rummaging in her bag for a lipstick.

"Harry! He kissed me!"

"Oh, that. Don't worry, it's all part of the act. You don't mind, do you?"

"Well—I think I do, really. That wasn't in my contract," I added.

"Your contract wasn't in your contract," said Charlotte blithely. "Now. Harry's leaving in half an hour," she said. "He's meeting a couple of friends for a drink first. He's told me to make absolutely sure that you turn up after him, and after *me,* for maximum impact."

She looked at me, affection spilling from her green eyes.

"I hope you've found something to wear. Oh, Christmas, Penelope!" she cried, catching sight of the Black Watch coat. "Surely not?"

Surely not, indeed. I ditched the coat and borrowed a slim-fitting but understated black peacoat from Charlotte, who had, in turn, borrowed it from Aunt Clare.

"She need never know," said Charlotte breezily. "She hasn't worn it in a decade and a half."

She expressed delight and amazement over my dress and shoes.

"Where on earth did you find them?" she gasped.

"My fairy godmother delivered them."

"Ah. I see."

That was one of the best things about Charlotte. She accepted everything without explanation.

She and I took a cab to the Ritz together, but Charlotte went in ahead of me.

"See you in five minutes," she said, sweeping in through the revolving doors.

I paid the cab driver with shaking hands, and for a moment stood outside the Ritz, trying to breathe deeply and fix a smile onto my face like they say you should do when preparing to make your big entrance, but the doorman bowed to me and leaped forward to help me through the door, so I wasn't able to linger for long. Inside, the hotel wrapped its charm around me like a cloak. I caught sight of a sophisticated and beautiful woman in the reflection of the mirror in the reception and I realized with a shock of recognition that it was me. I tottered briefly in my heels and pulled my dress straight and beamed at the man behind the desk in concierge.

"I'm here for the Hamilton dinner," I said firmly. Half of me expected him to laugh and tell me not to be so silly and I was still a little girl and where were my parents.

"Of course, Madam."

He led me down a long, shiny corridor that made me feel as though I were stepping inside a birthday card (it took all my self-control—and the knowledge that I would most likely fall over—not to waltz) and we ended up outside a closed door marked PRIVATE.

"May I take your name, Miss?"

"Oh. Um, Penelope. Penelope Wallace. Miss Penelope Wallace. I am Penelope Wallace." What was wrong with me? I sounded deranged.

He opened the door.

"Miss Penelope Wallace!" he announced, then melted off, leaving me standing in the doorway like a fawn in the headlamps of a speeding car. In fact, nobody even heard the announcement of my name over the din of corks popping and breathless chatter and jazz from the piano player in the corner of the room. *Charlotte?* I thought helplessly. She was nowhere to be seen. The combination of low lighting and swirling cigarette smoke made me feel like an actress on a first night waiting for the rest of the cast to feed me a line. I shuffled a few paces in, and fairly grabbed at the nearest glass of champagne. George Rogerson, who was, according to Harry, a terrifically committed host, spotted me and quickly detangled himself from a crowd of Marina's friends and waded across the room toward me. But someone else got to me first.

"My goodness! If it isn't my little friend from the train, all grown-up. I've been worrying about you."

And I nearly passed out, for sauntering toward me, more wicked and delicious than even I remembered, was Rocky.

A silence followed his words—the sort of silence where you can hear everyone's brains whirring away as they tried to work out who on earth I was. He looked me up and down and actually ran his hand down the side of my face.

"Don't you look nice," he said, smiling softly.

"I see you two know each other, how terrific!" exclaimed George, beaming.

"We met on the train," said Rocky. "She was worrying about something quite trivial, weren't you, Miss Wallace? Whether or not one should be oneself at dinner parties, wasn't it?"

"I shouldn't bother, Penelope, such a dreadful effort," laughed George.

"Penelope. Is that your name?" asked Rocky. "How strangely fitting."

"What does that mean?" I widened my eyes and took a huge mouthful of champagne, and quite ruined my previously sophisticated air by spilling some down the front of my dress. Thank goodness, there was Charlotte, sitting down at the far end of the room, talking to the Wentworth twins. I felt a wave of relief that they were here; at least I would have a couple more people to say hello to.

"Beautiful shoes," said Rocky, trying to keep a straight face and glancing down at my legs.

"They're Dior."

"Damn. I'd have thought girls who shop at Dior would be able to afford their own train tickets."

"I could!" I bleated. "I lost my ticket! And I had every intention of paying you back!"

Rocky smiled and was distracted by a beauty in a dazzling yellow and black cocktail dress.

"Where's Harry?" I asked George as calmly as I could.

"Oh, he and Marina have gone to find a pack of playing cards. Apparently Harry's got some fabulous new tricks up his sleeve. Missing him, are you? I'm just the same with Marina. If she leaves the room for so much as a second, I start to fret."

Knowing what I knew about his future wife, I was hardly surprised. George turned back to Rocky.

"Penelope and Harry have been inseparable since last Christmas. We're all wondering when we're going to be hearing the chiming of church bells."

"Is that so?" asked Rocky, an amused smile playing on his lips.

"Oh, I don't know—"

"Don't be so coy, darling—he's mad for you. Please excuse me, new arrivals. Ah! If you want to talk books with someone, you must meet Nancy. Nancy!" George lumbered off.

Charlotte was beside me in a flash.

"You look radiant," she said. "And did I see Rocky Dakota talking to you a moment ago?"

"Yes," I admitted. "I met him on the train. I had no idea he was going to be here tonight."

"Why in the name of jumping Jeremiah didn't you tell me you'd met him?" hissed Charlotte out of the corner of her mouth. "He's not the sort of man you bump into every day, is he? Christmas! You'll be telling me you had Sunday lunch with James Dean later."

There was a soft cough behind me.

"Won't you sit next to me at dinner?" said Rocky, sliding up to me. "I'm bored sick of everyone here but you."

"Charmed!" trilled Charlotte. He turned to her at once.

"Hello, I don't believe I've had the pleasure," he said, holding out his hand. In her heels, she was almost as tall as he. *Oh no,* I thought, heart hammering. *Please don't let him fall for Charlotte.*

"Perhaps I could sit between you two," suggested Rocky. "The Wentworth twins frighten the hell outta me. You know Helena can bite her own toenails?"

"That's nothing," said Charlotte quickly. "One of my friends was at school with Kate. Apparently she once sleepwalked into the housemistresses' bedroom, took off her pajamas, and got into bed with her. The only reason they all found out was because the fire alarm went off two hours later and Kate emerged from Miss Gregory's bedroom like a furious cat."

"Lucky Miss Gregory," said Rocky, looking at Charlotte with respect.

"They're both far too pretty for the real world," went on Charlotte. "Looking like that makes a girl very lazy. After all, no one's going to care what you're talking about as long as your face is that good."

"Very true," agreed Rocky.

Goodness, but looks like *his* were powerful stuff. He had the most divine way of making one feel like a little girl and a thoroughly cosmopolitan woman at the same time, and I had never known *anyone* to make me feel like that. He was wearing an immaculate charcoal gray and black suit with a bright green and pink silk shirt that no Englishman—except perhaps Bunny Roger—would have gotten away with. His shoes, I noted in amazement, were blue and black suede—Charlotte could barely tear her eyes away from them. We relaxed under the spell of his intoxicating accent to such an extent so that when at last Harry reappeared, spraying cards into the air with one hand and catching them in the other, I had almost forgotten about him. I had also drunk three glasses of champagne on an empty stomach.

"Penelope!" Harry spotted me and his eyes widened in surprise when he saw who I was talking to. "Are you all right?"

"Quite fine, thank you." I managed a stiff smile. If Harry was going to go swanning off with Marina before the night had even begun, then I was certainly going to spend as much time as I could entertaining myself.

Rocky stuck out his hand. "Rocky Dakota."

Harry gave him a wintery look and shook his hand.

"How do you do?" he said, then frowned. "Ah! I've been looking for that, so sorry!" He leaned forward and plucked a potato from behind Rocky's ear. I glared at Harry, but Rocky was laughing.

"That's real clever," he said. The uncomfortable silence that followed was broken by a stout man in tails barging up to Rocky and dragging him across the room to meet his wife. Harry and I were left alone.

"Where's Marina?" I asked pointedly.

"I don't know. She said she needed some air." A shadow of despair crossed Harry's face. "And why on earth didn't you tell me you were so thick with Rocky bloody Dakota?"

"I'm not." I blushed. "And how come everyone but me knows who he is?"

"Oh, Penelope, don't you know anything?" asked Harry infuriatingly. "He's an agent and a producer. For actors, singers, that sort of thing."

"Singers?"

"He's made more money than he knows what to do with. He's just bought himself a place in Cadogan Square. Apparently he had a Chevrolet shipped over here from Los Angeles—"

"I know!" I squeaked. "I saw him getting into it at Didcot! I've never seen a car look so out of place!"

"He's never been married," went on Harry primly.

"So?"

"So don't you think that's a bit odd?"

"Not at all," I said firmly.

Yes, must investigate further, I thought.

I lost Harry again as Marina reentered the room. She looked as willful and as powerful as she had at Dorset House, her red hair piled on top of her head with a diamond-studded comb, her wide mouth never still for a second. She saw me and blew me a kiss.

"There she is," said Harry softly, "the girl who rips my soul apart."

"Sounds painful," I snapped. I didn't see what gave Harry the right to criticize Rocky when he was fawning over the ridiculousness that was Marina.

"You're so bloody tall, Penelope. Oh, it's the heels, of course," he said absentmindedly.

I rather liked the way that he couldn't resist pretending that he hadn't planned it all.

"My fairy godmother has wonderful taste, don't you think?"

For a moment he glared at me, and then he couldn't help himself, and his face broke into an unfamiliar smile—all boyish and pleased and quite unlike his usual self-aware smirk. He looked very young suddenly—young and vulnerable and sweet.

"I couldn't resist the heels," he admitted. "Even though they make me look ridiculous. I know I said I didn't want you to tower over me, but actually I think it's pretty sexy."

"Gosh, Harry!" I wasn't sure I knew how to react to words like this from him. I changed the subject quickly.

"So how did you get them into my—"

Harry placed his fingers on my lips.

"I'm a magician," he said. "Don't ask silly questions."

The conversation at dinner was fast and furious and peppered with noteworthy exclamations like *No! But I only saw her last week in Monte Carlo! She looked like a Polish whore, I tell you!* and *Well, my dear, I've said it before and I'll say it again, I wish I could live in a mud hut and be done with interior design altogether!* I was supposed to have a man called Ivan Steinberg on my left and Harry on my right, but just as we were sitting down, George reshuffled things and I found Rocky in Ivan's place.

"Steinberg's plane's been delayed," explained George. "Won't get here until we're on to brandy, at the earliest. Thought I'd move Rocky up your way, since you seem to be such good chums."

"First sensible idea you've ever had, Rogerson," said Rocky, sliding up and holding my gaze. We sat down, and in my flustered state I knocked my glass of Chablis all over the table and onto Rocky's beautiful suit.

"You clumsy oaf," he said, not unkindly.

"Oh, goodness!" I gasped. "I am sorry!"

"Don't be. The laundry service in this hotel is exceptional."

"Staying here, are you?" asked Harry.

"Sure am."

I think Harry would have liked to think of something smart to say to this, but he couldn't think of anything, so instead he drained his first drink of the evening and reached over for the bottle to recharge his glass. Unfortunately, Marina, sitting diagonally across from him, caught his eye, and he lost concentration and sent the bottle flying.

"What's wrong with you, Delancy?" asked George with a bark of laughter, retrieving the bottle and whipping a napkin onto the soaked tablecloth.

"He's in love, of course," drawled Rocky, nodding in my direction. "Can't ya see it?"

I noticed Marina flush.

"Don't embarrass him, George," she said. "It's just a little spill. You know what, guys, last week at the races, my plate of prawns slipped right out of my hands and into the princess's lap. You know what she said to me? She said, 'Marina, dearest, I don't believe I ordered the shellfish.' " She put on a very good impersonation of the princess to deliver this line and everyone, including me, roared. Marina, sensing an audience, was off. Just like the last time, I found myself fascinated and horrified in equal measures: She was like trifle—irresistible, but too much made one feel distinctly queasy. For every time that Rocky looked at me and smiled, I fidgeted and grabbed at my glass and sipped and gulped and refilled, and before long I realized I had drunk too much, but of course, it was too late.

" . . . Next day, I found him rummaging around in the garbage looking for her diamonds!" Marina concluded.

Everyone roared again, and a great tidal wave of laughter filled the room and swamped Marina in praise. She laughed herself, and her eyes watered slightly. I felt an unexpected and most unwelcome rush of affection for her.

"In this country we call it rubbish, not garbage, darling," said George fondly.

"Ah, well. It's all trash to me," Marina said lightly, but I sensed her irritation and I felt sorry for George. He was a curious character, like something out of a book. The way he spouted on about the wine, the insistence with which he talked us through every mouthful of our starter (a cheese soufflé so stunning that I suppose it did merit *some* discussion), and the way he hung on every word Marina said made him difficult to take seriously, but for all that there was a softness about him, an unconscious kindness, that made him more teddy bear than Teddy Boy, I couldn't help liking him. I wondered if he was too stupid to notice the fiery looks that were passing between his future wife and her former lover, and I decided that yes, he was. Or maybe not too stupid, but too blindly in love. "I like George," said Rocky, as if reading my mind, when Marina had finished her story and we were allowed to talk among ourselves again. "He's good with her."

"I think so too," I found myself saying. Harry, overhearing us, frowned at me. I ignored him.

"So," went on Rocky, "tell me everything."

"About what?" I asked nervously.

"Oh, you know—what you were doing on the train the day that we met, what you like to watch at the movies, how old you were when you realized you could sing—"

"I can't sing!" I spluttered.

"No? Betcha can," grinned Rocky.

"My brother's the singer," I said. "It's all he ever wants to do—sing and play the guitar."

"I must meet him some time," said Rocky.

I laughed because I was starting to feel whizzy with champagne. Rocky would love Inigo, I thought. Inigo would love Rocky.

Between mouthfuls of soufflé, I started to talk and found that once I had started, I couldn't stop. I talked about Johnnie and Charlotte, and about Mama and Inigo and everything in between. Occasionally, Rocky interrupted me with a question—what actress would I most like to invite to

Magna for tea? (Grace Kelly, *naturellement.*) What did I miss most during rationing? (I lied here and said new stockings, but the true answer was Cadbury's chocolate.) Was my mother really only thirty-six years old? (Yes, and more's the pity, I said indiscreetly.) Then our main course appeared, and I felt a wave of fear and nausea. It was duck.

"Pretend it's goose," murmured Charlotte, sensing my unease, and I smiled thankfully at her and took another gulp of champagne. Charlotte was opposite me, sandwiched between two very beautiful boys of about twenty. They were obviously very taken with her, vying for her attention, telling elaborate stories about people she knew, filling up her glass, and lighting her cigarettes, and she responded amiably enough, but there was none of that fire, the nerves, the jittery legs, the spark that there had been when we had been out with A the T at the caff. These boys, with their two addresses and fast cars and their Garrick Club memberships, bored her.

"Sometimes I find it hard being eighteen," I said to Rocky. Waiters were clearing our plates away now. I was amazed to notice that I had eaten almost all of my duck.

"You hate being eighteen?" Rocky looked amused, but not in the edgy, self-conscious way that Harry did. Rocky was amused because he could afford to be. "Why would anyone hate being eighteen?"

"I don't know," I said. "Guilt, I suppose. That Papa died fighting somewhere I can't even imagine in the middle of the Pacific, yet I spend more time thinking about when I'm going to see Johnnie Ray or what to wear to parties."

"My dear Penelope, your father would expect nothing less. He fought and died so that you could think luxurious thoughts about pop singers and Yardley perfume."

I had one of my odd moments when I thought I might cry, so I drank some more and went on talking.

"It was hard, during the war. Mama kept it together until the news came through about Papa. Even then she refused to believe it. Inigo and I were so little that when she told us that he wasn't coming back, it didn't really mean much. We hated her being sad more than anything else. Still do."

"I guess the strangest thing about your generation is that you grew up with the war as your normality. That's something *I* can't imagine."

"You're right," I said slowly, because it was the first time that anyone had articulated this, although I had always felt it somewhere inside. "When it ended, it seemed completely unreal to me. I think I was a bit scared of what would happen next. Isn't that craziness? Scared of life without war?"

Rocky lit a cigarette and passed it to me. I took it with shaking hands and our fingers touched.

"Frightening to think what you all will do with yourselves," he said, shaking his head. "All this freedom after all that deprivation!"

"Sometimes I think I want to do something mad, something outrageous. I talk to Johnnie all the time, and imagine myself with him. My friend Charlotte and I, we just want to be different, I suppose. She's much more successful than I am in that sense. She just doesn't really care what anyone thinks. She'll wear strange hats and make them look right, or she'll spend all her money on one pair of silk stockings. I can't even eat a whole packet of sweets myself without feeling bad."

"You will, darling, you will. And if you can't, your children certainly will."

Children! Heaven forbid, I thought, and hastily changed the subject.

"So how do you know Marina and George?"

Rocky leaned in toward me.

"Ah. That's an interesting question. Unfortunately for me, you're the type of girl who makes a guy feel bad unless the truth is told."

I wasn't entirely sure whether this was a good or a bad thing.

"What's that supposed to mean?"

"Marina was auditioning for a movie I produced."

"Was she any good?"

"She was wonderful," confessed Rocky. *Oh, terrific,* I thought, wanting to throw all my toys out of the pram or whatever the expression was. I had always imagined that the reason Marina wasn't a famous actress was because she wasn't any good.

"How come she hasn't been in anything big yet, then?" I asked Rocky.

"Ah. There's a question." Rocky shook his head and lowered his voice. "She's trouble. She's a difficult, spoiled girl and she drinks too much."

"Drinks too much?"

"Of course. If your whole life's a dinner party, then what do you expect? She can't be trusted, but I believe she'll sort herself out one day. It may take longer than any of us expect, but she'll wake up to the truth soon enough."

"So she auditioned and you became friends?"

Rocky nodded. "She's vulnerable and self-destructive. I've always found myself attracted to people like that."

"A-attracted?"

"Oh, no, nothing like that's ever gone on between us," said Rocky quickly. "She's far too difficult, even by my standards. But it was I who introduced her to George."

"You did?"

"It was a funny thing. I arrived for a week in London and invited them both to a dinner at Harry's Bar. I couldn't believe they'd never met before. Two months later, they were engaged."

"Gosh," I managed. "Did Marina ever talk about—er—anyone—anyone else?"

"Oh, no, she was dead set on George the moment she met him. George confided in me that there had been some other guy the year before that she had been involved with, some jazz fan with no cash. I don't know what happened to him."

Charlotte, listening intently, raised her eyebrows.

"Poor thing," she said rather loudly. "The jazz fan, I mean."

"Ah, he'll be okay," said Rocky. "If you're into jazz, you gotta get off on being lonely."

George plainly believed in keeping his friends close and his enemies closer. How odd it all was, that Rocky was unaware of the fact that the jazz fan in question was sitting between Kate and Helena Wentworth right now.

"I used to read what they said about me in the papers, but I've learned to turn a blind eye to it nowadays," Helena was saying. "And you can't trust a soul anymore! At Marina's engagement party I met this this awful girl who said she was George's cousin, then wouldn't leave me alone all evening. She kept on and *on* at me—who designed my dress? what did I think of the party?—until I was ready to scream. I mean, there's only a certain amount of time that one's prepared to waste with people like that. I told her that I never spoke to the press at private parties, and the next day she stuck the knife in. *Helena Wentworth turns orange after eating nothing but carrots for two weeks in order to fit into Chanel couture dress borrowed from Princess Margaret* was about the worst of the lot. *Evening Standard.* I'd have thought they'd have better things to write about."

"People always say that when they can't imagine for one moment that anything could fill the public with more excitement than reading about themselves," Rocky whispered to me.

" . . . She was this fat little thing, voice like a foghorn," went on Helena.

"Hope Allen!'" I cried gleefully. "She and I studied English together for a time. When she was twelve, Patrick Reece used to take her to the theater and offer her cocaine in the interval."

Everyone barked with laughter. *Holy Moses,* I thought in horror, *what was I saying*? But they all loved it. I had offered them something scandalous, something they could feast on later with friends.

"Don't you just love Paddy Reece?" boomed a blond man down the other end of the table. "I must invite him to the box at Lords this summer."

Helena was anxious not to move off the subject of herself.

"It was *cabbage*, not carrots, and the diet lasted a month, not a fortnight, and actually it was Tania Hamilton she borrowed the dress from, not the princess," said Kate.

Everyone roared again and Helena yelled and threw a bread roll at her sister. Harry looked over to me, raised his eyes, and grinned. Rocky clocked the look.

"He loves you," said Rocky.

"Oh, no. He's—well, we're—" I faltered, knowing that I was supposed to be encouraging Rocky to think what he thought. But how could I, when all I wanted was for him to tell me that I was the prettiest girl in the room and could he please walk me home?

"It's not what you think, he and I," I said falteringly.

Charlotte gave me a warning look.

"They're crazy about each other," she said. "But Penelope's very un-American, Mr. Dakota. You won't get any gossip out of her."

Too right, I thought.

The next half an hour was a bit of a blur as Rocky talked about James Dean and Marilyn Monroe and the film he was working on for a big studio, but I couldn't stop thinking about Marina and Harry. Eventually I stood up.

"I must find the bathroom," I muttered. "Please excuse me."

I was very drunk indeed and it took all my self-control to walk sensibly across the room and out into the corridor.

"Ladies' room is down the stairs, turn left, Madam," said the man on the door of the private room.

"Oh, thank you so much."

Grabbing hold of the bannister, I took the downward journey gingerly. Such was the extent of my concentration that I did not hear the pounding of feet behind me until they were right upon me. Someone grabbed me by the waist and I yelped.

"Penelope!" It was Harry.

"Help!" I cried weakly, collapsing against him.

"You're drunk and you're flirting disgustingly with Rocky Dakota."

I giggled. "I wasn't flirting. I don't know how to flirt. Gosh. Was I flirting?"

"You're not funny."

"But you're right, I am drunk. Help, Harry, what shall I do?" I leaned my weight onto the door of the ladies' bathroom and, finding it not as heavy as I had anticipated, hurtled inside, heels skidding all over the polished floor. I collapsed into giggles, made worse by the distinctly unfazed face of the lavatory attendant, all smiles, soap pump at the ready. Harry followed me in.

"Sir, the gentlemen's room is next door—"

"I am quite aware of that," said Harry, taking a crisp note out of his pocket and handing it to her. "Get this girl a glass of water, please."

"No. I want to go back to the table. I want to talk to Rocky again." I stood up and lurched forward.

"Not on your life. We're going to sit here until you're sober."

I collapsed onto a brocaded chair next to the basin, head between my hands.

"I'm going to be sick."

"No, you're not," said Harry ominously.

His tone must have been pretty severe because I decided against it. We sat together in the ladies' room at the Ritz for twenty minutes, while I waited for the world to stop spinning and sipped at a glass of water. I can't recall exactly what we talked about—Harry and I—but I know that I felt an odd relief that he was with me.

"I hope Mama's okay," I found myself saying, apropos of nothing.

"Why on earth wouldn't she be?"

"I don't know. She would be appalled if she could see me now."

"So would my dear mother," admitted Harry. "She thinks you're the most wonderful creature ever to have entered our lives."

"Can't think why—"

"Neither can I," said Harry, utterly without humor.

"Thank you very much! I'm the voice of sanity in your housh-hold—I mean housh-shold. I mean household," I spluttered.

He didn't need to respond, but when I fell forward, he held me for a few minutes, absentmindedly stroking my hair and sighing occasionally. I closed my eyes and felt as though I could fall asleep forever.

"Come on, then," Harry said eventually. "Please, Penelope, for the sake of my pride and your Johnnie Ray tickets, can't you just make the smallest effort to pretend that you find me even a fraction as attractive as that bloody American?"

"Bloody Marina is a bloody American!" I cried.

Harry shook his head. "We better get back." He looked sad in that moment, sad and small, but so very familiar. I reached out and took his hand—I just couldn't help it.

"Everything will work out, you know," I said earnestly. For a second Harry gripped my hand so hard I opened my mouth to howl in pain. He stared at me.

"Do you really think so? Do you believe that?"

"I don't know. I think so—"

"I'm a fool."

"But you're good at magic."

"Oh, shut up."

When we walked back through the door, people had started to move around the room. The voices were louder, the smoke thicker, the atmosphere hotter. Marina was sitting on some young man's lap, shredding petals from a rose. Charlotte was talking to Rocky and eating chocolates from a silver bowl.

"He loves me not!" exclaimed Marina loudly.

"Don't you believe it, darling," said the young man.

They looked up at Harry and me.

"Well!" said Marina. "Where have you two been? We were about to send out a search party."

"Penelope was feeling a little faint," said Harry, stifling a yawn. Crikey, I thought. He can't be *bored*. I looked at Marina, my dislike for her growing with every moment that passed. She was looking at Harry in that horrible, challenging way again. Her eyes mocked us. I was now at that liberating stage that comes after the room has stopped spinning, but before all sense of self-awareness has been regained. I caught sight of Harry and myself in the long mirror that ran along the back of the room. We were up to her poxy challenge, I thought. We sat down together, and I poured us a coffee to share. Charlotte crouched down next to me for a moment.

"Well done," she said in an undertone. "That was a stroke of genius, vanishing for as long as you did. You got Marina pretty cross. Where were you, anyway?"

"Powdering my nose," I giggled. "What do you think of Rocky?"

"The least boring man in the room," said Charlotte finally, and coming from her, I recognized this as a huge compliment. "He's also the best dressed," she added. "You see the cut of his trousers? I've never seen anything so wonderfully crafted in all my born days. And his *tie*!"

"You talked about nothing but clothes?"

"Art, Penelope. The suit that Rocky Dakota is wearing is nothing short of *art*. It'll be hanging, framed, in Dorset House in a hundred years' time, alongside that painting of the orange squares."

I could believe it, absolutely. Everything about Rocky looked as though it should be framed. Harry slid up to me and handed me another glass of water.

"Drink this," he said. Against Rocky, Harry, with his careless hair and odd eyes, appeared even more chaotic than usual. *Imagine you're crazy about him,* I told myself firmly. *Imagine he's not just your friend.*

"Darling," I whispered, "thank you for looking after me." I glanced at Marina, who was pretending not to look at us.

"Move closer," I instructed. "Marina's looking."

Harry shifted forward in his chair, and I wrapped my hand over his. We stared at each other and tried not to laugh. He moved even closer.

"What can we do?" I whispered. "To get her really annoyed?"

Harry smiled at me and pushed a strand of hair out of my eyes. For a moment, that something that had floated in the air in the Long Gallery was back again and I didn't want to move away. Ever.

"I don't know, sweetheart. I'm wondering whether I really care anymore."

"What do you mean?"

"I think perhaps, if I kissed you—"

He didn't need to say anything more.

I stumbled into my bedroom at Aunt Clare's three hours later, and found an envelope on my chest of drawers. Ripping it open, I found my precious tickets inside with a note from Harry.

Thank you, I think it worked.

On the floor above me, I heard him crashing about in his room. I pulled off my lovely heels and my dress and my stockings, and, being the good girl that I am, wiped off my makeup with some cold cream. My head was spinning again. Before Harry and I had left the Ritz, Rocky had taken me aside.

"Perhaps I should take you out some time. You English kids, you and the magician boy and your friend Charlotte. When I was a teenager in America, I had a very clear idea of how English kids should be. You lot come pretty close."

I climbed into bed, my mind full of the Ritz and Rocky and Harry and Marina and champagne and blistered feet and kissed-off Yardley lipstick. Acting had been so very easy, I said to myself—effortless, in fact. There was another thought that kept on coming back to me, another thought that couldn't be pushed away but that I didn't fully understand until the next day. The other thought said that acting was only ever easy when you weren't acting at all.

FIFTEEN

Marina Trapped

I DON'T THINK that I have ever felt so wretched as when I awoke the morning after the night at the Ritz. At six o'clock I had a headache so terrible that I felt certain I should die within the hour. When seven o'clock slouched around and I was still alive, I decided that I had to leave London as quickly as possible. The thought of seeing Harry over the breakfast table and answering Aunt Clare's inevitable machine-gun fire of questions filled me with horror. I brushed my teeth and packed—sighing and stuffing my beautiful dress into my case any-old-how, in the way that one does after something has been worn to unpredictable effect—and hurried downstairs, tripping over the cat and cursing the squeaky floorboards outside Charlotte's room. Goodness, I was thirsty; I simply had to have a glass of water before I left. I creaked open the kitchen door (funny, I had never been into the kitchen before, and very smart it was too, all modern and shiny and not at all like the rest of the house—Phoebe obviously ran a tight ship) and padded across the room. Running the water over my hand for a minute, I closed my eyes and tried my hardest not to think too hard about the night before. It was just too confusing, too awful to have been used like that in front of Marina, and yet it had been me who had encouraged him . . . or had I? I groaned to myself, wishing that the events of last night would sort themselves out into chronological order in my hurting head. Two full glasses of water later, I was about to turn around and leave the room, when I froze in horror at the sound of footsteps thudding down the stairs. *Please go away*, I wished silently. The footsteps got closer. Quite without thinking, I opened the nearest door, which happened to lead to the pantry, and hid inside. I couldn't say exactly what made me do this, only that I felt strongly that the desire not to see anyone outweighed the possibility of being caught somewhere stupid. The footsteps followed the precise route that I had taken. I could hear the tap being turned on, a glass being selected, and moments later, the contents being consumed. It could only be Harry, I decided. Charlotte always carried water upstairs with her at night, and Aunt Clare would never gulp like that. *Please can he not feel hungry,* I prayed, only too aware of the cold apple pie above my head. *Please can he not think to open the—*

"What on earth! *Penelope!*" Harry nearly jumped out of his skin.

"I was getting a bit of apple pie!" I barked, voice croaking, hating myself for minding about my knotted hair and deathly complexion in front of him.

"You were hiding!"

"No! I didn't realize you were in the kitchen."

"You little liar!"

I squeezed out of my hiding place.

"I thought you might be Charlotte. I didn't want to answer any questions about last night," I wailed. "I've hardly slept. I thought I'd take the first train home."

"How convenient."

"What does that mean?"

"Oh, I don't know. You've got your tickets, I suppose the job's done."

"Well—yes. I don't think I could have given you a better performance," I snapped, anger at being caught in the pantry making me sound more sarcastic than I had intended.

"Indeed. Oscar winning, I'd say. Rocky Dakota obviously thought so."

"What's he got to do with anything?"

"I heard him asking you if he could take you out sometime—"

"So what? Don't I deserve some fun?"

Harry considered for a moment.

"Not really. Anyway, he's all wrong for you. He'll spit you out when he gets bored."

"You should know," I hissed.

"What do you mean?"

"Marina. She obviously works on that premise. Get bored, move on."

Harry gave me a look of pure loathing, grabbed the apple pie out of the pantry, and walked toward the door.

"Enjoy Johnnie Ray," he said. "Oh, and Penelope?"

"Yes?" I said sulkily.

"Your blouse. It's open."

Horrified, I looked down to see that Harry was quite right—my blouse had come open almost to the waist, revealing nothing more than the black brassiere I had been wearing under my dress the night before. I was too annoyed to think of anything snappy to say, and Harry stalked off without looking back. Oh, how infuriating it was that he *always* seemed to have the last word.

Two minutes later I was clear of Aunt Clare's and marching toward Paddington. I wanted so very badly to stay wretched and furious—it seemed the only sensible thing to be feeling—but London sparkled after a light shower of rain, and the first buds were appearing on the cherry trees down Westbourne Grove, and Whiteleys had just changed their windows to display all kinds of delicious things: a lemonade set with ice crushers, huge plastic beach bags in gay colors, and a portable Roberts radio. *You were kissed, kissed in the Ritz,* I said to myself as I walked, and it made me smile, because even if it had been staged for Marina Hamilton, and even if neither of us was remotely in love with each other, I had still been kissed in the Ritz. It was more than most people could wish for, I thought. Even if Harry and I had rowed in the pantry and he had seen me in my underwear.

When I got home, I found Magna empty (Mama had left me a note explaining that she had gone into town with Mary to buy supplies for the weekend), so I rushed to the gramophone and played my Johnnie Ray records over and over again. I flung him and Rocky around in my mind— whom would I rather dance with (Rocky), whom would I rather sit up all night talking poetry and dreams with (Johnnie)—yet all the time, Harry's face rattled me more than either of them. My excitement at the thrill of being kissed turned to irritation, and a black cloud descended over me. How dare he, I thought, over and over again, remembering the way he had kissed me, so slowly and deliberately in front of Marina. And how dare I have been so drunk and so hopeless? He had gone too far, and I should have run from the room there and then. Instead, I had allowed him to kiss me again in the cab on the way home, then—horrors!—I recalled him kissing me again as he said good night to me outside my bedroom door. I was a silly little girl, I decided. By the time Mama arrived home, I had made up my mind that I should not talk to Harry ever again—he had made me act like a fool and he hadn't even the good sense to apologize. Mama, being Mama, did not even ask me about the party until after lunch, by which time I was so tired, I felt ready to collapse into my ham and eggs.

"I suppose you've had too much champagne, too little sleep, and too much to think about today," she said, hitting the nail on the head with un-nerving accuracy. Mama was amazing like that; I spent most of my teenage years assuming that she knew nothing about me, and all of my twenties re-alizing that she knew everything.

"It was a late night," I admitted, and then, knowing how she hated si-lences at mealtimes, I ventured a little more information.

"The Ritz was beautiful and the food was to die for."

"Well, that goes without saying, darling. Really, can't you tell me some-thing I don't already know? Like who you talked to, and whether there were any nice young men present?"

Usually I dreaded this line of questioning from my mother, but that afternoon, the urge to forget about Harry and talk about the dreaminess of Rocky was too strong.

"There was someone rather nice," I began falteringly. Mama looked up, startled.

"Goodness, Penelope," she said, astonished. "Who on earth is he?"

"Oh, some man," I said, blushing furiously and thoroughly uncertain that I should go on.

"So much information, darling, I can't keep up."

"He's very successful."

"Good. What does he do?"

"He works in entertainment," I began haltingly, regretting my use of the word straightaway. "Hollywood films, that sort of thing."

Mama frowned and I could see her wrestling with the fact that he sounded rich but worked in an industry she feared, so was therefore, by definition, ultimately unsatisfactory.

"He's written a film that James Dean's going to be in," I said.

"Gracious. He must be terribly pleased with himself."

"He said he'd like to take me—and you—out for dinner," I said, all in a rush, "which would be lovely, as he's very interesting."

"Where does he live?"

"America, most of the time."

"I see." Mama's lips tightened. "So he's American?"

"Yes. Oh, but, Mama, you'd think him *most* charming."

"How old is he?"

"Oh, I couldn't say. Perhaps forty?"

"Forty?"

"Y-yes."

"Has he been married before? Did he lose a wife to some appropriate disease?"

"N-no."

"Never married," confirmed Mama. "Forty years old and never married. Well, it's a very good thing that you had the good sense to tell me about this gentleman, Penelope. You *certainly* should not see him again."

"But why, Mama?"

She put down her fork and stretched out to me.

"Take my hand, darling." She was well aware that physical contact made disagreeing with her virtually impossible. I took her hand in mine, feeling it small and hot and heavy with the exquisite beauty of her ruby engagement ring.

"There are some things that I just know, aren't there? Things that I have a bare instinct about—the woman who worked for a while in the village shop, for example, I was the only person for miles around who could see that she was no good. Well, it's the same here. I don't trust this man, and I don't think you should, either."

"There's nothing wrong with him," I muttered, feeling tears pricking behind my eyelids.

"Penelope, he's unmarried at forty. I'm afraid that says all we need to know. The fact that he works in the films is another factor that can hardly be seen as counting in his favor."

"But he's rich, Mama! I thought you wanted me to meet a rich man!"

"Oh, darling," said Mama sadly, "not an American."

"But he only wanted to take me out for dinner," I said weakly.

Loudly, and on cue, the telephone bell sounded. Mama and I sat tight, awaiting Mary.

"Telephone for Miss Penelope."

Mama's eyes flashed. "Was it a gentleman, Mary?"

"It's Miss Charlotte, Madam."

Mama sighed with relief.

"Run along then, darling."

Charlotte could hardly get the words out fast enough.

"It's Marina!" she gasped.

"What about her?"

"She's called off the wedding! She turned up on the doorstep about an hour after breakfast, still wearing last night's dress, and smoking like mad. Well, luckily for her, the aged aunt was out at the races, so I bundled her into the house and gave her tea and crumpets—she ate the lot, the greedy pig, can't have been that distressed, I'd say—and she talked all about how silly she'd been and how she realized last night after seeing you and Harry together that she was making a terrible mistake and she didn't really love George, and all she wanted was to be with Harry forever."

"I don't believe you!" I gasped, my heart hammering.

"It's all true, honestly. And wait for the rest! An hour later, George arrived—"

"He didn't!"

"He did! He was terribly controlled and beautifully dressed, I might add, saying he just wanted to talk to Marina and make her see sense. He was so jolly nice and polite, I was quite ready to let him in, though Marina had eaten just about everything, so there wasn't much to offer him anyway—but she'd made us promise that if he appeared we were to pretend that we didn't know where she was."

"No!"

"Yes," said Charlotte impatiently. "He left ten minutes later. I hid Marina, just in case he decided to burst through the door like something out of the films. Harry's absolutely bewildered beyond belief," went on Charlotte. "He turned up half an hour after she'd gone, heard the news, and went into a sort of daze and says that he won't speak to anyone at all about the situation, and if any of the gossip columns call, we're to say that he's flown to Spain for a month."

There was a pause. My hands were shaking, I noticed. Actually, properly *shaking*.

"Goodness," I said slowly. "So the plan actually worked? She really was jealous of *me*?"

"You looked sensational last night," said Charlotte matter-of-factly. "It would have been virtually impossible for her not to be jealous. Marina was raving on about your 'bewitching smile' and how she nearly fell to the floor with rage when Harry kissed you. I must say, *I* nearly fell to the floor after that. It was so *utterly Vanity Fair*."

I giggled, feeling rather better all of a sudden. "Do you think so?"

"Of course."

There was a pause.

"Isn't Rocky Dakota wonderful?" I said.

"Dreamy. But far too old for us, despite his beautiful suit. Still, we should be able to sting him for a couple of decent dinners."

I laughed. "Didn't you like the way he talked?"

"He's very charming. But underneath all that chat, he thinks we're little girls, Penelope. Heavens, get him out of your head, for goodness' sake."

"He's about the only man I've ever met who *hasn't* treated me like a little girl," I said huffily.

"Ah, that's his great talent. Making girls like us feel old and sophisticated is a very clever thing."

"Why should he want to bother doing that, anyway?"

"Because we're his target market, of course!" said Charlotte instantly. She sounded so close, it was as if she were in the next room. "We're the ones watching the films he produces and buying the records he makes. I don't blame him for his interest in our lives—in fact, I think it's jolly flattering. But really, Penelope, you mustn't get any other ideas about him. That would be too silly for words."

There wasn't much I could think of to say to this.

"When shall we meet?" demanded Charlotte. "I'm suffering Magna-withdrawal symptoms of the most violent nature."

"Come down on Saturday. Mama's going off to stay with my godmother Belinda again."

I could hear Mama shuffling around loudly in the drawing room. This was a tactic that she frequently used when I was on the telephone—make me think that she was settling down in front of the fire, when she was actually stealing into the hall to eavesdrop.

"I have to go," I hissed.

Replacing the receiver, I wished that Inigo was with us and not at dreary school. He was much better at diffusing Mama's moods than I was. One of his most successful diffusion tactics was simply to turn on the wireless or the television set, because Mama, quite out of character, was utterly seduced by the BBC. No sooner had I sat down with my book (no chance of anything of any importance sinking in, of course) than the telephone bell rang again. Mama looked up, eyes sharp.

"Mary's left," I said. "You better get it, Mama." I felt certain that if it was Rocky, he would know how to charm her.

"Who on earth calls anyone at this time of day?" I watched her flounce out of the room and heard the delicate clatter of her little shoes on the hall floor.

"Hello, Milton Magna . . . Oh, darling! What on earth are you doing on the telephone? . . . Suspended! . . . What does *that* mean? . . . *What* were you doing? . . . You'll tell me when you see me? . . . Oh, Inigo . . . I'll have to send Johns and you know how difficult he's being at the moment. . . . It's just too careless, it really is. . . . How long will you be at home for? . . . Ooh, but that means you *could* come with me to the theater tomorrow night, darling, every cloud . . ."

She replaced the receiver without saying good-bye and I heard her hurrying back into the drawing room. Her face was flushed and animated, her eyes full of fire.

"Well?" I demanded.

"Inigo's been suspended from school. He's going to explain everything when he gets here. I imagine he's been answering back to Mr. Edwards again."

And I imagine he's been caught listening to the radio again, I thought.

"He's on his way home now," said Mama.

"Are you happy?" I asked her, straight out. She bit her bottom lip in an attempt to halt the broad grin that was spreading across her face and answering my question more effectively than any words.

"He's a very irresponsible little boy," she said cheerfully. "Go and tell Mary that it'll be a family supper tonight. Goodness knows how long he'll be here for," she went on. "I suppose we should wait and see what the inevitable letter from the headmaster says. I thought we could all go to the theater tomorrow night? Tickets for *Salad Days* are on offer this week. *We're looking for a P-I-A-N-O!*" she sang loudly.

"Shouldn't Inigo be made to stay at home and think about the error of his ways?" I asked slyly. I felt certain that had *I* been suspended from school, Mama's reaction would have been quite different.

"I think he knows he's gone too far," said Mama, assuming a serious expression. "But if the school is silly enough to think that sending him home is some sort of a punishment—"

"You're supposed to feed him bread and water and make him deliver food packages to the aged poor or something," I said, slightly irritated.

"Aged poor, my foot," scoffed Mama. "*I'm* the aged poor."

She honestly believed that, too.

Inigo arrived home just before supper looking sheepish, hair combed forward like Elvis Presley. Mama tried to be standoffish, but of course it was Inigo, so this lasted for about twenty seconds.

"I'm to stay home for a week," he announced, trying desperately to keep from sounding too gleeful.

"Are you sure they're going to let you back in at all?" I asked. I couldn't imagine for one moment that Inigo contributed anything positive to academic life.

" 'Course they will—they need me for the first eleven." He ran a few paces into the hall and bowled an imaginary ball at the portrait of Great-Uncle Lorne. I giggled.

"What's for supper, Mama?" he demanded.

"Fish pie."

"Grim. I should have stayed at school."

"Well, how about toast and anchovy paste and cocoa?" ventured Mama.

"And the wireless!" I added. "*Hancock's* on at seven!"

"Go and tell Mary she can leave early then."

Inigo and I raced off together, and for that moment all thoughts of Rocky and Harry and kissing at the Ritz felt a million miles away. I felt small again.

Like the rest of the country, we were brought up listening to the wireless, and I know now, as I did then, that wartime existence without the crackly familiarity of *Listen with Mother* would have been unbearable. When the television first opened its doors, most people were unconvinced. Mama, for example, was reluctant to embrace it, and deeply admired people like Winston Churchill, who claimed that it was a "peep show" that would destroy proper family time and the art of conversation. As our family had already been destroyed by the war and the three of us rarely talked about anything that extended outside the parameters of Magna, I was hard pushed to agree with this philosophy. Inigo, hot off the mark as ever, felt determined that we should have a set to watch the Coronation, and succeeded in persuading Mama that we were doing our duty to Queen and Country by flocking to Mrs. Daunton's niece's in the next village to watch our new queen being crowned, and by the time everyone had finished wiping their eyes and saying, "Isn't is wonderful? Oh, it can't have been better from inside the Abbey itself," Mama had been quite converted. But still she refused to let us have a television set, sticking resolutely with the wireless—her first love, and ours too. We were gripped daily by *Hancock's Half Hour* (Mama in particular), and nothing could have been more blissful, nor more of a comfort, than toast and the wireless. Sometimes we wouldn't talk for hours on end, all three of us gripped by a play, and yet we would say good night feeling far closer than we would on an ordinary evening. The wireless was part of the family, as comforting as an old friend. That night we didn't talk much, but we listened, and crunched our toast, and outside the night sky darkened and I heard an owl hooting, and I felt that warmth that comes from being inside and safe with one's family. When we finally switched the radio off, Mama forced Inigo to confess why he had been suspended, saying that if he didn't tell her then she would only find out from the headmaster.

"I was listening to Radio Luxembourg when I should have been in prep." he said. "I've been caught three times now. They don't understand—"

But Mama's mood had changed. Now that Inigo's suspension was to do with pop music, a different light had been cast on the situation. She shook her head.

"I don't *need* school," he said quietly. "I want to leave *now*, and get myself to Memphis—"

"No. I won't hear this again, Inigo."

"I feel so trapped, Mama, can't you see that? There's so much music inside me, I feel like I could explode with it all. But it's no good, is it?"

"Nobody's trapped," said Mama. "Stop being so dramatic!"

Ooh! I had to stop myself from shouting out things about pots and kettles when she said that.

"But there could be a way, Mama," persisted Inigo. "There could be a way that I could save Magna—"

"Singing? You could save Magna by *singing*? Inigo, I won't listen to this anymore, do you understand? I won't hear it anymore!" She stood up and actually stood over him, something that I had never seen her do before.

"The best thing you could do is try and finish school without being expelled. Try not to be sent home for doing silly things. Try and pass your exams and get a good report at the end of term. Give me something to feel proud of, for God's sake."

She delivered this little speech in a most un-Talitha way. She spoke through gritted teeth, voice steady, eyes steely hard. Inigo and I, who had heard it before through tears and hysteria, felt uncomfortable. It was the first time that we felt like she really meant it. She crossed the room to the drinks tray, poured herself an enormous brandy, and left the room.

"I could do it, you know," said Inigo quietly. His dark hair fell forward over his pretty eyes, and he pulled out his comb and swept it back again. He had got so good at these self-conscious gestures that I had almost ceased to notice them; they had become part of his makeup.

"You can understand why Mama worries," I said.

"But what choice have we? I can't see you marrying a rich man in the next two years. The house is crumbling, Penelope. You do realize that, don't you?"

"Of course I do!" I cried, close to tears. "You think I don't notice? Sometimes when I'm lying in bed at night, I feel like I can hear the place groaning, like a dying patient."

Inigo winced. "So no rich husbands emerging?"

"No, of course not. Although I did have a lovely chat last night with an American called Rocky Dakota. He's—"

Inigo's eyes widened. "Rocky Dakota? The film producer? *You* met Rocky Dakota?"

"Well, yes. And why do you have to sound so surprised?"

"I need to meet him."

"Why?"

"He's rich and he knows people. Why else?" Inigo stood up. "He could help me. He could help *us*. Don't tell me that the thought hasn't entered your mind, Penelope."

"Well, I suppose it did, briefly. I told him about you. I said you played the guitar and sang—"

"You get me to meet Rocky Dakota, Penelope. Get me to him and I'll make enough money for us to save Magna fifty times over."

He was so certain. I don't think it mattered to me terribly whether he was right or wrong. All that made sense was that he believed it. It was good enough for me.

"I'll see what I can do," I said.

For the next three days, Inigo, Mama, and I lived in comparative peace. We avoided certain topics of conversation—school, Elvis Presley, the state of the ceilings at Magna, Americans, and film producers—and concentrated instead on the garden and the wireless. We went to church, we picked flowers, we read the papers, and I plowed though an essay on Tennyson with Charlotte's help. Over the telephone she told me that Marina was being hounded by the press, and that George was telling everyone that he would fight to win her back, come hell or high water. Harry, on the other hand, had temporarily vanished.

"I think he's a bit shocked by what he's started," said Charlotte. "Aunt Clare keeps on saying how infra dig it is to be the third party in a breakup like this. She's convinced you're dying of a broken heart."

"I am," I said sadly. "Rocky hasn't called."

I thought of him every night before I went to sleep, and he filled my head from the moment I awoke. The telephone tortured me—sometimes with its silence, other times with the thudding disappointment that accompanied the ringing that was never he. On Friday night, Mama set off for the weekend.

"Look after the place, won't you, darlings?" she asked us, immaculate in her green wool suit.

"Yes, Mama," we chorused.

But as it happened, it wasn't Magna that needed looking after. It was who turned up that did.

SIXTEEN

The Intruder

I COULDN'T SLEEP THAT NIGHT. I would like to be able to say that it was because I was too worried about Inigo and Magna and Mama, but really it was because I couldn't stop thinking about Rocky, Johnnie, and Harry. Johnnie and Harry and Rocky.

"Rocky's not right for you, kid," said Johnnie, coming to me in my half-wakened state, eyes full of concern, but smiling all the same. "I'm the only man for you."

"Why do I loathe Harry for what he did to me at the party? It was all part of the plan, after all. I just feel so—so *used*, Johnnie. And what is it about Rocky Dakota? I know he's too old for me, but thinking of his face just turns me to jelly."

"Hell, kid, haven't I been doing that for years?"

"But he's *real*, Johnnie, I've had *real* conversations with him, not make-believe like we do."

"Make-believe?"

And so it went on. I glanced at my clock at three in the morning and decided that as Johnnie was only confusing me, I should try to immerse myself in Shakespeare. Of course, what I actually did was pull *Good Housewife* out from under my bed (not a great magazine for a girl like me, but I liked their short stories and they talked more about sex than the others) and settled back to read for ten minutes. I was so captivated by the final installment of a Joan Bawden domestic drama that I didn't hear the knocking until it was accompanied by the sound of the door opening and Inigo's skinny frame appeared in my room, pajamas buttoned up to his neck and glasses on, making him more John from *Peter Pan* than Elvis Presley.

"What are you doing?" he hissed.

"Reading a magazine," I answered in surprise. "What are you doing?"

"Can't you hear it?"

"What?"

"The noise downstairs!"

"What noise?"

"Shhhh!"

"I can't hear anything," I complained, but my heart began to hammer. Ghosts were one thing, but intruders were quite another.

"I think it might be a burglar," said Inigo, confirming my fears. "I think I heard footsteps in the hall."

"Footsteps!" I bleated.

"I'll have to go and find out." He pulled his cricket bat out from behind his back. "Lucky I bought this home with me. I thought you could bowl to me tomorrow. I need to get in some practice before the start of the season."

"How can you think about cricket at a time like this!" I demanded. Inigo was unbelievable sometimes.

"I was just pointing out that it was lucky I had—"

"Oh, shut up! What happens if they're armed?" I gibbered.

"Then they will have to content with my off drive," he said, swiping the air with his bat.

"Shall I come too?"

"You stay back here."

"We should have a code," I said quickly. "In case you get into real trouble."

"The code will consist of me shouting, 'Help!' at the top of my voice. Then you can call the police."

"Oughtn't we to do that now?"

"No. Let me deal with them." Inigo was raring to go.

"All right. I'll wait here," I said.

"No, come to the landing. That way you can look out for me from a safe distance. If they give chase, run into the Wellington Room and bolt the door."

I pulled on my dressing gown.

We crept downstairs to the landing, barely daring to breathe, and Inigo signaled that I should stay where I was while he went on to investigate. From our vantage point we could see that a lamp in the hall had been knocked over. The bearskin rug growled up at us threateningly. If I were a burglar, I wouldn't be too happy to wind up in a place like Magna, I thought. I gripped Inigo's arm.

"There!" I whispered. "There's a light coming from under the library door!"

"I hope they take Aunt Sarah's painting."

"Oh, I hope not!" I said in alarm.

Inigo's face took on a determined look.

"They aren't very professional. I just heard one of them knocking into something and saying 'ouch' like a girl. Right. I'm going in," he said.

"I'm coming too!" I whimpered, fear of being left alone outweighing the fear of what Inigo and I were going to find. I would love to have seen us both that night, as we stole down to the hall, Inigo's cricket bat raised out before us, eyes straining in the half gloom. The hall was spooky at night, the familiar faces in the portraits on the wall looked too knowing, the low windows dark with shadows and secrets, the animal heads all breathing. We hovered outside the library. Inigo pressed his ear to the door.

"I can hear pages being turned," he whispered incredulously. "Of all the cheek! Right, that does it!"

"No, you—"

But in he had marched.

"Right! The game's up! Hand over what you've taken and nothing more will be said of this!" he ordered, sounding jolly grown-up. I quivered outside the door, heart crashing, hands sweating—

"Good God, put that thing down, will you?"

It was a girl's voice. An American voice. Slowly, I stuck my head around the door, and my eyes nearly popped out of my head. Sitting in Mama's chair, a battered copy of Philip Miller's *Gardener's and Botanist's Dictionary* on her lap, was Marina Hamilton. She was beautifully dressed, as ever, but I noticed that her pert heels had trailed mud into the room, her tights were ripped, and her skirt was crumpled. Fido lay at her feet, and looked up at us as we came in with a sort of what-on-earth-are-you-two-doing? expression. *Traitor!* I thought, thinking irrationally that Marina wasn't the sort one would expect to be good with dogs. But then after this episode, I didn't think that I would ever try to predict anything about anyone ever again. I decided to stay put out of her line of vision for a moment. Inigo could find out what on earth she was doing.

"What on earth are you doing?"

Marina stood up and wobbled slightly, her eyes wild and slightly crossed, and I realized, with a rush of glee, that she was very drunk.

"I've come to see Harry," she said defiantly.

"Harry?"

"Yes! Don't pretend he's not here! Where is he? Where is she?"

"Who's she?"

"Penelope, of course!"

"By Penelope, I presume you mean my *sister,* Penelope?"

It took a minute for the meaning of these words to sink in.

"Oh, you're Penelope's *brother*? Well! I would *never* have guessed. Goodness, but you're divine! You don't have your sister's nose, do you?" She stood up and crossed the room toward him, catching her right foot on a rug and tripping slightly as she went.

"It's a pretty uncommon way to meet, but it churtainly is my pleasure." She grinned broadly. Inigo, bewildered, shook her hand.

"Who are you?" he repeated. "What are you doing breaking in like this? You know, I could call the police—"

"No. Oh, no, please!" Marina held her hand to her chest, her red lipstick quivering. It was a sensational show, and from behind the door, I was starting to enjoy myself, in spite of everything.

"Do you have a cigarette?" she asked Inigo huskily. He reached into the pocket of his pajamas and pulled out a packet. Stepping up to the fireplace, Inigo flicked open his lighter and lit it for her.

"Oh, thank you so much. You are a sweet thing."

I decided it was about time I said something, so I pushed myself out from behind the door, into the room.

"Oh, Penelope!" Marina reeled and nearly fell over for the second time.

"Hullo, Marina."

"You know this girl?" asked Inigo.

Marina composed herself and wobbled up to me. With the sort of high-class drama that one would expect from an actress of her caliber, she reached out and touched my cheek. Her hands were cold. "Heartbreaker," she said softly.

Inigo coughed and she turned back to him.

"Do I see whiskey on that tray?" she asked.

Inigo was already pouring her a double.

"Water?" he asked her.

"No, thank you."

She took a generous gulp of the stuff, then staggered back into Mama's chair.

"Where is he? Where's my love?"

"Your love?" repeated Inigo, looking at me in bewildered irritation. Marina ignored him.

"Oh! My poor, darling shoes!" she wailed, noticing the mud for the first time. She pulled out a handkerchief and stretched down to try and wipe them clean, but lost her balance and fell off the chair and into a heap on the floor.

"Gracious!" she giggled. "I fell!"

Inigo and I hauled her back up onto the chair. We could be here till dawn waiting for an explanation, I thought.

"I think I'll have a whiskey, Inigo," I said.

He poured us both a drink and poked at the fire and got it going a bit, so that after five minutes we were sitting in relative comfort. I flopped onto the sofa and wrapped an ancient traveling rug around my knees.

Despite (or perhaps because of) her inebriated state, Marina's hair looked magnificent; she seemed like a flame-haired version of Natalie Wood at the end of *Rebel Without a Cause*. Her elegantly cut wide-legged trousers were soaked and muddy at the bottom, but nothing could distract from the narrow curve of her tiny waist. Her generous bosom spilled out of a low-cut red blouse that had come unbuttoned to a degree verging on indecent, resulting in an overall effect that was, naturally enough, pure sex. Unlike Charlotte, whose appeal came from her very English brand of stylized chaos and breathless excitement, Marina was pure, unapologetic Los Angeles swish, even after too much to drink and a night walk on a muddy grass verge. Inigo gave me a look as if to say, *Well, she's your friend! You ask the questions!* I sensed that he was frustrated to have been caught looking about twelve in his glasses and pajamas, but then, who dresses up to confront intruders? Marina would, I supposed.

"What are you doing here, Marina?" I asked sensibly. It seemed like the right place to start, though I was fairly sure that I already knew the answer.

"Haven't you heard the news?"

"Eden set to succeed Churchill?" suggested Inigo. Marina giggled loudly.

"You're a doll, aren't you? No, *my* news, silly. It's all off. The wedding. George and I. I've called it off. Off, off, off, off, *off.* Don't you just adore the word 'off?' So expressive. So *off.*"

"Off?" repeated Inigo, dumbly. I supposed I should stop imagining that I would get any sense out of him now.

"So I've come to find Harry, to tell him that the whole engagement was an awful"—she pronounced it "are-ful"—"mistake."

"Harry?" exclaimed Inigo.

Oh, help, here we go, I thought.

Marina loaded her eyes and fixed me with her siren's gaze.

"I can't bear it anymore," she said.

"What's all this?" interrupted Inigo. Marina ignored him.

"Harry and Penelope! Penelope and Harry! Oh! Even your *names* sound romantic together!" She started laughing again, but it was hollow, mirthless laughter that made me a little afraid. She shook her head in wonder.

"Who would have thought that I could be jealous of someone like *you?*"

In her defense, I don't think that she meant this unkindly. It was, in fact, a perfectly reasonable question and I half admired her for speaking it out loud. She stood up again and started to pace the room, her feet creaking over the library's ancient floorboards. I sensed the ghost of Aunt Sarah looking on, gripped.

"I can't marry George because when I saw you with Harry the other night, I nearly died," she said simply.

"You and Harry?" spluttered Inigo in my direction. I glared at him.

"The way he kept looking at you when Rocky was talking to you, the way his eyes lit up when you walked into the room, the way you sneaked off together after coffee, the way he kissed you—oh!" She covered her eyes with her hands as if the scene was being replayed on a screen in front of her. "It was too much. I realized then that if I didn't get him back, I might as well stop living. You'll never guess what I did," she added, looking a little bit guilty.

"What?" demanded Inigo.

"I set the birds free," she whispered dramatically.

"The birds?" Inigo was thrown.

"Oh, my word, the *birds*!" I cried, suddenly realizing exactly what she was talking about.

"The parakeets Harry gave me for my engagement. I just couldn't bear to see them locked up anymore. I set them free on the way out of town."

"Where?" I demanded.

"Richmond somewhere. I don't know. I asked the driver to stop where he thought the birds would be happy and I just opened the cage and off they flew. They were kinda confused to start with, didn't understand that they were free. I guess they're not used to it. It made me so happy for about five minutes. Then I got back into the cab and we drove off again and I thought, how silly! They probably won't last a day in this weather."

"Oh, I wouldn't bank on it," said Inigo comfortingly. "Who knows, maybe there'll be thousands of wild parakeets all over London in fifty years' time."

"Oh!" cried Marina, pressing a hand to her heaving bosom. "Oh! That makes me feel so much happier! D'you really think they might survive?"

"Certainly not," I said witheringly. I felt cross with Marina. Those birds would have looked marvelous in the knot garden.

"He doesn't want me anymore," moaned Marina dully, swiftly returning to the topic of Harry.

I opened my mouth to tell her that there was nothing to worry about, that he had never stopped loving her and that I had been nothing more than a pawn in his game, but stopped myself. Let her think that he loved me, I decided. It was rather fun. Harry had got himself into this, so he could provide all the explanations. So instead of confessing, I said, "Don't you think you're being a tiny bit overdramatic?"

She stared at me, incredulous. "Can you imagine the horror of losing the man you love to another woman?" she demanded.

"But how do you think *he* felt when you ran off with George? You can't have loved him that much, to agree to marry another," I said indignantly.

"I was *blind!*" cried Marina, flinging her hands up into the air this time. "Blinded by what I thought I wanted: money, success, a rich man—someone to pick up the bills and open doors and adore me. George is a sweetie, but he's not Harry. He doesn't spark like Harry. He doesn't fill me with *passion* like Harry. He doesn't make me want to take off my clothes and *fling myself at his feet* like Harry."

Even I was taken aback by these words, and Inigo, who clearly had no trouble accessing his imagination for this image, blushed to his very roots. Despite my role in the affair, and the fact that I was supposed to know the answer, I couldn't help asking, "Just what is it about Harry that you find so irresistible?"

"Everything," said Marina miserably. "He's the most alluring man I've ever met. He has that certain something that very few people have. I suppose *I* have it, so I recognize it in other people," she added, entirely without irony. *Tally ho!* I thought, *back to the old Marina.* " . . . I'd been tearing myself to pieces ever since I heard that he had taken up with *you.* Everyone said how well suited you were, how charming you were, how pretty and sweet. *Well!* I thought, *At least she won't have my intelligence.* Then I hear that you're studying Shakespeare and that you and Charlotte can't get enough of Tennyson!" (*Gosh!* I thought, *I like that rumor!*) Marina was rattling on now, stopping only to drain her whiskey. "The worst thing of all was hearing about this place, Milton Magna. I heard that Harry came here for an afternoon and he—I heard he—heard he—he—*performed* for you."

"Performed?"

"Magic," whispered Marina. She was certainly enjoying herself now. "Magic," she repeated. "It's how he seduced me. And he did it to you too. Here at Milton Magna—the very name of this house has haunted my very soul. The place where you first kissed, the place where you first laughed together. I couldn't stop torturing myself, so I decided I had to see you with him again, one more time. I made sure that you were invited to the Ritz. I needed to convince myself that he really, *really* loved you. So you were. And he does." She sat down again and absentmindedly opened a box of After Eight mints that had been sitting by Mama's reading lamp since Christmas.

"How did George take the news?" I asked her.

"Oh, calm as a cucumber. He won't talk to me, of course. In a few months he'll be counting his lucky stars that he didn't marry me. I'd have ruined him," she said simply, "even if I hadn't been in love with another man." She bit into a mint. *Funny,* I thought idly, *she chews just like the guinea pig.*

"Do you want to explain why you're here?" managed Inigo, removing his specs and pulling forward his hair. Marina looked down at her hands.

"Where else was I to go? This afternoon—heavens, was it only today? it feels like another century ago—I turned up at Harry's mother's house in Kensington, and was told that he wasn't at home. Charlotte was a darling, she plied me with tea—I couldn't eat a thing—and suggested I wait until he returned. By eleven o'clock, he was still out and I had a vision, a sudden flash of realization that he was with you at Milton Magna. I told Charlotte I was going back to Dorset House, but really I went to Claridge's and ordered myself a bottle of Moët, drank the lot, and took a taxi all the way here. It cost me fourteen pounds"— Inigo gasped admiringly at this—"and the paparazzi followed me nearly all the way, vultures that they are. My nice taxi driver threw them off the scent when we got close to your place. He dropped me at the bottom of your drive. I had to walk up to the house alone, and I'm afraid I wasn't wearing the right shoes." She started to weep again. "When I got to the front door, I found it was open, so I just walked in. I suppose I thought I would find myself another drink, then go and find Harry."

"But you got distracted by the *Gardener's Dictionary,*" I couldn't resist saying.

Marina ignored me and picked up another book from the shelf in front of her.

"*The Constant Nymph,*" she whispered. "H-H-Harry used to call me his nymph. I'm afraid I wasn't very constant." She pulled out a handkerchief. "Now he's lost. I am undone."

"Well, he's not here," I said frankly.

"Don't pretend! I know he's here!" Marina stood up again, and lurched again, and steadied herself with her mint-free hand.

"Why would I have to pretend to you?" I said. "I promise he's not here. I have no idea where he is, but I expect we can find him tomorrow."

"Why isn't he here?" wept Marina. "I came all this way, *all this way!*"

"In a taxi,"added Inigo.

"In a *taxi!*" agreed Marina. "And I tore the hem of my pants fighting my way up your driveway. I've ruined my shoes! I don't *do* this sort of thing, do you understand what I'm saying, Penelope? It's not usual. It's not like me." She looked genuinely distressed.

"Sometimes doing things we don't normally do can be great fun," I observed.

"And sometimes doing things we don't normally do can be a pain in the ass. Don't patronize me just because you've got the guy."

Inigo's eyes gleamed.

"Lucky Mama's not here," I muttered, nearly swooning with the horror of imagining Talitha waking up to the sound of Marina's shrill American tones echoing around the house.

"Your mother? I've heard she's one of the great beauties of all time," said Marina.

"Apparently," I said.

"Do you take after her?" she asked Inigo.

"Oh, I don't know, people say that there's a slight resemblance."

"They're identical," I said wearily.

"You're a doll," said Marina. "I like your hair."

Inigo blushed again. *Please no,* I thought. *Spare Inigo.*

"Do you think perhaps it would be a good idea if we showed you upstairs?" I asked her, bracing myself for another outburst. To my surprise, her eyes drooped.

"I'm so tired," she admitted. "I came all this way! I came to find him!"

"We can all look for him in the morning," I said, mother to infant.

"Where is he?" she asked again, her voice slurring. She closed her eyes and her head lolled onto the back of the chair.

"Inigo, I'll show her to the Red Room," I said in a low voice. "I don't think she's going to remember much of this conversation in the morning."

"You've got a lot of explaining to do," said Inigo, draining his whiskey.

So had bloody Harry, I thought, leading Marina upstairs.

"Whoops!" she giggled, catching her foot on the rug on the way out of the room, and grabbing at the back of my nightdress on her way to the floor. She brought me down with her and for a moment we struggled together on the rug, Marina giggling so hard that I found it virtually impossible not to join in, in spite of myself. I clambered to my feet.

"Oh, I've torn your nightdress!" she wailed.

"Oh, don't worry, I think it was already ripped."

"No one should go to sleep in a ripped nightdress," said Marina, sounding remarkably sober all of a sudden. "I'll have you sent a new one next week."

The next morning I overslept and did not make it down to breakfast until half past nine. I wondered if last night's episode had been no more than a particularly surreal dream, but I dressed with more care than usual, in case it hadn't been. Walking into the dining room I was nearly asphyxiated by the Chanel No. 5 and frying bacon. It's not Sunday, I thought. Marina was sitting at the table, relaxed and beautiful in full makeup and a black-and-white-checked blouse and skirt, finishing a plate of food. Beside her sat what looked like a glass of fresh orange juice. Inigo sat opposite her, reading the paper and spreading butter on a corner of toast. It was quite the most civilized of scenes; I half expected a small child to run into the room and hug them before setting off for the school bus.

"Oh, Penelope!" said Marina, looking up with a smile. "Would you like a cup of tea?"

"Yes, thanks. And what's all this? Bacon and eggs on a normal day?"

"Marina was hungry," explained Inigo.

"Orange juice?"

"I cycled to the stores and bought some oranges."

"I can't drink anything but freshly squeezed juice," said Marina. "I need my vitamin C."

She pronounced it "vite-amin." Inigo smirked, delighted with yet more Americana.

"You know, I am so sorry about last night," went on Marina conversationally, pouring me tea from the best porcelain, which had last been used on Coronation Day. "I expect you think I'm the most dreadful beast. I'm happy to say that I can recall very little of what happened once I entered your beautiful home. I remember meeting Inigo, and admiring your wonderful library, but apart from that"—she giggled coquettishly—"I've drawn a blank!"

How convenient, I thought.

"You came looking for Harry," I said, quite happy to fill in the gaps.

"Oh, yes, I know *that.*"

"You've left your fiancé, and the world's press tried to follow you and your taxi down here. You made your way up the drive in the pitch dark, and tore the hem of your pants."

"Oh yes, I know *that,*" repeated Marina, merry as daffodils blowing in the March breeze.

"Like we said last night, Harry's not here," I went on, "but you're not the only one who would like to know where he is. I suggest we call Aunt Clare's—I mean, the Kensington residence—after breakfast."

"Good idea," said Marina warmly. "Now, your woman Mary found me this marvelous Damson jam. It's the best thing I've ever spread on toast."

On cue, Mary shuffled into the room.

"You didn't tell me you were expecting Miss Hamilton," she said to me accusingly.

I gritted my teeth. Mary, like the rest of the world, was a sucker for red lips and red hair.

"I'm sorry, Mary. Can lunch stretch?"

"Expect so. Miss Hamilton says she can order in some beef for Sunday lunch," she said smugly.

"Sunday lunch?" I stuttered.

"It's Friday," said Marina. "I don't plan on returning to London until I've recovered from last night. If you show me the telephone, I shall call my man in London and have him send down a joint. So silly not to make the most of the glorious spring weather. Sugar and milk?"

I looked at Inigo, who looked away. *He wants her here,* I thought. *He's captivated by the whole performance.*

"Black and no sugar, thank you," I said.

After breakfast, Marina said she would like to take a bath and I showed her up to my bathroom.

"Oh, lavender oil, how charming," she said, turning on my bathroom taps. Then, just as the water spluttered out, the tears were back.

"Oh, Penelope!" she wailed. "I love him!"

The speed with which Marina was capable of switching from happy to miserable quite overwhelmed me and I blinked a few times, trying to readjust myself. Rocky was quite right. She *was* exhausting.

"Do you think he'll marry you?" she asked, sniffing. "No! Don't answer me just yet. Let me lie in the bath and pretend that he wants to be with me. Don't ruin my daydream. Please, Penelope. Say nothing. Say nothing."

So I said nothing, and excused myself and rushed downstairs and telephoned Aunt Clare's. To my amazement, Harry picked up the phone.

"Where have you been?" I demanded. "Your American Lady Love is here at Magna, using all the hot water, organizing Sunday lunch, and weeping every other minute. She wants you back, for goodness' sake."

"I know," he said simply. "Our plan worked."

"*Your* plan," I hissed.

"I knew she would come and find you," he said. "She's rather predictable like that." He didn't sound victorious, as I had expected. He sounded half-tired, half-something-else. Yes, that was it. Half-*bored.*

"Nothing predictable about turning up drunk in the middle of the night," I snapped. "Isn't this your cue to gallop up the drive and whizz her off into the sunset?"

"I suppose so." I could hear him yawning.

"You *suppose* so? Aren't you overwhelmed by happiness and triumph?" I wanted to shake him.

"Of course I am," he said, suddenly sharp. "But she made me *suffer,* Penelope. I'm rather enjoying the idea that she's having to put up with a bit of pain now."

"Oh, for heaven's sake! She thinks you love *me*," I said impatiently, "which was all well and good at Dorset House and the Ritz, but it makes me jolly uncomfortable at two in the morning in the library at Magna."

"Did you look beautiful when she saw you last night?" asked Harry lightly. It mattered to him, I supposed. He needed me to keep up the image he had created.

"No. I was wearing an awful nightie and a torn dressing gown. I looked a mess," I said smugly.

To my surprise, Harry laughed. "I wish I'd been there."

"So do I," I said with feeling. "I don't like the girl, but it's rather awful seeing her like this. She *needs* you, Harry."

"The only person she's ever needed is herself."

"Are you telling me that now that she's left George, you don't love her anymore?" I asked in ominous tones.

"Oh, I love her all right," said Harry grimly. "But I hate her too."

"Please, Harry, don't leave me to sort this out alone."

"Sit tight. Don't let her know that we were only pretending, *please,* Penelope. For your own sake too."

"If she's still here by the end of the weekend—" I warned.

"What will you do?" He sounded almost amused now.

"I'll tell her this whole thing has been one big act and I don't think she'll forgive you. The one thing I've learned about Marina is that she doesn't like being taken for a fool. Good-bye, Harry."

I replaced the receiver and nearly leaped out of my skin as Mary tapped me on the shoulder.

"I thought I'd do a Queen of Puddings tonight," she said thickly. "Miss Hamilton says it's her favorite."

Upstairs, I could hear Miss Hamilton singing "The Little White Cloud That Cried."

"Lovely voice she has too!" sighed Mary.

Personally, I thought it rather shrill. *And* she got the words wrong in verse two. Johnnie would have been horrified. . . .

SEVENTEEN

Drama in the Dining Room

CHARLOTTE ARRIVED just as Marina descended the stairs after the longest bath in Magna's history.

"I got the first train I could," she said breathlessly. 'They should name the train line after us. The Wallace-Ferris Great Western service. I feel I spend more time on the train than anyone else in the world. We were delayed at Reading. I nearly burst with frustration. And I *paid* for my ticket! I'm far too well behaved by half, nowadays. I blame bloody Christopher Jones."

"I'd blame Marina if I were you."

"Where is she?"

"Charming Inigo somewhere."

I was relieved to see Charlotte. With her around, the situation became less desperate, and more amusing. She was very good at cracking jokes at inappropriate times.

Against the odds, Marina had unearthed a set of ancient tongs from the depths of some long-abandoned cupboard, and had curled her hair, reapplied her makeup, and dressed thoughtfully for her weekend in the country in a tweed skirt and twinset, which would have looked quite dreadful on anybody but her. As it happened, she defined *alluring*. Inigo, who had been valiantly struggling through a geometry paper at the dining room table, decided to abandon his work in favor of a "stroll in the garden" with our American guest.

"Shall we take a glass of champagne with us?" suggested Marina.

"Why not a bottle?" said Inigo quickly.

"You should get that paper finished by the end of today!" I called out threateningly as he popped the cork. Inigo, quite rightly, ignored me.

"I shall need something to walk in," said Marina, looking down at her feet. Inigo raced to the cloakroom and found her a pair of wellingtons.

"Try these," he suggested, handing her my boots.

"Oh, Lord! These are men's boots, surely!" giggled Marina, pretending to fall over so that Inigo had to catch her.

"No, I think they're Penelope's," said Inigo.

"But they're *huge*!"

I could have slain him.

Half an hour later, Charlotte and I watched them wandering back to the house, stopping to pick daffodils en route. Marina appeared to be laughing a great deal, which foxed me, as usually I am the only person who finds Inigo funny.

"She doesn't seem to be missing Harry much at the moment," said Charlotte. We were sitting on the windowseat in my bedroom overlooking the drive, eating a bag of apples and smoking cigarettes out of the window.

"It comes in waves," I said. "And when it comes, watch out! She's like a different girl, terribly humble and afraid and convinced that she'll never get him back. Harry wants me to go on pretending for a while longer. He thinks it's only right that she should suffer a little bit."

"How disgusting," said Charlotte. "And he calls that being in love?"

"It's George I feel sorry for," I said. "There's something rather sweet about him. Rocky thinks so too," I added unthinkingly. Charlotte was on to me like a shot.

"Oh, well, if *Rocky* thinks so," she said slyly. "Tell me, has he telephoned? When are you going out for your terribly smart dinner?"

"I don't know. He hasn't called. I feel a fool, Charlotte."

"Give him time," she said. "These sort of men are far too important to call when they say they will."

"How do *you* know?"

"Just do."

Charlotte was one of those people who only ever found anything good in everything. Events that I had dreaded, she had embraced with never-ending *joie de vivre*. She had also been working far harder than Inigo or I could even dream of—the tips of her fingers were hard, like dried wax, from hammering the keys of Aunt Clare's typewriter. Sometimes, she said, she felt herself typing in her sleep. She never complained, but more than that, she saw light in everything. She *made* light of all the right things, and she realized when she shouldn't, which is one of the rarest gifts I ever knew in anyone.

"You will see him again, you know," she said, seeing my thoughtful expression, and again I thought, *Isn't that just like Charlotte?* She understood completely that the only thing that mattered was that I saw him. Never mind kissing him or even talking to him. She understood the ache that could be eased just with a look or a smile.

"Even if things don't work out, there's always Johnnie," she added, and unlike the rest of the world, I knew that she was being serious; she simply could not conceive of a reason why Johnnie Ray, world famous and only in England for a few nights a year, should want to spend his time with anyone but us. I loved her for that. And why not? We were young and the world spun for us alone.

"I suppose we should go downstairs and have some lunch," I said.

"Is Marina eating like a pig?"

"She won't stop. I think it must be a nervous reaction to the horror of her situation," I giggled.

"Rubbish. She's just greedy."

"Mary adores her," I said. "She calls her Miss Hamilton."

We stood up and Charlotte flipped her thick hair out from under the collar of her blouse.

"Do you have a comb?" she asked, and I said that I thought so, and crossed the room to my dressing table. Marina the guinea pig shot out from under my bed, so I picked her up and made a fuss of her.

"Look how tame she is now, Charlotte," I said, but Charlotte's eyes were fixed on something outside, her jaw open in astonishment.

"What is it?" I demanded. Not Mama back early, *please*. But no. The most sensational pale silver car was careering up the drive at the most sensational silver pace.

"Oh, my God!" breathed Charlotte. "It's a bloody Chevrolet!"

"Whose?" I whispered idiotically, and the word stuck in my throat, because who else would have a Chevrolet in the middle of Wiltshire?

We watched him get out, take off his hat, and march toward the front door.

"Help! It's him! Oh, Charlotte, what on earth is he doing here?" I whimpered.

"Come to find Marina, I'll wager," said Charlotte with glee. "Americans can never keep their noses our of other people's business."

Why, oh *why*, hadn't I washed my hair? I ran to my basin and splashed cold water on my face. Charlotte snapped into action.

"Put this on," she ordered, hurling a pair of red trousers and a black sweater at me as the doorbell rang and Fido began to bark.

"The trousers are too big!" I hissed.

"Hitch them up with a belt. Too big is always good—it makes you look like you've lost weight."

"What about my hair?"

Charlotte grabbed the comb from me and messed around with my mop for a few minutes.

"You'll do," she said. "Get those pearls off, and for goodness' sake, put some red lipstick and powder on. Don't you just hate it when men turn up unannounced?"

"I can't say I have a great deal of experience in this field," I gibbered. "Suppose he wants to take us out for lunch? What shall I do? Oh, help! Look!"

But it was too late. From our vantage point, we could see the front door being opened and Marina stepping outside to greet him.

Charlotte and I fled my bedroom and stood just back from the gallery, looking down at the scene emerging below. Marina looked Daphne du Maurier–beautiful, still dressed for her walk, radiant and mysterious in a pale gray wool cape. She seemed to register very little surprise at Rocky's arrival; rather, she smirked a bit and held out her hand to be kissed, which I thought jolly affected. Rocky looked heartbreaking in a long black coat that must have cost about a hundred pounds and a red-and-black-checked scarf wound around his neck. His hair was Brylcreem-advertisment perfect despite the blustery day, and he carried a light brown leather case and a newspaper under his arm. I felt curiously detached from myself; watching him and Marina standing in the hall was like watching an alternative ending to a favorite film.

"I suppose you want me to ask you what you're doing here," I heard Rocky say.

"I could say the very same to you!" said Marina.

"Where's little Penelope Wallace, havoc maker?" asked Rocky, shaking off his coat, and my heart jumped and Charlotte nudged me in the ribs.

"How did you guess I was here, anyway?" demanded Marina.

"You're as easy to read as Salinger," said Rocky.

"I suppose George sent you," said Marina dramatically.

"All George told me was that your jazz-fan boyfriend is the same man that Penelope kissed at the Ritz. That was all he needed to tell me for me to work out where you were."

"Congratulations, Perry Mason," said Marina, removing her cape and tossing it onto the hall table.

"I suppose you've terrorized that sweet girl into thinking that she has to give him up?"

Suprisingly, Marina had the insight to lower her voice at this point, so I missed most of what she replied, but I caught the phrase "doesn't love him like I do."

"He's not so old," conceded Charlotte in a whisper.

"I told you!"

Gosh, but he was handsome. The hall at Magna that dwarfed and made fools of most people seemed the perfect fit for Rocky. He held out his arms to me as Charlotte and I descended the stairs.

"How are you, girls?" He smiled, kissing me on both cheeks.

In that moment, I didn't think to ask him what he was doing rolling up unannounced. I didn't think to wonder what his reasons were for anything. The only thing that struck me as remotely important was the fact that ten minutes after Charlotte and I had been talking about him, he was standing next to me, as real and as shake-makingly intimidating as ever.

"Do you want to stay for supper?" I asked him, trying to keep the glee out of my voice.

"I can't think of anything nicer," he said.

I led Rocky to the drawing room and poured him a scotch.

"Good girl," he said, taking it from me. He chucked it down his throat in one gulp. Everything looked too small for him, even the double dose of whiskey.

"What a place!" he exclaimed, noticing his surroundings for the first time. He gave a great kick of laughter and prowled around the room.

"My God! This is the kind of England I read about when I was a kid. I kinda assumed there was none of it left. Seems I was wrong."

Not that wrong, I thought, covering up a huge tear on the back of the sofa with an equally ravaged cushion. *Help—Mary would go spare if I didn't let her know that there was yet another glamorous guest for dinner.*

"Would you mind terribly if I left you here for a minute or two?" I asked Rocky politely. "I need to talk to Mary about dinner."

"Who's Mary?" asked Rocky, eyes glinting.

"Oh, she's just the cook."

"Wonderful. Are we having spotted dick? Or frog in the hole? Suet pudding?"

I giggled. Rocky sloshed his ice around in his glass.

"You're so pretty when you laugh. It's hard to believe you're behind all this mess."

"Me!"

"Yeah, *you.* I know Marina better than I know myself. She's far more concerned with the fact that the jazz fan finds you so darn pretty than she is with the fact that she really loves him after all. You've got right under her skin."

"It was never meant to be like this," I said awkwardly. I clenched my teeth together to stop myself from running into his arms and yelping out that he was the only one I had ever wanted from the start.

"I kinda understand the way she feels, you know," he said slowly. "I always want what I can't have."

"You do?" I whispered.

"All the time," he said.

The blissful tension of our eyes locking and my blush spreading up my neck and into my cheeks was broken when Inigo plowed into the room.

"Marina says Rocky Dakota's here!" he hissed. "Why didn't you tell me he was turning up?"

"She didn't know it herself," drawled Rocky, standing up and offering his hand to Inigo. I had to hand it to my little brother. He composed himself without turning scarlet and without stammering.

"You ever met Elvis Presley?" he asked quickly.

"What does an English kid like you know about Elvis Presley?" asked Rocky, genuinely surprised.

"Everything," said Inigo, taking out his comb.

Marina collapsed into bed and Inigo monopolized Rocky all afternoon with his incessant Elvis Presley chat, and Rocky responded by firing questions at Inigo: How long had he been listening to Elvis? Did he feel Elvis was going to make it in England? How many records had he in his collection? Did he like Johnnie Ray like me? Why not? Charlotte and I arranged ourselves prettily by the drawing room fire and pretended to play Scrabble, but their dialogue was too thrilling not to be a part of. Inigo, after all, must have been the only boy in England dyeing his hair to be like Elvis and able to sing "Mystery Train" in perfect imitation of the man. For both Rocky and Inigo, I felt it was a sort of dream meeting; it was impossible to tell to what extent each was using the other. What they had in common was their passion: Inigo's for Elvis and escape, and Rocky's for making money.

"So, you girls, how do you feel when you look at Johnnie Ray?" Rocky asked us, taking it upon himself to haul us into the conversation while he poured himself another double whiskey. "You wanna mother the guy? Is it because he wears a hearing aid? You feel sorry for him?"

"Gosh," I said. "It never even entered my *head* that we might feel like that."

"Oh, no," agreed Charlotte breezily. "It's all about sex, isn't it, Penelope?"

I went scarlet. Rocky raised his eyebrows at me and I wriggled my toes frantically.

"Is it, kid? You feel that pull toward him? Like you wanna get *close* to him? Close to him like that?"

"Of course," I admitted, and Charlotte and I collapsed giggling.

"Gee," said Rocky. "Does the magician know how you feel?"

"Oh, yes," I said. "He knows absolutely everything." As usual, the champagne confused me with that giddy feeling that I could say or do what would normally stay firmly inside my head.

We sat down to supper that night, a curious party of five, but the force of Rocky's and Marina's presences meant it felt as if there were many more of us in the room. Mary had polished and set the best silver; I held my breath wondering how everything was going to taste. Marina had slept all afternoon and had joined us for drinks before dinner in a green and white sequined gown that would not have looked out of place at the opera house. For someone whose heart was aching, she had thought awfully hard about what to wear. She slid into her chair, between Rocky and Inigo, not meeting my eye in a very deliberate way. We were only a few minutes into our prawn cocktails (like bits of India rubber in a watery pink glue) when the sparks began to fly. Marina, unsettled by the fact that Rocky was still deep in conversation with Inigo and not concentrating on her, cleared her throat. If she could have tapped her glass with her fork and not looked absurd, I think she would have done.

"So I suppose we're all going to sit here and act like nothing's wrong," she said loudly. We all fell silent and I noticed a spark in Charlotte's eyes. She loved a bit of a scene.

"Sure," said Rocky lightly. "We're having dinner, right? Charlotte, would you pass me the water?" He pronounced it "wah-der." I felt my heart jump a bit.

"So you're quite happy to watch me falling apart at the seams?" asked Marina with a bark of her famous sob-laughter. She abandoned her food and reached for her cigarettes. Inigo flipped open his lighter.

"What the hell else do you expect us to do?" said Rocky quietly. "You wanna go make it up with George? We can be with him in a couple of hours if we leave now."

For a second, I sensed Marina flipping this option over in her mind.

"No!" she whispered. "I don't want to see George. I've left George. I can't ever see him again. I need to see Harry. I need Harry!" Her voice rose hysterically. As if taking cue from some invisible director, she stood up and crossed the room. Staring out of the window, she clutched her hand to her chest.

"I never, ever imagined anything could hurt so much," she said. Rocky continued to spoon up the last of his prawn cocktail.

"Really?" he said absentmindedly. Charlotte stifled a giggle and he caught her eye and grinned. Marina turned back to us, her eyes full of fire.

"You!" she said, pointing a red fingernail at me. "*You!* This is all *your* doing! You seduced him! You *tricked* him into believing he loved you! You stole his heart! *You. Stole. His. Heart!*" This last phrase was uttered with Cleopatrian passion, every word a statement within itself. Charlotte actually leaned forward in her chair as if she were at the theater, and Rocky began to clap slowly.

"Very good," he said in a bored sort of voice. "Do you do a matinée tomorrow afternoon?" He was devastating when he was sticking the knife in, I thought.

Marina, cued up for tears, decided to change tack.

"You know nothing," she said simply. "Nothing at all. You're just some rich guy with an empty heart! You can't bear the fact that I'm aching for Harry and not for you. You can't *conceive* of how I could love someone who can't offer me what you think you could. What the hell are you doing here, anyway?" she taunted. "I don't believe you give a damn about George. This is all about you. *You* wanting *me.*"

"On the contrary, Marina, I couldn't afford you," said Rocky idly, stretching across the table for the remains of my prawn cocktail. "Excuse me, kid. May I?"

I nodded. Rocky scooped up the rest of my starter.

"Damn good," he said. "Where's Mary? I like the sound of her."

Possibly because she had been lurking outside the door, Mary, ears burning, emerged only seconds later.

"Shall I clear?" she asked, looking straight at Rocky.

"Oh, sure, Mary. That was delicious. You have quite a talent."

She blushed and mumbled something about "never feeling appreciated" until Inigo glared at her.

"Why don't you sit down, Marina?" suggested Charlotte. "It's pork and carrots from the garden, next."

Marina ignored her and stubbed out her cigarette. Mary ignored Inigo and lurked around the back of the room, pretending to polish something.

"You still haven't told us why you're here," Marina said to Rocky.

"Right now, I just want to enjoy my dinner. If you're determined to upstage, I think you should do so elsewhere."

Marina frowned as if she hadn't quite heard right.

"Are you asking me to leave the room?"

"Just a suggestion," said Rocky.

Marina gave a strangled sob and fled upstairs, taking with her a full wine glass and Inigo's remaining cigarettes. Mary ambled out after Marina, her face bright red with excitement. *Oh, well,* I thought. That may have quelled Mary's admiration for her.

"Oughtn't we follow her?" I said doubtfully.

"Ah, leave her to stew," said Rocky. "You can always tell the ones who were never spanked as a child. Spoiled little bitch."

"But she looks amazing," sighed Inigo.

"The crazy ones usually do, kid," said Rocky. "It's a cunning disguise. You better get used to it if you're gonna make it in the music business."

Inigo picked up his glass and pretended not to look thrilled, but I could see he was, and I felt half-excited too, and half-afraid that Rocky was raising his hopes. What on earth would Mama think if she were here? Having Rocky to supper was a revelation to me. I realized that he was the first man to have eaten in the dining room since Papa died. It was something that I could see was not lost on Inigo, either. Instinctively, he sat up straight, he used his knife and fork, he dropped his exaggerated chewing routine—in short, he behaved. I wanted to scream with laughter, it was so strange. The focus of the room seemed to center around Rocky, even when he was not leading what was being said. He filled the room with something that I thought had been lost years ago, after Papa died. No, that's not right. He filled the room with something that I *did not even realize was missing.*

"Tell me, Penelope," he said. "Your family been here since the dawn of time?"

"My father's family," I said.

"Who was your *farther?*" asked Rocky, imitating my accent.

It was a funny question. Who was Papa? He was a million things that I would never know, and a million things that I had made him as a result of never knowing.

"His name was Archie Wallace," I said, as ever his name feeling high and strange in my throat.

"What did he do? Before the war, I mean." Rocky spread a thick layer of butter on his bread, which struck me as terribly cavalier.

"He worked in the city," I said. "Stocks and shares."

"Oh, yeah?"

"He wasn't frightfully good at it," I went on, faltering slightly. Charlotte gave me a whisper of a smile and I spoke a little louder. "He—he hated wearing a suit. He only did it for us. Well, for the family, just because it was what he felt he should do. Really, he was suited to being outside."

"And war's always been a great excuse to get the hell outside," said Rocky without irony.

"He was very brave," said Inigo suddenly, sounding about twelve. Unthinkingly, I stretched out my hand to him.

"He was very brave," I repeated in a whisper. Why couldn't I learn to talk about Papa like other people talked about their fathers? My heart crashed against my chest and Rocky, to his eternal credit, sensed my unease.

"I couldn't have done it myself," Rocky said. "I got this awful knee injury in a car smash when I was nineteen. Woulda been no good to anyone in a battle. So I figured that I could do something for the ones who weren't fighting, but hoping: the women, the kids, the injured. It made me feel better about not being out there. So I started making radio shows, making TV shows. Got rich so quick I was blowing my nose on twenny-dollar bills."

Inigo laughed loudly.

"Doesn't it make you feel guilty?" blurted Charlotte, which was something that I was wondering but would never have had the nerve to ask. "Making money that way? When people are dying by the thousand?"

"Not one little bit," said Rocky cheerfully. "If I could take people out of their heads for a little while, if I could give them a dose of fantasy, that was all that mattered. You can't put a price on escape."

In my head I could hear Johnnie sighing with agreement.

"That's why I want to get out of here," Inigo said restlessly.

Charlotte looked from Inigo to the ceiling. "You should be careful what you wish for," she said. "This place—Magna—I sometimes feel that it knows you want to get out."

"Goodness, Charlotte! Whatever do you mean?" I asked her.

"Oh, I don't know. I suppose what I mean is that I'd sell my soul for good shoes and a stack of good pop records. Who wouldn't?"

"And?" asked Inigo, baffled.

"Well, maybe we're just too modern," said Charlotte. "This perpetual craving we have—music and the cinema and good clothes—when this house is the most triumphant work of art any of us will ever know." She picked up her wine glass, uncharacteristically self-conscious. "I don't know," she said. "It's just how it strikes me sometimes."

"Here, here," said Rocky and he raised his glass. "To Milton Magna. May her pretty ghosts haunt us long after we leave her gates."

"To Magna!" we repeated, and sloshed our glasses into the air and into each other's glasses.

After dinner, Charlotte, Inigo, and I showed Rocky around the rest of the house. Like Charlotte, he had a beady eye for a good book and an interesting painting, but he was unafraid of admitting to not knowing things, too. He fired questions at us, and I am ashamed to say that Charlotte stepped in and answered more than Inigo and I.

"Tell me about the carvings on the staircase," he said, examining the detail on the horses' hooves.

"They're medieval," I said with the usual flourish.

"They're unusual. Why are they so ornate?"

"Um—"

I didn't want to tell him that I had ceased to notice the carvings a long time ago and that to me, it was simply the staircase, part of the familiar route from my bedroom to the hall. I remember being very hard on myself later that night as I lay in bed and recalled Rocky's questions and my halfhearted answers, but now I see that it would have been odd for me to have been any other way. Magna, to me, aged eighteen, was my home, and what I loved about it was not what anyone else would love about it, after all. What Charlotte had was a newly developed eye for beauty.

"Oh! I wondered that, the first time I came here," she said in answer to Rocky. "I looked it all up in this wonderful book my aunt has called *Great English Houses*. The ornamental design was commissioned by Wittersnake, the original owner of the house, who apparently had seen a similar design in a Dutch palace."

Rocky looked impressed and Charlotte gave me a pleading look.

"Do let's show him the Tapestry Room!" she cried. She turned to Rocky. "When I have my own house one day, an entire floor is to be based on the Tapestry Room. You've never seen anything quite so delicious."

Rocky grinned. "You should charge people for the tour," he said. Charlotte tossed her hair over her shoulders.

"How much have you got?" she asked, spinning off in the direction of the East Wing. Rocky and I lingered behind her at a slower pace.

"Don't you think someone should make sure Marina's recovered?" I said. "After all, she hasn't had anything to eat this evening. Do you think we were rather cruel to her?"

"Not nearly cruel enough," said Rocky cheerfully. "When we've finished looking around the house, I shall pack her into my car and take her back to London with me."

"I shouldn't think she'll be very pleased about that," I said, trying to hide my disappointment.

"That is of no consequence whatsoever. She's got away with far too much already. I came here to get her out of your hair and to give her a plain talking-to. Both of these things can be achieved by putting her in the car and driving back to town."

How I hated Marina! Now she had the pleasure of sitting in Rocky's wonderful car all the way back to London, something that I would have happily given my right arm to do.

"She came to find Harry," I said. "I don't think she wanted to leave until she had talked to him."

"Gee, Penelope, you sound as if you *want* her to get back with him!" said Rocky, looking at me from under his sooty eyelashes and smiling softly, and I felt the whole world swaying around me.

"N-no!" I stuttered. "I just think that I—oh! I don't know *what* to think anymore."

"She won't take him from you. That much I can promise you."

"How do you know?"

"I've already told you. She doesn't really love him and he doesn't really love her."

I bit my lip to stop myself from saying anything.

"*He* loves you," said Rocky. "The magician, I mean. I could see it. At the Ritz that night. She's lost him but she's damned if she's gonna accept it."

"This is the Tapestry Room," I said, thoroughly rattled.

An hour later, Rocky and Marina left Magna. She left without much fuss at all, climbing meekly into the passenger seat and waiting for Rocky to bid farewell to us all. Once inside the car, she opened her handbag and fished around frantically for something, and everything spilled out all over the seat of the car. She rescued her hip flask before anything else, her hands trembling. It was only then, I think, that I realized Marina was a drunk. In that moment, she seemed to shrink in front of me.

"Good-bye, girls!" called Rocky to Charlotte and me. "Keep sweet and beautiful!"

"Look after Marina," I called out suddenly.

"Oh, she'll be fine," said Rocky. I was glad that he said that. He could say anything and I would believe it. I didn't want him to go. I wanted to throw myself sobbing into his arms to stop him from leaving, but instead I smiled and waved and tried to push memories of waving good-bye to Papa out of my mind.

"Well!" said Charlotte as the glorious car roared off into the night, lighting up the drive and scattering rabbits into the hedges. "I can see what you mean about *him*!"

"I can see what you mean about *her*," added Inigo dreamily.

"Oh, shut up, Inigo," I said.

You see, it didn't really matter if Marina was a fool or a drunk or a silly pain in the neck. Boys just simply didn't mind. She was that powerful. You had to admire her for that.

EIGHTEEN

In the Garden and Out of Touch

FOR THE REST OF THE WEEKEND I had to keep asking Charlotte whether Marina had really been at Magna, for after she left, the memory of her arrival seemed nothing short of absurd. By contrast, the memory of Rocky at Magna felt entirely plausible. He had left evidence of his fleeting visit that filled me with longing—his whiskey glass in the library, his forgotten cashmere scarf on the hall table—yet all the time I found it impossible to place exactly what the longing was for. It wasn't as if I felt drawn to Rocky in the same way that I was drawn to Johnnie, which was, if I may be frank, utterly to do with Johnnie's monumental sex appeal. With Rocky it was more that I just liked being near him. I wanted to be *close* to him, yet I wasn't sure how I would feel if he tried to kiss me. He made me feel like a little girl and something in me adored that.

That evening, Inigo took a copy of the *New Musical Express* to bed and Charlotte and I made ourselves mugs of cocoa in the kitchen and, deciding that we were not a bit tired, set up camp in the ballroom with a stack of records and a pile of rugs to keep us from freezing to death. Listening to Johnnie and talking about Rocky was an odd sensation—like overdosing on delight—and I was relieved that Charlotte was staying because without her to share how I was feeling, I felt I may well have exploded with the effort of keeping it to myself.

"Why do you think he's never married?" I asked, opening a packet of chocolate sandwich biscuits and dipping one into her cocoa.

"I don't know. Maybe he's never been in love. Maybe he was let down."

"Who could let *him* down?" I sighed.

"He was wearing the most beautiful clothes," said Charlotte. "He must have more money than he knows what to do with."

"Imagine if he married Mama and saved Magna," I said idly. I don't know what made me say Mama and not me, but there it was, something in me had made me say it. Was it Rocky's age, or the fact that he made me feel just like Papa had made me feel when we said good-bye? I didn't know.

Charlotte raised her eyes at me. "Not such a silly plan," she said seriously.

We let the idea hang in the air for a moment and I felt the whole universe suspended. The pale moon was nearly full and shone through the ballroom windows like a silver ghost. It was a clear, clear spring night and the sky was peppered with stars and possibilities.

"Oh!" cried Charlotte suddenly. "A shooting star!"

We clambered to our feet and opened the window.

"It's a sign," she whispered. "We must find another one. Make a wish."

We stared out at the stars for the entire duration of "Walkin' My Baby Back Home" and then, just as Johnnie sang the last line, we caught one. I closed my eyes and breathed in. What to wish for? I wanted to wish for a man as beautiful as Rocky to love me, but something stopped me. Instead, I wished for the one thing that seemed even less likely than a marriage proposal. I wished for Mama to be happy again.

The next morning, Charlotte left on the early train and I telephoned Harry to tell him that there was no need for him to come and collect Marina, as the job had already been completed by somebody else.

"Who?" demanded Harry.

"Oh, just Rocky Dakota," I said breezily. I could hear Harry's sharp intake of breath.

"What?"

"Rocky came down here to get Marina, so you don't need to bother. She's back in London by now, so I expect she'll come knocking on your door any moment now."

"Why the hell does he need to go sticking his nose into other people's business?" snarled Harry. "Why didn't you tell him that I would be down to get Marina?"

"Because I didn't know that for certain!" I snapped back. "You told me to let her sweat for a while. When were you planning on coming to get her, anyway? Next week? Next month?"

"I was going to take the train to Westbury this afternoon."

"Well, like I say, no need. Rocky swept her off in his Chevrolet." I hoped Harry couldn't hear my jealousy.

"No doubt you wished it was *you* in the bloody car with him."

"That's neither here nor there," I said, unable to issue a denial. "Marina was drunk and mad, and she hates me."

"She doesn't hate you," said Harry. "She only *thinks* she does."

"Oh, what's that supposed to mean?" I demanded, but I thought about Rocky and how he had said exactly the same thing about Marina's love for Harry. How I hated talking to Harry on the telephone! I don't think we had ever managed a civilized conversation in all the time we had known one another.

"Do you still want her to hurt a bit?" I asked him.

He sighed. "Of course not. I'm not *that* much of a bastard, Penelope. It's been pretty hellish trying to pretend that I don't want her, I can tell you. I've been terrified she'll move on again. Perhaps she already has," he added ominously.

There was a short silence; then, on cue, I heard a distant, persistent ringing noise.

"The doorbell," said Harry needlessly.

"Off you go then. That'll be her, won't it?"

"I should think so. Nobody else would be crazy enough to leave their bed in this weather."

"Good-bye, then," I said stiffly.

"Good-bye."

There was a pause while both of us waited for the other to put the receiver down.

"Before you go," said Harry quickly, "I just wanted to say thank you.

You know, for everything, really. I can't deny that this whole thing has rat-tled rather out of control. You've been pretty marvelous, Penelope Wallace, actress *extraordinaire*."

"I've got my Johnnie Ray tickets," I said, embarrassed. Praise from Harry was not something I was very used to.

"Front row," he said.

"Front row," I echoed.

"Not long to go now," said Harry.

His words stuck in my mind long after I had replaced the telephone. It was what I had always felt but had never really believed until then. *Not long to go.* Until something, anything, *everything* happened to me.

Later that night, Mama arrived home and Inigo was driven back to school.

"Please, darling, make it through to the end of term, at least," said Mama, kissing him good-bye. "No more Radio Luxembourg," she added sternly. There was not much grumbling from Inigo—in fact, he even man-aged a cheerful wave from the car window as Johns lurched off down the drive, and I realized that meeting Rocky had made him impervious to the outside world. The short time Inigo had spent talking to Rocky had re-placed his restlessness with a steely calm and a willful determination. Mama seemed unsettled by his lack of grumbling.

"Do you think he's feeling quite normal?" she asked me.

"I shouldn't think so, Mama. When is Inigo ever normal?"

"I hope he's getting over this silly pop-music bug."

She didn't need me to respond to this. She knew there wasn't a hope.

I spent the rest of the afternoon weeding the fruit cage. Mama stood about watching me. (She did a great deal of watching in the garden.) I didn't men-tion Rocky's and Marina's visits to Mama because I knew she would have been horrified by the idea of not one, but *two* Americans in the house. There was a part of me that hated keeping anything from Mama—I would nearly always prefer her to know everything rather than rattle on in igno-rance—but my feelings for Rocky outweighed my honesty. I didn't want her to poison my mind with her prejudice, and I use that word in the truest sense. She was afraid of America and Americans. They represented change, and the modern world, and Inigo leaving us. If that wasn't a good enough reason to hate the place and the people, then what was? As I weeded, I kept half an eye on Mama, trying to guess what was going through her mind. I wondered if she trusted me; I wondered sometimes how much she actually *liked* me at all. In the past few months, I had felt more and more distant from her, less and less able to understand her. There were only seventeen years between us. When I was growing up, it had felt like only seven. It felt like seventy now. I reached for a trowel and began digging away at the border around the kitchen garden.

"Careful!" ordered Mama. "There's no need to hack away, Penelope. The garden is a living thing, you know."

She liked saying this. When she stood up to straighten her back a few minutes later, some of her gypsy-black hair had broken free from the head scarf she always wore when she stepped into the garden. Her cheeks were flushed pink from the energetic March breeze and there was a smudge of earth on the end of her nose. She could have been photographed right there and then for the front cover of *Country Life,* and she would have had every bachelor in England swooning at the newspaper stands.

"You're so lucky, Mama," I said suddenly. "You never get watery eyes and a red nose in the cold."

She laughed.

"It's true," I protested. "You suit the cold."

"Oh, Penelope," she said, shaking her head.

We stood together not saying anything for a short while, and all the time the wind roared around us and the daffodils blew and skidded about like drunk dancers at a Dorset House party.

"I've been thinking—" began Mama.

"Yes?"

"Oh, I don't know," Mama said restlessly. She pulled off her gloves and knotted her fingers together, looking worried. Framed against racing gray clouds with the dizzying swoop of the back lawn and the pond behind her, Mama looked like a beautiful Agatha Christie heroine about to break down and confess that yes, she did it, she killed him.

"What is it, Mama?"

"Sometimes I feel so small, don't you?" she said. "Especially at Magna. Like the house is too big for us—like it's swamping us. I have these odd nightmares, you know. I dream that the walls of the house just get wider and wider, until all of us are quite lost. I look for the front door, but it's grown so tall, I can't reach to let myself out." She had to talk quite loudly as the wind was so strong, which seemed fitting with what she was saying. She closed her eyes.

"Funny," I said. "With me, it's quite the opposite. I dream that Magna closes in on us, lower and lower. Inigo and I have to run and hide under our beds because the ceilings are falling down on our heads."

"Where am I when this is going on?" demanded Mama.

"Oh, you're with us, too," I said, but I lied, because oddly, Mama was never in my dreams about Magna.

Mama took out her powder compact and cried out in horror.

"What a sight!" she cried. "Why didn't you tell me I had a great splodge on my nose, Penelope?"

"I rather liked it," I admitted.

Mama dug around for her handkerchief to wipe the splodge off her face, but a sudden gust of wind took it out of her hands and off across the lawn. I lumbered off after it, hearing the *thud, thud, squelch* of my wellingtons on the grass. On and on went the hanky, cheerful and light as a child's balloon. Every time I nearly had it, it took off again. It was heading toward the pond.

"Hurry!" yelled Mama, mildly hysterical. "That one was one of the embroidered set of five Archie gave to me on my wedding day!"

But I was too late. A strong surge of wind sent the small square of lace straight into the pond. I waded in after it but it floated off, out of reach. I looked around for a large stick, but by the time I had found one it was too late and the hanky was irretrievably floating toward the center of the lake.

Mama looked distressed.

"Oh! Can't we do something?"

"With any luck it will float into the reeds and get stuck somewhere we can reach it."

"Oh, what does it matter?" asked Mama bleakly, and on cue, the heavens opened.

The sudden burst of energy had inspired me.

"Race you back to the house, Mama."

"Oh, don't be silly, Penelope."

But once I started to run, she couldn't resist the challenge—it was the competitive child in her that she had tried her hardest to squash, but never quite succeeded in destroying entirely. We ran from the pond to the back door—which was quite a distance, I might add—drenched within seconds as the rain fell harder and harder. Mama won because I slipped over at the last moment.

"And I've got shorter legs than you!" she cried triumphantly, whipping off her sodden head scarf. She was quite cheerful for the rest of the day after this. At teatime, she bought up the subject of Marina the guinea pig.

"I thought we could ask Johns to build some sort of outdoor hutch for your rodent," she said. "It really isn't on, keeping her upstairs. Not in a house like Magna, darling. Queen Victoria herself slept a night in your room, you know. December 1878, I think."

The roof is falling off and you're worried about the guinea pig in my bedroom? I wanted to scream.

"I bet she froze to death," I said sulkily.

"I shouldn't think so. She was a plain woman. Plain women don't tend to feel the cold."

"Plain but powerful," said Inigo, buttering a stale crust of bread.

Four days later, I went for tea with Charlotte and Aunt Clare. I had not heard from Harry since our last phone call, which had left me puzzled rather than relieved. After all that conspiring and discussion, the lack of communication felt odd, although there had been times over the months that had passed that I would happily have given my right arm *not* to talk to him. I half expected him to answer the door to Aunt Clare's flat and bundle me into the kitchen to talk about our next move. But there was no need for that anymore. He had got her back. He had won. *We* had won.

* * *

As it happened, Charlotte answered the door.

"We're midparagraph," she said wearily. "Come in."

Until that afternoon, I don't think that I had ever seen Charlotte look tired. Her long hair fell lank and greasy over her hunched shoulders and one could have packed enough kit for a two-week holiday in the bags under her eyes. I realized then how much of her appeal was in the glow of her skin and the brightness of her eyes. Without this, she almost looked quite ordinary. I don't think I completely understood how hard she had been working until I saw her then, and I felt suddenly ashamed. Charlotte was doing something substantial, something important. She was recording her aunt's stories for her, keeping them perfect, intact, forever. Whether or not the book went on sale for the rest of us seemed somehow irrelevant.

"We've been up since six," she explained, thudding back onto her seat and staring at the paper she had just fed into the mouth of the typewriter. "Aunt Clare wants to finish by tomorrow night."

I sat down quietly. Aunt Clare was lying on the daybed, her eyes tight shut, her arms stretched up into the air. Despite the fact that she had the gramophone playing softly in the corner, the room seemed quieter than usual.

"He was to become the only man I was ever to love with all my heart," said Aunt Clare. "No, no. Scrub that. *He was the only man I ever loved.* That's enough, isn't it? I mean, one can't state it more clearly than that."

She opened her eyes. "Half an hour, Charlotte," she said. "Then we'll carry on. Oh, good afternoon, Penelope," she said, giving a start. "I didn't hear you come in. I was away with the ghosts of my beautiful youth." She sat up. "What a *strain* this book is becoming," she sighed. "I can't think how anyone writes more than one of the damn things in a lifetime."

She gave me a small smile. "I suppose it's rather like childbirth—the mind chooses to forget the pain the body has gone through," she added.

"One would never write a single word if one knew the horrors that lay ahead," agreed Charlotte.

"But if you sell copies by the sack load, you may well forget the horrors," I said quickly.

Aunt Clare smiled. "You *are* encouraging!" she said. "Let's have tea, shall we?"

"Is—is Harry at home?" I asked falteringly.

Aunt Clare's face softened and I am certain her eyes filled with tears.

"Oh! You poor child!" she said, pulling out her handkerchief. "You poor child!"

"Has something happened to him?" I demanded, suddenly frightened.

"Who knows?" Charlotte shrugged. "He and Marina have vanished without a trace."

"Oh," I said. "Well, as long as he's alive and well—"

"Hear how brave the dear girl is!" said Aunt Clare. She pulled out her handkerchief. "I could *murder* him for what he's done to you, truly I could, Penelope." She stretched out her hand to me. I felt uncomfortable.

"I suppose he's always loved Marina," I mumbled. "I was never going to be more than a friend to him—"

"Nonsense!" snapped Aunt Clare, suddenly animated. "I never knew Harry as happy as he was with you, never knew him to be *himself* like he was with you. I knew from the moment you first walked into this room— I said to myself—there she is! The girl I never thought would appear has—has—"

"Appeared?" suggested Charlotte, stuffing a crumpet into her mouth.

"You agree with me, don't you, Charlotte?" demanded Aunt Clare.

"Oh, yes, Aunt. Of course. But you know, the only thing that really matters now is that Penelope realizes that she mustn't lose him."

I gave Charlotte a kick under the table, but she didn't respond.

"I have lost him," I said, hoping I sounded woebegone enough for Aunt Clare and practical enough for Charlotte.

"You haven't," said Charlotte. "But there's no point in running after him unless you know that he's the one."

"The one?" I asked stupidly.

"Yes. The one."

"The one what?"

"The one you'll love forever. The one you can't imagine ever being without," said Aunt Clare. She stood up. I noticed that her neat suit, usually such a snug fit, was almost hanging off her that afternoon. She had lost a great deal of weight recently, I noticed with surprise.

"Oh, Charlotte, cut me another slice of Battenburg, won't you?" she sighed.

"Goodness, Aunt Clare, you do look slim," I said.

She looked down at her hands.

"Do I? You see what this book is doing to me?"

"They should suggest writing one's autobiography as a solution for the overweight," said Charlotte. "And as for Harry, he's vanished with Miss Hamilton. She rolled up here on Sunday evening—"

"High as a kite, I might add," interjected Aunt Clare through a mouthful of cake.

"High as a kite," echoed Charlotte. "And Harry packed a small case and disappeared with her. He said he thought they might go to the coast for a few days, somewhere away from London where Marina won't be recognized."

"Anyone would think she was Marilyn Monroe!" I couldn't resist saying.

"Well, she's not. The Monroe woman always looks rather vulnerable to me," said Aunt Clare. "Nothing vulnerable about Marina. You know what she did, Penelope? She and Harry raided the wine cellar before they left. A whole case of liebfraumilch they took with them. Liebfraumilch! I ask you!"

I wanted to giggle.

"How vulgar can one be?" Aunt Clare went on. "I suppose they did me a favor—I'd been trying to get rid of the stuff ever since I was given it last summer. I would have thought Marina might know a little better. Still, one man's poison, etcetera, etcetera." She coughed.

"Do you think Marina's drunk it all by now?" asked Charlotte.

I pictured her and Harry on the seafront in Brighton, which was hard as I had never been to the place, but I had always imagined it being rather romantic in the windswept, pebbles-in-your-shoes way that English beaches can be. Something in me felt irritated that Harry had taken Marina there— he could at least have driven me to the sea on one of our planning meetings.

"Harry's always thought of Brighton as a rather romantic place," said Charlotte. "He likes pebble beaches and hot drinks, and watching the seagulls steal people's ice cream cones."

"What do you think they'll do next?" I asked. "When they tire of Brighton?"

"When he tires of Marina," corrected Aunt Clare darkly, "which he will—he will come home, tail between his legs, begging for you to take him back, Penelope."

"I've never seen Harry with his tail between his legs," observed Charlotte.

So we talked on, as we always talked at tea, yet there was something new with us in Aunt Clare's study that afternoon. Something I couldn't define, but something odd that I sensed in the ticking of the clock and the rays of dappled sunlight that crept into the room and shot bright into Aunt Clare's eyes.

"Do pull the curtains, Charlotte," she ordered. "It's too bright."

I never imagined that the sun could be too bright for Aunt Clare. At times, she had seemed too bright for the sun.

Twenty minutes later, I excused myself and left Kensington Court for Paddington.

"I hope Harry's all right," I said to Charlotte as we stood on the doorstep.

"Do you?" she asked.

"What?"

"Do you really hope he's all right?"

"Well, yes," I admitted. "I mean, I know that the whole idea was to get Marina back, but now that that's happened I find it difficult to imagine what's going to happen next."

"It's just as I thought, then," said Charlotte with a huge grin. She no longer looked tired.

"What is? Why are you being so odd, Charlotte?"

"You love him, of course."

"What?" I breathed.

For a split second, everything seemed to fit into place and the uncomfortable sensation that I had felt for as long as I could remember, of everything moving too fast, of not being able to hold onto myself at all, vanished. Then just as suddenly, it was back again.

"You're wrong," I said crossly. "I don't understand you, Charlotte."

"Nothing to understand. It couldn't be simpler."

"But it's not *true*! I wish you'd stop coming out with big statements that bear absolutely no relation to the truth. I think you do it for fun."

I sounded angry. I *was* angry. Charlotte just laughed.

"Methinks the lady—" she began.

"Yes. The lady *is* bloody well protesting," I snapped. "You think you know me so well, don't you? Well, you don't. This just proves it."

I turned and walked down the steps of Kensington Court, around the corner, and onto Kensington High Street, then all the way up to Notting Hill, Queens Road, and Paddington without looking back.

NINETEEN

Such a Night

IN THE SIX MONTHS that I had known her, I had never fallen out with Charlotte, and the prospect of not being her friend appalled me. Equally, her suggestion that I was secretly in love with Harry filled me with a fury so violent that I refused to telephone her for four days. With every new morning, I felt convinced that *she* was going to call *me,* but the telephone remained horribly, wilfully mute, and I began to wonder if she had simply decided that she had had enough of me. It was not a good time. I sat at the dining room table, and plowed through yet another essay, this time on *The perceived notion of the Lady of Shalott as a coquettish, shallow temptress*—adjectives which only served to remind me of Marina—and I wondered for the fortieth time where she and Harry were.

I think everything would have been bearable if Rocky had called, or written, or even whizzed up the drive in his lovely car for tea. I don't know what it was in me that assumed I would see him again—dumb optimism, probably—but I found it impossible to imagine that he might have vanished back to America without saying good-bye. I begged Mary not to tell Mama about Rocky's and Marina's visits, and although she had pursed her lips up very tight, she had agreed that it would be beneficial for everyone if not a word was spoken. I expect she thought that Mama would blame her for allowing strangers into the house. Personally, I felt certain that the only person likely to get into any trouble would be me. Mary, who had always pretended to disapprove of Americans to appease Mama, was finding it hard to forget Rocky.

"Such a presence!" she said to me, wiping away a tear as she chopped an onion. "And such smart shoes!"

Mama had been spending every waking hour in the garden, doing very little of any worth. Her financial concerns filled me with frustration. She was prepared to acknowledge that we couldn't go on as we were, and yet that was exactly what we *were* doing. Yet her fear of money was everywhere. Sometimes, when she opened her purse, her hands would tremble as though what was inside was contaminated. On another occasion, when I asked her for two shillings to buy stamps from the post office, her eyes shone with defiance and she gave me a ten-shilling note and told me to treat myself and Inigo to an ice and a magazine.

"But—" I began.

"Penelope, you take what you're given," she said ominously. I didn't enjoy my ice cream that day. Inigo did. He was quite capable of divorcing extravagance from guilt—a quality that I envied in him.

"You seem irritated, darling. Is anything wrong?" Mama asked me on day four of my "Not Speaking to Charlotte" campaign.

"No," I said quickly. "I've got rather a lot of work to get through."

"Isn't Charlotte helping you?" asked Mama slyly.

"We've had a slight row," I found myself admitting.

"Oh?"

"I think she thinks she knows me better than I know myself," I said, anger at Charlotte making me say more than I wanted to. Mama laughed.

"Oh, she probably does, darling," she said lightly. "Girls like Charlotte always do."

I was fairly speechless. Part of me was maddened by Mama, but another part of me was itching to pick up the telephone, so I waited until Mama had drifted off before stealing out of the dining room and into the hall. (I expect you are thinking that I spend most of my life making telephone

calls—Mama certainly thought this—and before I met Charlotte, I don't
think that I had ever made more than a handful of calls to friends. She was
the first person I had ever met who I can safely say was addicted to the telephone, and the addiction was catching. It made her lack of communication
over the last few days even more irksome.)

Charlotte answered straightaway.

"Hullo?"

"It's me. Penelope."

"Goodness, you sound serious, Penelope. Are you all right?"

"I'm not in love with Harry!" I blurted. "I think you were jolly unfair to
hurl that at me. I've never been in love with him. Surely you can see that,
Charlotte?"

There was a silence while both of us digested what I had just said.

"Hmmm," said Charlotte. "I think we'll have to agree to disagree." She
often came up with these little phrases, and she put on an irritatingly good
American accent when she used them.

"It's not a case of agreeing or disagreeing!" I hissed. "It's the truth, and
I'm sorry if that disappoints you in any way."

"The only thing that's disappointing is that you can't see it yet. Still,
there's time."

I felt myself flushing with annoyance.

"Why is it that you think you can dictate who I can and can't fall in love
with?"

"Oh, I can't," said Charlotte quickly.

"What about Rocky?" I asked. "Do I love him too?"

"Of course not."

"What do you mean, 'Of course not'?

"I mean, of course not. Oh, there's no doubt you've got a thumping great
crush on him, but then so have I. So would the whole country if they could
only see the way he pours champagne, or the way he looks at you when he's
talking, like he doesn't care about anything else in the world. He's absolutely, unavoidably delicious. It doesn't mean we're in love with him. We
just like being with him and we like the idea of him paying us attention.
That's quite different."

I tried to grasp what she was saying, but none of it seemed to make any sense.

"I've missed you," went on Charlotte. "Aunt Clare's been crippled by a terrible stomachache—too much talking, I'd say—so I've been roaming the streets staring at beautiful jewelry and wishing I was rich. Not much fun on one's own, I can tell you."

"Why didn't you telephone me?"

"I thought you needed some time to think."

"About what?"

"About you and Harry, of course."

"Can we *stop* talking about me and Harry?"

Charlotte laughed. "You *are* easy to tease," she said. "I won't mention it again if it upsets you that much. Oh, except to say that he sent me a postcard from Brighton."

"What did it say?" I asked, curiosity getting the better of me.

"It just said, 'Please feed Julian.' I suppose he thinks he's funny."

"It *is* rather snidge," I admitted.

"You know there's only one thing on my mind at the moment," said Charlotte.

"I know. Me too." I felt a shiver of excitement.

"Johnnie," we both said together, and exploded into giggles.

So Charlotte and I were friends again, and Harry was alive and still in England. The fact that he had mentioned Julian in his postcard was strangely uplifting—as if he was trying to let us know that Marina hadn't changed him as we feared she would. As long as Harry was happy, I thought, the world could breathe out again.

The next morning I woke up at seven o'clock with the sun in my eyes and my head full of birdsong. I pulled on the dress that Charlotte had made for me and walked with Fido to the village stores for a pint of milk and packet of Force and some pear drops. Dew sparkled along the verges and the fierce sunlight of the April morning heightened the whiteness of my arms and legs in the frail material of Charlotte's dress and I felt alien—a creature of the winter coming out of the underworld. As I passed the village green, I saw three girls of around my age sitting on the old bench and eating white-bread sandwiches and sipping milk from a pint bottle. They looked to me as if they had been up for the whole night. Having been sent away to board for five years, I had always rather envied the freedom of the girls who went to the school in the village—who always seemed part of a gang, always seemed to be laughing at some private joke. Fido, scenting cheese and ham, ran over to the girls and started begging for food.

"Fido!" I hissed, desperately conscious of Charlotte's dress. If Mama knew that I ventured outside the grounds wearing so little, she would have been mortified. Fido ignored me.

"Bloody dog!" I muttered under my breath and called his name again. By now, he almost had his nose in their food. The prettiest of the girls laughed and fed him a crust.

"Careful! Nearly got my hand!" she giggled.

I marched up to Fido and grabbed him by the collar.

"Sorry," I said. "He's never been very well mannered."

"We all love dogs," announced the second girl, a cheerful-looking blonde with saucer-round eyes and a smoky voice.

"Sweet," said the third, a mousy-looking type wearing acres of pink lipstick, and as she patted Fido, I noticed she was wearing a Johnnie Ray Fan Club badge on the lapel of her coat.

"Oh!" I cried. "You're a member of Johnnie Ray's fan club!"

Six beady eyes fixed on me. "You like Johnnie?" demanded the mouse.

"I love him," I corrected her automatically. "I'm going to see him next week."

"So are we," said the blonde quickly. "Where you sitting?"

"Oh—I—I don't know," I said, embarrassment preventing me from admitting that I had front-row seats.

"You don't know?" The mousy girl looked at me in amazement. "You're going to see Johnnie and you *don't know where you're sitting?*"

They looked puzzled, almost disgusted.

"Are you all going?" I asked them.

"Of course," said the blonde, not without hauteur. "We never miss Johnnie."

"Maybe we'll see you there," giggled the pretty one. "I've got me mum lookin' after Kevin that night, after all."

"Kevin?"

"Her son," explained the mousy one sagely.

I was a bit shocked.

"We always wait for Johnnie afterwards," went on the mousy one. "Last time he kissed Sarah."

The blonde blushed and covered her face with her hands.

"It's true!" she wailed. "I never washed for a week afterwards!"

"He kissed you!" I whispered incredulously. So it was possible. Charlotte was right.

"We wait at the side door, sometimes the front. We never know which one he's goin' to leave by so we look out from both. He has to get out some'ow, after all," said Sarah. She pulled a packet of cigarettes from her coat pocket and they all took one. Then they sat there, lighting up and leaving lipstick over their cigarettes while I stood by as if I were interviewing them. Behind the bench where they sat squinting and smoking stood the church, and behind the church stretched the fields that Mama had rented out for half the price that she should have. The bleating of newborn lambs and a sudden onslaught of fit-to-burst birdsong from the silver birches on the green made me heady with the shock of spring. Someone had altered the scenery overnight, and the village was another country compared to what it had been yesterday. The blonde girl was offering me a cigarette.

"Oh, no, thank you," I said quickly.

"Don't you smoke?"

"Oh, sometimes. Not this early in the morning."

I could hear a bat squeak of disapproval from Mama sound in my head. Was it right to sit on the village green and smoke with these girls? I feared Johns or Mary or Mama herself emerging and looking horrified. I knew that Charlotte would have had no such reservations.

"We're just standin' at the back of the Palladium this time," admitted the mouse. "We couldn't get the money for our tickets in time, so we just pay a couple of shillings to stand. Better than nothing. Still get to see 'im. And maybe get a kiss on his way out the building."

Sarah picked at the peeling paint on the bench.

"Your dog's eaten my sandwich," she observed coolly.

"Oh, rats, I am sorry," I gasped, pulling Fido away.

"He's spat out the tomato, Sarah," giggled the one with the big eyes.

"At least I'll be thinner for Johnnie."

"I'm Penelope," I said, aware of my smart voice and my long name.

"I'm Lorraine," said the mouse, sticking out her hand for me to shake.

"Deborah," said the prettiest.

"Maybe see you at the Palladium, then," I said awkwardly.

For some reason all the girls started to giggle and look preoccupied by something, and I realized that it was time for me to go. I dragged Fido away as, on the other side of the green, a gang of fifteen-year-old Teds appeared, suits immaculate, hair perfect. I kept my head down and walked on—and hated myself for doing so.

"Hey!" I heard one of the girls yell, and automatically I turned around.

"Say hello to your brother from us!"

They laughed some more, leaving me stunned. While Inigo had always been fairly famous in the village (he was too good-looking not to be), I was amazed that they knew I was his sister. I wandered back over to them.

"You know my brother?" I asked.

"Kind of," said Deborah.

"What's your brother into?"

"What do you mean?"

"Does he like Johnnie?"

"Oh no!" I laughed. "He won't listen to anyone but Elvis Presley."

"Who?" asked Lorraine.

"Elvis Presley," I repeated. The name, now so familiar to me, must have sounded odd to them. "He's big in Memphis, Tennessee," I explained. "Inigo—my brother—thinks he'll be big over here too before the end of the year."

I felt quite smug, dispensing this information.

"What's he sound like?" asked Lorraine suspiciously.

"Like no one," I admitted. "Like no one at all."

They said nothing, just looked into space as if they were all wondering what no one sounded like. I smiled again and moved away, and this time, just before I got to the edge of the green, they called out again. I swung around.

"We like your dress!" shouted Lorraine.

"Thank you!" I shouted, uncertain.

"Where d'you get it from?" called Deborah.

I remembered what Charlotte had said to me, *Girls will understand these dresses. Girls will want to wear them.*

"My friend makes them!" I called back. "She's going to be a famous clothes designer!" I awaited more giggles but they never came. The girls just nodded and stubbed out their cigarettes. *They didn't laugh.* I supposed that meant they believed me.

"Send our love to Indigo!" yelled Sarah.

Charlotte and I decided not to congregate at Aunt Clare's before we went to see Johnnie. Instead, we arranged to meet at Lyon's Tea Shop before the show. Johns was driving to London to fetch some spare parts for the car, so I had a lift all the way there and arrived twenty minutes before Charlotte. The whole of London seemed to be on fire that night; it was as if everything had altered because the city knew that I, Penelope Wallace, was going to see Johnnie Ray in the flesh for the first time. I had agonized over what to wear, taking into consideration the fact that I wanted Johnnie to notice me over every other girl in the audience, but also that I was not confident in anything very different from what every girl of my age liked to wear—a neat little blouse and stacks of lipstick and a full skirt, nipped in as tight as you dared at the waist. At the last minute, I decided to wear the pearls that my great-grandmother had left me in her will and Mama had stipulated were only to be worn on special occasions. If this wasn't a special occasion, then nothing was. I carried the little evening bag that my fairy godmother had left me for my night at the Ritz, which made me think of Harry. I smiled, knowing that wherever he was, and whatever he was doing with Marina, he would be thinking of me tonight, and wondering how my seats were and if I cried when Johnnie walked onstage. I fancied that Harry would have given anything to be with Charlotte and me. He so admired our devotion to Johnnie; it utterly fascinated him.

I ordered chips and ice cream and waited for Charlotte to arrive. The room was full of girls, some so young that they were accompanied by their mothers, and many of them wearing the fan club badges. The air was stifling hot—hot with steam and pots of tea and chatter and anticipation. I remember having to force my lips inward to try to stop smiling like a fool. The only thing that I could think was that *this was it*! This was the night I had been waiting for, and in less than an hour I would see Johnnie for real. The whole room seemed to breathe in when Charlotte arrived looking like the only girl that Johnnie would ever want to kiss. She wore a pale blue dress, belted high, and made demure by a sugar pink cardigan. She was wearing her painted shoes, the gold-and-green-spotted pair that she had designed at Magna. She had shaken off the tired eyes and weary shoulders of my last tea at Aunt Clare's and was pure dynamite once again, her long hair thicker than ever and lying loose down her back. Since every other girl in the room had piled her hair on top of her head in a chignon of some sort, and no one had ever seen anything like the green and gold splodges of paint on Charlotte's feet, she was pretty well stared at when she sat down. As usual, she looked entirely oblivious.

"Goodness, I'm too nervous to eat!" she wailed, but her green eyes widened as my chips arrived.

"Well, maybe I could squeeze in something," she conceded, and ordered a glass of wine and a hamburger.

"Where are the tickets?" she demanded, and I pulled them out of my bag like pieces of priceless treasure.

"Do you think everyone in this room is in love with Johnnie?" I asked.

"Of course. But no one else has seats as good as ours."

I had never been to the Palladium before. Charlotte had been once to see *Cinderella* with Aunt Clare and Harry two years before, and had fallen asleep halfway through the performance.

"I only woke up because Harry was making such a racket in the seat next to me. He got the giggles over the man playing the pumpkin and that was that," said Charlotte as we followed the stream of girls down the street and toward the front entrance of the theater. I had never seen anything like the crowds, and judging by the faces of the policeman, neither had they. There looked to me to be thousands of us. The most electrifying thing was knowing that everywhere I looked, people were there for Johnnie, and no one else; it was like meeting a long-lost branch of the family that one had always known existed, but had never actually encountered in the flesh before. We stood in neat groups, grinning from ear to ear because we just couldn't *not*, and wondering whether the girls in line ahead of us were prettier than we were, and if Johnnie would fall in love with them and not us. Just as we were nearing the entrance of the building, a tall girl with thick spectacles standing just behind us whirled around and hissed. "Papers! Over there!"

Charlotte and I turned around, and sure enough, two men with cameras and another two with thick notepads lingered at the edge of the throng, talking to two fans and scribbling furiously.

"Stupid, they are, talkin' to them," said the girl with glasses. "They'll only make them sound silly."

"He's just like no one else," I heard one of the fans saying to the reporter. "I won't marry until I marry Johnnie."

"She's in for a long bloody wait," giggled our new friend. "Everyone knows Johnnie likes blondes." She had an unbelievable accent.

"Where do you live?" I asked her, full of curiosity.

"Lancashire," she said. "I hitched my way here."

"Hitched?"

She laughed at me. "Yes. Stuck out my thumb and hitched."

I opened my mouth to reply but there was a great surge forward, and Charlotte and I found ourselves propelled up the steps of the building and into the entrance, where we stood blinking for a moment, our eyes adjusting from the bright April sunlight to the seasonless gloom of the foyer. Charlotte moved ahead of me, taking me by the hand.

"Follow me!" she commanded, and I surged forward again, my legs following automatically. I have never held anything as close as I did those tickets. The girls around me, while sweet as pie in their skirts and sweaters, had a wild glitter in their eyes. It was quite clear to me that they would steal, push, punch, collapse, and hitch for Johnnie—and I knew this because I would too.

Charlotte and I sank into our seats and stared up at the ceiling, then back at the crowd behind us and, giggling nervously, opened a bag of pear drops and listened to the low hum of excitement growing more and more urgent. Several girls came right up to us and asked how we had got such good seats and could they buy our tickets off us. One girl, who looked no more than thirteen, asked if she could exchange her coat and shoes for my ticket. I shook my head and she ran off and up the aisle without another word, a crowd of her friends pressing around her and staring back at Charlotte and me. There were boys there too (as there were wherever there was pop music), but it was the girls who had the power, the girls who defined the atmosphere that night, and we jittered for Johnnie's arrival with the blissful, magical urgency that one can only feel when one is young and modern and full of desire. Desire! It was the only word for it. Occasionally, an adult face swam into view—an usherette or someone selling ice cream—and I felt the gap between us, the brilliant youthquakers, the teen mob, and them, the sufferers and the forty-somethings, open up like a great chasm between us. They may as well have been three hundred years old—they may as well have been from another time entirely. They were nothing like us.

By the time the curtain rose for Johnnie, the excitement had reached fever pitch and Charlotte and I had become creatures I had never known before. As the piano became visible on the smooth blackness of the stage, the screaming accelerated and I felt a wave of energy that had started in the soles of my feet rise up through my body like mercury and set the tips of my fingers on fire so that I had to throw my hands into the air as if they were separate from the rest of me—I had no choice, it was simply happening, and I was watching and following.

"Johnnie!" yelled Charlotte, her words lost in the greatness of the noise from the crowd behind us.

"JOHNNIE!" I screamed, really screamed. It was like shouting against the roar of a tidal wave, but we couldn't stop. For there he was, beautiful, unreal, skinny as a rake, trembling like he had been shot through with electricity—Johnnie Ray. He smiled, and we felt weak; he spoke to us and we nearly collapsed. He started to sing "The Little White Cloud That Cried," and I would have not been surprised if the roof of the Palladium had caved in under the strain of such need for him. I looked at Charlotte and saw her cheeks soaked with tears, and she looked at me and we both yelled with laughter, for neither of us, for all that we had longed for this evening, could have prepared for the way that we felt at that moment. All around us, in the great velvet womb of the Palladium, girls stood up and screamed—possessed with a religious fervor; if Elvis was to become the King, then here was our John the Baptist, wailing and proclaiming on the stark wilderness of that stage—honey, locusts, and all. He held us in the palm of his hand, and there was no place in the world that we would rather have been. When Johnnie stood on top of the piano and beat the keys like a madman, unleashing his demons and driving us on to want more, more, *more*, I closed my eyes and framed the image forever.

Charlotte turned to me at the end of the song.

"Bloody amazing!" she said.

"Oh, help, I love him."

"I know," said Charlotte. "Isn't his suit divine?"

(To be truthful, I had barely noticed what Johnnie was wearing—it simply wasn't important to me—but Charlotte's eye for detail had missed nothing. She even remarked on the color of his shoes on the way home—why on earth she spent any time studying his footwear instead of his glorious face, I do not know.) As he started "Whiskey and Gin "and the cheering and the shrieking filled my senses, I thought of Mama, shattered and torn by the war and Papa's death, and I wished with all my heart that she could understand how it felt to be us that night—how it felt to feel eighteen and unbeaten, eighteen and alive.

"He's coming down!" yelled the girl behind me, and sure enough, halfway through "Walkin' My Baby Back Home," Johnnie descended from the stage and the noise grew so great that for a moment I felt almost afraid. Charlotte and I stood, transfixed, hands halfway up to our faces, waiting to see what he would do next. He came closer to us, closer and closer, until he was right beside us. Then, without warning, he leaned down and kissed me on the cheek.

"Hey, kid," he said, smiling. I said nothing, just stared, my mouth wide open while all around us the crowd roared and girls fell over each other trying to get to him, ripping the place apart with their screams.

"JOHNNIE!" filled my ears and my chest, and he smiled at the girls behind us, winked, and then, just as quickly as he had come down and spent that split second inside my life, breathing my air, being *my* Johnnie, he was back up on the stage again, wailing into the microphone, wringing his hands and shuddering with the emotion of the song.

"It happened!" Charlotte muttered, over and over again. "He found us! He kissed you!"

"I don't believe it!" was all I could manage in reply.

"Harry must have *known*," said Charlotte. "He must have known that these seats—well, that's why all those girls were so desperate to sit here—" she trailed off.

I knew she was right. Harry had known all along that if we sat where we sat, Johnnie would come right over and kiss us. He arranged it for us. It was then that the oddest feeling came over me. Johnnie started to sing "Cry" and my head was suddenly filled with the oddest, most jumbled-up feelings I had ever felt, and the more they jumped around inside my head, the more I struggled to join them up to make them into a proper picture.

On the way out of the theater, much to my astonishment, I heard someone calling my name.

"Hey! Penelope!" I turned around to see Deborah and Sarah, two of the girls from my episode on the village green.

"Oh!" I said. "Hello!"

Charlotte raised her eyebrows at me, questioningly.

"We're going to hang around and wait for him," explained Deborah in a low voice. "You want to come too?"

I opened my mouth and Charlotte spoke.

"Yes." She stuck out her hand. "Pleased to meet you. Charlotte Ferris."

Deborah glanced down at her shoes.

"Are you the girl who makes the dresses?"

"Yes, I suppose so."

They looked at her with new respect.

"Come on," ordered Sarah.

TWENTY

My American Heroes

WE STOOD OUTSIDE the stage entrance for what felt like an hour, but in fact was no more than about ten minutes. There were a large number of girls out there with us, all of whom looked as if they had done this sort of thing a million times before; some had seventy-eights and posters for Johnnie to sign, while others were just singing his songs and swaying, smoking and giggling in groups. Johnnie had fired everyone up. Some of the girls actually pushed through the barriers and a number of policemen appeared and pulled them away. I stood back, my mouth slightly open, amazed. Johnnie had unleashed something wild in us, something that had been there all along but had been squashed down by the war and our parents. He made us unafraid. All of us girls made a curious collection that night—all of us dressed up to the nines in what we imagined Johnnie would like best, filling the city night with the smell of cheap scent (Yardley's Fern on forty or so girls was asphyxiating beyond belief) and even cheaper lipstick—all of us desperate for something that we didn't know all that much about: a man, and love, and to feel grown-up and beautiful. Every so often the door would open and some unfortunate sound engineer or stagehand would venture out, prompting hopeful yells followed by wails of disappointment.

"Maybe he'll come out around the front," suggested Charlotte.

"We've sent Lorraine to check," said Deborah, who had an answer for everything. "If he comes out, she whistles, high as you like, and we bomb around the front in time to catch him. Personally, I think we're going to be lucky out here."

I had my doubts. Sarah, who had plastered herself in so much pancake powder and rouge that her unquestionable good looks had been entirely destroyed, was rustling around in her handbag. At length, she pulled out a bottle of gin.

"Swiped it from nan's bag," she giggled, unscrewing the lid. "You want some? It keeps out the cold. She took a big swig herself, carefully so as not to smudge her lips, then wiped the top of the bottle with her coat sleeve and passed it to Charlotte. Naturally enough, Charlotte accepted the offer.

"When in Rome," she muttered under her breath to me, taking a large gulp. "Ugh! Gin really is the most hideous sin of a spirit. What I'd do for a brandy," she muttered.

"You want some?" Deborah asked me. "Or do you not do gin? Not posh enough for you, eh?"

"Don't be stupid," I said, idiotically, and grabbed the bottle. Goodness, it was strong! I nearly choked, and my eyes watered, but I looked away so that none of them noticed. I passed the bottle back to Deborah, who passed it to Sarah, and before long nearly all of it had gone, because honestly, it was the only thing to do. I agreed with Charlotte. It was a horrible drink with the most insufferable aftertaste. Of course, it was also addictive. After another ten minutes, Lorraine appeared, striding toward us in a cream trench coat. They may have been girls from the village, but they certainly knew how to dress up. Lorraine looked at Charlotte and me with amusement.

"Oh, you made it!" she said. "Where were you sitting?"

"Front row," said Charlotte promptly. "Johnnie kissed Penelope."

There was a stunned silence.

"That was *you*?" wailed Sarah. "In 'Walkin' My Baby'? Why didn't you tell us you had that seat when we asked you the other day?"

"I didn't know it was any different from any other seat," I confessed.

"Bloody hell, and you call yourself a *fan*!" exclaimed Deborah, infuriatingly.

"How did you get your tickets, then?" asked Lorraine, full of curiosity.

"A friend," I said quickly. "He—er—got them to thank me for doing something for him."

"Tell him I'll do whatever it is, next time," sniggered Sarah.

"Yeah, how far did you have to go?" demanded Deborah, to gales of laughter.

I grinned. "It's not like that."

"Aw, come on!" Lorraine looked at me with new respect and offered me another swig of gin. As I drank, I felt like Marina. I suddenly wished that Harry was here to see all of this—to see us standing in my heels, gin-drunk on the corner of Argyll Street, waiting for Johnnie Ray under the dirty glow of the starless London night sky, my mind dizzy with the thrill of Johnnie's kiss, my heart surprised by the sudden swell of the incoming summer. That April night there were already cherry blossoms under our feet. Harry would have loved it, I thought, because although he had never understood our love for Johnnie, he understood what it meant to feel so strongly for something that it nearly sent you berserk. I pushed aside the feeling of missing Harry that had swamped me during Johnnie's songs that I associated with our afternoon in the Long Gallery, and hoped that he was happy with Marina. What was it about that afternoon that I guarded so preciously? It wasn't as if either of us had mentioned it since. . . .

"I don't think he's coming," moaned Deborah, after another five minutes had passed. Several of the other groups of girls had given up already, some of them sobbing quietly.

"He has to leave the building somehow," said Sarah impatiently. "Let's open another bottle, Deb."

We were the last group of girls left, an hour later, and certainly we were the most drunk. Charlotte and I flopped onto the pavement, and the others followed suit, crashing on top of each other in fits of laughter.

"Ow!" moaned Deborah. "You're on me foot, Lorraine!"

"What do we do now?" asked Charlotte.

"Go home, I suppose," said Sarah gloomily. "Bloody long way home, too."

"Hey, I'll swap you your shoes for me coat," said Deborah, prodding Charlotte's arm. She grinned.

"You can have them, darling," she said. "I don't want your coat, thanks awfully."

"Whass wrong with me coat?" slurred Deborah. Charlotte gave her one of her most shattering looks.

"There simply isn't enough time for me to discuss exactly what's wrong with your coat. I will try your gloves, however."

So we sat there, watching Charlotte try Deborah's gloves, and Deborah maneuver herself into Charlotte's shoes—not an easy task when one is as drunk as she was. I think another half an hour must have passed before the stage door opened again, and a man stepped out of the shadows.

"Johnnie!" cried Sarah weakly.

"No. He's gone, girls. You should get yourselves home to bed—it's gone half past midnight," said the man, small and dressed in uniform and about as far from resembling Johnnie as it was possible to be.

"Why didn't he come and say good night?" wailed Lorraine. "We've come all the way to London to see him."

"You girls'll catch your death," said the man kindly. "Shall I help you to find yourselves a taxicab?"

We staggered to our feet like newborn fawns, struggling to stay upright and holding onto one another as we started to sway.

"You tell him from us that we came all the way from Wiltshire to see him," said Deborah.

"You tell him—" began Sarah, but the man had already left us again.

"People are so—" she began, but her words were drowned out by the low throb of a car engine, and around the corner, blinding us all in the glare of the headlamps, came the huge, angular beauty of a foreign car. A car that belonged to the silver screen, a car that looked so out of place in London, it may as well have been a spacecraft. An American car.

"Christ!" offered Deborah, clasping her hand to her forehead. "The aliens have landed!"

"It's bloody Jimmy Dean!" yelled Lorraine.

Charlotte reacted quicker than I, which was not surprising, as my reflexes were steeped in gin.

"Shit! That's Rocky's car!"

"Rocky?" I repeated, my jaw dropping. "No!"

The car stopped just in front of us, and the driver's door opened.

"Maybe it's Johnnie's getaway vehicle?" cried Deborah hopefully, stumbling toward the vehicle, arms outstretched like a zombie.

"I'm afraid not," said that blissfully familiar American voice. "Penelope, Charlotte—what on earth are you doing?"

"Rocky!" I cried, and stumbled toward him. He caught me before I fell.

"Gin!" he said drily. "How extravagant of you girls."

"What are *you* doing here?" I demanded, unable to wipe the silly smile off my face, as my eyes drank in the beauty of his dinner jacket, the dark shadow of stubble across his jaw, and the wonder of his moustache.

"I just finished a dinner at Claridge's," he said. "The people at the table next door to ours were talking about Johnnie Ray at the Palladium and saying how there were queues of girls thronging around the stage door waiting to see him. I had a strange feeling I'd find you here."

Sarah hiccuped.

"But I didn't think I'd find you so damn drunk," continued Rocky, glaring at her. "Come on, then, you had better get in."

"What do you mean? We're waiting for Johnnie," I said petulantly. "Then we're going back to Charlotte's aunt's house."

"Not likely," muttered Charlotte. "I've just realized I've forgotten my keys."

"Waiting for Johnnie, my ass," said Rocky tersely. "If the guy has any sense, he will have left the theater before you guys even got out of your seats."

"But—" began Deborah.

"No buts. And who are this lot?" demanded Rocky of Deborah, Sarah, and Lorraine.

"They live in the village, they love Johnnie too" was the best I could manage.

"Right. You can all squeeze in, but let me warn you—if any of you throw up, you can get straight out again." I sensed he wasn't joking.

"Where's he taking us?" asked Sarah, gleefully piling into the back.

"He's quite safe, we know him," said Charlotte smugly.

"Red leather seats!" squeaked Lorraine. "Hey! The wheel's on the wrong side of the car!"

It was quite some feat, getting five drunk Johnnie Ray fans into the back of the car, but Rocky managed it. Deborah, Lorraine, and Sarah got the most terrible giggles and asked Rocky a series of ridiculous questions, the answers to most of which I was agog to hear.

"Who d'you have to bump off to get a car like this?"

He ignored this one.

"What kind of car *is* this, anyway?"

"It's a Chevrolet."

"Lord, I'd love Jack to see this."

"Jack?" asked Rocky.

"My son." Deborah blushed. "Gone to stay this week with a friend of me sister's up north. She's got a little boy called Kevin. Gets on with Jack, does Kevin. They like Johnnie Ray too, but London's no place for kids."

"How old are you, Deborah?" asked Charlotte, on behalf of me, Rocky, and herself.

"Eighteen. And Jack's only a baby, before you go thinkin' bad things about me."

I looked at her with a funny sort of respect. Through a mist of gin, she seemed much wiser than I. Yet Mama was the same age as Deborah when she had me, I realized with a sudden jolt. Both babies with babies, no matter what your background or the size of your house.

"Is this the same car that Johnnie has?" demanded Lorraine, who obviously felt Jack and Kevin were not gripping topics of conversation for the back of a Chevrolet.

"I have no idea, nor do I care."

"How can you not care about Johnnie?"

"I don't like the guy's wailing, all that continual weeping, sounding sad on the radio, breaking hearts in mono—it drives me crazy after a while."

Deborah laughed. "Breaking hearts in mono!" she exclaimed. "That's good."

"How d'you get the car 'ere in the first place, then?" persisted Lorraine.

"I had it shipped here from New York."

"Do you live in New York?"

"Sometimes."

"Do you have a wife?"

I sharpened my ears for the answer to this one.

"No," Rocky replied evenly. "Nor do I have any grandparents, pets, or children. And after tonight, I thank the Lord for that."

"Who do you most admire in the movie business?" asked Sarah conversationally. She seemed to be sobering up quicker than the rest of us.

"Myself," said Rocky automatically.

"Why are you here and not in America?"

"Business. Why are you?"

"We *live* here!" said Lorraine, who was as stupid as Deborah was sharp. She looked at him curiously.

"Are you famous?"

"Not at all."

"Are you rich?"

"Rich enough to be driving five girls all the way from London to Wiltshire in the middle of the night."

Charlotte and I, side by side in the front passenger seat, nudged each other.

"And what, may I ask, would you have done if I hadn't driven past the theater?" Rocky asked us without glancing our way.

"I don't know," said Charlotte dreamily. "Sold our bodies and souls to the cruel night, I suppose."

"Speak for yourself," I said primly. I saw Rocky fighting a smile.

We reached Westbury at five in the morning. The trio in the back had fallen asleep for the last hour of the journey, as had Charlotte beside me, her head lolling about on my shoulder. I stayed awake, if only because I knew that I would curse myself forever if I forgot any moment of a drive from London to Magna with Rocky.

"Wake up," I whispered to the backseat. "We're here!"

"Where do you girls live?" Rocky asked a sleepy-eyed Deborah.

"Oh, we'll get out on the green," she yawned. Giving a stretch, she dug into her bag.

"Can we give you anything?" she asked. "You've been so kind, driving us all the way home in your lovely car. I feel like a film star or something."

"Just promise me you won't go hanging around after singers for the rest of your lives," said Rocky, opening the door for them.

"Oh, I couldn't promise that," said Deborah.

The village green was eerily still. An owl hooted from the depths of the cherry tree and the shadow of a fox crossed the road in front of us. Now that we were out of London, the night was alive with stars and the moon looked as if it had been through one of Mary's vigorous washes; it glowed as white as Marina Hamilton's teeth. Charlotte climbed into the backseat of the car for the last part of our long journey. Rocky and I said nothing for the five minutes that it took to drive back to Magna. *Why is he doing this?* I thought. *He doesn't have to be here with us.*

"You should stay the night," I said.

"First sensible thing you've said tonight, kid."

Rocky bundled us out of the car and we crept into the hall—Mama never locked any doors, which Rocky found horrifying.

"I'll show you to the Wellington Room," I said, stumbling over a cricket bat. "Charlotte, you know where you're sleeping."

"Sure do."

I was achingly conscious of Rocky following me upstairs and I wished with all my heart that I had not drunk quite so much gin. I felt terribly weary and unaccountably sad all of a sudden, as if I had been smacked in the head. Rocky, sharp as a razor, sensed the horror of my hangover.

"Gin will make you feel more disgusting than any other spirit," he said, sitting down on the bed. "I suggest you get some sleep and drink a stack of black coffee tomorrow morning." He looked exhausted all of a sudden, his kind brown eyes small with tiredness. He gave a great yawn, like a lion. I wanted to collapse into his arms and say how sorry I was for putting him so far out of his way with such a long drive, but instead I hovered at the door like a child looking for approval.

"I expect Mama shall jump out of her skin when she sees you tomorrow," I said in a high voice. "Don't worry, I shall explain everything to her. Once she realizes that you were our knight in shining armor, she'll forgive you everything."

"As far as I'm aware, I don't have reason to beg her forgiveness," said Rocky evenly.

"Oh, you're American," I explained.

"Ah," said Rocky. "So the fact that I rescued her daughter from the streets of Soho won't come into it at all."

I grinned. "Not at all."

There was a pause, and I supposed I should leave and make my way back to my room, but something in me went on to ask: "How's Marina?"

Rocky looked surprised. "Oh, Marina? You didn't know?"

"Know what?"

"Well, she's back with George, of course. Just like I said. Decided that she couldn't live without him. They've already taken off to the States. So your magician might come back to you after all. I'd give him another chance if I were you. Marina's a powerful drug, but I don't believe he ever stopped loving you. How could he?"

"Oh," I whispered, too dumbstruck to say anything else.

When I awoke the next morning, I convinced myself that I had dreamed that last part of our conversation. After all, if Marina was with George, where was Harry? Rocky must have it wrong, I thought. But somehow, I couldn't imagine Rocky ever having anything wrong. He was simply the most right person I had ever encountered.

Although I set my alarm clock for eight, which was only three hours after I had gone to bed, I must have slept right through, for when I awoke, the sun was streaming through the window in a triumphant caught-you-out-there way. *Horrors!* I thought, fixing together the events of the night before. It was eleven o'clock. I dressed quickly and padded across the landing to Charlotte's room. There was no response when I knocked, and when I pushed open the door, she was still curled up in bed.

"Leave me alone, I'm dying," she croaked.

"You'd better hurry up about it. It's gone nine and Mama must have met Rocky by now." I crossed the room and pulled open the curtains.

"It's raining!" I cried in surprise, for the sunlight had been infused by a heavy downpour, the sort that you get in April, falling at a slant and lightning-bright in the sunlight.

I raced downstairs and into the dining room. For a moment or two, I stood at the door, looking in at the scene before me. I knew instantly. Rocky had been lost to Mama. I suppose it had to happen, but that didn't stop it from hurting, and it started to hurt straightaway, because I knew that there was no questioning it. She was laughing at something he had said; her whole body rocked forward toward him instead of recoiling back, back from everything, which was the stance I had known Mama for as long as I could remember. They were sitting together on the window seats, framed by the newly rich green of the lawn, while unbelievably, behind them, in the brilliant morning sky, shone the faint curve of a rainbow.

"Look!" I heard myself exclaiming, and I rushed over to join them, pointing at the sky.

"How glorious!" said Mama. She turned back to Rocky. "Do you get wonderful rainbows in America?"

He laughed at her, which was something that ordinarily she couldn't handle at all. "We sure do," he said.

"Penelope, darling, Rocky's been telling me all about last night," said Mama, smiling at me and taking my hand. "How lucky that he happened to drive past the theater when he did! He says the place was awash with drunks."

I blushed. "Sort of. We were fine. We just wanted to meet Johnnie."

"Won't you stay for lunch?" Mama asked Rocky. "We're not having much, just a chicken pie, but we'd love to have you."

Rocky looked at me and I knew that he was asking for my approval. There was a light but friendly challenge in his eyes, as if to say, *Go on! You said she hated Americans, but I'm doing pretty well so far!*

"Of course you should stay, Rocky," I said.

Knowing that I couldn't have Rocky for myself was one thing, but knowing that the reason for this was because he was falling in love with my mother was quite another. He stayed for lunch and I tried not to stare as he held Mama's eyes in his for longer than he had ever held mine, and she actually blushed for the first time in living memory. There was something fascinating about Mama that day; she was like a butterfly emerging from a cocoon, fluttering toward Rocky's light with hesitant new wings. Shattered by Johnnie and gin, I excused myself after lunch, saying that I was going to have a lie-down. Upstairs, Marina the guinea pig rushed out to greet me and I fed her one of Mary's carrots and stared out of my window until the light faded from the sky and the sunset spilled an inky pink and red over the horizon. At four o'clock I turned on my bedside lamp, opened my notepad, and began to write. I didn't stop until eight, when I was called for supper. I called the story *Cry* after Johnnie's song, and I felt, somewhere deep inside myself, that it was the best thing I had ever written. It was certainly the most true. I folded it into an envelope and walked down to the postbox in the village straightaway. The day that I always knew would arrive was here, but it didn't hurt like I thought it would. Certainly, it ached, but it was a peculiarly sweet ache, like giving away your last pear drop to someone you know will appreciate it more than you. Not that I'm comparing Rocky to a pear drop, really, but, oh, I think you understand what I mean. That evening, Charlotte telephoned me.

"You'll never guess what's happened," she said.

"What is it this time?"

"Marina's vamoosed back to America with George."

Although I had already heard this from Rocky, it still shocked me.

"I don't believe it."

"*I* do. Harry hasn't reappeared. I suppose he can't face us all after this. I feel rather sorry for him, which is saying something. I don't think I've ever felt sorry for Harry before in my whole life."

He and I both with broken hearts, I thought. It was never supposed to be like this.

The following week was a revelation for me, for Mama, and for Magna. Rocky, who had been booked to fly back to America the day after he dropped me home, postponed his flight and said that he would be in England until the end of the month. He telephoned us every other day, and he came down to see us for dinner on Saturday night. Not once did Mama and I talk about him when he was not with us. It felt forbidden, as if talking about it was recognizing the one fact that Mama was too frightened to admit: He was replacing Papa. He was making her happy. What did I do? I wrote a great deal in my diary, and walked through the bluebell woods thinking hard about it all, and found that I could see the picture far more clearly now than I had that day on the train when I first encountered Rocky, or that evening at the Ritz, or even the night that he had driven us all home only a week ago. I could see, for the first time, that there had never been any serious possibility of Rocky falling for me. I was too young (though when one is eighteen and delirious about a man of forty-five, one feels terribly, terribly grown-up, and not at all like the guileless ingenue that he sees one as at all), but more than that, Rocky understood very little about what was important to me, and me to him. The twenty-seven years between us had included a war that I could barely remember and that he would never forget. But Mama . . . she instinctively understood things that I couldn't begin to comprehend. And I suppose, above almost everything, was the fact that had always been there, staring me in the face. She was just too beautiful for him *not* to fall in love with. I felt, for all this, oddly proud of Mama. It amazed me how little it actually hurt. Then I started to realize that the reason it hurt so little was because it wasn't actually Rocky that I was missing. It was somebody else. Only once I realized who it was, it started to hurt more than ever.

I invited Charlotte to Magna on Saturday night, when I knew Rocky was coming for dinner again. I wanted her to see for herself what I had told her about on the phone. Of course, I was also hoping for news on Harry and I hated myself for hoping. Inigo was also home, and full of excitement at Rocky's presence. Rocky had barely taken off his coat before Inigo ushered him into the ballroom.

"I've been playing guitar," he announced, pushing back his black hair. He seemed to have grown up a great deal since the beginning of the year, or perhaps since he had last seen Rocky. He looked taller, more like a man, and less like the little boy I had always known.

"Let's hear you," said Rocky.

Inigo looked hesitant, and I knew he was worrying about Mama.

"She won't be down for twenty minutes," I reassured him, knowing that Mama was currently soaking in the bath, waiting for the moment to make her entrance.

"You don't want your mother to hear you play?" he asked Inigo.

Inigo looked uncomfortable.

"She doesn't like me playing the guitar. She thinks it's never going to get me anywhere."

Rocky shook his head.

"I've chosen the ballroom," Inigo went on, "just because the echo sounds nice in here. Kind of like a record."

"Ah, no," said Rocky seriously. "If you're any good, you'll sound good anywhere. Why not play to us in the library?"

Inigo looked a bit taken aback, but agreed straightaway, so we all trooped into the library and took our places—Charlotte and I sat on the daybed, she in her painted shoes. Inigo pulled his guitar out of its case.

"I thought I'd play you an Elvis Presley song to start with, just to get you feeling good," he said, as if we were an audience of five hundred rather than three. Rocky laughed.

"Go ahead."

Inigo cleared his throat and looked down at his feet, and I sensed him charging himself full of confidence and I felt terrified for him, yet absolutely convinced that if anyone could pull off the feat of playing to a man like Rocky in a room like the library at Magna, then he could. His fingers struck hard at the guitar and he started to sing, *really* sing, and his voice was like a record, perfect and dangerous and shot through with conviction. He chose a song that Luke had sent to him only a couple of weeks before, called "Heartbreak Hotel," and it had an incredible range—one minute high and raw, the next low and tender. When he sang, Inigo's eyes never left our faces; he was unafraid of challenging us to look away, which, of course, none of us did. He was better than I had ever heard him, spine-tinglingly magical, and I felt a flutter of sorrow as I realized that this was the start of the end— that Inigo's life was going to change forever if he carried on performing like this. As he came to the end of the song, I couldn't resist looking at Rocky for his reaction. His face looked unchanged, unmoved, and for a second I felt alarmed. Surely he couldn't expect anything more than that?

"You got another one, kid?" Rocky asked him simply.

"Um, yes. Of course." Inigo grinned and broke into "Mystery Train," which was, if anything, even better than the previous song.

"Okay, play me that one again," ordered Rocky, lighting a cigarette, certainly more animated this time. Inigo grinned, pulled out his handkerchief to mop his brow, then tossed it at Charlotte, who caught it and pretended to swoon. This time when he played, Charlotte and I sang too, at the tops of our voices, thumping our legs with our hands, clapping, and whooping. We did not notice Mama until the end of the song, when we heard the sound of clapping, and we all turned around only to see her standing in the doorway of the library, tears streaming down her face.

"Mama!" cried Inigo, putting down his guitar at once and stumbling toward her. But before he could get to her, she had run from the room with a stifled sob. Moments later, I heard the sound of her footsteps in the hall, then the dull thuds as she raced upstairs.

"May I go after her?" asked Rocky at once.

"Let me," I said. "Charlotte, pour Rocky a drink, will you?"

Charlotte, who was used to dramatics, nodded.

"You were *that* good," she said to Inigo. "I would cry, if I were your mother."

But Inigo didn't smile. "She makes it so hard," he said, full of frustration and really shouting the word "hard" through clenched teeth. "I feel awful now."

"No one should feel awful after a performance like that," said Rocky. He spoke evenly, without much emotion, but I sensed that what he was saying was a big deal.

I found Mama upstairs at her dressing table, removing her makeup with cold cream and a tissue.

"What are you doing, Mama?" I asked her, aghast.

"Taking off this filthy stuff," she said, scraping away at her beautiful cheekbones. "I can't think why I was wearing it in the first place."

"I don't understand," I said, but I think I did. Her bedroom, usually so tidy, was littered with clothes—stockings and dresses, shoes and blouses lay scattered all over the carpet and bed. It looked like my bedroom before I went out to meet someone exciting, and I realized that Mama had been agonizing over what to wear for Rocky. For the first time since Papa had been killed, it had actually mattered to her that she should wear something to please someone else, rather than herself. I moved a Dior skirt off the bed and sat down.

"Did you—did you think Inigo played well?" I asked her falteringly.

"Of course he played well. He plays better than all the records he feeds himself with," said Mama, ladling more cream onto a fresh tissue.

"Aren't you—aren't you a little proud of him?"

"Of course I'm proud! How could I not be *proud*? I'm the boy's own mother, for goodness' sake, Penelope!"

"Why don't you show it, then, Mama?"

"What? And encourage him to leave us? To go to America like Luke?" She wiped even harder at her eyelashes.

"But he's so *good*, Mama. You're not being fair on him. He could have a real chance, and I know Rocky thinks so too. He could make proper money."

"Why can't he stay here and do it?" Mama rubbed at her mouth, and the tissue was stained bloodred with her lipstick. Now clean faced, she stared at herself in the mirror. A huge tear plopped onto the glass top of her dressing table.

"He might only have to go for a short time," I said. "Then he would be back to see us, back to Magna, and perhaps he'll make enough money to keep the place going. Can't you ever think of the good side of things, Mama?"

"I don't want this place," said Mama. There was a silence while both of us took in what she had just said. "I don't want to live here anymore."

I felt a wave of sickness pass over me.

"Mama, don't say that! You don't mean it! Magna's our home, it's everything—"

"It *was* everything," said Mama. "It was everything when your father was here too."

"Oh, Mama! Don't start—"

But she wasn't listening. She stood up and started pacing in front of me, but I don't believe that she was aware of moving at all. Irrationally, I noticed how loudly the floorboards were creaking.

"I loved the place," Mama hissed. "I loved it because he loved it. I could have lived happily ever after at Magna if Archie had stayed with me," she was talking quicker and quicker—it was as if the truth was dawning on her and she needed to speak it before it crept away again. "But what do I want with the place now? We rattle around the house like three little skittles waiting to be knocked down—every corner I turn I'm reminded of him, everywhere I look, I see his face. I'm thirty-five—"

"Thirty-five! That's right! You're thirty-five!" I interrupted. "Do you realize how young you are Mama? How *young*!"

Mama's face crumpled at these words, and she slumped back onto the chair in front of her dressing table again. Without her makeup, she looked like a little girl of twelve. I have never seen anyone look so lost and I had never loved her as much as I did in that moment. She looked down at her hands and twisted her wedding ring around her finger.

"Thirty-five years old and what am I to do for the rest of my life?" she whispered. "Sit here and watch the house die because I can't ever sell it or leave it? Because when I gave my heart to Archie, I gave it to this great mass of stone too?" She spat out the word "stone," and it fell heavily between us. "Sometimes I—sometimes I think he shouldn't have married me at all. Maybe he would have been better off with someone else, someone older, someone with more confidence—"

I was crying now, quietly, because I hated scenes, and the last thing I wanted was for anyone to hear what was going on.

"I remember when we were first married, Archie warned me that it wasn't all going to be parties and long baths. I didn't really hear him—I thought I'd arrived in Paradise—I'd never seen such an unbelievable building. I thought he was quite mad. Now I know exactly what he meant. Once the gold starts to fade, you're left with nothing but steel bars."

"But Rocky, he's rich—"

"You think he might marry me and take on this place," said Mama with a sad smile.

"Well, it's not such a silly thought—"

Mama shook her head. "It's out of the question, Penelope. Not just because I could never live at Magna with another—a man who wasn't your father—but because I could never marry again. Never. I hate myself for thinking, even for one second, about Rocky Dakota. An *American*, too!" She gave another sob. "Thank goodness Inigo played the guitar tonight. It made everything clear again. I want that man out of my house before he whisks Inigo off to Hollywood."

"But, Mama, he's been so wonderful to us!" I cried. "We can't throw him out now, not before supper!"

"We certainly can."

"But don't you like him? Don't you like *talking* to him?"

For a second Mama's eyes filled with pain.

"I'm sorry, Penelope. Would you go downstairs and tell him that I feel it would be inappropriate for him to remain here?"

Charlotte and Inigo were loitering in the hall, pretending to play backgammon.

"Is Mama okay?" asked Inigo.

"Of course not," I snapped. "You shouldn't play the guitar in the house at all, Inigo. You know she can't stand it. Go up to her and say you're sorry."

Charlotte stood up. "Should I be here at all?" she asked me under her breath.

"Oh, please stay," I begged her. "Where's Rocky?"

"In the library."

He was standing by the fireplace with a glass of whiskey in his hand.

"What's going on, kid?" he asked me, his voice full of concern. Lovely Rocky, with his soft voice and his kind eyes. Rocky, who could have made Mama happy.

"She thinks it would be inappropriate for you to stay for dinner," I said bitterly. "She thinks it would be best if you left."

He drained his whiskey. "Tell her she looked beautiful tonight," said

Rocky. He crossed the room to where I was standing, trembling with the strain of the last few minutes.

"She needs you," he said simply. "Look after her."

Five minutes later, we heard the scrunch of the Chevrolet taking off down the drive.

We had duck for supper, and none of us mentioned Rocky's name. Mama talked of the garden. We were back at the beginning again, I thought in despair. No pain, not even the pain of realizing that Rocky had fallen for Mama, could compete with the agony of realizing that she was incapable of returning that love.

TWENTY-ONE

The Lost Art of Keeping Secrets

INIGO RETURNED TO SCHOOL the next morning without a word to me about the night before. Like Mama, he was quite capable of closing himself up when he wanted to, and I feared he had been more affected by the events of the night before than I could ever know. There was a great weariness at Magna, as though something had altered that could never change back again. Mama, determined not to mention our conversation of the night before, spent the day outside in the garden with Johns. Mary arrived at lunchtime with a terrible cold. I wanted, more than anything, to get out of the house.

"Come to London tomorrow," begged Charlotte. "We're celebrating the end of Aunt Clare's book. She's holding a small gathering at teatime for the chosen few. Champagne and cakes. Naturally, she's hoping you'll be there."

"Does Harry know about it?" I asked, trying not to sound too hopeful.

"I shouldn't think so. I imagine that even if he did know about it, he'd run a mile."

I smiled. "I'll come," I said, "if only for the tea."

"I—I took the liberty of inviting Christopher."

"You did? Was that at Aunt Clare's request, or have you been missing the old dandy?"

"Oh, shut up. And anyway, he's not as old as Rocky," said Charlotte after a pause.

*　　*　　*

Yet for the first time ever, I set off for Aunt Clare's without a hunger for cakes and scones. I wore my smartest tea dress—Aunt Clare would expect nothing less—and carried a bunch of early bluebells from the fairy wood, and even though I knew that Harry was not going to be home, I felt more nervous than I had ever felt in my life. I bought a paper on the train and tried to concentrate on pompous articles about flying saucer sightings—of all things—but found myself incapable of taking anything in. I had a dim sense that if only I could see Harry, this great feeling for him would be cured once and for all. He was too short, too weird looking, too in love with Marina—and I felt certain that if I could only be with him one more time, the ache for him would vanish. He would be just my friend again, the only boy with whom I would happily spend half an hour in the ladies' bathroom in the Ritz, or having a picnic in the Long Gallery. For the tenth time since boarding the train, I checked my reflection. I looked paler than ever, but what else could I expect after nights on end with so little sleep? Rubbing rouge into my cheekbones, I wondered where Rocky was and if he had forgotten all about Mama already. He was most likely back in America, maybe enjoying breakfast with Marina and George, laughing over the English and their funny ways. Yet somehow that scene didn't ring quite true. *Wherever he is,* I prayed, *make him happy.*

It was one of those London afternoons that makes one feel like dancing as if in a musical film—the cherry blossoms were at their sugary peak all the way down Kensington Church Street, and the blue sky was merry with puffball white clouds. I thought how odd it was that Charlotte and I had only really known each other in the cold, and I wondered if the heat suited her personality as much as the winter months. I felt at once comforted by the noise and bustle of London—Magna had felt quieter than ever since Rocky had left before dinner that night—and because I had arrived early, I stopped in to Barkers to look at the new season's hats. In the record department I could see Bill Haley and His Comets' new record *Rock Around the Clock*, and in a fit of generosity, and because I felt like he had been given a raw deal of late, I bought it for Inigo. There was just time to pop to the post office and send it off to him at school before tea. This simple act, combined with the bliss of the sunshine, should have soothed my nerves, but alas, as I stood on the steps of Kensington Court, I felt my legs trembling. There was nothing for it but to ring the bell and go in. *He's not even there, I told myself again.* In my head I heard Johnnie singing "Whiskey and Gin." *Help me, Johnnie,* I thought. Phoebe answered the door.

"They're upstairs," she said, taking my coat. She looked even more miserable than ever, her skin greasy, her blouse practically hanging off her skinny frame. Miserable without Harry, I thought, with a pang of empathy. She took the bluebells from me and I fancied I saw them sigh and hunch in her fist. Never was there a girl so suited to unhappiness. I made my way up to Aunt Clare's study and, taking a deep breath, opened the door. The quiet emptiness that had filled the room when I was last there had utterly vanished, replaced by a carnival atmosphere. The room was packed. I was thankful that no one took the slightest bit of notice when I walked in. Charlotte extracted herself from the crowd.

"Do come and meet Patrick Reece, the great theater critic," she said to me with a wink. "He hasn't seen Aunt Clare in years, but he couldn't resist turning up this afternoon."

"Terrified he's going to appear in the book, I imagine."

"With good reason," whispered Charlotte. "He makes up most of chapter twelve."

"How do you do?" interrupted Patrick, flashing me a beaming smile. "So nice to see some young here."

"Yes." I couldn't think of anything else to say. I kept thinking of Hope Allen and cocaine and the engagement party at Dorset House and Harry and I playing Dead Ringers.

"I suppose you know Harry too?" asked Patrick. *Was he a mind reader?* I wondered in alarm.

"Yes, I know Harry," I said with a forced smile.

"You're in love with him, I presume?"

I felt the heat rise. "Whatever makes you say that?"

"Oh, I don't know. Those wonderful two-tone eyes he has. Devilishly attractive to the ladies, I gather."

I was saved from a response to this by Aunt Clare, who bustled up in a magnificent red-and-black-striped dress with matching shoes. There was none of the weariness of my last visit. She sparkled.

"You mustn't monopolize this dear girl, Patrick," she scolded. "Penelope, dear, go and get yourself a glass of champagne, won't you?"

Gratefully, I slipped off to find myself a drink, but not before overhearing Aunt Clare's next comment.

"Delightful child, so intelligent! Archie and Talitha Wallace's eldest, you know," she murmured.

"Talitha Orr, that was?" demanded Patrick throatily.

"Indeed."

"Gracious, she looks nothing at all like the dam and everything like the sire. How jolly interesting. Is she engaged, Clare?"

"Not at all, and more's the pity. I longed for my Harry to fall for her, but it seems he was too smitten by the ghastly American girl."

"Ah."

I missed Aunt Clare's next comment and nearly sent Phoebe and the drinks tray flying in my rush to get to Charlotte. She was taking a break from the throng just outside the hall and stuffing her face with a currant bun.

"Sorry to dump you with him," she apologized. "I'd had him for nearly an hour. Goodness, right now Aunt Clare's study has to be the bad-breath capital of the world. Men over sixty simply should not be allowed to drink champagne, it's just *too* hideous."

"What's happening next?"

"Aunt Clare's going to read an extract from the great book," said Charlotte, "a passage that I've selected about a chance encounter between her and a tiger cub in India. Once that's over, I suggest we scout around the room for any remaining drink and get happily sloshed."

"I should go home tonight," I said. I didn't like to think of Mama at Magna on her own at the moment. Charlotte ignored this.

"Come upstairs and let me show you some of my new designs," she said.

On the way out of the study, we bumped into Christopher.

"I heard you were going to be here," I said delightedly. "I like your jacket."

"Rather beautiful, isn't it?" agreed Christopher. "But then, it should be. She charged me enough for it."

"Who?"

I looked at Charlotte, who had the grace to have gone slightly pink.

"I think it turned out rather well," she said.

Christopher looked at her with genuine affection. "She's a talented girl, loath as I am to admit it. I've had nine compliments on the jacket already this afternoon."

"And eight of them were from Patrick Reece. You know he tried to push some cocaine on me when I arrived? I thought those days were behind him."

We stayed in Charlotte's room for longer than was strictly polite, but eventually Charlotte decided that the breath and Aunt Clare's reading could be put off no more. Reentering the study was like walking into a furnace—the voices had grown louder with drink and the windows were foggy.

"Open the window, Phoebe," ordered Charlotte, "and get me another drink." Once Charlotte had her glass in hand, she tapped on the side with a teaspoon, but it didn't begin to cut through the wall of gossip.

"Excuse me!" said Charlotte, and again, louder, "EXCUSE ME!"

Everyone fell silent and looked at Charlotte in amazement, as if she had just taken off all her clothes.

"I'd like to introduce the reason why we're all here this afternoon," said Charlotte in her clear voice. "She's an angel and a slave driver to boot. The one and only, once met and never forgotten—Her Serene Highness—Clare Delancy!"

There was a great whoop of applause and Aunt Clare moved over to the fireplace where Charlotte was standing.

"I've been with this remarkable book from the start," Charlotte went on, "and I thought it would be rather nice for everyone if tonight, Aunt Clare read an extract from her memoirs."

A few people murmured in agreement.

"If you would all take a seat or remain standing just for a few minutes," said Charlotte, "Aunt Clare will begin."

Aunt Clare picked up the manuscript, looked at the passage Charlotte had selected for her to read, and placed it back down on the table. Charlotte frowned. Aunt Clare sighed and smiled.

"I would like to read you an extract that my darling niece hasn't even heard," she said, pulling two pieces of paper out of her bag. They were covered in smudgy blue ink.

"I had to wait until I'd finished the rest of the book until I wrote this bit," she said. "I hope you don't mind, Charlotte."

Charlotte looked bemused. By this stage, the room was simply humming with people—some were standing in the corridor peering in as far as they could. I had been squashed rather further into the room than I would have liked and felt a wave of sudden claustrophobia. I felt awkwardly giant, for next to me stood a woman half my height and five times my age with the most enormous head of white hair and long fingernails, while on my other side was an eccentrically dressed man of sixty-five-ish who can't have been far off dwarf status, and as the exception that proved Charlotte's bad-breath rule, he smelled overwhelmingly of peppermints and snuff. I tried to move my feet a little and nearly toppled over. I caught Charlotte's eye and saw her trying not to giggle.

"I'd like to read you the prologue to my story, because it is, in many ways, the most important story in the whole book," began Aunt Clare, headmistress to pupils, and the force of her presence and the richness of her voice was such that the whole room fell silent at once. "It is simple truth and it happened in 1936. What more could anyone want from a prologue?" She glanced down at the typed page and began to read.

"*I always felt there was a resonance in the fact that my years exactly matched those of the war and of the century, and as a result, I measured the world in the same way that I did my own existence. When I was ten, the world around me was ten and growing fast. Equally, the century and I began the Great War as children of fourteen. We ended it women of eighteen.*"

Aunt Clare paused here and for a second I thought I saw a flash of uncertainty in her expression. *She's nervous,* I thought, *and thank goodness for that.* She cleared her throat and went on, a little too fast at first, then slowing down as she progressed, so that every sentence could be captured in the imagination of her audience. I don't think that there was one person left in the room by the time she finished. Of course, we were all physically there, but everyone's mind had run away with Aunt Clare. Everyone was with her in 1936.

"At thirty, I met the only man I have ever truly loved, outside the opera house at Covent Garden. I was pleased to be on my own; freedom was a rare and delicious treat for me at that time. A man who looked barely old enough to be out of school, carrying an empty birdcage, asked me if he could be so rude as to steal a cigarette. Certainly, I said, and he ended up repaying me by taking me out to dinner. We talked of everything but opera, laughed a great deal, and drank endless glasses of Chablis, and he grew up in front of my eyes. He was just nineteen and so alive with that elusive, inquisitive lust for existence that I felt myself transforming in front of his eyes. I talked in a way I had never talked to anyone: I laid my soul down on the table between us and let him hold it up to the light and ask what it meant. I want to see the world, I said. Go, he said. I'm married to a man who detests travel, I told him. Leave him behind, he said. I have a seven-year-old son, I retorted. Better and better, he claimed. A boy of seven is the perfect companion on any journey. I imagined for a blissful few hours that I would be with him forever, but when midnight came, he said he had to drive home, to his parents' house in the country, and could he stop a taxi for me? Of course, I said, and I sat in the back of the cab on the way home, imagining that any moment it was to turn back into a pumpkin. I never forgot that evening. Not only because I met him, but because I realized that it was possible for the world to spin just for you, even if only for the length of time that it took to have dinner. For those few hours, I experienced a happiness so acute it felt half holy: a happiness made all the more intense because I knew it was a limited happiness, just passing through. I did what I had suggested to him that I might do; I did what I never imagined I would ever have the courage to do. Harry and I left Samuel for an entire year and opened our eyes to the rest of the world. What follows is an account of that year, and none of it would have happened were it not for that evening with a stranger in Covent Garden."

Aunt Clare stopped for a moment and you could have heard a pin drop.

"I never saw him again, though I heard his name occasionally, and it was in India the following year that I read of his engagement in the papers. He married an astonishingly beautiful girl of seventeen."

I bit my lip and choked back the tidal wave of saltwater that threatened to spill from my eyes. As if feeling it too, Aunt Clare's eyes hit mine for a moment, and her eyes smiled, infinitely kind.

"He was killed, of course. The war saw to that. Yet my memory of him is as clear today as it was the morning after our meeting. I think of him still, and in writing this book, the boy with the birdcage has never been far from my thoughts."

She stopped here and placed the manuscript down on the table in front of her. Her hand was shaking a little. And I knew in the way that you realize you have known all along: Aunt Clare's birdcage boy was Papa.

The guests showed no sign of leaving when Aunt Clare had finished reading. If anything, they grew louder still, clattering their teeth on champagne glasses, ordering Phoebe to find more cakes and scones. Charlotte and I moved, without speaking, away from the noise and into the morning room.

"Goodness," said Charlotte, who was looking rather white. "I don't suppose you saw that one coming. I certainly didn't."

She stood by the window looking down onto the street. "Aunt Clare certainly hasn't lost the ability to hold an audience," she added.

"It's quite all right," I said, and my voice sounded high and unnatural. "I think I knew all along that there was something unspoken between Aunt Clare and me. I suppose you did too."

"She didn't dictate that passage to me, Penelope," said Charlotte in sudden panic. "You have to believe her on that count. She would have known that I would have told you."

She was right, and I did believe her. It all made sense, of course. Mama's diary entry the night that I had first mentioned Aunt Clare's name. Her remark the other night: *Maybe he should have married someone older than me, someone with more confidence.* She must have known about their evening outside the opera house. Papa must have told her about the one woman who had stirred him before he met her, and, being Mama, she had never forgotten it.

"You know nothing ever happened between them—what she read there was the absolute truth," said Charlotte, watching me carefully. "Oh, darling Penelope, don't cry!"

Of course, tears take their cue from lines like this, and I found that once I had started weeping, it was impossible to stop. I cried for Papa, and for what we lost when he was killed. I cried for Mama and for Magna and for Inigo. But most of all, I cried for myself, for realizing too late that it had been Harry all along, and for pushing him away from me every time he nearly got close. Then, to my horror, the door creaked open, and Aunt Clare's white blonde head peered around at us.

"*Penelope!*" she cried, and it was the first time I had seen her truly shocked.

"Why did you have to read that bit?" demanded Charlotte, and it was the first time I had seen her truly angry. "How could you do that to her? In front of a roomful of people?"

Aunt Clare just sighed and placed her hand on my shoulder.

"I could never tell you," she said. "And the oddest thing about it was that to anyone else, it would appear that there was nothing to tell. There *was* nothing to tell, just that I once spent an evening dining with a terribly nice man who happened to be your father. Yet of course, to me, it was everything," she said simply. "Oh, Charlotte, do open the window—it feels like the house is on fire."

"It's quite all right," I said truthfully. "I suppose it's just so jolly, oh, I don't know—*maddening*—that Papa had to be killed." I blew my nose. "Sometimes I feel so, so *cross* with him for not staying alive."

"For goodness' sake, Charlotte, get the child a brandy."

Charlotte poured me a double and I took a great gulp.

"I seem to have drunk rather a lot this year," I said with a half laugh.

"Comfort yourself in the knowledge that however much you've drunk, Marina Hamilton will have drunk more," said Charlotte.

"I won't have that girl's name mentioned in this house," said Aunt Clare ominously.

"Was—was Papa very like me? To look at, I mean?" I asked Aunt Clare. I knew the answer, of course I did, but I needed, very much, to hear it from someone other than Mama.

"Oh, you're very like him," said Aunt Clare. "That wonderful long nose and those exquisite freckles! I knew right away, as soon as I first set eyes on you, do you remember?"

"Did you think him very handsome?" Charlotte asked her.

Aunt Clare paused before answering.

"I wouldn't say that he was handsome in the usual way," she admitted. "He was too rare for that, too unusual looking with that strange coloring and those long eyelashes. Goodness me, Charlotte," she went on, much her old self again, "who on earth ever fell in love with anyone who looked *handsome*? What a ghastly bore handsome is."

I remembered Charlotte and myself in the back of the cab, a few moments after we had first met at the bus stop.

Is he the most handsome man in London? I had asked her of Harry.

Of course not! she had responded. *But he's by far the most interesting.*

"Do you mean he was funny? Mama says that she never had a straight face for longer than five minutes when Papa was alive. She says he made her laugh more than anyone else in the world." ·

"He liked words—liked the way he could twist their meaning to make me laugh."

"Ooh! You do that, Penelope!" cried Charlotte.

"Do I?" I was absurdly pleased.

"There was a *lightness* about him," said Aunt Clare. "That's the only word I can think of to describe it. You have it too."

"What do you mean?"

Aunt Clare stretched her hand out toward my whiskey.

"He struck me as being terribly good at living, which is the greatest gift anyone can ever have. A talent for life."

"You mean he seemed very happy?"

"Not just happy," said Aunt Clare. "Nothing as straightforward as that."

"What do you mean, then?"

"He was at ease with himself, he was at home in his own skin. I remember seeing the waitress light up when he asked her where she got her pretty shoes."

"He was charming, then?"

"More than that, too. It wasn't because he was handsome, but because he made people feel as though they were in the right place at the right time when they were with him. I don't think for a moment that he was aware of this. It was instinctive, his talent for living brilliantly."

"Brilliantly?" It seemed an odd choice of word. No one had ever called Papa brilliant before.

"For living brightly."

"So why did he have to die, then?" I asked. I didn't mean to say it out loud. It sounded so stupid. But Aunt Clare looked at me and smiled.

"One thing I've realized," she said slowly, "the people who are good at living are very good at dying too. I don't think he was afraid of death."

"You—you *don't*?"

For a moment it was as if someone had lifted a great weight from my shoulders and I felt almost dizzy with the relief of it, my head light with what Aunt Clare had said. Yet what was I doing, filling myself up with romantic notions about my father from a woman who had only ever spent a few hours with him? What could she know about the man's soul? However much I loved Aunt Clare, I couldn't allow myself to be drawn into thinking that she understood Papa better than anyone else. It wasn't possible.

"How can you say that? You hardly knew him," I said sadly.

But she took my hand in hers.

"He wasn't afraid," she said quietly. "I just *know*. He wasn't afraid."

And I believed her. Not because I wanted to, but because I knew it was true.

Charlotte came with me in the cab to Paddington. We didn't speak much. My mind swam with images of Papa and Aunt Clare, Papa and Talitha on their wedding day, Papa fighting, Papa dying.

"I wish Harry was here," Charlotte said suddenly. And just the mention of his name sent the adrenaline pumping into my fingertips.

"I miss him too," I said, unable *not* to say it. Charlotte looked at me with a sideways grin.

"Oh, I never said I *missed* him," she said. "I just wish he could have been here this afternoon. Gosh, Penelope, you're coming closer and closer to confessing it to me, aren't you?"

I didn't smile. I didn't say anything. Missing Harry was the least amusing experience that I had ever had. Especially when he was aching as much as I was, but not over me at all. The cab rattled up Kensington Church Street.

"He'll come back, you know," said Charlotte. "They always do."

There's never any warning that something extraordinary is about to happen, is there? I got the 6:15 train home, as usual, and collected Golden Arrow from his usual spot. I quickened my pace as I rode past the deserted village green and threaded up Lime Hill toward the drive. It was dark, so I kept the estate wall close to my left as I pedaled along the road, and I hummed Johnnie Ray songs and tried to push the strange but powerful sense of dreadful urgency that was swamping me as I made my way home. I don't know which of my senses picked up the changes first—was it my eyes, seeing the sky redder than it should have been, or my ears, hearing the unmistakable sound of distant voices shouting? Was it the taste of something different but undefinable in the night air, or the prickle of fear that touched my skin? I reached the bottom of the drive and found a policeman coming toward me, shining a powerful torch into my eyes. I shielded my face and applied the brakes to Golden Arrow.

"What's happening?" I asked him. "What are you doing here?"

"Stay away, Miss," he said firmly. "This is no evening for a young girl like you to be snooping around this place."

"I *live* here!" I cried, trying to squash the rising panic in my voice. "What on earth is happening?"

"You *live* here, Miss?" repeated the policeman, suddenly concerned.

"Yes! I *live* here!" I repeated, slightly hysterical.

"I should come down to the station with me if I were you, Miss," he said, but I remounted the bike and pushed off toward the house before he could say any more. I think he shouted something after me, but I couldn't hear—the only thing that mattered was getting home, home, *home*. My legs pushed around and around, faster and faster, my heart crashed against my ribs, and I clenched my fingers over the handlebars and rode on. I came to the turn in the drive, the point where Charlotte and I had stood that first day that she had spent at Magna.

"It's like nowhere else," she had breathed.

My first thought that night was how spectacular it looked; the front lawn and the lime avenue lit up under an orange sky that hurt the eyes with its thunderous, glorious brightness, the house itself more alive, more powerful than I had ever known it. Magna was on fire. There was a triumph in the red glow that swept methodically along the roof; there was beauty in the theatrical leaping of the flames that had taken hold of the house and danced with the falling timber and the crackling walls, and Magna was a willing partner in that dance. There felt to me to be no shout of fear from the burning house, only a laughter, a joy, in its destruction, an exultation in the majesty of the display. *Mama!* I thought with that cold, sick feeling of dread, and I cycled on, closer and closer to Magna, until the heat from the house was so great, and the smoke in the air so thick, that I had to stop again and gasp for air. In front of me stood a familiarly stout figure.

"Mary!" I gasped. "Oh, Mary!"

"Miss Penelope!" she cried. "Oh, it's terrible! *Terrible!*"

"Where's Mama?" I cried. "Mary! *Where's Mama?*"

"She's in London. She telephoned me only a few hours ago to say she was staying with friends and would be back tomorrow. Back to *this,*" Mary went on. She coughed so hard that she actually staggered and I leaned forward to catch her.

"How can she come back to this?" she gasped. "There'll be nothin' left of the place by mornin'. Nothin' at all!"

"She's in London?" I shouted. "Mary, are you quite sure?"

"As sure as I've ever been. I came over five o'clock as usual. She'd gone then. Johns had taken her to the station. She'd given 'im the rest of the weekend off."

"So she's not inside?"

Mary shook her head. "I can promise you she's not inside."

"Oh, my goodness! Fido!" I shouted. "Where's Fido?"

"Johns has 'im!" said Mary. "Yer mother suggested 'e take 'im home with 'im since she was goin' to be in London for the night. Said you were staying away too," she added, not without a note of accusation in her voice.

"I was," I whispered. "I just got this feeling I should come home."

We were interrupted by another policeman.

"Think you two ladies should stay clear," he said firmly. I didn't hear what he said next. I stared straight ahead at Magna, watching the flames shoot out of the downstairs windows, transfixed with the same dumb sense of the smallness of self that I had while watching for shooting stars with Charlotte. My eyes burned with the red-hot power of it all, and I stepped back with the shock of it. I saw figures dancing on the lawn in front of me, Mama and Papa as they were on the summer evening that they first met; I saw Inigo and me as children, running toward Magna on the day the war was over, shouting with excitement for the end of something that we couldn't conceive of living without; I saw Charlotte and me walking through the orchard and dreaming of Johnnie; and I saw Harry and me lying on the floor in the Long Gallery listening to the wind and the rain bashing against the East Wing. Then I thought that I saw Rocky coming toward me, and I felt something in my head shut down, and a lightheadedness soothed me with the idea that this was all a dream, all a dream.

TWENTY-TWO

The Occasional Flicker

WHEN I AWOKE, I was in the Dower House, in the bedroom that Inigo and I had shared during the war. For a moment I wondered if I was eight again, and if the war had ended at all.

"Mama?" I croaked.

"Penelope!" came her voice from the bedside. "You're awake at last!"

I was awake all right. Daylight streamed through the window. I sat up.

"What time is it?"

"You fainted," she explained. "Mary and a kind policeman helped you walk up here. You slept through the night. It's seven o'clock in the morning."

"Magna! The fire!" I flung myself from the bed and ran to the window.

"Darling, you must slow down—the shock—"

"It's still burning!" I cried. "Can't they do something?"

Mama sat down on the end of my bed. She was desperately pale and wearing her best frock with a fur shrug around her shoulders. She had obviously not changed from the night before.

"How did you hear about it?" I asked her, my throat dry, the smell of smoke thick in my hair.

"I was in London," said Mama. "I decided that I couldn't bear to be in the house on my own for another night. I called Johns and he drove me to the station."

"Who were you going to see?"

Mama flushed.

"He called me just after you left. He said he would love to take me out for dinner, but he quite understood if I never wanted to see him again."

"Rocky?"

Mama nodded, looking away from me, her fingers pleating the quilt Mary had made for us during what she described as "the long, dark evenings of 1943." I had not seen the quilt since we moved out, and it filled me with childish memories to see it now. Inigo and I snuggled up in it listening for bombs overhead, Mama wrapping her legs in its warm coverings on the nights when fuel was rationed. Mama saw me staring.

"The quilt," she began, "remember how you loved it?"

I realized then how Mama still saw the war years. There was fear, but always, always hope. It wasn't until the very end, when Papa had been killed, that hope died. Everything before that was clouded in romance, and giddy anticipation of seeing him again. It wasn't until we had moved back to Magna that we had word of Papa's death. The Dower House, to her, would forever be a place of cocooned dreams.

"Rocky telephoned?" I asked her. She nodded.

"I decided that I should go for dinner, if only to say that I was sorry about the way I treated him the other night. Now I can't imagine what would have happened if I had not gone," said Mama. "I would—I would have been killed."

"Not necessarily," I said, horror at the truth of what she was saying sinking in. "I think you would have escaped all right, Mama,"

"But perhaps not," she said, shaking her head. "Perhaps not."

"How did you hear what had happened?" I asked her.

She looked at me, eyes tired and smudged with mascara.

"Well, it was a funny thing," she admitted. "Rocky and I went to dinner at Claridge's—such a treat," she couldn't resist adding. "And afterward, we decided to take a walk. London was so beautiful last night, you know," she added, forgetting that I had been there too. "It must have been after midnight when I realized that I was too late for the last train home. Rocky said that he would drive me back to Magna," she added. "We arrived at half past two. What a sight greeted us when as we came up the drive!"

I was struck by Mama's choice of words here. There seemed little horror in her voice, more incredulity than anything else. There was none of Mary's "it's terrible!" from her, no fainting like me.

"I had no idea that you were going to appear," she went on. "Rocky said that it was too much for me to have to watch the house burn. He spoke to Mary and asked her if there was anywhere else that he could take me. We ended up here." She crossed the room and straightened the photograph of Inigo and me on the chimneypiece.

"I was so frightened when we arrived back here to find you," she went on. "You were shaking like a leaf. It must have been the most awful shock, darling."

"And not for you, Mama?"

"Of course!" she said, her voice cracking. "It is—it was Papa's house. He would never have let this happen—"

"What about Inigo? He *must* be told," I said, pulling on my shoes.

"Rocky drove straight to school to break the news to him," said Mama. "He left an hour ago. He should be there by now."

I said nothing, but I had to admit to myself that Rocky was the right person to tell Inigo.

"What shall be left of the house?" I whispered. "Oh, gosh!" I said with a sob. "Marina!"

"Who?"

"The guinea pig!" I felt tears stinging my eyes. Marina, the pet Harry had given me to look after, the closest thing I had to him—what had happened to her last night?

"Oh, darling, don't worry about her," said Mama with a smile. "Funnily enough, I decided yesterday that it was time for her to move outside permanently. I put her in a box and handed her to Johns just before I left for London. He was to take her home with him to show her the new cage he's been making."

"Oh, thank goodness," I muttered, and it wasn't until later that I thought how odd this was. Why on earth did Marina need to leave my bedroom while Johns finished her new hutch?

"You were right about Rocky," said Mama quietly, and I think it was the first time that she had ever admitted to me that I was right about anything.

"What do you mean?"

"He is wonderful. Of course, I knew it from the moment I first met him, but I was afraid, Penelope. So afraid of—of—"

"Being happy?" I asked her.

"Happiness can be frightening when one is not accustomed to the sensation."

"So now that Magna's burned to the ground, you think you might be happy?" I sounded harsher than I meant to. "What about Papa? His home! *Our* family home, Mama! Now it's over, it's gone!"

"Just like your father is gone!" shouted Mama, animation turning her face whiter still. "I never wanted the place to die like this! But I couldn't go on living there, either. Your father would never, ever have wanted me to. He used to say to me that Magna only felt real to him when I was there with him."

"He would have done something," I cried. "He would have fought the flames, he would have done *anything* to save it! It was in his blood, Mama. It's in our blood!"

"No!" screamed Mama. "*We* were his blood, not the house! The house trapped him, owned him, frightened him like it did me. Oh, he loved Magna," she went on, her voice rattling now, "but he would have done anything to get away. He never said anything to prove it, but sometimes there was something in his eyes, just the occasional flicker of doubt as to whether he had taken on something too big for him. You understand that, don't you?"

Mama walked to the door. "Something had to change," she said. "Something *had* to change."

It was the first time I had heard her sound certain about anything for years.

But I shook myself away from her grasp and shot out of the bedroom and down the stairs. None of it would be true unless I saw it for myself; nothing about the fire was real until I saw what had happened to Magna. Mama rushed to the door and shouted after me, but her voice sounded like something unreal, like a sound from a wireless, fake. I turned out of the Dower

House and ran and ran toward Magna. I heard my feet thumping rhythmically on the solid earth beneath my feet, and it gave me strength. I looked down at my feet as I ran, and I saw the glowing patches of bluebells swim into focus as I raced up the drive. I felt the sun warm on the back of my head, and the unexpected brightness of the morning hurt my eyes. I rounded the bend into the courtyard and had reached the bench by the pond where we had sat that winter's night—Inigo, Charlotte, Harry, and I— eating hard-boiled eggs and drinking champagne in the snow. Now the air was soft, too warm for my thin woolly. I pulled it over my head and walked slowly, slowly toward the house.

How could it have only taken one night to change everything? I had read of houses being destroyed by fire overnight, but had never believed it was possible. Surely someone was able to put these infernos out before they took hold? Yet the fire at Magna was *still going*. It looked smaller now than it had last night, yet there it was; I could see it calmly smoldering through the blackened windows of the Morning Room. I walked, without any thought, up to the front of the house, and stood where the front door had been. No more. It had caved in to reveal the hall, or what had been the hall, indistinguishable from the chaos of the rest of the ground floor. Knowing I shouldn't, I stepped inside. A rumble in front of me, and a huge chunk of the hall ceiling crashed to the floor, still red with heat, still hot with the exertion of damage.

I stepped back. I could see the sky through the hall ceiling, the blue and white spring morning laughing down on the blackened shell of Magna. It felt as though the house, for the first time ever, was naked, ashamed, unable to hide anywhere. Last night it had seemed to burn with a cackle of laughter under the midnight sky. Now it looked—there was the word!—it looked *hungover*.

Three firemen were loitering about, one of them drinking from a thermos flask. Just behind them was a huge pile of objects that had obviously been salvaged from the house. Mama's desk from the Morning Room was stacked with stuff from the kitchen—a whisk, a blackened saucepan, and Mary's singed copy of *The Lady*. Ironically, Mama's W.I. calendar for 1955 had flapped open to December to reveal a photograph of a blazing Christmas pudding sitting above a fireplace. We would never see another Christmas at Magna now.

"Miss Penelope?"

I swung around to see Johns, his pipe in one hand, and a weeding fork in the other. I stepped back and he nodded slowly and walked away from the house, toward the pond. I followed behind him, wondering if he was real; it seemed impossible that Johns could exist now, on this morning of all mornings. Was there a Johns without Magna? As if reading my mind, he bent down and started to fork out the weeds around the bench. Without thinking, I knelt down and started to help him, knotting the tough stems around my fingers, listening to the resistance of the roots in the earth as they were pulled from the ground.

"You leave these too long, you'll 'ave nothin' but trouble in no time," muttered Johns. "Best keep on top of the garden, 'specially this time of year, what with new shoots all over the place."

"Yes," I said in a whisper.

How long we worked together I don't know. It felt like no more than five minutes, but it could have been an hour. Occasionally, we looked up when another police car or fire engine swept up the drive, but I said nothing. My throat was dry; I felt afraid of trying to talk.

"Won't be much good they can do now" was all that Johns said. No one bothered us. I don't know that they even noticed us. The more time passed, the harder it became for me to talk. I didn't know what to say, didn't know how to begin. I took my lead from Johns, and Johns, it seemed, was unwilling to say anything, until I stood up and announced that I had to go, that I had been out for long enough, and that Mama would be waiting for me at the Dower House.

"Won't you help me with sommat, just for a minute, Miss Penelope?"

"Of course, Johns. What is it?"

"Won't you come with me, just to the pigeon house? There's a coupla birds need checkin' in there. Frightened last night, they were. I'd like you to be able to tell your mother they're all right."

"Certainly, Johns."

I followed him silently, through the gate and into the garden. The sunlight blasted on the path; white blossom exploded from the apple trees. In the garden, not one shoot, not one petal or new bud, cared whether the house stood or not. It was another country altogether. Johns tidied as we walked, as he had always done. He had gone from seeming absurd to seeming the most sensible of all of us: getting on with his job, and his job had always been outside.

Harry's doves were perched together in a line in the pigeon house, a little away from the rest of Mama's doves. How like Harry they seemed, and I swallowed, imagining what he would have to say if he could see what had happened to the Long Gallery. None of the birds seemed any more flustered than usual—Johns filled their trays with seed and they all flapped around his hands, making the usual racket.

"They seem to be fine, Johns," I said, relieved.

"Ah."

"I really should get back—" I began again.

"One more thing, Miss Penelope," said Johns. "Just one more thing."

I said nothing, but stood and watched as he bent over and pulled a small box out from under the seed bins.

"Found this 'ere this mornin'," he said simply.

"What is it?"

"You take it. You see fer yerself."

It had been tied up with several pieces of string and ribbon, some of which I recognized as the ribbon from the Fortnums ham that Charlotte and Harry had brought with them on New Year's Eve. I heard Mama's voice, *Oh, I'll save the ribbon, it's too pretty to throw away.*

"Oh, that'll be something of Mama's," I said to Johns, feeling uneasy. "Something she probably tied up and forgot about—"

"Sure to be," said Johns. "You just take it back to 'er, won't ye? Shouldn't leave these sortsa things hangin' about in the pigeon house fer too long."

"Thank you, Johns," I said. And I knew.

*   *   *

I don't know how I knew, except to say that perhaps I had known all along. I hurried back through the garden and out of the gate, clutching the box to my chest. It wasn't very heavy. It rattled a little as I ran. When I got to the clearing at the top of the drive, when Magna was all but obscured by the lime avenue, I crouched under the copper beech tree.

The layer of tissue paper on top of the contents of the box blew away when I opened it and I was too late to catch it. Underneath was something soft, something neatly folded, something that was so familiar to me that I would have known it merely from its touch or smell. Mama's wedding dress. With shaking hands, I pulled it out of the box and held it up. The sunlight gleamed on the thin, pink material, making it translucent, a fairy's dress. Carefully, I placed it beside myself on the ground and pulled out what had been packed away underneath it. Everything was quintessentially Mama. She had saved last year's ration book, her *Pirates of Penzance* record, several photographs of Papa, and, discarded from its ugly frame and lining the bottom of the box, lay the reproachful sight of Aunt Sarah's watercolor. Funny, I thought. Away from the majesty of Magna's ancient tapestries and Inigo Jones ceilings, it looked rather good. I balanced it against the trunk of the tree and reached into the box again. There was a letter in the bottom. A letter whose handwriting I recognized instantly. Aunt Clare's. Yet it was addressed not to Papa, as I expected, but to my mother. *Talitha Wallace, Milton Magna, Westbury, Wiltshire.* The date on the envelope was just a month ago. April 1955. I sat quite still for a second, my mind whirring. Then I read, slowly and carefully, and hearing Aunt Clare's voice in my head all the time.

My dear Talitha,

I can't tell you how relieved I was to hear from you. Since meeting Penelope it has been bothering me very much—how you've been since the war, how on earth you've managed Milton Magna on your own. It must have been hard for you to write to me, and I thank you very much. We should have de-Rebecca'd each other years ago. It is never too late, not even now.

Funny how often you came into my thoughts. Talitha Orr—the luck-iest girl in the world, the girl who won Archie. Whenever I saw your pho-tograph together in the paper, I would search your faces for some flaw, some sign that you were not as happy as everyone said you were. I searched in vain. Even after I read of Archie's death, I envied you. Isn't that strange? To envy a widow as young as you. But at least you had him for a while, even if your time together was short. All that changed when I met Penelope and I realized how awful it must have been for you. To lose your husband and be landed with a house like Magna . . . The weight must indeed be great. And your letter was so sad. You have held yourself back for so long. The idea that I have haunted you is so ridiculous to me. So futile. You are far too young to live like this. Life is long and full of pos-sibility if you set yourself free.

A great house is a remarkable thing, but all great houses are built for men, by men. Any house, great or small, ceases to seem real when the peo-ple you love are no longer there. Free yourself, because you are too young not to.

Yours with great affection,
Clare Delancy

P.S. Penelope is such a dear girl. My son once said that he is not good enough for her. Perhaps you could persuade Penelope that this is not the case?!

I liked the exclamation mark. I placed the letter back in its envelope and put the envelope back in the box, but as I was doing so, I noticed one more thing. Another photo. It was a one I had never seen before, although it was of Inigo and me, sitting together, laughing by the pigeon house. I flipped it over. *July 11th 1941 (21st birthday),* Mama had written. *Penelope and Inigo.* She had drawn a rather wobbly heart shape in pencil next to our names. For some reason, it was this, above everything that had happened and every-thing that I had seen, that filled my eyes with tears.

*   *   *

Inigo and Rocky arrived at the Dower House later that afternoon. Rocky looked tired but still impossibly glamorous. I wanted to run into his arms and wait for him to tell me that everything was going to be all right, because somehow, just having him in the same room made everything better. It was always the same with Rocky: First you were knocked sideways by his height and his charm, then by that unmistakable kindness. He poured Inigo and me a stiff drink.

"I don't think any of you guys should go near the big house for a few days," he said, giving me a look. "There are still men out there trying to work on saving as much stuff as they can. I think you should leave them to it. I need to go up to London for a few days, but I can be back here by the weekend. If you want me to, I can take a look at the insurance for you, get the papers worked out. It's a complicated business, but I can help you, if you want me to."

"All my records," said Inigo dully. "I suppose it was impossible to save anything."

Rocky lit a cigarette and said nothing. Later that evening, I took Mama's box to her bedroom. Neither of us mentioned it. We didn't need to.

Rocky took care of everything, despite having to spend most of his time in London. New furniture arrived for the Dower House in vans from Peter Jones—smart, modern sofas, an American refrigerator, and even a television set.

"You can't let him pay for all this stuff, Mama," I gasped. "It's too much."

Mama agreed with me and tried in vain to send it all back.

"I suppose it must give him pleasure," she said. "Helping other people."

I couldn't disagree with Mama. Rocky was the only true philanthropist I had ever met. It was what made people suspicious of him. It was hard to believe that he only ever wanted the best, for everyone. Of course, in our case it made matters easier for him that he was madly in love with Mama.

"I expect he'll want to marry you," I said, testing the idea on for size.

"Don't be ridiculous, Penelope," said Mama, frowning. "Not everyone thinks the way you do. He's just a very generous man."

"Indeed," I added wryly. "So you don't mind all this American stuff? The new cooker, and the fridge?"

"It's not ideal," sighed Mama, "but Mary tells me the washing machine *is* a marvel."

The first few days after the fire were nothing like you might imagine them to have been. I envisaged tears and drama, delayed guilty regret from Mama, sinking despair from Inigo and me as we realized that our childhood and our home had gone forever. I was quite wrong. Rocky was careful not to overwhelm us with details, but he let us know that we would be receiving enough money from the insurance to keep us living quite happily at the Dower House for the next few years. I didn't ask him any questions. Above everything that had happened, I was aware only of his kindness. Watching Mama and Rocky was like watching the unraveling of a fascinating, slow-moving film. I felt much of the time that Inigo and I should be passed a paper bag of popcorn when he arrived for dinner—their friendship was such a delicate, butterfly-ish thing. Rocky bought Mama presents, not always expensive gifts, but sweet little things that he thought she might like— a bag of sugared almonds from Fortnums, a sweet-smelling candle from a shop he knew on the Portobello Road. He was the least sentimental man I knew—he had a practical answer for everything—yet when Mama talked, you could actually see his face softening, mark his eyes smiling. He found her fascinating and frustrating in equal measures (which, of course, she *was*), but Rocky was not afraid to challenge the frustrating part, much to Inigo's and my delight. He pulled her up on things—her views on America, her petulance at dinner one night, her criticism of Inigo's love of music— and she actually listened to him. In return, she teased him, she made him laugh with her outrageous impression of Mary and her tales of life in the village during the war. It took me two weeks of observing them both to realize that they were the perfect combination. It took Mama a great deal longer than that to admit it. Almost more than anything, I felt grateful that Rocky understood me. One evening, as I lay on my bed reading an article about the joys of Spain in *Woman and Beauty* and wondering if Harry had ever been there, I heard a light knock at the door.

"Come in," I said.

Rocky stood awkwardly in the door.

"Hey, kid," he said.

I put down the magazine.

"Hello," I said.

"I was wondering," he said, "not that it's any of my business, of course, but what happened to your magician?"

"Oh, he's not my magician," I said lightly. There was a pause.

"Ah," said Rocky. "As long as you're all right with that?"

"Oh, quite fine, thank you," I said.

Rocky didn't believe me, of course, but he knew when to leave me alone. I wasn't quite fine about Harry. I had never known hurt like it: the constant, persistent ache, the continual, dull longing. I lay awake at night scribbling into my notepad and driving myself crackers with memories of how cavalier I had been, how presumptuous, how *ridiculous* not to recognize that I had been falling when I was, and now it was too late. One evening, Rocky came to dinner smelling of Dior pour Homme and I nearly passed out.

"Are you feeling well, Penelope?" asked Mama.

"Yes," I muttered.

It wasn't until nearly three days after the fire that Rocky suggested that Mama go with him to look at Magna for the first time. He took with him a hip flask and a handkerchief, but she needed neither. On the same day, I went up to London to see Aunt Clare. She had written a letter to me asking if I would pay her a visit as soon as I could. She didn't mention Magna in the letter. "Everything will work out right, you'll see, Penelope," was the closest she came to mentioning the fire. I wondered why on earth she wanted to see me so urgently; for a fleeting moment I wondered if it was something to do with Harry.

Aunt Clare answered the door, which was unheard of.

"Penelope!" she said, kissing me hello. "Do come in. We're quite alone, which is something of a novelty, isn't it?"

"It is, rather," I agreed. "Where's Phoebe?"

"Oh, I gave her the day off. She's not herself at the moment."

Has she ever been? I wondered.

It was a curious fact that I had never spent any time at Kensington Court between eleven in the morning and four in the afternoon. Sitting in Aunt Clare's study at midday on a sunny morning felt wrong, somehow. It felt like a different place entirely.

"No tea, I'm afraid," she said, reading my thoughts. "Would you like something stronger? I've rather taken to gin at this time of day."

I grimaced, thinking of the stage door of the Palladium.

"I'm fine, thank you."

Aunt Clare poured herself a large gin and tonic and sat down.

"Now. How is your mother?"

I laughed. "Uncommonly well. Surviving beautifully without Magna. She's free, just like you said she would be." I felt the heat rising in my face. "I know about your letter to her."

Aunt Clare didn't give me the thrill of looking remotely surprised.

"I found it. Mama was never much good at keeping secrets. I'm amazed she managed to keep her communication with you to herself for as long as she did."

"She's a great believer in fate, isn't she? She felt that you becoming friends with Charlotte was too much of a sign for her to ignore."

She crossed the room to her writing desk and pulled out an envelope addressed to Clare Delancy in Mama's trademark peacock blue ink.

"Don't open it yet," she said, her voice strange. "Open it when I'm not here."

"When I get home?"

"No, no. When I'm gone."

"What do you mean?"

Aunt Clare sat down. She held out her hand to me and I sat next to her, a sudden dread filling up my soul.

"I may not be here much longer," said Aunt Clare. She spoke lightly, without difficulty. "I'm dying, Penelope."

Everything went blank. Blindly, I pulled my hand away from her and found myself standing up, though my legs had turned to jelly.

"How—what do you mean?" I whispered.

"Oh, it's something I've known about for quite some time," said Aunt Clare. "Nothing anyone can do for me now, or so they say. Once it takes a hold, etcetera, etcetera. Still. I've had longer than they predicted last summer. But these past few weeks have been—difficult. I don't want to wilt away here. I always said that when it got to this stage, I would go abroad. Paris, perhaps. The Tuileries in spring cannot be bettered."

"It's not real. It can't be!" I crashed down onto my chair again, and in that instant I knew that it was real because I found that I had started to cry.

"Oh, dear girl," said Aunt Clare. "Please don't cry. Really, you mustn't. I've had a wonderful life. No one could ask for more. Don't cry."

She was beside me, her hand over mine.

"Does Charlotte know?" I sniffed.

"No. She knows nothing except that I am thinking of moving to Paris for a few months. I didn't want her to be thinking about it when we were working together. I needed her to be fresh and alive and aggravated with me when I asked too much of her. I didn't want her to think she was working with a dying woman. My book is all life, all new limbs and adventure. Oh, no. It wouldn't have suited to have told Charlotte."

"But surely she should be told—she'd want to say good-bye—"

"She wouldn't. Not Charlotte."

I knew she was right.

"She hated me at times, for pushing her so hard to finish the book. But I had to push her—you can see that now, can't you? We had to finish what we'd started before it was too—well—too late, I suppose."

"And you did," I said. "You finished it."

Aunt Clare nodded. "It never mattered to me if it was going to sell five copies or five thousand," she said. "I wrote the book for me, and for the people I love—after all, a little self-indulgence never did anyone any harm. As it happens, I think it's done my Charlotte a great deal of good. She was a stranger to discipline before I got my hands on her."

I had never heard Aunt Clare refer to Charlotte as hers. I swallowed.

"And Harry?" I asked her.

"Harry's known from the start."

I was so surprised I stopped crying.

"What?" I blinked.

"I told Harry because I couldn't not. He knows me too well. I wouldn't be able to hide it from him like I could with Charlotte. And I knew it wouldn't change us, and that's what made it all right. We still argued. I continued to despair over Marina. He still refused to get a proper job. But he spent great chunks of his earnings as a magician on me. On doctors, specialists. Nothing that's come to any good, but he's *tried*. That's the only thing that matters. He tried."

"Where is he now?"

"He'll join me in Paris," said Aunt Clare evenly, "if I ask him to."

"You will, won't you?" I begged. "Say you will!"

"I will. I promise you that much."

"He'll be lost without you," I whispered. "He needs you. To—to tell him he's being silly, to keep his feet on the ground—"

"I think I've trained Charlotte rather well in that department," said Aunt Clare.

"If only he weren't still so in love with Marina."

"Oh, he's not." Aunt Clare's reaction was instant. "Not at all. He never has been in love with her. He just thought he was."

"But what's the difference?" I felt angry all of a sudden. Why did Aunt Clare always talk in riddles like this? Why did she have to be dying? And why did she have to go to Paris to do it?

"He's only just working that out for himself," she said quietly. "I regret that your mother and I will never be friends." There was sadness in her voice now, real sadness. "But it all worked out as it should, of course. I got to live, now she shall too."

I reached out for Aunt Clare's drink.

"Don't you think it was a terrible thing? To destroy a house like Magna?"

"Far more terrible to go on living there. Debt is the terrible thing, Penelope. It swallows you whole, but—" she turned to me, her eyes wicked, full of fun, "Harry will have a nice surprise when I'm gone."

"How's that?"

"Oh, I sold a piece of china I never believed was worth anything for the

most extraordinary amount the other day. Well, enough to keep Harry in
smokes for a while, as he likes to put it. Christopher Jones spotted it when
he was here for my reading. He nearly burst with the excitement. Said he'd
never seen a piece its equal in such wonderful condition."

"What? And in the meantime, let him think he's poor as a church
mouse?"

"Of course!" exclaimed Aunt Clare. "I can't have him thinking he's got
money to spend. He might lose his mind and start thinking he can afford
Marina Hamilton again."

"And what was the piece?" I asked her.

"Oh, you won't remember it. It was an ugly thing, really. The little milkmaid that used to sit right here—"

I laughed, in spite of everything. I laughed.

I only stayed another ten minutes. I imagine Aunt Clare didn't want me
to have to sit around and make conversation with her now that I knew it
would be the last time. I didn't want to, either. She saw me to the door.

"Aunt Clare, does Phoebe know? Your—your secret?" I asked, hating
myself for sounding trite.

"Oh, yes, she's known all along."

"I see. That would explain her misery."

"Oh, no," dismissed Aunt Clare. "She's naturally like that. Always has
been. And worse than ever now that Harry's left."

Harry. I couldn't believe he wasn't about to saunter through the door
clutching his magic bag, humming a jazz tune, and making snide comments
about Johnnie Ray. I wanted to see him so much, I almost felt capable of
conjuring him up, as a traveler in the desert sees water.

"Just one thing," said Aunt Clare.

"Anything," I said, meaning it.

"Look after Charlotte for me. I know she's still infatuated with that Andrew boy. He's not right for her, but she'll take her time realizing it. There
will always be part of her that loathes me for keeping her away from him.
But you see, Penelope, sometimes experience knows best."

She looked thoughtful for a moment. "She's mentioned Christopher
rather a lot since you introduced them. You know, he hasn't changed a bit

since the day I met him. Still such a pretty man, and still quite unaware of it."

"Charlotte claims he irritates her."

"Well! Need we say more?"

I took a taxi to the Ritz and sat at the bar to read the letter Aunt Clare had given me. It felt like the right place to read it, and just being there made me feel that Harry was with me too.

Milton Magna, Westbury   *March 2nd (approx.)*

Dear Clare,

I hope you don't think it queer that I am writing to you. What am I saying, of course you do. (Typical Mama, I thought. Her letters always read like this—a stream of consciousness, utterly unplanned.)

My daughter, Penelope, has become friends with your son and niece, and apparently you spoke of knowing of Archie and me, and of Milton Magna. Oh, I can't think what I'm doing, sending this to you—perhaps I read too much into the coincidence of their meeting, perhaps I am seeing it as a sign. At any rate, I am here, with the draft whistling through the window, writing to you.

You were the one woman Archie spoke of with any affection, the only person to have moved him before he met me. How I hated you for it! Just after we first met I asked him if he had ever considered marriage before, and being Archie, he just couldn't resist being honest. He told me of the evening of your strange encounter—how you had met outside the opera house and had talked for hours. Just talked. He said you were older than he was, and married with a son, and yes, rather beautiful. He said that if you hadn't been married, perhaps he would have seen you again. How wretched I felt hearing those words! How sophisticated and worldly and intimidating you seemed—how untouchable. You became my one demon, my own private Rebecca. I feared Archie bumping into you more than anything else in the world.

Oh, he loved me. He loved me more than he loved you, of that I have no doubt—I had his children; we were as inseparable as twins. And yet nothing could erase the fact that he had felt something before, something that didn't come to anything, but oh—something! (She had underlined this word several times, and as I read it, I could hear her saying it.)

Anyway, after Archie was killed, I couldn't bear to look at his clothes hanging, no, weeping, at me from inside his dressing room. At the back of the wardrobe, I found a suit I had never seen him wear before. I felt faint, I tell you, because something in me just knew. I pulled it down, and emptied the pockets. Nothing, except for a ticket to the opera. It hadn't been torn. Unused, because something even better than La Bohème *happened that night. He met you, Clare.*

None of this matters. None of this means anything. You didn't steal my husband, I hadn't even met him. Perhaps that's what's made it harder to bear. You were then, as you are now, blameless.

I am thirty-five years old, but I feel a hundred and thirty-five. I live in a house I don't like, but I'm too frightened to say I don't like it. I don't understand my children because I don't understand myself. And why I'm telling you all this, I can't think! I can't think why I didn't tear up the ticket and put you out of my mind. Penelope told me that you had described me as a "sensational beauty." It suddenly struck me that you might have loved him too. I'd never thought of that before.

So here is the ticket for you. Perhaps you will throw it away, thinking me very odd indeed. Perhaps you will weep over it for days. I suppose I will never know. Penelope is so fond of Charlotte, and Harry.

Yours, freezing cold as usual,
Talitha Wallace.

Funny, I thought, putting the letter away and pulling out my handkerchief, how the best months of my life had also been the saddest. As I left the bar, I could see Kate and Helena Wentworth arriving for a late lunch with a large party of equally beautiful girls. As usual, Helena's voice rang out above everyone else's.

"I don't think I'm asking for much," she was saying, "just a good-looking

man with excellent taste, his own airplane, a private income, and an obsession for Italy and me."

The girls around her exploded in hysterics. The funny thing was that,
knowing Helena, she wasn't joking at all.

I heard Aunt Clare's voice in my ear.

"Hear, hear!"

I was up in London again the following day to see Charlotte. We met in a
café in Knightsbridge, and I was struck for the first time by her resemblance
to Harry. It was there, all right; I had just never seen it before. It was in the
sparkle of her eyes, the tilt of her head, the way she talked, and I realized
with a stab of pain that the longing for him was there worse than ever.
Would it ever, *ever* leave? I had become used to the ache now; it was with
me all the time, and never seemed to lessen. Time was no healer, I decided,
but it was a great accommodator.

"I think Mama will marry Rocky before the end of the summer," I said,
biting into my hamburger.

"Shall you be pleased?" asked Charlotte.

"I think so."

Charlotte paused.

"How is it?" she asked me slowly. "Not having Magna?"

It was the first time anyone had asked me the question, although I had
tried to figure it out for myself a million times.

"It's partly terrible, like someone dying," I said. "But there's another side
to it all, a part of it that feels like being set free," I confessed, and hearing
the words spoken, I bit my lip, for it felt like a betrayal. "Whoever set fire
to the place knew exactly how we all felt," I added.

"What on earth do you mean—whoever set fire to the place?" asked
Charlotte, leaning forward and stealing a chip from my plate. "Do you
think someone—someone started the fire *on purpose*?"

"Oh, yes," I said. "I knew that right from the start."

"Who, for goodness' sake?"

I laughed. "Inigo's entire record collection was saved, and Marina the guinea pig and all my notebooks with my stories. And my beautiful fairy godmother outfit that I wore to the Ritz. Oh, and Mama's wedding dress," I added.

"Ah," said Charlotte.

"You do see, don't you?" I asked her.

Charlotte bit her lip.

"He heard her say that she hated living there and he saw a way out for her. For all of us. He took it," I said.

"Very American of him," said Charlotte.

"Of course, I don't really have any proof," I said. "I could be utterly wrong. But it was all too perfect to be true. Mama being out of the way, all the animals taken care of—"

"He must have been shaking in his boots when you turned up!" said Charlotte. "Imagine if you had arrived before the fire started!"

"Somehow I don't think he left any stone unturned," I said. "He's not the sort of man who would, is he? He says he can help Inigo with his singing—you know—put him in touch with the right people to make his own record."

"So I suppose Inigo can forgive him anything?"

"He doesn't think like me—he never questioned what happened," I said. "Inigo sees it as a miracle that Mama wasn't at Magna when it happened. He thinks we were lucky. He's so fixated by music that everything else seems secondary to him."

"A the T was arrested last week," said Charlotte with a grin. "He and Digby were caught tearing up the seats in the cinema after watching *Blackboard Jungle*. He wrote me a card telling me all about it. He says he wasn't to blame."

I laughed. "Mama says she'll never talk to Inigo again if he gets into trouble for rioting in the aisles."

"Rioting in the aisles," said Charlotte thoughtfully. "We *must* do some of that before the week's over." She looked at me carefully. "How are you, anyway?"

"I don't know," I confessed. "It seemed so awful at first, and I've always been so much more sentimental about the house than Mama or Inigo. I kept on thinking about playing records in the ballroom and the night Marina descended upon the place and all the Duck Suppers we've had since the war ended and how I would never again sit on the window seat in my room looking out over the drive and—and—it's odd," I confessed, "but I think I only ever really appreciated Magna since meeting you and Harry."

"Don't be silly," said Charlotte briskly.

"Oh, but it's *true*. In the short time that we spent there, I loved the place much, much more than I ever had in the years before that. I mean, Inigo and I felt sometimes that it was rather like a prison. Every dark corner frightened me—it seemed so old and so *dark*. We would much rather have carried on living in the Dower House after the war."

"Houses like Magna are much easier to admire when you don't have to clean your teeth in them," said Charlotte, pushing a slide into her thick hair.

And I nodded, because she was exactly right.

"I thought Magna was a dream house," admitted Charlotte, "but you know me, anything elaborate and romantic and ancient sends me into raptures. But I could never have lived there all the time. It was like a museum, somewhere you stepped inside and pretended to be someone else for the time you were there. It wasn't *real*. That was what I loved about it, I think."

"It was real when *you* were there," I confessed. "Just as it was real to Mama when Papa was alive. Those times that you came to stay, the times when we stayed up late in the library, the times with Harry—" I felt myself about to cry as one feels about to sneeze, but I managed to choke back the tears. "For some reason," I said, my voice shaking, "for some reason I keep on thinking about—about Harry—and the Long Gallery that afternoon of that terrible storm—I—I don't know why—"

Charlotte handed me a handkerchief.

"He sent his love to you in his last postcard," she said kindly, and I felt her eyes sharpen for my reaction. "He wrote, *Do send my love to Penelope, not that she'll remember who I am after seeing Johnnie Ray at the Palladium.* It came from Paris. He thinks he's going to stay there until the end of the month. Apparently the magic scene in France is *magnifique*."

"And Marina?" I asked. "Did he mention her?"

"No," said Charlotte. "I read in the papers that she and George are hold-ing a cocktail party in Nice aboard some boat or other to celebrate their re-engagement."

"The party goes on. Somehow, I don't think we'll be invited to that one."

"Oh, I imagine we'll *definitely* be invited," said Charlotte breezily. "She can't afford to keep people like us at too much of a distance, you know. We know too much, don't we? What do you think *you're* going to do now?"

I closed my eyes for a moment, feeling the warmth of the afternoon sun on my face. My freckles would be in overdrive soon.

"I don't think I want to live in the Dower House much longer," I said.

"I don't blame you."

"It's not just that," I said. "I feel restless. I want to move, maybe go with Inigo to America—" It was the first time I had thought this, but saying it made me all the more certain that I had to get away for a while.

"No!"

"What do you mean, no?"

"You, Penelope Wallace?" Charlotte laughed hard. "Gosh, wonders will never cease."

"I thought I might go and find Johnnie," I said with a grin. "Want to come too?"

"Aunt Clare's gone to Paris," said Charlotte suddenly. "I don't think she's coming back."

"You don't?"

Charlotte shook her head. "Perhaps I'm wrong," she said slowly. "Per-haps I'm wrong. I think she'll stay out there for a while, at least."

I said nothing. Aunt Clare had chosen not to tell Charlotte. Far be it from me to betray her trust.

"I spoke to Christopher yesterday," she said, going a little bit red. "I'm trying to persuade him to go into business with me. Come and have a look at the spot I've chosen if you like," she added, her eyes lighting up. "It's on King's Road. We could walk there now."

We linked arms and set off and I thought of that cold afternoon in No-vember when Charlotte had first appeared in front of me in her green coat, asking if I wanted to share a cab with her. It felt like yesterday and yet like a hundred years had passed since that first afternoon in Aunt Clare's study.

"Aunt Clare always said we should follow our dreams," I said idly.

Charlotte stopped walking and turned to me with a grin.

"Couldn't we follow them in a taxi?" she said.

Epilogue

HARRY RETURNED TO LONDON two months later. He took Charlotte and me to lunch at Sheekeys. I wore the dress I had worn that night at the Ritz and prayed he wouldn't notice how much I was shaking. It was a balmy July evening, which felt odd, as I had never known Harry in the summer. It suited him. I had expected him to look older—tired from carrying around Aunt Clare's secret for so long—but I should have learned not to try and second-guess anything about Harry. He looked better than I had ever known him. He walked into the room and pushed his hair out of his eyes, and I saw the waitress double-take as she noticed their strangeness. He looked over to where we were sitting at the bar, sipping Coca-Cola through straws, and I felt tears stinging my eyes with the relief of seeing him. The utter relief of seeing him. The strange thing was that even though we were in the same room, I ached for Harry more than ever. I had never known someone so familiar, yet so utterly foreign to me. I wondered for a moment whether he was still obsessed with Marina, yet I just knew that he wasn't.

We sat down to lunch, and he told us how he was with Aunt Clare at the end, and how she had talked of us all. He told us how much he missed her. Charlotte cried and he took her hand and told her that Aunt Clare had said that the most important thing about writing her book had been the fact that she had done it with Charlotte's help. That made her cry even more. I just sat there, aching. I had never been aware of Harry's kindness before. To me he had always been aloof, difficult, brilliant—never kind. But that afternoon, I realized that he had done everything for someone else. It struck me that the Marina affair had kept both him and Aunt Clare beautifully distracted from her illness. While his mother disapproved and complained and tried to get him a proper job, she was still fighting. Harry would not have had it any other way.

An hour later, Charlotte left us to meet Christopher. When she had gone, Harry asked me about Inigo, and I said that he was going to America to play the guitar and become famous. My brother, the pop singer! Maybe one day he'll play the Palladium like Johnnie Ray. Harry said he didn't doubt it. Then he told me that he had planned to go to Italy from Paris, but something had pulled him back to London instead. I asked him what that was, but I think I knew. I knew because when I looked at him, I saw something in his face I had never seen before. I knew because we were still sitting together three hours later, while the waiters looked at their watches and started to lay the tables around us for dinner. I knew because Elvis Presley himself could have walked in and I wouldn't have looked up. We smoked cigarettes and drank red wine and talked about music and magic. And about the Long Gallery and the Dorset House. And of Aunt Clare and my father, and Mama and Milton Magna.

We talked of what was to come. And of the lost art of keeping secrets.

Afterword

WHEN ELVIS FINALLY MADE IT big in 1956, Johnnie Ray became something of a forgotten figure. To me, he will always be the ultimate pop star. I have never known anything like the crowds outside the Palladium that night that Charlotte and I went to see him sing. He was the forerunner. He died on February 24, 1990. He was sixty-three years old.